CW00794754

Libraries
ReadLearnConnect

THIS BOOK IS PART OF
ISLINGTON READS BOOKSWAP
SCHEME

Please take this book and either return it to a Bookswap site or replace with one of your own books that you would like to share.

If you enjoy this book, why not join your local Islington Library and borrow more like it for free?

Find out about our FREE e-book, e-audio, newspaper and magazine apps, activities for pre-school children and other services we have to offer at www.islington.gov.uk/libraries

ISLINGTON
For a more equal future

A Terrible Matriarchy
a novel

*To Sarah
and
Sheela

With love,
Easterine*

Easterine Iralu

zubaan

An imprint of Kali for Women

A Terrible Matriarchy
Published (2007) by
Zubaan
an imprint of Kali for Women
128 B Shahpur Jat, 1st floor
NEW DELHI 110 049
E-mail: zubaanwbooks@vsnl.net and zubaan@gmail.com
Website: www.zubaanbooks.com

10 9 8 7 6 5 4 3 2

ISBN (10): 81-89884-07-7
ISBN (13): 978-81-89884-07-9

This is a work of fiction. Names, characters, places and incidents are either the product of the author's imagination or are used fictitiously, and any resemblence to any actual person, living or dead, events, or locales is entirely co-incidental.

Typeset in AGaramond 11.5/16.2
at FACET Design, D-9, Defence Colony, New Delhi
Printed & bound at Raj Press, R-3, Inderpuri, New Delhi

To Preeti with thanks for not letting me stop at page 4...

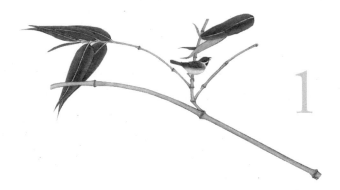

1

My Grandmother didn't like me. I knew this when I was about four and a half. I was sitting in her kitchen with my brother, Bulie, older to me by two years, when she served us food. Hot rice and chicken broth.

"What meat do you want?" she simpered sweetly, as she ladled out gravy and meat.

I quickly piped up, "I want the leg, Grandmother, give me the leg."

"I wasn't asking you, silly girl," she said, as she swiftly put the chicken leg into my brother's plate, "That portion is always for boys. Girls must eat the other portions."

I didn't understand why, and I didn't care to ask why not. I was also too hungry to sulk so I sat and quietly ate her food. Funny. At Grandmother's house it was always her food. I never thought of it as food. It had to be attached with the pronoun "her" to make it clear that it was food cooked and served by Grandmother so she had every right to do with it as she wished. Serving, for instance, chicken leg to my brother and none to me. I don't remember telling my mother about that incident. I think I knew even then, young as I was, that Mother would have that terribly hurt look on her face and then she would go dumb and then, come back with many questions. Questions that I did not always have answers for, like, how many pieces of meat did Grandmother serve me? What did her face look like when she was rebuking me? Did she take my brother in her lap? Did she take me in her lap? Why didn't she take me in her lap? Did I say all the nice things I had been taught to say or did I forget some? Did I greet her first or did she greet us first? Endless questions. Mother would have made a good interrogator. She never left out any aspects to be questioned. She covered everything meticulously. One thing about Mother was her meticulousness. She was always neat and orderly. So, it was a pain for her to pick up after me and my four brothers.

I was the youngest in a family of five children and Mother and Father made it seven. I sometimes felt I was an afterthought, and maybe Father and Mother didn't quite know what to do with me. Also, because I was a girl after four boys, they never seemed to be sure whether to buy me girls' clothing or let me wear leftover boys' clothing. So I have vivid memories of alternating between wearing new girls' dresses which felt tight and uncomfortable and short in the leg or old, torn-at-the-knees boys' trousers and stained t-shirts which were immensely comfortable. We never had enough to eat. My brothers were always hungry. We rarely had leftovers in our kitchen. My aunt, who was rich and had only two children, a girl and a sickly boy, threw away food because the children did not want to eat and she always made too much. Of course, she did not throw it away, as that would have been taboo, but she fed it to the pigs.

"Silly woman," said Father. "Doesn't she know I have five hungry mouths here? Why throw away good food?"

"Hush, Father, don't let the children hear you talking like that. We have enough to eat in this house," said Mother.

 2

But that wasn't true. I had often seen her scraping the pot and giving it to Leto, my eldest brother, or taking out meat pieces from her own plate to slip into Vini's plate saying she was full. The boys never refused. They never seemed to think that she might want to eat it herself. Oh well, that was Mother, and in later years, she still would not indulge herself. She thought it was sinful to eat the food one really liked or wear more than two new clothes in a year.

Maybe it was because she had to listen to Grandmother's rebukes if she bought anything for herself. When she went to church, Mother would throw an old shawl over her new blouse if she were wearing it for the first time. Mother was not the only daughter-in-law that Grandmother had. There were my two uncles whose wives were just as much in awe of Grandmother. They were not as poor as we, though, and they lived far away from Grandmother. So I suppose they had a better time of it than poor Mother. She always looked worried and nervous. And she was most worried about me. "Do you know your Mother was the prettiest girl in the village?" said one of her cousins visiting for a couple of days. I didn't believe him. Mother, with her face and clothes always wrinkled, how could she possibly have been pretty at any age? I thought she was born with that worried expression on her face. It was like she wanted to please and yet did not quite manage to and that set a constant, anxious look on her face. The person she feared most was Grandmother and I hated Grandmother with a vengeance because nothing my mother ever did seemed to please her.

"Nino, you sent the older boy to fetch water, I hear," said Grandmother quietly when we went visiting her. But there was an edge to her voice that made it sound like a veiled threat instead of a casual query.

"Mother, I could not leave my cooking. It was only once, Mother."

"Send the girl next time, that is girls' work. No man in my day has ever fetched water."

"Yes, Mother," said my mother timidly, ignoring altogether the look of utter dismay I threw at her.

The water-pot was almost as big as I, how did Grandmother think I would be able to fetch water in it? Why didn't Mother say that I was too small to go yet? Then I remembered that she had once said that I was small and Grandmother had said that she began to fetch wood at four. I was almost five so I guess Mother didn't have any excuses anymore.

"The girl must be made to work at home. Don't let her run about with her brothers anymore. That is not the way to bring up girl-children," said Grandmother on another visit. She always referred to me as "the girl."

"Why doesn't Grandmother call me by my name, Mother? Why does she only call me 'the girl'? Doesn't she like my name?"

"Don't say things like that, Dielieno, she probably thinks you are special as you are the only girl. She can't talk about the boys and call them 'the girl,' can she?"

I accepted that explanation but when she was still calling me 'girl' two years on, I said, "Grandmother, my name is Dielieno, remember you gave me my name? Why won't you call me by my name?"

She pointed her stick at me and snapped, "Don't be cheeky with me, girl."

I decided it was easier to let her call me anything she wanted. I wasn't sure if she would try to land her stick on me. When Leto and I went to her house with a basket of vegetables that Mother had sent, she sat down and put Leto on her lap. "Come here, my darling, let me see how big you've grown. My, my, you are a big boy now." I could see Leto didn't want to be carried. After all, he was turning thirteen next month. But he let her have her way. I readied myself to be carried next but instead she said to me, "Go bring in another piece of wood and put it on the fire, it's by the shed outside." I ran off and ran back,

Easterine Iralu

hoping that now I would be held and told that I had grown bigger. But she had forgotten all about it and had hobbled to the almirah to give a lump of jaggery to Leto. My brother saw me return and gave me a bit to lick at. "Enough, enough, it is for you," said Grandmother and closed the almirah with a loud bang. We didn't stay long after that.

One afternoon, my father's cousin, Atu, came to visit. Uncle Atu was great fun. He would put me on his lap and tickle me or let me tickle him. I was enjoying his company so much that I began to climb up on his right shoulder when all of a sudden I saw a shadow at the door and the unmistakable tap of Grandmother's stick on our wooden floor. I desperately clambered down but it was too late. The stick caught me on the back of my calf before I reached the floor.

"Girl, what do you think you are? A monkey?" her face was red with rage, "I've never seen such a badly behaved girl."

"Aunt, I was playing with her" my uncle quickly spoke up in my defence. "She wasn't bothering me, she is a child, don't be so hard on her, Aunt, she is a good child."

"No girl" she spluttered, "no decent girl climbs up a man's shoulder."

"Good heavens, Aunt, she is a mere child."

"They have to be taught young."

Uncle Atu kept quiet after that, probably realizing that he was only making things worse for me.

I slid away and stayed out of her way the whole evening. I was not going to keep quiet about it though. As soon as Father came home, I said loudly, "I hate Grandmother Vibano."

Father was shocked. "Why, Lieno?" he asked.

Before Mother could tell him her version I burst out,

"Because she wouldn't let me play with Uncle Atu today. We were playing and she hit me on the calf with her stick. Look, Father, the place where she hit is red still."

My leg bore an angry red mark and I saw the same pained look on Mother's face.

"Is this true?" he looked at Mother and she nodded yes.

Father looked angry but his face quickly changed expression and he said, "It is for your own good, your Grandmother would never do anything to you that is not for your welfare."

"No, Father, you don't understand, she hates to see me enjoying myself. You don't know how she is. She wouldn't let me eat Leto's jaggery when we were at her house."

"Lieno, that is not respectful to your Grandmother. You know she has had a hard life. She only wants to raise you to be a good woman."

I ran from the room, my eyes smarting with tears. I wanted my Father to take my side but he spoke up for Grandmother. That hurt deeply. How I wished Grandmother would die. It was a wicked, wicked thought but I thought it was even more wicked to hit a child for playing.

Mother's younger sister, Pfünuo, was very pretty. She would make me new dresses at Christmas time or for my birthday. One day, she came home to Mother and they stayed in the bedroom a long time, talking. That was not unusual. They often did that when she came but on that day she did not play with me or talk much to me. Her eyes were red like she had not slept the night before. Leto had red eyes like that when he went hunting and they were up the whole night. They locked the room and let me in only for a short while before opening the door and telling me to go play with the neighbourhood kids. Later, when Pfünuo had gone, my mother hurriedly took my hand and we went to Grandmother's house. "Play a while," said Mother so I happily made dolls out of the old clay leftover by my cousins in the yard. If I wet the clay with water, I could mould a car out of it. It was more fun to play with clay than with dolls. If Mother was distracted, as she looked tonight, she didn't

 6

scold me even if I got my clothes dirty with mud. "Come on, Lieno, we're going," called Mother after some time. So I ran to her. Halfway home, she stopped and said. "Oh no, my purse, I must have forgotten it in your Grandmother's house. Do run back and get it, Lieno, I have to get back home and cook dinner before your father comes home." I ran back to Grandmother's house and slowed down at the door because she did not like girls running. Her sister was there too. I heard loud voices. "That's right, it was her younger sister, she's gotten pregnant and they have to marry her off. Terrible! I hope her mother realizes that you have to raise girls on a tight leash so that this sort of thing doesn't happen. They let her run around too much. I just knew this would happen. Bad blood in that family, that's what my mother told me." It was my Grandmother's voice. I hesitated a bit and then walked in. They were startled to see me. Very nonchalantly I said, "Mother left her purse behind" and then I spotted it on the low stool so I grabbed it and said bye before they could stop me and ran off. "You think she heard?" my Grandmother was asking her sister. "No, she is too absent-minded, that child, she wouldn't have understood even if she heard."

When I mentioned to Mother what I had heard Grandmother say, Mother's face went very pale. She put a hand to her mouth and looked as though she would faint. "Bad blood, did she say that, Lieno?" I nodded yes, and Mother held my hand so I wouldn't slip off and she begged, "Please don't ever tell anyone what you heard, please Lieno, promise me?" I hated seeing Mother look hurt or worried so I bit my finger hard and showed it to her. "Oh, my child" was all she said and she gave me a little hug before letting me go. A week after that, Pfünuo was married but it wasn't in church and I was disappointed I didn't get to be the flower girl.

I remembered a bit of Grandfather. He was a nice friendly man who would try to teach us a lot of things. But I hardly remember them now. If we ran into his study, he would speak to us in English and we giggled because it made no sense to us. But one day he got sick all of a sudden and before they could get him to the hospital, he died. So they turned the car around and brought him home to lay him in a long coffin for he was a big man and there was a night-long vigil. The next afternoon they buried him but not before several people made many speeches for he was quite old and that was what they did when really old folk died. My brother Bulie and I thought he would come back after a few days and so we waited a long time at the grave. When Mother thought we were playing, we were actually at the grave digging up the fresh soil from the corner. "Seen anything yet?" I asked, while Bulie dug with a little spade. "I think it's a bone, I saw something white." After four days, we stopped digging because Bulie's spade wasn't very big. It was just a play-spade and in any case, he couldn't possibly have managed a real spade.

"When is Grandfather coming back?" I asked Mother one day.

"Back from where?" she asked in a very surprised tone.

"When he's finished dying, isn't he coming back?"

"Oh, Lieno, don't you know that when people die, they never come back? They go to another place. Their bodies turn into soil. That's why we bury them under the ground."

"Oh, is that so? No wonder Bulie and I couldn't find anything when we were digging," I said.

Mother looked shocked. "What? Where have you been digging?"

"Why, at the grave, of course, we were trying to help dig up Grandfather."

"Oh my God, don't ever let your Grandmother hear that. Ah, it's not your fault. You didn't know. And we never thought of telling you."

After that, it wasn't so much fun anymore to go visiting Grandmother because she was even more ill-tempered than before. When Grandfather was alive, he would chide her if she was too hard on us. He liked to call us to him and give us sweets, rock candy at Christmas time and funny little chocolates in animal shapes on Sundays. It wasn't every day that he would do this. It was only Sundays that we were given sweets so we always persuaded mother to take us to visit Grandfather then. Now that he was dead, no one remembered to give us sweets and four Sundays had already gone by without any sign of sweets. Bulie and I secretly agreed that it was pointless going to Grandmother's house now.

But Mother was even more adamant about going. We went on weekdays as well. When I got home from my aunt Pfünuo's house, Mother would be waiting and she would say "Hurry up and eat your food, we have to go see Grandmother."

"But we were there two days ago," I would protest.

"That's not the point, Lieno, don't you know she is lonely and we must keep her company? Don't you feel sorry for her?"

I didn't really feel sorry for her because Grandfather's death had not made her a nicer person. She seemed to have grown more sour, if that were possible.

One night, I was sleepless. Mother and Father were talking in low tones. I thought I would be able to fall asleep after some time as I usually did, lulled by their voices. But I just lay there unable to sleep. I was not listening to what they were saying because they would only be talking about how Bulie was doing in Math class or the field they were saving up to buy, but when they suddenly mentioned my name, my ears pricked up.

"Mother wants Lieno to stay with her from now on," said Father in a very decisive tone.

"She's too young to be of much help yet, Visa," said Mother.

"Yes, but that is how Mother wants it to be and we can't possibly say no to her." I was horrified. They were talking about sending me to live with Grandmother! What a horrid thought! I could not even bear to be with her more than an hour. If I had to live with her day in, day out, I would rather be dead. I hoped I would die tomorrow.

And I hoped that when my parents found me dead in the morning, they'd be sorry they ever planned to send me to live with Grandmother.

"It won't be so bad, dear. Bano will also be there. Lieno won't have to do too much work. Mother gets lonely, you know."

"Is it that or does your mother think we are not raising the girl properly? You know she has said that to me more than a dozen times."

"How can you say that of Mother? She is a widow. What could you possibly be thinking?"

Father's voice was cold with anger.

"I am sorry, dear, but I worry that Lieno is not going to turn out to be the ideal girl your mother so wants her to be. She is too full of life for that. But only I know what a sweet little girl she is. I don't want her to be with people who might misunderstand her and mistreat her."

"What! Are you saying that my mother could mistreat our daughter, her own granddaughter? Are you accusing my mother of meanness?"

"Please, dear, you know I don't mean it like that but the girl is still so young and may not know how to please Mother."

"Mother was right. You are not raising her properly. She will leave tomorrow for Mother's house and I don't want to hear any more arguments about this."

After that, they both went quiet. There was no way I could sleep, having heard that. Father began to snore loudly but Mother was sniffling and trying to stifle her sniffling. I did fall asleep though I stayed up a long time with so many thoughts whirling in my head. In my dream, I saw Grandfather walking ahead of me. I ran up to him, having quite forgotten that he was dead. I tugged at his hand and we were playing together when his face suddenly changed and he became Grandmother and she shook off my hand and gave me

Easterine Iralu

such a stern look that I woke up suddenly, in fear. It was so real, my dream, and I had to lie in bed a long time till I remembered that it was a dream. But the things I had heard last night came back to me and how I wished I had not woken up.

"**Bano**, get up and make the fire, and while you are about it, wake up the girl."

I could hear Grandmother's shrill voice outside our door. She tapped on the wooden wall and Bano's response was quick.

"Coming, Mother, I am awake, I am tying my hair."

Actually she had been snoring half a minute ago so I thought it was funny that she should pretend to be awake. She sat up in bed, stretched herself and then twisted her long hair into a rubber band. She shuffled out of the room in her slippers and soon, I heard her breaking twigs and blowing on the embers of last night's fire. We always buried a small burning log in the ash in the hearth so that we could start the fire with it in the morning. I got up on my own because I did not want Grandmother to wake me. I instinctively knew that would not be a pleasant experience. I splashed cold water on my face and stealthily slithered into the smoky kitchen. Bano had stuffed paper in the fire to get it burning and now the smoke from the fire filled the room. I choked a bit and began to cough. But when I coughed, more smoke got into my nostrils and down my throat and I felt quite horrible.

"Girl, are you sick?" asked Grandmother.

"No," I got it out between coughing. "It's the smoke."

"Humph," she snorted, "keep her away from me, we don't know what germs she might have brought from their house. Give her a good scrubbing down with the carbolic soap later."

I dreaded that because it was something that Father would insist on doing if we had sores or rashes on our skin. "It disinfects your skin and kills the germs," he would say. But it was a harsh soap that got into the sores and burnt your skin. Grown-ups tended to forget that your skin was tender and they would rub it in very hard till the sores bled or were very red. At least, one thing good was that if Grandmother believed that I was full of germs she would keep away from me.

Bano was boiling water for tea. The kettle was burnt pitch-black from the years of being used on a wood fire. It was so old, it was dented in places. "That kettle is older than me," Father would tell us with a big laugh. Bano brewed tea in an aluminum teapot and kept it by the fire to warm it. When she served us the mixture of weak tea, sugar and milk, Grandmother took out some biscuits from a jar and gave us a biscuit each. I knew it would be useless asking for more afterwards so I nibbled at my biscuit and drank my tea slowly, avoiding the temptation to dip my biscuit in tea. That way it would finish too quickly.

"Drink up, we have so much to do," said Grandmother.

I scalded my mouth with the hot tea because I was too scared to tell her that I was not used to drinking hot tea.

"Better bathe her before you start cooking," said Grandmother to Bano. "I'll make some hot water then," replied Bano.

"No need for that, she shouldn't be spoilt with warm water."

"But, Mother, it is very cold this morning," said Bano looking surprised that Grandmother should suggest that I be bathed in cold water.

"She has to get used to it," was all that Grandmother said.

I glanced at Bano and threw her a pleading look but she wouldn't look at me. "Come then," she said to me and led me to the bathroom. I was placed on the cold cement floor. She did try to ease the shock of a cold water bath by soaping me down quickly and rubbing my body very fast and then rinsing off the soap with cold water in small amounts. It was terrible. I was so cold my teeth were chattering and I thought I would fall sick and die of pneumonia. Better to be dead, I thought. Bano said something like "poor girl" and wrapped the towel around me very quickly. I felt my body heat return when she did that and then she held me tight so that I would gradually warm up. Then she carried me to the room and we raced to put my clothes on me.

I pulled on the wool socks that Mother had knitted for me and ran into the kitchen to sit by the fire. "No time for that," said Grandmother as she handed me a small water pot. "Go get some water for cooking."

I took the water pot and put it into a carrying basket which reached down to my knees and went out the back door. The cold wind went through my thin clothes and I walked fast because it was worse if I slowed down. Bano hurried out after me with her own water pot. "Don't worry, I'll help you," she whispered. At the water spot there were two women.

"I swear he is the father of the child. Haven't you noticed how much the child looks like him?" the first one was saying to the other.

"No, not Bito, it can't be."

"Well, you only have to look close enough and then you'll see how much the boy resembles him, even down to the fingernails."

"Doesn't her husband know?"

"I'm sure he does, but you know how it is, he'd rather own the child than expose his family to scandal. But she has a hard time of it, ever so often we hear raised voices because our houses are so close by, and he beats her sometimes."

 14   Easterine Iralu

The two saw us coming closer and began to talk of something else. Bano greeted them.

"What's Lieno doing with you this morning?"

"She's come to stay with us," Bano answered.

"Oh, does your aunt want to make a woman out of her already?"

Both the women laughed at this and Bano did not say anything.

"Don't worry, Dielieno, we won't do you any harm. You are to be pitied for being descended from that woman," the younger woman said in a friendlier tone.

I did not say anything either. I did not understand what they meant.

Afterwards, when we had filled our water pots and were walking away, I whispered to Bano, "What did they mean?"

Bano looked sternly at me and said, "You must not repeat what you heard to Grandmother, it will only make her hate you, I hope you understand me, Lieno?"

"Yes."

Young as I was, I was beginning to understand that other people did not like Grandmother but they did not let her know.

"The women seemed nice, don't you think?" I asked.

"Don't get close to them, they worm their way into people's hearts and get them to tell their darkest secrets."

I wasn't worried about that. My only secret was listening in on my parents when they were talking about sending me away. Ah no, I had forgotten that I had something worse to hide. If Grandmother ever found out Bulie and I had dug Grandfather's grave, she would do something terrible to me, I was sure of that. Suddenly I was not so calm anymore. I didn't want anyone to find out about that.

I had to peel the potatoes for Bano to cook along with dried meat, chilly and herbs. Grandmother always had good food at her house, at least that was something one could look forward to, mealtimes. Dried meat hung from spiked bamboo over the fire. There was some dried pork from Christmas that was very nice to eat now. But Grandmother never cooked much of it. We would get a piece or two of meat in our plates and we would want so much to eat more but would have to be satisfied with what we got. That was the way it was in Grandmother's house. No one ever got second helpings of meat. But Grandmother would always ladle out more gravy and meat to Bulie or Vini and Leto. If Pete was there, he would get more meat too but he didn't have as great an appetite as the others. I sat close to him when he got more meat so that he could slip me the pieces he didn't want. Oh, at those times, how I wished I were a boy for then Grandmother would love me and take me on her lap and give me all the meat I wanted to eat.

"Lieno, get me some more wood from the wood stack outside," said Bano.

I ran out to the wood stack and picked up the smaller pieces of wood. I didn't mind at all that Bano sent me on errands and made me do little jobs around the house. Bano was kind to me and I knew how hard she worked. I always liked to be of some help to her. I was a little confused as to who she really was. She was too young to be Grandmother's child because she was 19 while Grandmother was at least 75 and Father was now 40 or 41. Yet, she called Grandmother "Mother" and as long as I had known, she had always been here. Grandfather had been kind to her but I never saw affection for her in Grandmother. Yet Bano was good-natured, working hard in spite of being rebuked often by Grandmother or her sister who was stern but not as unkind as Grandmother. Oh well, never mind that, I thought to myself, I would find out sooner or later. Perhaps she was adopted. That might explain why she had stayed on, drudging for the elderly pair and now, here she was stuck to Grandmother whether she liked it or not. I forgot all about it when I heard Grandmother calling me. I ran to her in her bedroom.

16

"Bring me the yarn basket," she said brusquely.

I ran to get it from the kitchen. But on the way back I deliberately slowed down, trying to take as much time as possible over this one task because by now, I had learnt that when one errand was over, there was always one other to do.

"Faster, girl, you have to learn to walk faster than that," she scolded.

Not much escaped Grandmother's eagle eye. If I lingered over my food too long she would reprimand me. If I took longer than usual to return from an errand to my Father's house, she would be waiting with a long lecture. So I learnt to be slow but not too slow. That way I just about escaped being scolded and could rest up a little before the next task. Grandmother's house was like a little factory. The people who lived there were always occupied with some work or other. The old man who came from the village chopped firewood after a cup of tea had been given to him. His wife would either dig up the garden to plant sweet potatoes or garlic or beans and maize. On other days, she would sit and weave rough cloths for Grandmother which I thought were especially ugly because they were of no definite colour, just a sort of dirty white, like when white got old. When Grandmother died we found so many of these cloths in her tin trunk. No one would have them so her sister stuffed the coffin with some of them. But that was much later.

I had to take in the firewood that the man had cut and stack the pieces on top of the fireplace. I had to stand on a stool and place them carefully on top of the wood already kept there. It was not particularly difficult but I learnt to be careful after a sliver of wood pricked my finger and I bled a little. "That will teach you to be more careful," said Grandmother. I sucked the blood and tried to finish stacking the wood. My finger hurt but I pretended it was fine.

On the third day, Leto came to see Grandmother in the morning. I ran to him and clung to his arm.

"Go bring the potatoes inside, girl," said Grandmother looking very displeased.

I went out to do as she bid. At the door I stopped and tried to listen because I was sure she was going to say something harsh to Leto. Her face had that look. But she began to coo.

"Come to me, my darling, why haven't you been here for so long? Don't you know I have kept sweet potatoes aside for you? Didn't you say that my potatoes were the sweetest?"

Oh what a carrying-on there was! I was sure she had taken poor Leto on her lap but I dared not go in and look so I tiptoed off to get the potatoes. When I returned, Leto had his mouth stuffed with roasted sweet potato and Grandmother was stroking his hair and calling him sweet names.

"Mother wants me to be back early," said Leto trying to clamber off from Grandmother's lap.

I knew he didn't like to be held like a baby anymore. The others would tease if they saw him now.

"Why is your mother trying to keep you from me? You never come to see me as often as you used to when you were a baby," pouted Grandmother.

Leto hastily said, "She said I was to help Father cut the firewood before I went to school."

"All right, then, but you must come and sleep here with me when you don't have to go to school. I have many fine things here and I am just waiting to cook them for you."

Leto promised he would come as soon as he could and she finally let him go.

It amused me the way my brother had to extricate himself from Grandmother's clutches. With some revulsion I recollected that she was going on like a young girl with him, vying for his attention and bribing him with good food. The meat that hung on the spiked bamboo was not for us. It was for Leto and all my other brothers.

 Easterine Iralu

Father was sometimes served a plate heaped with meat. But, lately, the boys were getting all the meat and even Father had to be satisfied with smaller portions. "I should have been younger," joked Father, looking at the meat in Vini's plate on an afternoon when they had both been invited to eat. Grandmother served the food at every meal. Bano was not allowed to serve food though she had cooked all of it. One day, Bano took out a large piece of meat from the pot and popped it into her mouth. She laughed at the look of surprise on my face and said, "I need to see if it is tender enough, do you want some too?" We were alone. I said yes and she gave me a big piece. It burned my palm and I cried out involuntarily. "Hush! Go eat it in the back room," she whispered so I took it to the back room, juggling it so it wouldn't burn my hand. I quickly ate it and wiped the residue on my skirt.

In the afternoon, Grandmother would lie down if it were a hot day. Bano and I took turns to massage her legs and back. Grandmother was a large woman, much heavier than Grandfather who had been a tall man but quite thin. Grandmother's hips swayed when she walked and her calves were enormous. It was no easy job to massage her calves. After some time, I would gratefully give way to Bano. These days, Grandmother had got slower than before. So I suppose she was to be pitied. I guess Mother saw that there was more to her than I did. I only felt fear and awe of her. And she seemed to enjoy picking on me. In the morning, she complained I had made her bed wrong and got her blanket upside down. It was a big bed and I took ages to make it. I had to stand on the bed, then lay the blanket on the bed and fold it in from one side to the other. I did try to remember which side it was that she liked facing up but sometimes I got it wrong and then she would always know. Bano said helpfully, "Look at the tassels on this side, they are longer than on the other side. Grandmother likes to have the longer tassels at her feet." I measured the tassels the next morning and made sure the longer ones were at her feet. "Don't worry so much," said Bano. "You'll soon get the hang of it."

One of my other tasks was to feed the chickens in the morning and count them at night. The chickens came to me easily enough to be fed in the morning. But in the evening, they would hide behind the wooden posts and if I reported one missing, I would have to go back and count. The chicken shed was an outhouse and it was dark and smelly. I had a single kerosene lamp to help me count. The moment I went in with the lamp, the chickens would be frightened and fly off to the other corner. I had to wait and stand still till they settled and then only could I count. On lucky nights, the missing one would come out in the confusion and then I could report that all the chickens were there. But on some nights, more chickens would go missing and then I could not go back until I had counted them all. I would stand there in the chicken shed, getting more and more scared of the shadows cast by the lamp that looked like horned devils moving up and down as the lamplight flickered. But I was more afraid of Grandmother than the devils and forced myself to stay and count till I had got them all.

The first time two chickens went missing, I returned to the house and said, "Could count only ten chickens tonight."

"What?" Grandmother's bellow shook me out of my complacency. "You idiot girl, get back there and count them again. You are not to return until you can count all the chickens!"

I didn't understand. If two were missing, how would they reappear if I counted them again. Besides, I did not want to go back to the chicken shed which was dark and cold. Thrusting the lamp into my hand, Grandmother pushed me out of the kitchen.

"Count them again!"

I had no choice. With a sinking heart, I returned to the shed and counted the chickens once more. There were no more than ten. I counted three times more before I went back to the house.

Easterine Iralu

"I'm sorry, Grandmother, there really are only ten chickens tonight. I counted them thrice."

"Unbelievable! This child will be the ruin of me," she sputtered as she got out of her chair and took the lamp from my hand roughly.

I was so relieved that she was going herself. When she returned, her face was dark and angry.

"You are such a useless girl. If you lose any chickens tomorrow, you will be sleeping in the shed, do you hear me?"

I was speechless with fear.

"I said, did you hear me, girl?"

I managed to whisper, "Yes, Grandmother."

I felt like I had signed my own death warrant.

Every day and every night after that I tried to make sure that no more chickens went missing. I guarded those chickens with my life. In the afternoons, I chased the neighbour's black dog away because I suspected he had taken the two that had gone missing. I threw stones at him whenever he came into our yard. We became such enemies, the dog and I, that he would emit a menacing low growl if I so much as went near his owner's house. One time he snapped at me just barely missing my calf. I learnt to be careful. And I relentlessly chased him when he came near our fence so that he would turn away if he saw me at the fence. It was a pity because I actually liked dogs very much. More than cats. Much more than the mean grey slit-eyed cat that Grandmother kept. It would sit on Grandmother's chair the moment she got up and spit angrily if anyone else tried to sit there. The dark grey cat grew more and more like Grandmother. They were both fat and they both disliked me greatly.

When I had been at Grandmother's house for six months, Mother and Father came one evening. I was very happy to see them. They didn't come to see me often after I had gone to live with Grandmother and if I was sent to them, I had to return quickly if I did not want a scolding. I buried my face in Mother's lap and tried to stay there as long as I could.

"Go bring the tapioca inside," said Grandmother.

I got up and walked out to the back of the house where she had left the tapioca in the shade. I took some to the kitchen and Grandmother spoke in a gentler voice. I was quite surprised because she never used that tone when we were alone. She put the tapioca into a big iron pot and put them on to the fire to boil. Father cleared his throat twice. But he seemed unable to speak. Finally Mother said, "The children are getting ready to go to school, Mother."

"Ah, the year has passed so fast hasn't it?" responded Grandmother.

"Lieno will be six soon, so she is ready for school too," said Mother quickly.

"Oh, you mean the girl?" asked Grandmother, though she knew fully well that Mother meant me.

I was the only child not at school yet. Bulie had already been at school two years now. Grandmother gave him a new bag on his first day at school.

"We want to send her to school, Mother. All her age mates are going too," said Mother rather firmly.

"In our day," Grandmother began, "girls did not go to school. We stayed at home and learnt the housework. Then we went to the fields and learnt all the fieldwork as well. That way one never has a problem with girl-children. They will always be busy at some work or other, too busy to get into trouble. It is all right if boys have a spot of trouble now and then, but with girls, it is different. You would never be able to get rid of her once she has caused trouble. I really do not approve of girls getting educated. It only makes them get fancy notions about themselves and they forget their place in the family."

"Mother," Father spoke for the first time, "You mustn't think we don't respect your views on this subject. We took this decision for Lieno because she is a bright girl and now that we no longer have the field, she will have the time to devote to her studies. Of course, she will continue living with you and helping you in your house. And of course, we want to listen to what your decision is on this."

I waited with bated breath for Grandmother's answer. Oh how I longed to go to school with my brothers, even if it meant staying on in Grandmother's house. After a long while, she said, "I suppose there is no harm in trying it out for a few months. But she must stay here. I have already taught her things which she might forget if she went back to you."

So it was agreed that I would go to school that year. The next days were very busy. Mother and I went shopping for fabric and she sewed a skirt and blouse for me to wear to school. That meant I could sleep with Mother for two nights. What joy it was to be back home, to not be afraid that an adult would always be watching you and waiting for the first opportunity to scold you. But Grandmother fretted and sent Bano to inquire if we were done with the sewing, so I had to go back the next morning.

"I can't understand why your mother took so long to sew a suit of clothes for someone as small as you," she said as soon as I returned.

I kept quiet and talked of the other girls who would be going to school with me.

"Well, we will soon find out what a school is good for, if anything," was all she would say.

Mercifully, there were my usual tasks to do so I did not have to carry on a conversation with Grandmother. I went out to fetch water. The water at the water spot was murky because it was late in the morning and most of the women had already fetched water. I waited for it to clear but that took long. So I fetched it as it was and did not take it into the kitchen but emptied it into the water tin in the bathroom. Grandmother was so particular about the water we fetched. We had to be the first at the water spot. She often asked if there were other women there and who had been the first to fetch water, them or us. One morning, we were a little late and when we told her that Selie's wife had taken water before us, she was very angry. "Do you know that woman brews rice beer in her house? Heaven knows who else might have touched her water pot and to how many houses in that godforsaken neighbourhood it might have been to." That morning we had to cook with the previous day's water. In these and other matters, Grandmother was so particular about cleanliness. That was why she would never let Bano serve food. Not that Bano was unclean in her habits, but I guess Grandmother liked to eat food touched only by her own hands.

I was very excited about the thought of going to school the next day, and I quite forgot to take longer over my tasks as I usually did. Vimenuo was going with me, too. We were about the same age and I

     Easterine Iralu

liked her because she was as poor as me and she did not have so many pretty dresses. I had three good Sunday dresses that Mother let me use alternately. The other girls would sometimes tease us and say that we never had new dresses at Easter and we wore the same dresses we had worn for Christmas. We stuck together and preferred that. The other girls looked down on us. They never had to fetch water as we did, nor run as many errands as I did. They had servants to do those things. Vimenuo and I were just grateful we had one another. Now that I lived with Grandmother, it had become increasingly hard for us to have playtimes together. It was inconceivable for Grandmother to allow me to visit Vimenuo and play with her. Her family lived five houses away, in a decrepit old house—her mother and father and her two younger sisters. Vimenuo lived with her grandmother in the house next door. But her grandmother was sweet and good natured, and though poor, she would always give us a treat when we visited her— a boiled wood apple or sometimes an egg. Her father worked as a night watchman but he was drunk most of the time. Except for her father, the rest of her family members were very thin and looked hungry all the time. Mother sometimes sent them some meat or rice when we had more than we needed.

Grandmother did not like them. She said that they were low and I shouldn't mix with them or else I would become like them. Bad blood, she muttered beneath her breath whenever somebody mentioned them. But that wasn't true. I knew Vimenuo's mother was a kind woman. She would always dress neatly even if her clothes were old. Their house was always swept clean and tidy. Her father scared me though. He had red-rimmed eyes and would be asleep on the porch when we visited them in the afternoons. If he were awake, he wouldn't say much but when he called for Vimenuo, she would run to him in a terrified manner. Her fear was contagious. I greatly feared her father and preferred her to come to my house rather than

I go to hers. Fortunately, he spent long periods away from home, sitting and drinking in the drinking houses by the roadside where the women were loud and laughed raucously. Bano said that he was angry his wife had given birth only to daughters. He wanted a boy to carry on his name. I asked, "Aren't the three girls doing that?" But Bano replied that girl-children are never considered real members of the family. Their mission in life is to marry and have children and be able to cook and weave cloth and look after the household. If they got married, they would always be known as somebody's wife or somebody's mother and never somebody's daughter. That way they could not carry on their father's name. I thought hard about it but could not think of anything to replace that system, so I gave up.

The day felt longer than usual. However, I did not tire from my jobs and Grandmother was surprised when I finished ahead of time. "Ha, if only you would work every day with the enthusiasm you have shown today," she said when we were all seated for the evening meal. Grandmother continued to observe everything that I did. Soon it was time for bed and I went to sleep in the room I shared with Bano. It was a small, humid room but there was a crack in the window that sometimes let in a draft and then it could get very cold. I was glad Bano slept on the outer side and let me have the inner side which was warmer. I could not fall asleep for a long time. I thought about school and how it would be to learn to write and sing and draw as my brothers did. When Bulie went to school for the first time, he brought back wonderful drawings of houses and flowers and he was given a box of crayons to colour them. I was fascinated by the crayons but Mother took them from me and soothed me by saying that when I went to school I would have my own set. That was two years ago. Oh, how vividly I remembered that and now I was going to go to school. Maybe I would get my own box of crayons tomorrow.

 Easterine Iralu

I must have finally slept because when I woke it was to the sound of the red rooster crowing and Bano moving around, getting ready. I felt as though I had hardly slept and I idly wondered if I should try and sleep a bit more. Then I suddenly remembered that it was my first day at school and I jumped out of bed so quickly that I fell because I had slipped on the mat on our wooden floor.

"Lieno!" Bano exclaimed.

But I got up again very quickly and she saw I was laughing so she knew I was not hurt.

"Today I'll go to school," I said to her excitedly.

"Oh, is that why you have gotten out of bed so eagerly?" she laughed.

We heard a shuffling of feet from outside the door and the familiar knocking of Grandmother's cane on the wooden floor.

"Come on," said Bano, pulling on her clothes swiftly. "Let's go get water before she comes in and spoils your day."

We were out of the room in a flash and noisily went out the back door with our water pots. When we came back, Grandmother was struggling with the fire-making.

"Can't you girls get up earlier and start the fire before going for water? You know how it is always a great pain for my back to light the firewood and lean over to make the fire," she said as we came in.

"I'm sorry, Mother," Bano replied. "We didn't want to be late for the water."

"Well, see that you get up earlier tomorrow morning," said Grandmother testily.

But nothing she could say or do could take away my feverish anticipation. I finished everything in record time. Feeding the chickens, taking in the pieces of wood and stacking them on top of the fireplace and making her bed, after all that. I didn't want to forget anything because I was afraid she would stop me from going to school if I overlooked any of my jobs. I double checked to see if I had remembered everything.

Bano called from the kitchen to say the food was ready. By then, I had washed and dried myself and was impatient to get into my school clothes. But Bano had told me I must first eat and then put on my school clothes, for if I stained them with food, I would feel very bad about going to school in a stained shirt on my first day. So when she called I went very happily. Grandmother served my food very slowly or so it seemed to me. It was hot rice with a broth of lentils and garlic and some dried meat. It tasted wonderful and I ate hungrily.

"Eat slowly, girl," Grandmother admonished me. "One would think we never fed you good food."

"Sorry, Grandmother," I said between mouthfuls of food, remembering too late that she hated us to speak when we had food in our mouths.

Thankfully, she didn't notice. As we were eating, there was a heavy step on the floor. "Aunt," called out a familiar voice. It was Uncle Atu. He grinned at me after greeting Grandmother and sat down by the fire. Grandmother hastily served him food which he first refused but accepted when pressed again and he too sat down to eat with us. I was grateful he was not paying too much attention to me. I remembered the last time Grandmother had caught me playing with him and rapped me on the calf with her cane. So I didn't want him to show too openly that he was fond of me.

"Lieno is going to school today," said Bano to him.

"Oh is she? How wonderful. Is this your first day at school then?" he asked.

I nodded yes. He beamed and reached a hand into his shirt pocket and pulled out a one-rupee note.

"Here," he said, handing it to me. "You may buy sweets and eat them in school. The children who don't cry always get sweets: I know you are a good girl and won't cry which is why I am giving you money to buy sweets."

I looked at him with rounded eyes. A one-rupee note! I had never spent a whole rupee on myself. When Mother took me to the shops she would buy a lot of sweets for a rupee but share them amongst my brothers and me. Now I had a rupee to spend by myself. I was so excited.

"Humph!" said Grandmother in a decidedly grumpy voice. "I wouldn't have served you food if I knew you were going to spoil the girl with money."

"Oh Aunt, it is only for today. Here, Lieno, take it and put it in your bag. It is for you to spend and be good at school."

I whispered my thanks gratefully and took it from him before Grandmother could snatch it away. Of course she wouldn't do that because Uncle Atu was a grown-up but I had no doubt she would find some means of depriving me of it. I resolved to buy all the sweets I could with it and hide them from her.

After we had eaten, Uncle Atu said, "Get ready, I am headed the same way, I can take you to your school."

I was so happy to hear that and I dressed in a great hurry. But something felt very wrong when I put on my sweater. My neck wouldn't go through.

"Bano, what's wrong?" I cried.

She looked up from tying my shoelaces and took off the sweater. And then she laughed out loud and long.

"What?" I asked.

There were tears running down her face from laughing so hard,

"No wonder you couldn't put your head through. You were pushing it up your sleeve!"

Once that was sorted out I was ready to go. In my bag was a box of pencils and an eraser and an old copy that Bano had found from among

Grandfather's books and slipped into my bag. I felt like I had been doing this all my life. Uncle Atu took my hand and we set off. Halfway up the road, we met Mother who had hurried down to take me herself. But I said I would go with Uncle Atu and then she let me go after making me promise I would not cry. She turned to go and then stopped and called us back.

"Oh, I almost forgot to give you your box of crayons," she said, holding out a little box of colourful crayons.

How happy I was! It was better than Christmas.

"What a fine girl you are," said Uncle Atu and I couldn't stop smiling at that. "You know, Lieno, you are such a smart girl and I know you will do well at school. I know that very well. Don't let anyone discourage you. Will you promise me that?"

He had a sombre look on his face and I found it easy to say yes, I would do well at school.

Vimenuo was in the schoolyard. I couldn't see her mother anywhere. Then afterwards I spotted her talking to one of the teachers. Uncle Atu stayed on in the school long after the teachers had taken us to our classroom and made us sit and given us a sweet each. There were some children younger than I. They clung to their mothers and so the mothers had to sit in the classroom along with them. The teacher was a pretty young woman with her hair tied in a high ponytail. She smiled a lot and told us we were a fine group of children, and that she thought we would be even more fine if we let our mothers go out of the room so we could learn a song to sing to them when we went home. Some of the children let their mothers go after that but two or three began to whimper as soon as their mothers got up to leave. When all the mothers were out of the room, there was such crying in the classroom as the younger children began to cry loudly and the others slowly joined them. Finally the teacher could not make herself heard and so she picked up the crying ones in turn and spoke gently to them. But they would not stop so she asked the mothers to return to the room. Even then, some of them would not stop crying and had to go home for the day.

Vimenuo and I held each other's hand tightly because her mother was not there anymore. We didn't want to cry. We thought school was wonderful and we didn't want to be sent home at all. I especially wanted the pretty teacher to pat me on the head as she was doing to everyone around us particularly to those who cried the loudest. She looked around to see if there were any children who were not crying. It was then she spotted four of us, Vimenuo and I and two older boys, and she smiled at us and gave us extra sweets for being so good, she said. Then she stood at my desk and asked me what I had in my bag. I took out my crayon box proudly and placed it carefully on the desk.

"Ah, can you draw, Dielieno?" she asked.

"I think so," I said.

Then she gave me paper to draw on and a picture book as well so I could copy the pictures in it. The four of us sat and drew pictures. The two boys drew pictures of trees and cars and Vimenuo and I both drew flowers. Then I made a girl with a ponytail and a short frock with flowers in her hand. The teacher came by and asked, "Is that me?" I felt embarrassed and said yes in a whisper. The girl in the picture had big ears. "Oh I look prettier in that picture," she said happily so I didn't feel so shy. After an hour or so, I looked out of the window and saw that Uncle Atu had come by to look in on me. I waved back at him and he was relieved that I seemed to be enjoying myself. I wanted to tell him I could make my own way home and waved him away. But he didn't understand immediately. He thought I wanted something from him so I had to wave vigorously again. Then he smiled and waved at me and went away.

4

School was the best thing that could have happened to me.
There were sacrifices I had to make. Grandmother did not want me
to go to school so she tried to make life even more difficult by making
me get up an hour earlier. In that extra hour I had to fetch water
alone and make the fire. I was not to feed the chickens earlier though.
Because if they were fed earlier, they would trouble Grandmother
later when she was alone in the house and drying her paddy in the
sun. I did not complain because I liked going to school so much.
But I did not like going so early to the water spot by myself; it was
very dark and I could not see three feet ahead of me. I remembered
the stories the old women used to tell about the bigger water spot
which lay above the small one that we used. That one was not a
water spot actually, it was a proper pond.

One morning, a girl saw a man by the pond. He was half turned
away from her but she could see that he was very good looking. She
was a big girl and so she looked at him closely without fear. They
said she fell in love with him there and then because he was so
beautiful.

"Are you going to bathe so early?" she asked him because men do not fetch water. They only came to the pond to bathe. She probably forgot that only the middle pond could be used for bathing and the top pond was strictly for drinking and cooking.

He said, "No, I am here to take a bride."

The young woman was so startled by this reply that she forgot to scoop water into her pitcher. The man then walked away from her. He walked up to the wooded area above the pond and suddenly he was covered by a thick fog and she did not see him anymore.

"He was not any man of the village," said the young woman vehemently when she was questioned by her elder sister.

"I have never seen anyone more wonderful. As he turned from me and walked upward, I saw that his ankle was so well turned, almost like a girl's but there was nothing girlish about him. And he was fair, so much more fair than Neizo."

"Hmm, fairer than Neizo? You know, of course, that Neizo's father was a white man, one of the soldiers that came during the war, married Neizo's mother and had Neizo by her but was killed in the war. Could he have been a white man? If he was more fair than Neizo?"

Her sister had a slight smile on her face as she said this because they both knew the only white men around these parts now were spirits.

"No, not a white man," insisted the younger woman, "he spoke our language well. He had the accent of our village."

And they mused about it for some days.

But one evening, the younger woman suddenly caught a fever and grew steadily worse. She lay in bed burning and restless. In the end, they could not even get water down her throat. On the evening of the sixth day, she exclaimed, "Ah, you have come!" and she sat bolt upright in her bed. The setting sun was casting long shadows on the bedroom floor and walls. Her sister looked to see who it was she had spoken to but there was no one there. "Will you come sit by me?" raved her younger sister, her eyes fixed on the door. The older woman went to her and held her hand and felt her fever. It had left as mysteriously as it had come. There was a beatific look on the girl's face. "I knew you would come, my love," she continued and then she slumped back on to the bed. The older girl screamed when she saw the pallor that had quickly settled on her dead sister's face. She couldn't bring herself to close the eyes that had fixed themselves upon the door in death. The old women still said that it was not a good thing to go too early to the pond. The spirit of the white man was often seen there by early risers. In the years that he was sighted, young unmarried women died in great numbers.

I remembered every detail of this story whenever I went to fetch water early. Sometimes I heard hard breathing behind me when my water pitcher was full and heavy so I could not turn around to look. Another time, I was sure someone had tugged at my pitcher. But I never told anyone about it. I knew Grandmother would scoff at me if I told her. If she decided to send me earlier just to get the stories out of my head, it would be intolerable. Bano had gotten so sleepy these days, it was no use trying to wake her to get her to accompany me. So I bore with it and tried to sing and keep my mind off the stories when I went to fetch water. Some mornings, drunks would be staggering home. I welcomed the sight of these men and blest them for going home so late. A real man, even if he were dead drunk, was preferable any day to a spirit. Fortunately, the days were dawning earlier as spring brought winter to an end and there was more light in the morning after two months of darkness.

When the chickens were grown large enough to eat, we slaughtered one of them and Grandmother made me take half the cooked meat to my brothers. The boys were happy but they were

 Easterine Iralu

used to Grandmother sending them meat ever so often that it was nothing new for them. I envied them. I now knew that I would never be sent half a chicken. I rushed back to eat and dress for school. In my plate I found a piece of chicken meat and lots of broth. Slowly, I savoured my meat. Grandmother never left her pot unguarded so I could not get another piece. I should have got used to getting one piece of meat by now. But I always wanted more. I was a little late for school. In a hurry Bano helped me to dress and I ran onto the main road that led to the Mission School. It was still called that even though the missionaries who had set it up years ago were now long gone. But those Angamis who had been educated there had now taken it over and extended it to a High School as well.

At school, they gave us a lot of drawing to do. But after some time, our teacher made some of us learn the alphabet and count numbers. Each evening I came home and opened my bag and showed Grandmother what we had done at school. But she was never interested. She would look once or twice and gruffly tell me to change out of my school clothes and finish my chores. So I stopped showing her my work. But if I finished early, Bano and I would sit by the kerosene lantern and I would show her what I had drawn at school. One day, I discovered I could read. I then became very interested in leafing through Grandfather's old books. There were words I recognised in the musty books that were stacked up in a corner of the storeroom. Sometimes, Grandmother would tear out the paper to cover the fermented soya bean she made once every two weeks. The notebooks were brown and dog-eared now. When I learnt to read they became precious to me. I tried to tell Grandmother but she said roughly, "People can't eat books," and tore at the books fiercely. So I kept quiet about it. But I did take out some of the books that were not so browned by the smoke from the wood fire and I hid them under my bed.

When our teacher brought books with pictures and words to class for the first time, I spoke aloud the word I could read on the book, "ball." The teacher was so surprised. "What? Who taught you that Dielieno? Has your father been teaching you how to read?"

"No, I live with my grandmother."

"I thought your grandmother had not been to school. Has she been teaching you?"

"No, I learnt it by myself."

"What a clever girl you are! Look at that. You can read before we've taught you how to read!"

It was wonderful that the teacher was so pleased with my reading skills. Maybe I showed off a bit. She asked me to read more words and I could easily read *doll, cat, fish* and *horse* but had some difficulty with *elephant, girl* and *apple*. She sat me on her lap and made me read more words and repeat the words I did not know. After school she asked where I lived. I thought it best to let her go to my father's house because Grandmother would probably not like a teacher from my school visiting me. Two days later, Father came to see us and when he saw me he picked me up and carried me. "My clever girl," he said proudly. I hoped it meant that he would take me home. But he had something else to say. Carrying me into the house, he called out, "Mother, do you know what this girl has done?"

Grandmother frowned at me. "What is it now? She gives me enough trouble already."

"Mother, it is not anything bad but she has done so well at school that her teachers want to put her in a different class. They want her to be with the children who are a year older and can read and write."

"Humph!" snorted Grandmother. "She'll only get ideas about herself if she is put with older children."

Easterine Iralu

"No, Mother, she will do even better," said Father, "Lieno is a clever girl and may do better than the boys at school."

"I really don't know what it is your generation sees in school. Your children are not being taught the skills of life because they are too busy studying. I was doing such a good job of teaching the girl to work about the house. It was difficult enough. She has a stubborn streak to her. Now you come with all these plans for school. She will completely forget all I have taught her now."

"No, Mother, it will not be like that. I think Lieno is quite capable of learning what you are ready to teach her as well as what she is taught at school. I am so pleased because Vini and Pete are not doing well. They are both very lazy."

"They are boys. Boys will be boys. They will be all right. They should be taught to be manly. In my father's day, boys never did any work because they had to look after the village and engage enemy warriors in warfare. The household that did not have a male heir was considered barren. They were always in constant danger if there was a war. The women would only have one man to protect them. That is why we love our male children so much and we give them the best of food. And we should."

Father did not say anything after that. He said he would go home to eat and then leave for work. Grandmother offered him food. He refused at first but she forced it on him and so he sat down and ate with us.

"Oh Mother, you always make such good food," he said between mouthfuls.

"Isn't Mother a good cook, too?" I asked innocently.

Grandmother's face looked as though it would burst.

"Ah yes, but not as good as your Grandmother," said Father and she was immediately placated.

At school, I was put into a new classroom. Vimenuo was to be with the others. So I was alone in the new class with nine other children. The girls were bigger than I and there were five boys who were working at their books. I, too, was given a new book by the teacher. It had pictures and more words. My new teacher was older and she did not smile as much as my old teacher. She rapped on our desks with a piece of sharpened bamboo if we were noisy. The students were terrified of her. They had their noses to their books all day. I struggled to read the new words.

"Write down the words on the first page," she said to me.

I was aghast. I didn't know how to write, I could read the letters but I had never learnt to write. In any case I had never found the time to write.

"I don't know how to," I said.

"What?" exclaimed the teacher. "Who sent this child here? Didn't they say you could read and write?"

I didn't know what to say.

"I don't have time for this, I cannot be wasting time teaching you to write here. Don't they know this class is for the children who can already read and write?"

I felt very ashamed. To make matters worse, I felt something wet on my cheek and I knew I was beginning to cry.

"Stop crying," said the teacher in her harsh voice. "You will have to stay back after school."

Oh, could matters get any worse? If I were late Grandmother would be so angry. If she learnt the reason behind my coming late, she would try all she could to make me stop going to school.

There was nothing I could do to avoid it. I thought the teacher would stop me from coming to school if I explained why I could not stay back after school. So I stayed back and she taught me how to write. I was nervous but eager to learn fast so that I could go home before it was too late. When she finally let me go, I was a whole hour late. Grandmother was waiting outside on the porch.

                    Easterine Iralu

"What kept you so late? Out playing after school I suppose, with that no-good daughter of Zekuo's?" she shouted.

"No, Grandmother, my teacher was teaching me more things," I said.

It wasn't a lie, was it? I did learn extra things in that one hour after school.

"Don't talk back to me, girl!" she shouted.

I stepped aside to avoid the cane that she thrust at my back. But that angered her more.

"Stop dancing around like the little monkey that you are!" she shouted.

I steeled myself and stood still. I flinched when her cane landed on my calf and an involuntary cry escaped me. Grandmother always knew where it would hurt the most.

"Get out of that ridiculous outfit," she ordered.

I fled to my room and quickly threw my school bag on the floor. I buried my face in my hands and hot scalding tears wet my pillow as I sobbed my heart out. It was bad enough to appear a fool at school but to be beaten by Grandmother when I had done no wrong was too much for me. I felt a hand on my shoulder. It was Bano.

"Bano, Bano, why does Grandmother hate me so?" I asked between sobs.

"She doesn't hate you, Lieno, she doesn't, really, she wants you to be a good girl. It's her way of bringing you up to be a good woman."

"Well, I don't care about being a good woman. I shan't ever be a good woman, whatever that is," I said between sniffles.

"Oh, poor girl, don't go on so, come, I have some jaggery for you. Let's get you out of your school clothes and get you a treat."

5

I missed Vimenuo very much. The older girls in my class were not so much fun to be with. They preferred to be in a group of their own and if I tried to play with them, the oldest of them would wrinkle her nose. I knew that meant they did not want to play with me. There was one girl who was fat and ungainly. She was kinder than the others. When we played tug of war, we were a team, she and I, and the others were always on the other side. Because she was heavy we always won. The other girls did not like that. To make matters worse, the teacher said I was making very good progress in class. One day, she gave us back our work after correcting it and she said, "Dielieno has scored the highest marks, you others should be ashamed of yourself because she is so much younger than the rest of you." That did it. After the teacher left, one of the older girls hissed, "Teacher's pet" and the rest of them joined in. It never occurred to me to do badly at my lessons because I liked it so much and so when I scored higher marks, the others would always hiss at me.

The boys were not so bad. I don't think they disliked me. But two of them would tease me mercilessly, by taking my school bag away at the end of school and making me run after them to get it back. As I neared the one holding it, he would throw it to the other boy, so I would chase after them for a long time. I grew more anxious as I realized that they would make me late with their silly game and then I would get a beating from Grandmother. Suddenly I burst into tears from the unfairness of it all. Then the older boy instantly took the bag and gave it to me saying, "Hey it was only a game, here's your bag, stop crying, you can have this sweet, stop crying now." I took the bag and the sweet and ran home.

Yet I loved school and didn't want to stop going because I loved learning all that I could. So I didn't tell Grandmother or Bano about the way the girls behaved with me. At recess, I always sought out Vimenuo and we would play together and if either of us had some money, we would buy cotton candy or orange drinks which were so diluted they looked orange in colour but tasted like slightly sweet plain water. Grandmother did not believe that I should be given a little pocket money like the other children. My daily routine was to run home during recess and eat a bit of food before running back to school before the bell rang. My stomach hurt when I ran back after eating but if I didn't eat the whole day I would have terrible stomach cramps. It happened twice so I always came back to eat. Grandmother justified not giving me money by saying, "The stuff they sell in the schoolyard is so unclean. If she buys that she will come down with cholera and we will all be affected too." She said this to Bano in my presence. Hundreds of schoolchildren bought and ate sweets or *pakoras* from the shops without ever falling sick. But it was just one of those things that you didn't argue about with Grandmother. I got used to the routine.

One evening a man came to the house. I could not see his face properly because the sun had set and we had not lighted all the lanterns yet. Then he stepped into the light of the lantern by the kitchen and Grandmother said, "Damn, what do you want, Sizo?"

The man looked amused and said, "That's not a very nice way of welcoming a guest."

She turned around and almost spat out her words, "Didn't I tell you I don't want you to be interfering in her life?"

"She is my daughter, in case you have forgotten Vibano. But don't worry, I haven't come to take her away."

"As though I would let you take her away. After all the work I have put into her in the past years."

"Will you calm down? See, you are frightening the little girl. Is she Visa's daughter then? Come here, dear, have a chocolate."

I stood where I was, fascinated by the chocolate the strange man held out and fearful to make a move toward it in case Grandmother should hit me if I stepped forward.

"Grandmother, may I?" I asked softly.

She didn't speak but nodded yes. It was a big block of Cadbury's chocolate and my brothers and I had tasted it sometimes at Christmas time and also when some of Father's brothers came visiting. "You are not to eat that before dinner, girl," rasped out Grandmother as I took the chocolate.

"All right, Grandmother," I said and turned to the man and said thank you.

He laughingly chucked me under the chin.

It was sheer torture to imagine what the chocolate would taste like. I had to remember to make it melt slowly in my mouth. Vini taught us that was the best way to make it last and to get the full taste of it. I couldn't wait to eat the chocolate. I was also very curious about who the strange man was. He was not afraid of Grandmother and for the first time, I saw Grandmother looking flustered and visibly struggling to be in control. The man answered my unspoken question.

"You may call me Grandfather because I am your Grandmother's

 42   Easterine Iralu

younger brother. My name is Sizo. Can you remember that? Can you say it?"

"Sizo," I responded.

"No, not like that, you must say Grandfather Sizo and you may simply call me Grandfather when we are alone."

He looked as though he were not more than ten years older than Father. He must be a lot younger than Grandmother then, I thought.

"I am Bano's father," he continued.

"Oh!" I said in total surprise.

So this man was Bano's father, and she was not Grandmother's daughter though she called Grandmother 'mother'. Why was Bano living with Grandmother and not with this nice man who was her father? But I could not, of course, ask such questions.

Grandfather Sizo ate dinner and afterwards, slept in the spare room. It was a dark, damp little room below Grandmother's and often used by guests. Bano and I made up the bed and she dragged down his bag to the room.

"Bano, is that man really your father?" I whispered.

"Yes, but I have been here for as long as I can remember."

"Then who is your mother?" I asked indelicately.

"Don't you know, Lieno? Hasn't your mother told you?" she asked.

"No, never, and I never thought of asking her because I always thought you were my father's younger sister."

Bano looked a little pained and then she said, "Father never married my mother and I have seen her just three or four times. I was not allowed to call her Mother and I could not call my father 'Father' when your grandfather was alive."

I thought it was all very silly to make you call another woman and man Father and Mother instead of your real parents.

"You must not tell other people, Lieno, they would talk about our family and that is what Grandmother hates so much. She took me away because she did not want a scandal. You must never say anything of this to the women at the water spot."

"Of course not," I assured her.

It all seemed very silly to me and I didn't know what was to be gained by telling the women about it.

"Is your father married now?" I asked.

"Yes, he has three children by his wife. I have been with them sometimes but they don't live here. Father is a Compounder in Tening which is very far from here. He doesn't come here often. And he rarely brings his family to Kohima. His wife is a woman from those parts."

"What do you think he wants? Is he going to take you away?"

"No, I don't think he will do that. Your grandmother would never let him do that. He never tried hard to keep me when I was little. But when he comes, he does give me a little money."

I was surprised by this news but accepted it as it was told to me. I was only mildly curious as to who Bano really was and now that I did know, it didn't really interest me that her father had not married her mother. But I did feel sorry that she had to be brought up by Grandmother.

"Are you going to be making that bed all night?" Grandmother's voice sounded plaintively down the stairs. We both jumped. "Coming now, Mother," was Bano's quick response and we climbed up the stairs a little guiltily. Bano's father was sitting by the kitchen fire with a large mug of black tea. I knew it tasted bitter because I had once tasted Father's after-dinner tea which didn't have any sugar or milk in it. It tasted awful. It was one of those things that only grown-ups could like. Like the bitter vegetables and strong smelling seeds that Grandmother sometimes put in her meat broths and which went up your nose if you ate in a hurry and bit into

Easterine Iralu

one of them.

Grandfather Sizo didn't seem to be in a hurry to go to bed.

"Been a bad year for the village," he was saying to Grandmother when we came back.

"You mean it has been a bad year for you, don't you Sizo?" she retorted.

"No. I mean it has been a bad year for the whole village. The rain was unexpected when it came in the middle of the harvest and then, that hailstorm out of nowhere. Many of the villagers lost a third of their harvests. Now, the Government is saying that it will give grain to the villagers next year but they need someone educated to write the application. That's why I am here. Tomorrow I will write an application and take it to the Deputy Commissioner."

Grandmother did not say anything and so he went on.

"Do you remember the old man, Heurang? Well, he died last week. When mourners went to his house, they found that there was no grain in his house. The neighbours quickly brought food from their own houses and arranged his funeral. After his wife's death, he had been living on alone in their house and cultivating their field. His son never came back after going away to live in Dimapur with his wife and two children. Word was sent to him but he never came to his father's funeral. My guess is he died both of starvation and loneliness. Well, that is how hard life has been for the village this year."

When he finished, no one spoke for a long time. I felt so sorry for the people suffering in the village. Bano began to wash the dinner plates and the pots.

"Do you have enough to eat, Grandfather Sizo?" I asked in concern.

"Fortunately yes, Lieno. We live on my salary and we have some grain from the previous year's harvest so we will survive. It is hard for the older folks who are not able to work as much as the others.

When their small harvests get destroyed there is little for them to eat. Some of them live on lentils that are mouldy because they have been stored for a long time."

"Will you write about that in your application, Grandfather?"

"No, dear girl, the government officer will not have time to read about the woes of a little village. We will be lucky if they send a survey team for the fields and then send us some grain soon. It will save a lot of elderly people from starving to death. Oh they won't be allowed to starve to death. But they would be too proud to tell their neighbours that they have no more food."

"Off to bed with you, girl. She is getting impudent after having started school," Grandmother said in her irritated voice.

"I don't think that is true, Vibano," said Grandfather Sizo, "She seems to be a bright girl and very smart for her age, I think. I don't find her impudent at all."

"Humph!" was Grandmother's reply.

I got up and left before she could scold me. It always angered Grandmother when others praised me in front of her. She didn't think I had anything good in me. Countless times in the week, she reminded me what a clumsy child I was, how I could never remember to do anything properly and how other girls my age would have finished my work in a quarter of the time I took.

As I lay in bed, I thought of the starving man who was too proud to ask others for food. I didn't think I could do that. It must be so painful to die alone of hunger. I also thought it was wonderful that Grandfather Sizo was the man that the village had pinned their hopes on to write the application to the Deputy Commissioner. I saw how much I could do with my education if someday I could learn to write applications. Maybe I could save whole villages if I learnt to do that. I fell asleep with that happy thought. When morning came, I had overslept. Bano nudged me awake and whispered to me to get up and fetch water before

Grandmother found out I was still sleeping. I ran out without putting on a sweater. At the water spot, the water was already murky so I waited for it to settle. The murkiness swirled slowly around. So I became impatient, and took my pitcher and went to the big pond and fetched clean water. Few people were about, a young girl and three young women. We exchanged greetings but I didn't know any of them.

Bano had already started to cook when I reached home. "You're lucky my father's presence distracted her," she hissed at me. The morning passed quickly. We ate in another hour and I was ready for school.

Grandfather Sizo, seated in the kitchen, saw me in my uniform and asked, "Are you off to school now?"

When I said yes, he looked disappointed and said, "Then I won't see you when I go, because I am leaving this afternoon. Here, take this and buy yourself a packet of sweets," he handed a five-rupee note to me.

I was too surprised to take it. Grandmother was seated beside him. Her hand shot out and she grabbed the money, "Don't corrupt her with such a big amount. I will see that she gets it in small amounts."

"Oh, Vibano," said Grandfather Sizo.

"If she does not give you the money you must tell me, right Lieno?" he asked me. I was too scared to say anything but felt it wisest to nod yes and leave quietly.

"You better give her the money, I won't have that little girl cheated of a little pleasure in life," I heard him say as I was leaving.

"You know I don't believe in giving money to children," said Grandmother.

"All right, but that is her money, let that be clear," he said with a note of finality in his voice.

6

"I guess you are growing, Lieno. That's the second time I have had to take out the hem on your skirt. If you grow any more we will have to stitch you a new skirt."

Mother was bent over the blue skirt I wore to school. There was a white line where she had taken out the hem and she was now re-stitching it below that line. So now the white line showed up prominently like a pattern. Many of the girls at school wore skirts with the same kind of white line showing. Some wore skirts faded so blue that it was no longer the navy blue of the school's regulation uniform. But no one took much notice. We knew that the very washed out blue skirts had been passed down to them by their older sisters in the same school. I had one new shirt and when it got dirty I wore an old shirt of Bulie's which had a brown stain over the pocket which was hard to hide.

"You did very well in your mid-term examinations, your teacher was very happy with you," said Mother.

"Did she say anything else?" I asked eagerly.

"Well, she did say that if you kept up the progress you have shown, you could pass your final exams and go on to the next class in the new year."

"Oh, did she really say that?" I was very happy to hear that.

The final examination was a month away from now and I was trying to remember all that I had learnt during the year. I really wanted to pass the exam and go on to the next class. I did miss not being in the same class as Vimenuo but we compensated by playing together at recess and walking to school and going back home together.

Now that I was at Grandmother's I could not go to visit my Mother and Father unless there was some legitimate reason. Today it was the skirt hemline. Bano could have fixed that but Grandmother thought it would take her away from her other jobs. In the end, I was sent to Mother with the skirt. It took longer than expected because she had to darn a hole along the hemline. None of my brothers were home. They had gone out fishing with the neighbour's boys who were older than them and would go off on fishing trips on their own or with their father, a big man who used to carry me on his shoulder when I was smaller. The house was very quiet without them. Father was at work. Sunshine streamed in from the window and the little house looked pretty. The sunlight filtering in through Mother's hand-made curtains made the rooms look bright and colourful. Mother worked very hard to make the small four-roomed house look cheerful. She planted flowers in boxes in front of the house. But it was hard to keep it tidy with the boys always littering the porch with their toys and books. Father did not help much. He would expect Mother to clean the house and wash all the clothes and have cooked food ready when he got home. It was a lot of work and took all morning. Twice a month, Mother would sun paddy and would run in and finish her chores and then run out of the house again to chase birds or chickens away. She always got up early to fetch water. Luckily, the boys bathed at the lower pond and Mother preferred to wash clothes there as well so she didn't have to fetch much water for bathing.

"There, it's done now. Put it on and let's see how it fits," said Mother holding out the skirt.

I put it on over the frock I wore. It now reached down to my knees.

"It should last till the end of the school year," said Mother. "You are growing but not so rapidly that you'll need two new skirts in a year."

I stood on tiptoe to try and appear taller. "I am six and a half now Mother, and next year I will be seven."

"You are a big girl now, and Bano says you work very well. I am proud of you, Lieno. One day you will understand that it was not such a bad thing for you to go and live with Grandmother."

"But don't you miss me, Mother? Don't you and Father want me back?" I asked.

"It's not for long that you'll be gone, dear," said Mother soothingly but when I looked into her eyes, she had a tear running down her left eye.

So she did miss me. I was happy to see that tear though it pained me that Mother was sad.

"Besides, you are already learning so many things there," she added bravely. "Come on, let's get you back."

Grandmother was out on the porch sitting in the sun. "What took you two so long?" she asked.

"It's not very easy to take out hemlines from old skirts. I had to be careful not to tear the fabric," answered Mother.

"Humph, all that trouble for a little girl. I really don't understand why they have to send girls to school when it is such a bother for everyone else."

I crept away because I really did not want to listen to Grandmother's theory of why girls shouldn't go to school for the umpteenth time.

 50

"Put the kettle on, girl," she shouted after me.

"Yes Grandmother," I shouted back but not too loudly in case she interpreted it as an impudent response.

In the kitchen was Grandmother's sister who I called Grandmother Neikuo. She was peeling potatoes at the sink. The kitchen was dark and I stumbled over a low wooden stool. Being in the bright sunshine outside had blinded me and I carefully felt my way around the kitchen. I almost fell over Grandmother Neikuo as she squatted over the potatoes.

"Oh, I'm so sorry, Grandmother Neikuo, I didn't see you."

"Don't rush around, girl, that is not the way young girls should behave."

"Sorry," I repeated.

I went to the fire and put the kettle on the fire and stoked the embers with more wood to get the fire going again.

"Grandmother wants tea," I explained because Grandmother Neikuo had turned around curiously to see what I was doing.

"Careful with that fire, you don't want too much of it in case the firewood stacked there starts to burn too," she warned.

Grandmother Neikuo was not difficult like Grandmother Vibano and she didn't mind me. When she came, she taught me how to do things in a neater way. I was never half as nervous around her as I was around her sister.

Grandmother Neikuo had never married. I once heard my cousin say that as a young girl she had been engaged to a student of theology. But the man died before they could marry and so she never married. My cousin also said that she still kept the photograph of the young theologian in her bedroom behind the photograph of my parents' wedding. I had never seen it myself. We didn't visit her much. She preferred to come to us and help with the household work. Sometimes she would bring homemade plum jam when she came. Grandmother

Neikuo was very good to my brothers. She didn't seem to mind us girls either. So we liked her to be around. She kept Grandmother in good humour.

"No school today, Lieno?" she asked.

"It's Saturday. We never have school on Saturdays," I explained.

She smiled at her own mistake and said, "Of course, it is Saturday, I must be aging faster. I could not remember what day of the week it was today."

We both laughed at that.

"Is that tea water ready yet?" Grandmother's voice sounded sharply across the corridor.

"It's almost ready, Grandmother," I shouted back.

Grandmother Neikuo's photograph in our sitting room showed an attractive girl with a big smile. She had been photographed by one of the white men who had been in Kohima as aides to the Deputy Commissioner. In our home we had a copy of the photograph in a smaller frame. I had seen a copy of it in my aunt's house too. It was treasured by the family and every family member had a copy it seemed. There were few photographs of Grandmother and Grandfather. In one, Grandfather was squinting in the sunlight and Grandmother was looking solemnly into the camera. Neikuo was intimidated by Grandmother like the rest of us. She would not argue with Grandmother if she were angry over some subject. But she would try to change the subject and tell some other story of people they both knew. And then, Grandmother would be distracted sufficiently to ask about the other people. If we were sent away on an errand, I would return to find them talking about the neighbours and some outrageous thing that had happened to them. They gossiped endlessly when they were together. But if we came near, they stopped talking or changed over to some innocuous subject.

 Easterine Iralu

Nevertheless, Neikuo always seemed to me a pleasant person because she did not lose her temper as easily as Grandmother did and she had never hit me. Also, she was poorer. The cupboard in her kitchen was not very interesting. I never saw much more than a packet of flour or a bottle of cooking oil inside it. She kept a small garden and gathered herbs or brinjals from the brinjal bushes in her garden, to put into her broths. When she served tea, there were no biscuits to go with it and the tea in her house was weak and not sweet enough. I didn't like it but drank it to be polite. But she would invite us when her sugarcane grew high enough to be cut and then she would cut us very juicy and sweet stalks which we ate standing, with the juice dribbling down our shirt fronts.

"Do you want to give me a head massage afterwards?" she asked.

"If it's all right with Grandmother," I replied.

So after tea, she asked if I might give her a head massage and Grandmother said, "Okay for a little while."

Mother left shortly after tea. We sat on the porch on the wooden floor and Grandmother Neikuo untied her hair so that the silver gleamed in the sunshine.

She had very long hair reaching down to her lower back. It was soft to touch. I ran my fingers through her hair and impulsively said, "When I'm grown I want to have hair like yours."

"You won't get a husband then," she laughed, "because no young man would marry a girl with grey hair."

"Oh I don't want to ever marry, so that's all right," I said.

"We'll see when the time comes. That is what they all say when they are young."

I smeared my palm with coconut oil and kneaded it into her hair. I took each section and oiled it down the way I had been taught by Bano.

"Oh this is one of the pleasures of life! It feels so good I could pay for it," she half sighed.

"Not that you would have any money to pay," retorted Grandmother.

Neikuo laughed at that but there was a strained note in her laughter. Grandmother had this odd way of putting down Neikuo by reminding her she had no money and no earthly possessions. Usually it ended in a good natured way with Neikuo laughing. But lately I thought I could hear irritation in her voice before the laughter.

"Nor would you, had you not married a man who had some education and a job in the D.C.'s office," she retorted now, "and a fat pension that you could live on after his death."

Grandmother was shocked at this response, "Surely there is no need to discuss my financial status in front of this impudent girl. She might blabber about it to others."

Neikuo said, "Oh she is not like that, I can't believe that she would do that."

"Humph!" said Grandmother and that finished the conversation.

I had learnt to ignore the opinion Grandmother had of me. I tried hard not to give her any reason to think ill of me. I didn't linger around when she was gossiping with her sister. I tried not to talk too much to the women at the water spot. I greeted them when I saw them and answered their questions but if they asked things about Grandmother or Bano, I simply said I didn't know and if they tried to detain me, I earnestly said that if I were late I would be scolded. So I always managed to avoid being drawn into gossiping with them. The most they had got out of me was what we were going to eat for lunch or what we had had for dinner the previous night. They were very curious about Grandfather Sizo's visit. "What did Bano's father want?" they asked. I ignored the way they had referred to him as Bano's father and answered that he had come to write an application to the D.C. "Was that all?" they laughed. "Didn't he say anything about taking his daughter with him?" This was asked amid much smirking. I said I didn't know anything of what the grown-ups talked about. Then I put my pitcher in my basket and lifted it on the higher stone so I could carry it without any help. I said I was getting late and quickly walked home. I could hear them laughing behind me for a long time. Of course I knew by now that I should never talk of what went on with the women to Grandmother. She hated them fiercely. If she found out that I was often drawn into a little talk with them she would forbid me to greet them. And that would be so rude. I didn't want to do that.

Neikuo was snoring gently by the time I finished massaging her hair. "The pig," said Grandmother as she watched her sister with her mouth hanging open and the sun in her face. "Should I wake her?" I asked. "No, the sun will soon do that," was Grandmother's reply. "Go and see if the yam leaves are getting enough sun." I tiptoed off. Grandmother and Bano dried a great quantity of vegetables in season—yam leaves, mustard leaves and squash sliced into thin pieces. In the winter months, when we ran out of green vegetables in the garden they used these dried herbs alternately in the broth with dried pieces of meat. It always tasted very good. The yam leaves were in the shadow because the morning sun had moved away from the spot where Bano had dried them. So I moved them into the front yard where the sun was fierce though it was early winter now.

7

At Christmas time, I was allowed to go home to my parents for a week. Oh what joy! I slept in my little bed in a corner of my parents' room. Mother baked a cake in the ammunition box that had been left behind during the war by British troops. Almost every house had one of these. Ours had a glass window. It was a heavy box and could be opened from the side. But we were not supposed to open the box until an hour had gone by or else the rising cake would collapse and a brick hard confection would be the result. Mixing the cake was a long procedure of beating the butter and eggs, sugar and flour and baking powder into a smooth batter. Mother baked her cakes at night after dinner. All of us helped her and now even Leto was big enough to help beat the batter. He would often slosh it out of the pot so Mother did not like him to do it. But soon her arms would get tired and then, she would call him to help, reminding him to do it slowly. It was something we always associated with Christmas because we never made cake at any other time of the year.

This year we made two cakes. One was a little burnt but the other was just right. It rose beautifully and didn't sink in the middle. It tasted wonderful, just right, and as soft as it should be— not hard like cake that has been left inside too long. We also ate the burnt one after scraping off the blackened bottom bits. We had a small Christmas tree. My brothers had got cards from their friends and they placed them on the shelves. I got three cards, one from Vimenuo, one from the fat girl in my class and one from the older boy who gave me back my bag. The card from the fat girl was very big and pretty. It had the picture of a house with lots of roses in front. Inside, my name was written in a childish scrawl. But, if you looked carefully, you could make out she had rubbed out the name of another person to whom the card had been sent before and she had written my name over it. Lower on the card, she had rubbed out, until the paper tore a bit, just a little bit, another name that was on the card, and she had written her name over it. It read, "with best wishes, from Lanuo." I didn't mind. Mine was the biggest card in our house. Mother and I had bought her a smaller card. Vini didn't think it was right to give her a card smaller than hers. He said that if people gave you big cards it was because they expected a bigger card in return. Mother said it was all right and that I could send her a big card next year, a brand new card.

On 23rd December we went to Church in the evening because it was White Gift Service. There were quite a lot of people in Church. I wore an old dress and though I begged and begged, Mother would not let me wear my new dress. "That is for Christmas morning," she said adamantly. "I don't have time to make you another dress for Christmas." So I went in a dress that looked neat and clean but one could still make out it was an old dress. I didn't feel so bad afterwards because Vimenuo was also in church in an old dress of hers that I recognized. We sat in different pews but I ventured to smile at her and she smiled back. During the service we kept glancing at each other and smiling when we could make eye contact. I think Mother saw us do this. She looked sternly at me. We were taught to look straight ahead at the preacher, sit still throughout the service and not go out to urinate as some of the other children did. So we always trooped to the toilet before leaving home for church. Then we would not have the excuse of wanting to empty our bladders if the service got boring. Still, it was much better than going to church with Grandmother.

On the Sunday mornings that we went to church with her, Grandmother would seat us in front of her and that effectively prevented me from casting sideways glances at Vimenuo. It surprised me that Grandmother could look at me and at the preacher at the same time. If I so much as moved an inch, she would know and I would get the cane on my palm when we reached home. I was amazed at how much fun church could be when Grandmother was not there. I did not move around but I could look at all the other people from where I sat and see what the other girls were wearing. In front of the pulpit was a row of benches where the old men sat. Two of them habitually dozed during the sermon. It was quite amusing to watch them nodding their heads as the service progressed and, then, fall into deep sleep. Sometimes, they began to snore. But as soon as that happened, they woke up from the snoring. But if they snored loudly, the preacher would look at the man seated next to them and he would immediately nudge them awake.

After the service, we children were all given sweets. Vimenuo and I held hands.

"Can you come to see me tomorrow?" I asked.

"I don't think your Grandmother would like that," she said.

"I'm back with Mother and Father for Christmas," I said.

"Oh," her face brightened instantly, "When should I come?"

"In the afternoon," I said, "I will have finished helping Mother then."

 58

It was soon time to go but I didn't mind because I had tomorrow to look forward to. When we were home, Bulie and I played hide-and-seek, and I screamed loudly each time he found me. Pete and Leto joined us and it was such fun. Vini had gone to a friend's house to sleep over. Leto lifted me up to the ceiling and Bulie could not find me at all. Then I had to come down but I couldn't without Leto's help. We had such a wonderful time. After some time, Mother insisted we had to go to bed and so, reluctantly we did. The next morning, I woke very early and joined Mother when she went to fetch water. It was cold but it was not too dark and there were other people about. When we finished making tea, the others were all awake. It was one of those crisp mornings when it felt so good to sit by the fire and warm up with a cup of tea. Mother and Father always drank their tea very hot but I couldn't drink it like that. So I took an extra cup and poured my tea into it and then back into my own cup. I did this several times to cool the tea. It worked. I could soon drink my tea without difficulty and Mother gave us cake to eat with tea.

Then I helped Mother to make food. While she cooked a big pot of rice, I cleaned the green mustard leaves we were going to boil as a side dish. There was meat in an earthen pot which had been cooked yesterday and left in a cool place. There was plenty of meat and it was to last us through Christmas. The meat tasted very good. It always tasted better the next day after being left to get cold overnight because the gravy formed a glutinous base which tasted delicious with steaming rice. In most houses they would eat hot rice and cold meat all of January because that was the time it tasted best. Mother cooked a much larger pot of rice than Grandmother did. The boys were growing and had hearty appetites. If there was meat, they ate more than usual. "How much of a help you are now, Lieno," said Mother as I took out the plates and placed them near her so she could ladle out rice and meat into them. My brothers came running into the kitchen as soon as I called them. They ate very well. Leto had grown so much bigger. He was fourteen and in another year or two he would be considered a man. Pete was thin and ate with little appetite. Bulie had become fatter in the time I had been away. Vini was taller too and as strong as Leto. Vini was 12 now and Bulie had turned 8. Pete was 10. Mother used to say that when Pete was small he almost died of pneumonia and after that he had always been a sickly child. That would explain why he didn't like to play games for long. He never had a great appetite like the other three.

"Mother, can I have some more meat?" Leto held out his plate and Mother put more meat into his plate.

"You're eating a man's share now," said Mother proudly, "and you are able to do a man's work as well."

Turning to me she continued, "When your father went to cut firewood, Leto was with him and he was able to cut half a stack, that is very good."

I said yes, too. I knew Mother was saying this more for his sake than by way of informing me. It was her way of telling him she was proud he had done a good day's work. But if she had said it directly he would have been embarrassed so she was saying it in this manner. I noticed that both Father and Mother spoke in this way when they wanted to say something nice about the boys. It made the boys work harder at what they were doing and especially if it was manual work, they were proud to work extra and be praised. But they never made Pete work much. Father said he had weak lungs. Once when we were playing he collapsed, gasping. We thought he was joking but his face began to turn blue and he stopped breathing. Frantically we called Mother, and Mother called Father and they held him and put cold water on his forehead and rushed him to hospital. We heard that the doctor gave him three injections and sent them home

Easterine Iralu

with instructions that Pete was not to be allowed to do anything that was too stressful or tiring which meant he could not play vigorous games with us and he was not to exert himself at all. After this episode we were all so frightened that we would be the ones to make him stop if he began to tire. We had never seen anyone collapse the way Pete had that evening. It was like watching him die in front of us. We did not forget that for a long time.

After food, I helped Mother clear up the dirty plates and she washed them. It was a fine day again. In winter, the days were short but we always had a few hours of fierce sunshine. Mother wanted to finish knitting the sweaters she was making for Leto and me. We were the only two who would get new sweaters. Vini would get Leto's old one which was small for him now and Pete and Bulie would get Vini's and Pete's old sweaters respectively. "Actually I don't know why I trouble myself to knit them sweaters," said Mother. "The boys hardly wear them. When they begin to play they peel them off and leave them on the playing field. Vini lost a very good sweater last year because he forgot to pick it up after he had finished playing." It didn't stop her knitting though. I liked the new sweater Mother was making for me. It would match my new pink dress. I had my cousin's white shoes to wear with it. My aunt often handed down her daughter's old shoes or frocks to me. She was three years older, and so, by the time I got to use it they would look a little less fashionable. But I didn't think so much of things like that. It felt like a brand new dress to me. Vimenuo envied me my rich aunt. But they never visited us all that much or sent us many things. At Christmas we would get a packet of used clothes from her. Sometimes, Mother threw away things that were really too old to be used, trousers torn at the knees and fraying at the hem. My aunt probably thought we were much poorer than we actually were. Her husband was a busy man. He was an important government official and he travelled a lot. They had a car and often drove to the market or to church in their car. If my aunt came visiting she would bring biscuits or some fruits but she would always say she was so busy and did not have time to sit. Mother would ask her to have a quick cup of tea but she would have some excuse or other.

Once she invited us to dinner at her house. It was an awkward meal with her husband's relatives. My cousin did not want to play with me. When asked who I was, she answered, "Oh, just one of Mother's relatives."

I felt ugly and poor when she said that. I ran to Mother and said I wanted to go home.

"But we haven't eaten yet," said Mother. "We can't possibly go before eating."

"I'm not hungry, I think I have a stomachache," I said.

Mother got my aunt to feed me before the others and I went out to be alone in the dark, waiting for them to finish so we could go home together. We didn't go to my aunt's for a long time after that.

"Lieno, Lieno," someone was calling my name from afar.

It was a small voice.

"I'm here," I said, "come here, over by the kitchen."

It was Vimenuo, holding a small packet. Shyly, she came forward and held it out to me. "That's for your Mother. It's biscuits my Mother made."

The packet was still warm and lined in plantain leaves. It was fried cookies made of pounded glutinous rice.

"Look Mother, Vimenuo's Mother has sent you these," I said and ran to Mother with the biscuits.

Mother took them and thanked Vimenuo profusely.

"Don't forget to take back a gift for her when you're ready to go home," she told Vimenuo.

 62   Easterine Iralu

Then we went off to play. I couldn't find anything to play with because I had been away so long, and Mother had got rid of my old playthings. I used to have a fine collection of empty cans of shoe polish and bottle caps and plastic spoons and old bottles of medicine that Mother was going to throw away. Vimenuo and I used to set up house with these. My collection had long since been swept into the garbage dump. So we ended up playing with her doll. It was a cloth doll. Some of the stitches were coming apart at the sides. We set up a hospital for the doll and I was the doctor. We operated her by begging Mother for a needle and thread with which we inexpertly sewed her together again. It was such fun—the things you could do with a girlfriend! Later, when the patient was better, we fed her some leftover cold tea from the teapot in a broken cup. Then Vimenuo and I went to see if we could pick any of the wild yellow sunflowers that were blooming profusely outside this time of the year. In the plot of land adjoining ours we found a big patch of yellow flowers and we brought back enough for her mother and mine. Mother put her bunch in a big brown vase and placed it in the tiny sitting room. "Why, thank you, my dears, I must give you some tea and cake now," she said. So we sat in the kitchen and washed our hands and ate cake and drank tea together. How wonderful it was to be home and be loved. I didn't care about being rich if I could always be happy like this.

"Vimenuo has to go home now," said Mother in her no-nonsense voice when the sun began to set.

"Oh Mother, couldn't she sleep here?"

"No, I don't think her mother would like that," said Mother.

So we both put on warm clothes and took her back, Mother and I.

At the door of their house, Vimenuo's mother asked us in but Mother said we couldn't stop. But she insisted and we went into the house, "Just for a bit," said Mother, "I have to cook rice before the boys back."

Vimenuo's mother was so pleased we had agreed, she busied herself in the kitchen and served us tea and more of her rice biscuits. After tea, Mother stood up and insisted we absolutely must leave so Vimenuo's mother could not ply us with more food. She was a nice woman but Mother thought she was hard to get away from because she would try to make you stay for as long as possible if you went visiting.

"It's not that I don't like her. She is a sweet woman but I always have so much to do and besides, your Grandmother wouldn't approve," said Mother when we were on our way home.

"Why Mother? Why wouldn't Grandmother approve?" I asked.

"Oh well, you should know that they are not what you would call 'respectable' people. Her husband is always drunk and they never have much to eat. Your Grandmother thinks he steals her chickens but that is not likely."

"Of course not," I said heatedly, "the chickens sometimes fall into the nearby river if they are small and then they drown. I know Vimenuo's father is too drunk to be able to steal anything, let alone chickens. Grandmother shouldn't say that of them when she doesn't know for sure."

"Well, don't let her hear you speaking of her like that, okay?" cautioned Mother.

When we reached home, the boys had returned with Father. They had gone fishing and brought back some fish.

"There were more but Vini scared them away," said Leto.

"How did you do that, Vini?" asked Mother.

"He fell into the river just when we had our poles in," said Leto with irritation in his voice.

"Oh goodness," said Mother in alarm, "you could have drowned! How deep was the water Vini?"

"It reached well above my shoulder," Vini was pointing to his neck. "I think it came up till here, I couldn't breathe," he finished.

"Your father must teach all of you how to swim if you are to go fishing with him again," said Mother firmly as she put away their wet clothes and shoes.

The fish were not very big but there was enough for a meal for us.

"Where is Pete?" asked Mother anxiously because he had not come home yet.

"Oh, he got tired so often, he told us to go ahead and that he would come with Uncle Avi," Leto responded.

"I'll meet him on the way," I said, skipping out so that Mother would not be able to stop me.

"Lieno!" she shouted.

"I'll only go till the top of the steps, Mother" I replied.

Running to the steps I peered in the semi darkness to see if Pete and Uncle Avi were coming. I must have waited a full ten minutes before I saw them. Uncle Avi was carrying Pete on his back and they slowly climbed up the steps. I ran down halfway and offered to carry the bag. Uncle Avi laughed and said, "It's heavier than you, girl."

I tugged at it but it was so heavy I could not even budge it.

"Leave it alone, Lieno, we will get home sooner if you don't bother with that," he said.

Pete was grey in the face. He looked haggard and waved at me weakly.

"Can you walk?" I asked.

He waved back at me and indicated that he could not walk. I trudged along by their side. It was worrying to see Pete like this. I hoped his sickness would not come back again.

Mother had reached us now.

"Oh my poor boy, come to me," she held out her arms.

But Uncle Avi said, "Let it be, it will be better if I carry him all the way home."

At home, we let him lie on a long couch in the kitchen and Mother ran around and made him some soup and after some time, the colour came back into his face. But he lay there quietly for a long time. Uncle Avi had gone home because it was getting dark. Mother still fussed over Pete. The others went to sleep and I got tired and sleepy, too, so I went to sleep but not before assuring myself that Pete would be all right. He was not as tired as before. He said he had a tight pain in his chest before but that it was gone now. When Pete got ill like now, he looked like a shrunken old man. It was as though he had shrivelled up and suddenly become old. I imagined he would look like that when he grew old and had children and grandchildren. But I didn't tell him that. It did not seem like a kind thing to say. I wanted him to get better and be able to play as hard as the rest of us did.

"Merry Christmas!" shouted Mother, waking all of us up. We had gifts to open so it was very exciting to wake up. Mine was a doll. It was not very big but it was beautiful with blue glass eyes and curly yellow hair in a ponytail. I was so pleased with it. Leto got a book of cars. Vini got a plastic aeroplane which he was thrilled with and Pete and Bulie both got plastic cars. So we were all very happy with our gifts. Christmas was the only time when we got gifts. We got little gifts on our birthdays but of course that was different because it was our birthday. Christmas was more special because you got a gift though it was someone else's birthday. I was so glad I had not worn my new dress to church a few nights ago because I could now wear a brand new dress. "Come and eat now or you will never be ready in time for church," shouted Mother from the kitchen. Carefully we kept away our gifts and raced to the kitchen. It was just tea and Vimenuo's mother's biscuits. After the service we would join the others for a Christmas feast on the church grounds. Mother was carrying our plates in a big bag. That was what we always did every Christmas.

We had to go early to church or we would be standing throughout the service. People who never attended church on normal Sundays would all show up on Christmas morning and if we were late we would not get a place to sit. So, we were in church a little after the first bell had been rung. Normally it would have been tiring to sit for such a long time in church. But today, I was happy to watch people as they came to attend service in their new dresses. All the girls wore new dresses. Many mothers wore something new like a body-cloth. If it was a new blouse they didn't quite cover it up with their body-cloths and you could see they were wearing new blouses. My mother wore a short coat which I couldn't remember seeing before. She had her hair up in a bun but not as high up like Aunt Sini's. We sat in our usual place and across from us sat Vimenuo and her mother. Her father walked in a few minutes later with a surprised look on his face as if he didn't know what had brought him to church in the first place. His was not the only new face there. Many of the people sitting in the middle pews were people who came only on Christmas day. On the Sunday after Christmas the pastor would anxiously announce that the church was too small for the congregation and members should consider extending it. But the plan would fizzle out a few Sundays later because the congregation would dwindle down to the usual worshippers and they never filled more than half the church.

They had decorated the church with fresh boughs of holly which the young men and girls had brought in from the forest. It looked very pretty. There was a lot of singing during the service. Different groups of people in different age groups got up to sing. When the old men's choir sang, two of them went flat and everyone laughed because their friends glared at them. They managed to finish their song amid much laughter from the rest. Fortunately, the preacher did not preach a long sermon. He knew by now that people were impatient to start the feast. So he spoke for about twenty minutes on the birth of Christ. The last hymn was sung and the last prayer was pronounced and then people poured out of the church and formed themselves into groups, the men standing in the sun and talking and the women hurrying to the kitchen to help serve the food.

At Christmas, it was always the men who cooked; they slaughtered a cow and a pig, cut them into huge pieces and cooked them in great pots. Mother called us together and our family sat in the shade because the sun had grown too hot already. Two young men came by with a big pot of rice and a heavy wooden spoon. They served rice in our plates and then went around serving everybody else. Then another two came by with meat and another pair with gravy. Almost everyone had come with their own plates and cups except the new folks. But the church had extra cups and plates that they could use after the pastor had urged them to stay back and participate in the feast. After the feast we didn't go home immediately. There were games for the children. Those who won were rewarded with sweets. The boys wrestled with others their age and Leto overpowered a boy who was a little taller than him. We shared the sweets he won. Vimenuo and I won two sweets each in a game where we raced six other girls. We had one leg free and two of our legs were tied together. It was very difficult and we kept tripping and when we finally got the hang of it, we were already in the race. We came second.

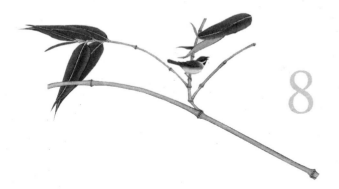

8

The day after Christmas, Bano came to call me back to Grandmother's. "Couldn't I stay till New Year?" I pleaded with Mother but she said Grandmother was probably missing me which was why she had sent Bano. But she did tell Bano that she would bring me herself in the evening. So at least I had one more day. I dreaded going back to Grandmother's house. It was not so much the amount of work to be done but the way Grandmother made us feel as though we were constantly being watched. I was clumsier when she was around and so she would always find something to scold me about. I went round our house and tried to fix images of these much used and much loved rooms in my mind. Mother and Father had the biggest room in the house. Yet it always looked like it was not big enough to accommodate the books and old papers which were cluttering the shelves. Many of the papers had belonged to Grandfather. In a corner of the room, Mother had her sewing machine which she covered up with a lace cloth when she was not using it. In another corner were trunks piled one on top of another. Some held body-cloths which Mother's mother had woven. She died when Mother was sixteen. I had seen photographs of a very dark haired, elderly woman who had a kind smile on her face. I loved to peer into the contents of the trunks even though Mother and I had done that many times. There were old tablecloths which we never used but still kept in the trunk. Maybe Mother hoped to use them someday. My old baby dresses were also kept there, a pink lace dress and a blue embroidered one. Leto's old cap was there too. Mother told me that these pretty dresses had been given to her by a friend of her mother who had since died and so she couldn't bring herself to throw them away.

The boys shared a room smaller than the main bedroom. They slept in bunk beds. Clothes were strewn everywhere. Vini's and Bulie's new toys were kept on a small table above which was a medium sized mirror. Pete had kept his car by his pillow. There were old schoolbooks on a heap on another table. I knew Mother could not throw these away before sorting out who could use the books. I suppose she would store Bulie's old books for me to use in the following year. I liked the window outside the boys' room. There was an old tree with its branches almost reaching into the room. I knew that Vini sometimes climbed out of the room on a flimsy branch and onto the tree. But I could not tell Mother this because he had threatened to box my ears if I did. When it was very windy, Father sometimes said he would cut down the tree. But the boys would beg him not to.

The storeroom was not a real room. It was called that because we stored things we didn't use every day but could not throw away. It was the little room behind the sitting room and it had no door. Once in two months, Mother would tidy it and clean it thoroughly.

The sitting room was the next smallest room in the house. It could seat six to eight people on a hard sofa set. The sofa set had belonged to Grandfather and Grandmother and we got it when

Easterine Iralu

they got a new set. On the shelves were photographs, one of Grandmother Neikuo smiling at the white man, and one of the seven of us when I was a baby. It already looked old now because the black and white photograph had turned brown. There was also a photograph of Grandfather's funeral. Mother always kept flowers on a vase in the middle of the room on the little low table. Today it held the yellow flowers Vimenuo and I had picked. But they had wilted somewhat already. At Christmas, Mother liked to put poinsettias in the vase. We had several tall poinsettia plants by the house and though the flowers didn't last long we could change them every two days. The Christmas tree was a short branch of a pine tree. I knew they had cut it from one of the two pine trees we had in the garden. The leaves were littering the floor now. But the fragrance of pine was fresh and filled the room. After Christmas, when Mother took the tree out, I knew the house would look very bare.

It was only at Christmas that our house looked pretty. But when a month passed you didn't really notice anymore, because Mother shone the wooden floor so well that every one commented on how shiny it looked. There were old magazines on the table, so old I knew them by heart. A copy of *The Illustrated Weekly of India* dated December 1960, *Time* magazine, February 1959 and *Life* magazine, December 1955. We had always had these magazines on display and when new visitors came to the house, they would pore over them avidly. But people who had come before would glance through the magazines and ask, "Got anything new?" There were pictures of Princess Anne in the *Life* magazine. She was riding a horse and looked very sweet. She had large curls in her hair and a flowered clip across her fringe. "That's Princess Anne," said Father to me when I was old enough to talk.

I saw that Mother had thrown out the picture frame of three elephants given to us by an Indian friend of my aunt's husband. At first, it looked out of place in our sitting room. But it had been there for so many years that it seemed to be a part of the room and the spot where it used to hang by a nail looked oddly empty. In some places the fabric of the sofa set was very thin. I could see the threads coming away.

The bathroom and toilet were not part of the main house. Father had built this behind the kitchen, a few feet away from the house. At night, it was dark and scary to go to the toilet. Mother would let me do it outside the house when I was small but when I turned five, she said I was a big girl now and should go to the toilet. I hated waking up in the middle of the night with that terrible urge to go. I learnt early to avoid drinking too much water at night. It was frightening to go to the toilet at night. There was no electricity there. If I took a candle on a windy night, it would blow out on the way if I didn't cup my hand around the flame. Once, when it was very windy and my candle blew out I thought I felt something scurry across the floor and step on my toes. How I screamed! "It must have been a rat," my Mother assured me but I was too frightened. I didn't believe it was just a rat. It must have been an early spirit.

Mother's flowers in their boxes were dry now. The roses were blooming and some of the geraniums. But the flowers were at their best in spring or summer when there was enough rain.

"Lieno," Mother called, "we have to get ready."

How soon the time had passed; I'd had a whole week at home! But it didn't seem that way at all.

"Come on," Mother called again so I went to her and we packed my clothes and shoes into a little cloth bag.

"Is that all?" asked Mother.

My belongings looked beggarly. But that was all I had brought with me from Grandmother's house. My new dress was made for

    Easterine Iralu

me when I was with Mother. And my new shoes were not really new. I had worn them on two Sundays while at Grandmother's house.

"Take some cake for your Grandmother," said Mother as she put a little packet into my bag.

"Oh, couldn't I stay till dinner?" I begged.

"No, I promised I would take you myself and if we tarry beyond dinner, your Grandmother will be angry with us both."

I didn't want Mother to get into trouble so I stopped begging and put on my shoes.

"Humph! I was about to send Bano again," said Grandmother when we reached her house.

"Sorry, Mother, I took a long time to finish my work," apologised Mother.

"Mother made some cake for you, Grandmother," I quickly handed over the packet.

I knew she would be placated if someone brought her a gift. Grandmother liked to be given things.

"Thank you," she said with no trace of surliness in her voice now. "Nino, you can take back some bananas for the boys. Take a whole bunch from the shed yourself," she said to Mother.

"Oh, but you will not have much for yourself then," Mother protested.

But Grandmother insisted so Mother took a knife into the dark shed and cut a bunch of yellow bananas. Soon after that she left because the sun was setting and Father and the boys had not returned from their outing.

"You look thinner than when you left, girl. Weren't they feeding you properly there?" Grandmother wanted to know.

I gave her the answer she wanted to hear, "Oh Grandmother, no one makes food as good as yours."

She laughed then, raucously, and rapped me with the cane, gently though, and said, "Off with you, put away your clothes and come and press my legs."

I hurried to the room, grateful that she was in a good humour and quickly changed my clothes, and ran back to the kitchen. She was sitting on the large chair that used to be Grandfather's. I pressed her calves and she sighed a bit. Bano was clearing the firewood and sweeping the twigs into the fire. It made the kitchen smoky and Grandmother coughed.

"Stop that, Bano, it's not good for my lungs. You should know, stupid girl."

"Sorry, Mother, I didn't think it would be so smoky," she said and blew into the fire.

The dry twigs instantly caught fire and the flames crackled loudly.

Bano and I got the plates and Grandmother served us food before taking out some for herself. It felt lonely in Grandmother's big house. I missed my brothers and parents. We were quite alone tonight. Grandmother Neikuo had not come by so it was just the three of us. After dinner, Bano and I washed the plates and cleared the remaining food. Then we went to the bathroom together and washed our feet and brushed our teeth. I washed my face and dried it on the rough towel hanging on the wall. We went back to the kitchen to warm ourselves by the fire. We always did that otherwise it would take too long to warm up once we were in bed. Grandmother wanted red tea so Bano made her a big mug from the water that was already boiling in the kettle. We were both tired and having stifled my yawning three or four times I couldn't bear to stay up any longer.

I found the courage to ask, "Grandmother, may I go to bed? I am so sleepy."

"What? Already?" she roared. "Your parents must have let you play all the time that you were there."

I was dismissed and I didn't much care what she thought. I was too sleepy to try and explain that I had helped Mother with the housework.

"I am glad you are back," breathed Bano when she came to bed. That was nice to hear and I felt guilty because I had not given any thought to Bano when I was at my father's house. Now, I felt very sorry for her. To think she could never go anywhere for Christmas, not to her father's house because she was not allowed to call him father and not to any other place away from Grandmother's harsh presence. "I am glad to come back and find you, too," I responded sincerely. I fell asleep almost immediately. I was dreaming I was fishing with Vini and Leto and Pete. We could see a big fish in the water when Pete suddenly fell into the river. He struggled to come out but the current was too strong and it was very deep. Leto was desperately trying to hold out his hand to him but Pete was too weak to catch it and in the end he was dragged under by the current. I woke up screaming.

"What is it Lieno? What? Wake up please, you must be dreaming!"

I woke to the sound of Bano's anxious voice. I had tears in my eyes. My dream had been so real.

"I dreamt Pete was dying. Oh I am so glad it was just a dream."

"Hush now, nothing bad will happen," Bano soothed me.

I tried to get the image of Pete's body sinking under the river waters out of my mind. But it had been so vivid, I could not help seeing that image again and again. I must have fallen asleep again because I woke to the rooster's second crowing and Bano urgently shaking me awake.

We got our water pitchers and went to fetch water. There was no one about.

"It's the holiday season now, so people sleep late and get up late. But of course, your grandmother would never hear of us getting up late," said Bano when we were filling up our pitchers.

A Terrible Matriarchy   75

"Have you always only lived here, Bano?" I asked.

"As long as I can remember," she replied.

"Don't you sometimes want to go home?" I continued.

"Where is home, Lieno? This is home for me. I don't know of any other home and it was a nice place when your grandfather was alive. Besides, I am used to your grandmother's ways and I know how to work in such a way that she will not be shouting at me all the time."

I thought hard about her answer. She was right in a way. Grandmother's house was the only home she had ever known so I could see how she would not be homesick for the mother she never knew or the family she never had. I understood that I felt lonely because I longed so dearly for Mother. But Bano looked to Grandmother as her mother and so she didn't have the same longing as I. I was glad in a way because it would be so sad if she were to be homesick and want to be with her mother. I did wish Grandmother were kinder to her. I could bear her being nasty to me so long as she was kind to Bano. But Grandmother did not seem to be capable of feeling that way for anyone. I remembered that she would often shout at Grandfather when he was alive, calling him an old fool. She could snap at Father too. But none of the boys ever felt the sharp edge of her tongue. She simpered with them. She tried to feed them great quantities of food when they visited her and if she were stronger she would have carried them in her arms all day long. Bano wove men's cloths occasionally. "I think Mother wants to give them to your brothers," she said with a crooked smile. "I heard her say so," she added.

9

The days grew warmer. I was so grateful for that. Winter was such a hard time in our hills. Some days it would stay foggy all day. Those were the most awful times. Because the old women said that spirits were about on foggy winter days, I was always frightened when we went to the water spot because the water reflected shadows that I dare not look at closely. Grandmother would insist that we do the washing even on foggy days so Bano and I took our washing to the water spot. But if she ran out of soap and had to go back home to get another bar, I hated to be alone by the water. I would remember that the spirits liked water, that there were spirits of the water that showed themselves to young men and frightened little girls. Sometimes, I would hear a cough and look up only to find, to my great relief, that it was another woman come to wash clothes. But few women washed on days when there was no sun. So it would be young mothers come to wash their babies' diapers because they had run out of a change. Sometimes Bano would take a long time to return because she would have to go to the shops to buy soap if we were out of soap at home. I often irritated her by asking, "Are you sure we have got enough washing soap?" when we were about to go wash clothes.

Now that it was almost springtime the fog had disappeared.

"You have to get ready for school," said Bano to me the next morning.

"I still have four days to go," I asserted.

But she said, "You should wash your school skirt and shirt and see that your skirt isn't too short for you. If it is short, your mother will have to stitch you a new one."

So I washed both and when they had dried, tried them on. My skirt would last me for a month or two. After that, if I grew some more, Mother would have to make me a new one. My shirt was alright for me too. It had been a little long in the sleeves last year. So it fit just right this year. One of these days Mother and I would go shopping for my books. That was something to look forward to.

"Did you ever go to school, Bano?" I asked.

"Yes, for a few years. Your grandmother tried to prevent it but your grandfather insisted that I should go to learn to write my own name and read the Bible. I will always be grateful to your grandfather for that. I learnt to count and read a little before I stopped going. But I still remember what I learnt at school."

"Why did you stop going?" I wanted to know.

"Well, it got more difficult. I often heard your grandmother and grandfather fighting over my going to school. So, I took the decision to stop going because I could see that it was the cause of all their arguments. Your grandfather still wanted me to go but I said I was tired of school. It was not true but I realised it was what I was expected to do. There are times in life when you have to sacrifice some things that you really like in order to bring peace into the family."

I found Bano's answer strange and I felt very sorry for her that she could not continue going to school when she had liked it so much.

"Didn't you tell your father?" I asked her.

"What could he do even if I said I wanted to continue going to school. He had given me up to them so he had no power really to make decisions for me. I don't regret it too much nowadays."

I thought it was a funny thing to say. I knew I would not be able to live with the loss if I were stopped from going to school. I loved to learn all the new things that were there to learn, to count numbers and to add them up, to learn to put letters of the alphabet together so that I could make words on my own. I would soon be as good as Bulie or Pete at making words. I supposed Bano did not feel the way I did about learning.

When school reopened we had a new teacher, a pretty young woman with short curly hair and very pink cheeks. I liked her immensely and the others liked her, too. She was not as stern as the other teacher and would giggle at our drawings and our school work especially when we made drawings of her with a curly mass of hair and two red dots on her cheeks. She wore short skirts and tight sweaters. The male drawing teacher liked to stop at our classroom window and chat to her every now and then. She would giggle a lot when he came by. We did get some work done though it was not as strenuous as the previous year when we were working under the teacher who was not as pretty. Six months after school started, our pretty teacher stopped coming to school. We wondered if she was sick because she didn't come for a whole week. Then we got a new teacher and he was a man and very strict. He carried a thin bamboo stick which the boys said hurt more than a big stick. He would hit them on the palm with it if they were naughty. Our pretty teacher never came back to school. We all wondered what had happened to her.

I mentioned it to Grandmother when Bano was there.

"Miss Sobu never comes to school now," I said.

"Humph, good thing she quit school before someone got it into their heads to chase her out," was Grandmother's reply.

I was amazed. "But why Grandmother? What did she do?" I asked.

"You should not have your mind polluted by hearing what she did," was all that Grandmother would say.

I was about to ask more questions when Bano threw me a warning look so I stayed quiet. Miss Sobu was probably two years older than Bano. She always looked good in her red high-heeled shoes and matching sweaters. How we loved looking at her. Now I was really curious to know why she had to stop teaching. All of a sudden Grandmother burst out, "That silly girl is pregnant with the Drawing Teacher's child. They are getting married of course. But how those two fooled the school with their goings-on. The school authorities should think twice before employing young fashion-minded girls to teach again. How she must have corrupted the morals of the young!" I was quite shocked at this news. It wasn't the first time that such a thing had happened. We often heard of some girl getting pregnant and having to marry outside the church. But Grandmother was suggesting that Miss Sobu had corrupted our morals by being our teacher. I thought long and hard trying to remember the days when she was our teacher. I couldn't recall her ever teaching us anything that would "corrupt our morals." In fact, I wasn't even sure what our morals were. I vaguely knew it was something to do with not stealing and not telling lies and now I knew it included not getting pregnant before you were married if you were a big girl. Miss Sobu had never taught us to do any of those things if that was what Grandmother meant. I felt that she was being very unfair to Miss Sobu but I knew it was not my place to say anything in her defence so I kept quiet, determined to ask Bano more about it when we were alone.

"Bano, why was Grandmother so angry at Miss Sobu?" I asked in a whisper when we were both in bed.

Easterine Iralu

"It's because Grandmother thinks that she will be a bad example to other young girls in the community. They will all want to dress up like her. And then they might get pregnant before they are married and that will be a terrible burden for their parents."

"I understand all that but why does Grandmother think that she was capable of teaching us bad things?"

"It's just the way your grandmother is. She thinks that there are only two kinds of people in the world. In the first group are those who are upright and go to church regularly and come to all the community gatherings. The others are those who do not go to church regularly and are fond of drinking and whose daughters sometimes get pregnant before they can get married. She is convinced that only those in the first group will get to heaven and the rest will all go to hell. There is no way they can be saved. In fact, she wouldn't dream of being in a heaven where such people could also turn up. Well, she is too old to change now, Lieno, you'll just have to tolerate her as she is."

Bano was right. Grandmother's views were to be tolerated. I had learnt that early on. In the beginning I had many questions. But she didn't like my questions at all and she would be very short with me, calling me an impudent child. Bano also told me that Grandmother did not like girls who were too pretty because she thought they would go wrong sooner or later. So I should not hanker after pretty clothes if I wanted to go on staying in Grandmother's house. That was alright with me because I never had many pretty clothes, for one. Nor was I a particularly pretty child. My hair fell to my shoulders and I often had it in a ponytail or two plaits. Vimenuo said I had nice eyes but Grandmother always felt that I did not have my father's blood in me and had missed out on his good looks. She frequently said that I was as plain as my mother. I took it as a compliment because I knew that so long as she thought I was ugly, I would be safe from the many lectures she gave Bano on men and their wily ways.

Soon, we both fell fast asleep. But in the night I was woken by the sound of a woman's loud scream. I sat up and listened. The scream came again. It was followed by wailing. It was a frightening and desolate sound. I wondered if I should wake up Bano but it was so dark outside, I decided not to. Let morning bring whatever bad news there was to share. Perhaps it was just one of the women from the drinking houses. They often brawled with one another or with their men and they would shout and scream at each other on the road. Very often the screaming would lead to blows. But we watched or listened from afar, too frightened to go near. I wondered what it felt like to give someone a blow or to get one. It was terrifying to think of. Sometimes the men left behind broken beer bottles. Bano said she had once seen a big woman hitting a man with a bottle. If we peered out of the window from the sitting room during the shouting, we could see figures drunkenly hitting out at each other. But Grandmother hated us to watch when a fight was in progress. She said it was vulgar and we should not be so curious about watching vulgar people hit one another. I did not hear the screaming again. But there was a low wailing and other voices had joined in. I really wanted to know what was happening. Now it sounded much closer to us.

I must have fallen asleep again because when I woke, I could hear Neikuo's voice in the kitchen. It was unusual that she should come so early. I quickly got up and went into the kitchen. She was talking to Grandmother who was already up. I braced myself for a scolding for getting up late. But they were deep in conversation.

"It was last night. The man had been sick for two days. Apparently it had happened very swiftly. He simply bled to death," Neikuo was saying when I came into the room.

Grandmother was drinking her tea and listening gravely.

 82   Easterine Iralu

"That sort will always die early. It is hard for the wife and children but she should have known better than to marry a scoundrel like that," she said loudly.

I could not control my curiosity any longer.

"Who is dead?" I addressed my question to Neikuo.

"Oh, the child does not know, does she?" she asked Grandmother.

"No, she has only just got up."

"It's our neighbour, Zekuo, the father of the little girl who goes to school to with you," said Neikuo.

My heart sank. It was Vimenuo's father. Zekuo, that was his name. Sometimes her mother called him by that name if he was at home and she wanted to ask him something. We often heard the women from the drinking houses calling out that name and laughing uproariously. So that was what I heard in the night, the wailing and the screaming. Our women screamed at the death of their loved ones. It was usual to hear mourners scream the name of the deceased when they came to mourn him. So it must have been Vimenuo's mother that I heard screaming in the night. I felt so sorry for Vimenuo. Of course he had not been a good father at all but she was just seven and to lose your father so early must be hard. I wanted to go to her and hold her hand.

"May I go with you, Grandmother? She is my best friend, the dead man's daughter. You may remember she has been here once last year." Grandmother was surprised at my boldness.

But Neikuo spoke up, "Of course you may come with us. Now go and fetch water and finish your work soon."

I ran to the water spot and scooped water hurriedly into my pitcher and walked back quickly, careful not to spill any. We drank tea and I changed into a clean frock and put on my shoes. Neikuo was wearing her black body-cloth. They always did that, the women. If there was a death, they went in their black body-cloths. Hers was completely black with four lines of navy blue on the border. The men also wore black body-cloths with red and green stripes on the border. Their cloths were more colourful than what the old women wore.

We took the longer path because Grandmother could not walk up the steep short cut. So we went to their house by a roundabout route that took us on to the main road and then we climbed down a flight of steps to enter their front yard. There was such a desolate air about their house. Men were already working outside, putting up a tarpaulin sheet to give mourners shelter from the sun or rain. A wood fire was glowing in the middle of the yard and burnt-out logs lay on the fire. So, people had come to stay with them in the night, I thought. I felt a twinge of guilt at not having woken Bano when I heard the screaming. In the left corner of their narrow yard, three men had dug a grave already. There was a fourth man working on lining the grave with flat rectangular stones. They always did that, laying flat stones on the bottom of the grave before placing the coffin in the earth. Then the coffin would be laid on top of the stones. The smell of earth was very strong when we passed the open grave.

Inside the house, Vimenuo's father was laid inside a coffin with black satin cloth pinned all around it. Vimenuo was sitting by her father's coffin. Her eyes were red and swollen, I could see she had been crying a lot. She looked at me and acknowledged my presence. But I suddenly felt shy and could not go to her and hold her hand.

"Is this why you said you would not look after me, Zekuo? I did not know you were meditating on this. The younger ones should stay and look after the old ones, how could you forget that Zekuo?"

Neikuo was standing at his head and mourning him loudly in the chant that old women knew how to do so well.

"Who will look after me now? Hei, Zekuo this is not the way it should be, we still need you, our son, our son, who will take your place now?"

 Easterine Iralu

Neikuo's chanting brought tears to my eyes and I could not see anything through my tears. When she began to mourn him loudly, others joined in and the house was full of the sound of wailing again. The women gathered round his body and called his name and some of them beat their cloths on the floor. Grandmother did not join in the mourning. She sat down heavily in a low chair and looked grim. Vimenuo's mother was very pale as she rose to mourn her husband.

"Zekuo, Aunt Neikuo is here, won't you speak to her? You always liked to joke with her, what is wrong with you today? Zekuo, won't you greet your aunt?"

Her voice was hoarse from the hours of weeping she must have done. The women always tired themselves out with their grief.

When Zekuo's uncle walked into the room, Vimenuo's mother rose up and with great sobs she went to him, "Ah, see what had become of us, Uncle," she wept, and everybody wept with her.

Zekuo's uncle stood at his head and cried out loud, "My son, my son, this is not the way it should be, you have consented to the spirits too early."

He continued to mourn him chanting out his grief. People wept afresh for it was very sad to see a grown–up man weeping.

Then a group of men and women entered the room. They were from the church. The leader spoke clearly and the weeping of the women subsided because he spoke with authority. "Our brother has gone the way of all mankind. He has gone earlier than usual. We understand the deep loss the family feels. We will pray for the family after I have read from the scriptures: 'So will it be with the resurrection of the dead. The body that is sown is perishable, it is raised imperishable; it is sown in dishonour, it is raised in glory; it is sown in weakness, it is raised in power; it is sown a natural body, it is raised a spiritual body.' Our dear Heavenly father, we are in deep grief today because our dear brother Zekuo has left his earthly abode to be with you in your heavenly home. We feel the loss that only you can soothe, we feel the emptiness that only you can fill, so we pray for you to comfort the grief of his family, of his wife and children and all his near and dear ones. We ask you to remember only his goodness and to grant that his funeral be conducted well. Provide for the young family that is left without a father and a husband. Always be with them in the lonely hours ahead of them. We commit them and this day into your hands. In Jesus' name we pray." Everyone in the room joined him in a loud amen. When he had finished praying, some of the women began to whimper but he opened his hymn book and said, "Hymn no. 343" and began to sing the hymn loudly. The weeping women did not resume their mourning but slowly picked up their hymn books and began to sing softly with the others.

They sang many songs after that, songs that were sung only at funerals. "In the sweet by and by", "Face to face with Jesus" and "He the pearly gates will open." The singers were from the church, old and young, women and men, about twelve of them. I recognised their faces from church. They sang for at least an hour and a half. Vimenuo's mother looked as though she wanted to weep again. But in that time, someone led her away to the kitchen to feed her some chicken soup. Vimenuo was also taken away by a relative. She looked in my direction but I was too nervous to get up and follow her. Funerals were such solemn events, they made everyone nervous. I peered at Vimenuo's father lying so peacefully in the coffin. He didn't look like himself today. He was not wearing the dirty checked shirt that he was so fond of using on most days. He was clean and shaved and lay in a white shirt and black suit. He had a thin black tie around his neck. I had only seen him once dressed like that when he was alive. That was the Christmas two years ago when he had gotten up to sing with the other men in the men's choir. Then he had worn a white shirt and

Easterine Iralu

clean black pants. I could not see if he was wearing the same black trousers as he had worn on that day because he was covered up with several body-cloths. The cloths reached up to his chest and were folded over, men's body-cloths with the red and green stripes on the border and patterns down the edge in blue or green or red thread.

The group from the church had brought a wreath which was laid at the foot of the coffin. It was made of pine leaves and the fragrance filled the room. Pine always reminded me of two things, Christmas and funerals. The singers began to tire after almost two hours of singing. And when they got up to leave, a man stumbled into the doorway of the room and loudly cried out, "Zekuo, you bad man, are you going to leave us? This is not the way, you cannot leave without telling your friends, Zekuo, you are a bad man."

He wept loudly over the body. His eyes were red–rimmed and he struck the floor with his body cloth several times, sending up a flurry of dust. He looked unkempt and I heard one of the women whisper, "They were together the night Zekuo fell sick. They were always together, drinking at one or other of the houses."

I recognised him as the man who had come with Vimenuo's father to their house when we were playing. Vimenuo's mother had said something harsh to him and he had laughed and said, "Woman, men take a long time to settle down. Don't fret about it, he will soon be tamed."

Vimenuo's mother had left the room hurriedly when he said that and busied herself with taking out the clothes drying in the sun. But I saw her shoulders slump when the man laughed and she seemed to be controlling herself with difficulty. I wondered if the man remembered what he had told her a month ago. He continued to cry loudly and he stood at the head of the coffin talking to his dead friend. But soon, he was led away and as he left the room he said, "We will meet again, my friend."

They buried Vimenuo's father in the late afternoon. The Pastor said a prayer over the coffin and Zekuo's brother gave a short speech thanking all those who had come to the funeral. He thanked the people who had given them gifts of sugar and milk and tea and money to help them host the mourners. Then he added, "Please do continue to pray for my brother's family as my sister-in-law has three young children to care for. She will really need your prayers. If Zekuo had been here today, he would have known what words to use to thank you. I am younger than he and yet I have to suddenly fill in for him and make the speech that the older one usually makes. If I have forgotten to thank anyone, please forgive me. All of you know my brother was a man who was free with his words and sometimes with his fists. If he has hurt anyone with his words in his life, I beg you to forgive him before we lay his mortal body in the soil. Thank you all."

The gravediggers laid the coffin in the grave with some difficulty because the wooden coffin was heavy and it slid from the hands of the two men in front so that it hit the edge of the grave with a thud. "Careful there," shouted an old man and the two men pushed the coffin from its awkward angle back into proper position and they managed to get the coffin into the grave the second time. "Dust unto dust," said the Pastor as he sprinkled soil over the coffin and then he read from the Bible and said a short prayer. When he had finished praying, he turned to the four men and said, "You can now fill up the grave." All of us stepped away from the opening and the men began to throw the soil into the grave vigorously. One of them mumbled, "Hurry before it gets dark," and they shovelled the rest of the soil over the grave. Then they pounded the soil down till it settled. Vimenuo and I were sent to fetch the wooden cross where her father's name was painted with his date of birth and date of death. One of the men took it and stuck it into the fresh soil at the

     Easterine Iralu

head of the grave. It read: Zekuo Solo, born 12-1-1932, died 20-2-1965. We placed the flowers and wreaths over the grave.

"There, Vimenuo, it looks very nice now, and you can plant flowers when the rains come and then your father will see that from heaven and he will be happy and he will know how much you love him," said Zekuo's friend who had been crying loudly before.

Vimenuo did not say anything but she took my hand and pulled me toward her house. I saw that her eyes had filled up with tears again. I didn't know what to say so I squeezed her hand hard and she squeezed back.

10

For some days after Vimenuo's father's death, people could speak of nothing else. There were stories of people who saw him on their way back from the fields in the late evening. They said he appeared to them near the stream on the way home, his face turned away from them. But of course they knew it was him immediately; he wore the checked flannel shirt that was his favourite when he was alive. Those who saw him always sighted him in the evening, at dusk when shadows disappear and a tree in the distance can look like a tall spirit with arms upraised. So, other people thought they had been deceived. But a man and a woman were together when they both saw him. It being too early in the evening for them to have drunk any rice brew, that story was accepted and it soon spread in the village. They saw him walk away from them and turn toward the road that led to the church.

Then something else happened. The old woman, whose drinking house he used to frequent, found him seated by her hearth. At first she forgot that he had been dead two weeks, because he was sitting in the same spot that he used to sit when he came to drink, and looking the same as before. When she realised that it was his spirit, she cried aloud. The other guests came running in from the outer room. But they stopped short when they saw Zekuo sitting by the fire. Then the lady of the house recollected herself and spoke to him and said, "Zekuo, we understand that you are longing for us and want to come back but yours is a different road now. You must not return again. This must be the last time, do you hear Zekuo? It will be the worse for you if you return."

The spirit did not reply but he got up and pulled on his body-cloth and walked out the front door. One of the men asked, "Should you have been so harsh with him?"

But the woman replied, "He is no longer a man, don't you see? He is a spirit and that is the way to speak to the spirits of the dead who are not at rest but try to return to the world of the living. They haunt the places they always frequented when they were alive and they seek out the people that were their constant companions because those are the ones who would feel sentimental about them and help them to return. But he is dead, he is no longer the Zekuo who was our friend. So I had to be harsh with him, don't you understand?"

All who were present agreed with her because no matter how close they had been with the dead man in life, no one wanted to encounter him now that he was dead.

"This is more usual with those who die young. They want so desperately to live out their life to the full and when their lives are cut short, they try to find ways to return," said the woman.

She spoke with knowledge of these things because she was not a Christian and her village had thrown out the few who refused to become Christians in their village. Those who remained still clung to the old religion. She then took out a dao and struck at different places in the wooden doorway saying, "Yha! Now try and cross that doorway, you spirits."

Those who had been there that night spread this story and for a long time, people feared to venture out after dark lest they meet Zekuo's unhappy spirit. When Bano and I went to the water spot, we walked close to each other. At night, we ran from the dark outdoor toilet into the bedroom. If she needed to go, she would always pull me to go with her. It was just as well because when I needed to go, I could take her with me, too. Grandmother was the only one unaffected by these stories. "He didn't deserve a Christian burial, that man," she said angrily when Neikuo was with us one evening. We were talking about the many stories being told about Zekuo by people who had seen him or seen his body-cloth or heard his cough. He had had a peculiar way of coughing that you could instantly recognise.

Neikuo was not as uncharitable as Grandmother. "He accepted the Lord before he died and the pastor says that he begged for his name to be reinstated. You know that the Church cannot deny those who repent at the eleventh hour. At least he repented. He was a hard one, that one."

"How are you so sure that he repented? Why is he back to trouble people who have done him no harm in his life? Didn't Mother tell us that the spirits of those who have found no rest return to trouble people? If he came here, I wouldn't hesitate to let him feel my cane on his back."

Neikuo laughed at the way Grandmother was carrying on.

"Don't worry, Vibano, I don't think he will try to come to you. Have you forgotten that the dead only show themselves to those who were close to them in life? I can't remember that you and Zekuo were particularly close at any time," Neikuo ended with a smile.

Grandmother did not smile in response but she said rather sourly, "Well, I am angry that people like him want to trouble people even after they are gone. These two girls will not go anywhere alone after dark. I am tired of them running in from the toilet as though the very devil were at their back."

Easterine Iralu

Bano and I looked at each other furtively.

"It will pass, Vibano, it will pass," said Neikuo by way of soothing her sister. "Have you forgotten that at this time last year it was the old Bangladeshi man who was haunting the village after he had hanged himself. There were so many who saw him carrying his water pot and singing to himself on the road. Why, there was a young girl who said that he even slapped her on the bottom!"

"How silly people will be," snorted Grandmother.

It was quiet the week after that. Many people believed that the old woman at the drinking house had done a good job of sending Zekuo's spirit on its way to wherever it was supposed to go. No more sightings were reported and Bano and I felt braver when we went to the water spot or when we suddenly had to go to the toilet. It was nice to know that Bano was grateful for my presence. I didn't feel so unwanted in Grandmother's house when I knew that Bano welcomed my company. Now we studiously avoided telling each other spirit stories after dark. As all this was going on, Grandfather Sizo came to visit again.

"What is it this time, Sizo?" barked Grandmother when he came into the house.

It embarrassed me the way Grandmother was so uncivil to him.

Sizo laughed and said, "Don't worry, Vibano, I have come to talk about my daughter."

"What daughter?" she asked dangerously. "You have no daughter in this house."

"You don't have to be like that, Vibano, I haven't come to speak on my behalf. You can greet me civilly and we can talk about it after dinner." Sizo was very calm when he said this, almost as though he were placating a recalcitrant child.

"You mean you are planning to stay?" asked Grandmother rather unpleasantly.

"Well, certainly, seeing that it is a whole day's journey to go back home," replied Sizo. "But of course if you don't want to host me, I could always go to Neikuo's house or to Visa's house but it would look odd, wouldn't it? And you don't want tongues to wag in the neighbourhood and have folk wondering why I am not being hosted by you, now do you?"

He was smiling pleasantly while he said all this and it made Grandmother look foolish to be so annoyed.

"You can stay, but don't try to worm anything out of me," she said, still trying to maintain her superior position.

It was funny how Sizo could make Grandmother feel so unsettled. It wasn't anything that he said or did. He was always courteous when he spoke. But Grandmother would be so prickly, like her grey cat that rose on all fours and whose hair stood on end when we tried to remove her from Grandmother's chair.

"Ah, it is Dielieno, isn't it?" said Sizo as he turned to me and lifted me onto his lap. "My, you have grown. You are so much more heavy now," he said admiringly.

"She's too big to be carried now," snapped Grandmother.

"No she is not, nor is she too big to eat a slab of jaggery all by herself." As he said this, Sizo reached into his bag and took out a big piece of jaggery which was wrapped in a dried plantain leaf.

"Is all of that for me, Grandfather?" I asked in surprise because we were used to sharing anything that big between the five of us.

"Of course, of course," he said. "It is all for you. You have passed your exams and gone on to the next class, haven't you?" he asked.

"Yes, I have and I am with bigger children now."

"I knew you were a bright girl, I always knew. Now you just keep studying hard this year too and when you have been to school for ten years then you can be a teacher and you will get lots of money and you can build your own house."

 94 Easterine Iralu

"Will I really, Grandfather Sizo?" I asked in wonder.

"Oh yes, that is what I did," he said with a twinkle in his eye.

"That girl must not eat all the jaggery by herself, do you hear me, girl?" Grandmother said to us both in a loud voice. "You are not to spoil her when you come visiting, I will not have that Sizo," she finished.

I clambered down from Grandfather Sizo's lap saying, "Yes Grandmother," and ran off to get ready for school. But first, I ran to my room and hid the jaggery in the room. If I kept it in the kitchen I might never see it again. Before I left for school, I remembered to thank Grandfather Sizo because Mother always taught us to thank people when they gave us things and she said we were to thank them without being prompted by anyone. When we were smaller, she would ask, "And what are you supposed to say?" every time someone came to the house and gave us a sweet or a gift. Now we were old enough to say thank you without her reminding us.

"Have a good day at school," Sizo was saying as I went off.

"Don't put ideas into her head," snapped Grandmother at him.

"She's all right, that one, she will do all right," he soothed her.

"Ah, you fool."

I ran off very fast, not wanting to hear anymore. At school, I felt like I was in another world. There was no Grandmother breathing down my neck. My teacher liked my work and he was not too hard on those children who did their homework and could spell right. I liked numbers and managed to get most of my sums right. Then Vimenuo was there at recess. So it was nice to be at school. This year they were giving us two breaks because we had a longer school day. At the long break, Vimenuo and I ran home to eat and ran back but during the short break we simply played together or went to look for four-leaf clover. I had found two this month. She hadn't found any yet. I said I would help her find one because I did not like her not to have any when I had two. In the second week we found a four-leaf clover for her. Actually, I had found it but I wanted her to pluck it so I called her and told her, "Why don't you look here? I'm always lucky with this spot." A few moments later, she gave a happy cry and held it up. We collected all the four-leaf clover we could get because the bigger girls believed that if you found these you would pass your exams. Some of the teachers often got angry to see these leaves fall out when they were correcting our notebooks. We heard that the Headmaster was planning to punish anyone who was found with clover in their books. We were careful to remove the clover when we got home and put it away. I had clover from last year which I kept in the small Bible that Mother had given me.

"Where is Grandfather Sizo?" I asked innocently when I got home from school.

"He's at the D.C.'s office. He will come in the evening," Bano told me. "Do try to be quiet, Lieno, your Grandmother's not feeling well today," she warned.

I nodded yes and tiptoed to the room to change. I didn't want to be mean but I felt great relief on the days Grandmother fell ill because she would not be around to find fault with me. I had also learnt that it didn't pay to slack off because she always found out when I had not done some job or other. The next day, I would have to explain why I had not taken in the wood so that it had gotten wet from the overnight rain. Now, I learnt to finish the tasks that were assigned to me. It was not all that difficult to do if I were left in peace to do them. Bano had the worst of it though. She had to be by Grandmother's side most of the time and massage her legs and also make food for her, not the food we ate but something else that she craved like egg soup with salt and ginger. Some times she would stop eating rice and eat porridge instead which came in a yellow and red tin labeled *Champion Oats*. Bano boiled this into a pulp and Grandmother ate it with milk and sugar. It looked very good and Bano would give me a little bowl of it if there was any left over.

Just before sunset, Sizo was back with some fish he had bought in the market. I didn't particularly like fish because it was difficult to eat with the bones. But he said that he would cook it himself and would make us ask for seconds. He did not boil the fish which is how Mother and Bano usually cooked it. He cut it into small pieces and covered the pieces with salt and some Madras curry powder. Then he put a lot of oil into a frying pan and heated this on the fire. When the oil began to smoke, he pulled the pan out of the fire and put the pieces of fish in the oil. The fish sizzled and crackled. He fried the fish for a long time and then put it in a plate lined with paper so that all the extra oil was absorbed. The fish was crispy and we could eat all the small bones. It was delicious and when we asked for more, he laughed and said, "See, what did I tell you? I knew this fish was irresistible." Grandmother was the only one who didn't have any of the fish. She said that oil made her head swim. By the time Sizo came, she was out of bed, though she looked worried and tired. "I'm not sick," she insisted so all of us avoided asking her questions on how she felt and we talked about other things.

When it was time for bed, Sizo and Grandmother remained seated at the hearth. I waited but they soon sent me to bed.

"Bano, you should go as well. Sizo and I have things to discuss," said Grandmother so Bano joined me in the room.

We were not too bothered about what the two of them were discussing. It was probably land and property or some other such boring topic that grown ups went on and on about. After some time we heard Bano's name mentioned. There was just a thin partition between our room and the kitchen. If we were very quiet in the room, it was possible to eavesdrop on conversations in the kitchen.

"He is a good man, Vibano," Sizo was saying. "He has a field and some cattle. She will probably not get a better offer."

"Why not?" Grandmother's voice was belligerent. "I have raised her in a perfectly respectable home. Why should not a better man make her an offer? I don't like the idea of her going to live in that village of yours."

"Tening is a town now. We have electricity and a school. If Bano had had some more education, she could have worked as a teacher there. Anyway, that is not the point. Do you realise that it has been thirty years since you have traveled to Tening? Much has happened since then. People have moved out and got educated, they are building a new road to the town and the Nagaland Transport Service has provided a bus service thrice weekly between Tening and Kohima. This boy now, he is from a good family and they would not ill-treat her. I would be there to see to that."

Bano looked at me open-mouthed. But I was too young to understand the significance of their conversation.

"Lieno," she whispered, "They are talking about marrying me off." Bano was so surprised that she spoke in a loud whisper. We both sat up in bed and listened intently.

"Think it over, Vibano, I have to give the boy's family an answer in two weeks when they return," Sizo was saying in a calm voice.

Grandmother did not seem pleased by the idea at all. "She will get other offers. This is only the first. That is the way with our people. There is no shame in refusing this one. They should understand that is how these things go. Why did they come to you and not to me?"

"Oh, it was not like that. They spoke of you as her mother and they inquired if I would ask for your consent to their offer."

I felt sorry for Sizo because he was trying so hard to placate Grandmother. "Perhaps you should listen to your dreams before you say anything on the matter," said Sizo in the end.

Then we heard the scraping of chairs on the wooden floor and we knew the conversation was over and they were getting up to go to their respective bedrooms. Soon, the house was quiet except for Grandmother's snoring and the odd sounds from the rats scurrying about in the kitchen. Bano and I lay whispering.

"Do you want to marry?" I asked her.

"Not just now but after some years, yes it would be nice to have a house of my own," she whispered back.

"Do you know this boy?" I asked in a whisper.

"I think he is the one who was there on my last visit."

"Is he handsome?"

"I really don't remember."

"Do you want to marry him?"

"It is not up to me, Lieno, it is up to your grandmother and what she decides."

We fell asleep after that because it became too late and we were wearied by our thoughts. In any case, since it was really up to Grandmother to decide, we felt reassured that this marriage might not happen as she didn't seem to like the idea at all.

In the morning, Sizo was getting ready to leave.

"Aren't you going to the D.C.'s office today, Grandfather?" I asked.

He laughed and said, "I will go next time. The D.C. is not willing to see me this time."

I didn't think there was anything much to laugh about in that but he seemed to find the fact very amusing. I liked Grandfather Sizo very much. He was full of life and he was kind to me. I wished that Grandmother were nicer to him. Then he might come more often. He might even come to live in Kohima with his family. I was sure he missed living here. Bano came out of the kitchen with a packet.

"Mother says this is for your children," she said and put it into his hand.

"Thank you, Bano, look after this girl well, won't you?" he said with a big smile.

Then he slung his bag on his shoulder and was soon gone with a wave of his hand.

Easterine Iralu

11

Bano and I talked and talked about the offer of marriage that she had had. What would Grandmother say, we wondered. Bano was very young still, she would be twenty this year and though some girls got married as early as eighteen, it was still scary to think of marrying and having children of your own. She was very unsure herself. She had never gone to stay in her father's house for long. The last time she had been there was three years ago to attend the wedding of Sizo's sister-in-law. They had stayed three days and returned the day after the wedding. The boy's family must have noticed her then. She tried hard to remember him.

"There were two boys," she told me. "Both were very nice and one would come to the house very early to help. He wouldn't talk to me but he would stare a lot and I felt shy and tried to work indoors as much as possible so I wouldn't bump into him. It is probably that boy."

"Was he older than you? Did you like him?" I asked eagerly.

I did not want her to marry someone she didn't like.

"He was at least two years older and of course I liked him but you don't show a boy that you like him when you do. He would think I was some cheap girl if I did," she said a little heatedly.

I found that funny. If you liked someone I didn't understand why you should hide it. People were funny when they grew up. They hid their real feelings and were polite to each other even if they didn't feel like being polite. I promised myself I wouldn't be like that. I would never marry a boy I did not like. And I would not be bothered to be polite to everyone.

We didn't find out anything about the matter from Grandmother. We were both too nervous to ask her about it because we would have had to confess that we had been eavesdropping on them. And if that happened she might not allow the two of us to share a room. Or worse, she might move us out of our present room to the room downstairs which was damp and dark. So we waited for Sizo's next visit. He came as he said he would, exactly two weeks later. This time he brought honey in a bottle, some bamboo shoot and long beans. He had a big slab of jaggery for me again. I left for school soon after and when I returned he was at home, chopping firewood. Sometimes the man who chopped wood for Grandmother would fail to come for a week. Then Bano would have to chop the wood. He was an old man and when he returned he would say he had been ill the whole week. He always came back though I often imagined him lying dead in a dark room when he didn't come for long periods. His wife would not come on the days that he was ill and it made Grandmother angry that she lost two helpers at the same time. Of course, he did not chop wood all the time he was with us. Grandmother did not have that much wood. The old man also did work on the shed for the chickens and repaired the holes in the bamboo walls through which the neighbour's dog could come in and steal our chickens. He also repaired the old furniture in the

Easterine Iralu

house, the broken arm of a chair or a table with a leg missing. This time he had not come for three weeks. So it was a great help that Sizo was chopping wood. Men could chop wood so effortlessly and have a big pile ready in no time. He swung the axe up and down in neat strokes and soon, there were big pieces on one side and slivers all over the yard. I brought out my basket and gathered all the slivers of wood because we never threw away any bit of wood and I brought them in and kept them close by the fire so Bano could use them to get her fire going in the morning. After Sizo had finished, I brought the big pieces in slowly because they were heavy to carry. "Good girl," he said as I took in the big pieces, "I can see you are a good worker." I smiled up at him. Grandmother never praised me for the work I did so I thought it was just not good enough. But Sizo was so different. I wished I had gone to live with him instead of Grandmother. After all, he was my grandfather in a way.

We ate dinner shortly after and then Bano and I went to bed early so the grown ups could talk. We were too excited to sleep. We lay in bed quietly and listened to the conversation of the three, brother and sisters. Neikuo was there as well and it was difficult to hear them because they were speaking so softly. Grandmother said something but it was not very clear.

Then Neikuo said, "Yes, yes, another might come and then again, it might not come. Some girls have been known to refuse a first suitor only to have to marry someone much worse because none as good as the first one would court them afterwards."

We looked at each other. So, Grandmother was opposed to the marriage.

She raised her voice now, "There will be other families who would covet her simply because she has grown up in my care as my own daughter. See how well Bino has married. Zeu's family is as good as ours."

"Well, you can't really expect the same for Bano, as Bino," said Neikuo drily. "It made a lot of difference that your husband was alive and wealthy when your daughter was being courted."

Sizo did not say much. It was as though he had given up on the alliance and was listening to what Neikuo had to say without much hope of it changing Grandmother's mind.

"Oh, I don't think it was my husband's wealth as you put it, they were richer than us. But it was the fact that Bino had been at home after her five years of schooling and she was well versed with household work. Men hesitate to court a woman who has too much education. They also do not like to take someone as wife who is not often seen at home." Neikuo was defeated but she would not give up without saying her piece, "Oh, I think things have changed considerably since our days or even since the days when Bino was a young girl. I suspect you are being selfish here, Vibano, the truth is, you want to keep Bano for as long as you can because she is such a help now."

Grandmother was outraged at this accusation, "How dare you suggest such a thing? I do think of her welfare and that is why I am saying no to this offer."

That was the end of the conversation and the meeting broke up suddenly. Sizo was bidding Neikuo goodnight but Grandmother had stormed off to bed.

The next morning, Sizo was packed and ready to leave.

"Oh won't you stay longer, Grandfather?" I asked.

He smiled and said, "I have to go, Lieno, the D.C. doesn't like me any more."

I knew he was making some sort of a joke but could not quite get it.

"Well, then, do come back when he gets to like you again," I said.

He laughed a little and said he would. This time he called Bano to a corner and they quickly exchanged some words. I had never seen them do that before. Then he hurriedly left, before Grandmother could come out and catch them, I suppose.

We didn't hear any more about boys who wanted to marry Bano for the rest of that year. Vimenuo and I talked about it when we were together. I made her swear not to tell anyone about it. She said her mother and grandmother knew about it already and that they thought Grandmother should not have refused the offer. It was surprising how quickly others got to know about news like that. I thought it was only Grandmother and Neikuo and Sizo who knew about it. Bano and I were not supposed to know. But this was how it was. If someone was pregnant, people got to know of it and they would tell each other much before the woman got round in the belly. And if someone was being courted, women knew about it and even before the family of the girl had given their consent, they would go around saying, oh yes, the wedding is to take place in April and they will be slaughtering three cows. I remembered that the two women at the pond were teasing Bano when we went to wash clothes.

"Ah, so you are going to be a matron then, hey Bano?" the older one said.

The other said, "Don't be choosy, in another five years, the offers will come for Lieno, not for you and you will be sorry you refused this one."

"Oh, it is not up to me to decide," said Bano modestly. "You know we girls have no say in these matters."

The younger woman laughed and said, "That is not true, don't listen to anyone who says that. A woman can say no if she doesn't want the man and she can say yes if she will have him. No one can force you to marry a man you don't want. You would do well to remember that next time, Bano."

Bano kept quiet but she blushed at their words and would not be drawn by them to talk about it.

"No matter if you don't want to tell us. We have our own ways of finding out about these things so you don't have to feel obliged to tell us."

They both laughed uproariously at that. Poor Bano was blushing furiously at their words and I suddenly felt a deep dislike for the two women. Did they eavesdrop at people's houses in the night? How did they find out the secret things of other people?

"Who told your mother about it?" I asked Vimenuo.

"Oh, she just knew, you know how it is with grown ups, there are so many things that they get to know," she replied.

I knew what Vimenuo meant by that. It was hard to hide things from grown ups, especially women. Some of them sat by the pond all afternoon and exchanged gossip about other people. The two women did that. Their children were grown–up so they did not have to look after them. The older one lived alone now that her husband was dead and her children were all married. The younger one had two daughters. They were both grown up but were still unmarried and they did much of the housework so their mother was so often at the pond talking to her friend and laughing raucously. But it occurred to me that many other women did not do that. They still spent a lot of time at home, working. Mother, for one, did not spend time at the pond gossiping about other people's lives. Later, Vimenuo and I talked about being married. We both agreed it would be quite terrifying to be pregnant and carrying a baby inside you. I had never seen my mother pregnant because I was the youngest but Vimenuo had two sisters younger to her.

"I can't remember seeing Mother pregnant with Ate because she is just two years younger to me but when Riano was born, I was six. It was so gross the way Mother would move around the house with her big stomach. She could not pick up things from the ground in the last month and I was forever picking up things for her. The

Easterine Iralu

night of the birth, they did not send me away to my aunt's house so I heard Mother crying in pain and I was so scared for her. Later Grandmother came out with a basin full of blood and she flushed it down. I was sure either Mother or the baby had died. But when I went in to look they were both well."

"Where was the blood from?" I asked curiously.

"How am I supposed to know?" responded Vimenuo. "I don't even want to find out."

We stopped talking about it then and played in the house until it was time for her to go home. It was one of those rare days when she was allowed to come and visit me on a Sunday afternoon. Sundays were one of the few days I enjoyed at Grandmother's. She said her father had taught them that it was a sin to work on Sundays so we cooked and ate and went to church after that but did no work. Of course it meant that we worked extra hard on Saturdays. But it was always worth it to be able to rest from work for one day and to sometimes be allowed to go visiting. Vimenuo had been to us just twice in my one–and–a–half years of staying at Grandmother's house. "Must children always make so much noise?" Grandmother would complain when we played. I am sure we never made so much noise. I especially warned Vimenuo to be quiet and she was so much in awe of Grandmother she would never think of being boisterous at our house. Furthermore, she was a quiet girl by nature and it surprised us both that Grandmother thought we were noisy. Her two younger sisters were so noisy, Grandmother would not be able to abide them for even ten minutes in the house. But then again, they would not be allowed to come to her house in the first place.

Two things happened that year. The first was Bano's marriage which did not take place. The other was Pete falling very, very sick. He could not go to school for a month and a half. He was taken to hospital when he stopped breathing. He had been playing with

Bulie. I think they had been wrestling when Bulie pushed him to the floor. Bulie was stronger than Pete though Pete was older than him. In the next minute, Pete was flailing his arms and turning blue in the face. At first they laughed because they thought he was trying to distract Bulie from winning the wrestling match. But when he stopped flailing his arms and lay down quietly they realised something was wrong and called Father and Mother. The doctor was very strict this time. No more wrestling for Pete. Not for a long long time. No school and no activity. His lungs were too weak and needed time to get stronger. It was a very strange time for all of us. Bano said I should ask to go home but Grandmother would not let me. She said the worst was over and what could a little thing like me do to help. Neither Father nor Mother had asked for me to come and be with them so I stayed on at Grandmother's. I was, however, able to go and see Pete in the hospital where he spent two weeks in the children's ward, looking very pale and weak. Mother let us eat some of the chocolates and biscuits and oranges that people brought for him. The children's ward was full of other sick children so we were not allowed to visit Pete frequently. Outside the ward there was a little garden with some pink roses and two pine trees. The children who were stronger could play in the sunshine for some time. Pete was too weak to play. Sometimes he watched the children playing from his bed where he lay with two pillows to prop up his head. Sometimes he simply slept slouched over the pillows. Mother was with him constantly. When he came home, he had to be helped to sit up in bed. Pete could not sit for his exams and he could not be promoted to the next class in the new year.

Easterine Iralu

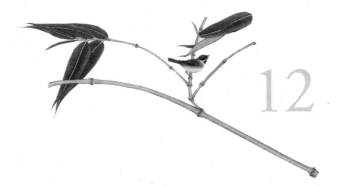

Vimenuo and I were nearly eight when we both got mumps. I don't remember it hurting a lot but we had to stop going to school for a week and my mother put black plaster with dots on my jaw. The next day, Vimenuo also had the same plaster on her jaw. I laughed when I saw her and she laughed back and said, "Your face looks round as the moon." It went away after a few days but the school would not let us attend classes for a full week because mumps was very contagious, they said. The medical bus came thrice to our school and all the students were rounded up and vaccinated against small pox. Some of the younger students ran off and the male teachers had to give chase and bring them back wriggling and crying. Eventually, all the students were innoculated. The students who missed the vaccination were sent letters and their parents were instructed to take them to the Primary Health Centre and get them vaccinated.

Pete had missed the vaccination at school and he was taken to the Health Centre by Mother the following week. He was still very thin from his illness but he could attend school. His teachers were told that he needed supervision in school so that he would not run about too much and get an attack. So, they resorted to taking him to the teachers' room during recess to feed him tea and biscuits and prevent him from playing too much with his friends. How we envied him. We were sure the teachers always had fine things to eat.

The boys in our class were still very naughty. It was as though they learnt new tricks every year. When the teacher came to class one morning, he found they had put glue on his chair. And when he stood up to leave, the chair stuck to his trousers so it was a toss up between walking to the teachers' room with the chair or taking his trousers off along with the chair! Afterwards, the headmaster came to our class looking very stern. He demanded to know who was responsible for the prank. No one would own up to it. So he marched off all the boys to his office and made them hold their ears and run round the school courtyard. After that, they never tried anything on the teacher. Of course they continued to plague the girls in the classroom but they had learnt that they could not get away with plaguing a teacher.

Leto was now in the ninth standard. He was almost as tall as father. He had turned fifteen and he refused to let Grandmother carry him when he came to visit her. His visits became less frequent and it was Bulie who delivered anything that Mother wanted to send to us. Bulie was ten and very big. He was bigger than Pete and he often went with Father when he went to chop firewood from the forest. Grandmother would simper and try to bribe Bulie with sweets and food when he came. But Bulie was rough and he plainly said that he didn't like being carried now that he was a big boy. "Oh, none of you are like Leto," said Grandmother plaintively.

Grandmother snored even more loudly these days. We would be woken in the night by her snoring. "It is too much," I told Bano. She agreed with me and said that perhaps Grandmother was sleeping on her side less than before. We were both heavy sleepers but we were often woken by her snoring. So Bano made a concoction of

Easterine Iralu

herbs and boiled it and gave it to Grandmother to drink because she had heard that it stopped snoring. It seemed to help. She stopped snoring for some nights after that but on Saturday she began to snore with a vengeance. So we resigned ourselves to it. "Some people choke themselves to death on their snoring," Bano said as she told me about Grandmother's uncle who was a terrible snorer. When he was 95, he died because he had choked on his snoring and they had to bury him the following day. If Bano was asleep, I would listen to Grandmother's snoring and if I didn't hear it for some time, I would imagine she had choked to death. It frightened me no end to think of being the one to find Grandmother choking to death in bed. But in a few minutes the snoring would begin again and then I felt a great relief and could sleep again.

One afternoon, Neikuo suddenly fell ill. She said she became very dizzy and fell in her kitchen. The doctor came to see her and prescribed a lot of medicines. All the grown ups came to her house to discuss how to take care of her and who could be with her. Mother could not come and stay with her. Nor could my aunt Bino.

"I'll be all right," Neikuo insisted weakly from her bed.

Now that she was laid up in bed, I could see how frail she had become. Her veins stood out on her hands and her neck looked very thin.

"You cannot be alone, we can't allow that," said Father very firmly.

"I'm sure I will be all right," she said again, "I remember your grandfather also had these dizzy spells and in two days he would be his old self again. I am sure all I need is a little rest and then I will be fine."

"Oh, I have no doubt you will be fine soon," Father replied, "but we must have someone nearby. There is no way we can allow you to be in the house on your own."

"Bano?" asked Mother enquiringly.

"No, Bano has to be with Mother, hmm, maybe Dielieno? Why not? She is a big girl now."

So it was decided that I would go to stay with Neikuo for a few days until she was mended.

I had a room to myself because Neikuo was not used to having someone sleep in the same room as her. Her house was very old. It was her Father's house and she had stayed on because she had never married while Sizo had married and chosen to settle in another town. Otherwise, it would have been Sizo's house. It would still be Sizo's house when Neikuo died someday. There were lots of rooms but the rooms were dark and musty. Neikuo was 73 this year and not as active as she used to be. I found the house depressing but Neikuo was an easy person to be with. She never complained and if I did some thing wrong she would laugh and say, "Ah Lieno," and tell me how to do it properly. With everyone gone, it was very quiet in the house. I had to close all the windows and doors in the house before dark. That was one of my jobs in Neikuo's house. Then I had to fill the lamps with kerosene so that we could light them in the evening. Her neighbours had had electricity installed in their house already but Neikuo feared she might not be able to afford to pay the electricity bills so she used kerosene lamps. She bought kerosene for two rupees a litre from the corner chop. We burnt two lamps every evening. We burnt one first to use in the kitchen for our evening meal and then we burnt the other one so I could use it in my room. I waited till I got really sleepy before I blew out the lamp because I didn't like being awake for a long time, listening to strange noises in the house. Sometimes the tin roof creaked in the wind and it was an eerie sound like an old man groaning. I also noticed that if it was very quiet in the afternoon, the upstairs rooms would creak as though someone was walking around. "It's house sounds, nothing to worry about," said Neikuo when I asked her about it. But it still kept me up at night if I were unlucky enough to be sleepless.

112

On Friday, when I got back from school, Neikuo had a hot cup of tea waiting and she gave me roasted pumpkin to have with my tea. She always had very sweet pumpkin. On the food shelf, I could see the half she had kept aside to roast the next day. "So how did your day go?" she asked and when I told her all that happened, she listened carefully and she laughed and asked more questions. "Get me the little box under the table," she said to me when I had finished my tea. It was a small black cardboard box. There was a fine layer of dust over it which I brushed away with my hand. But the dust made me cough so I got a damp cloth and took off the rest with that. There were letters and photographs and three or four official looking letters inside the box.

"That's Father when I was four," she said showing me a picture of a distinguished looking man standing very straight and holding up a spear.

"Why is he holding a spear?" I asked.

"That's because he was travelling. Father was a *Dobashi* when he was working for the British Government. He travelled a lot from village to village to interpret for the British officers."

"Did he speak English then?" I asked in surprise.

Neikuo laughed at the thought of her father speaking in English, and she said, "No, he didn't speak any English but he spoke Assamese and would communicate to the village elders what the British Government wanted them to do. Usually, it was things like organising a work force from the village to work on the road or to carry loads. Once he was sent to collect taxes but the people revolted and he was almost killed. The village elder helped him to escape to Kohima where he reported to the D.C. and they abandoned the plan of taxing that particular village. He was very lucky to have escaped being beheaded. Still, he did live very long after that. He died some seventeen or eighteen years after that photograph was taken."

It was fascinating to hear Neikuo tell stories from her life. It amazed me that her father had lived in an age when people cut off the heads of their enemies and there were no roads nor buses nor cars. Just narrow paths that led from village to village that turned into muddy tracks in the rains. She took out another photograph. It was of a middle-aged woman with two teenage girls wearing white waist-cloths. "Can you recognise those two girls?" she asked. I couldn't and I told her so. "That is your grandmother on the right and that's me on our mother's left. That is our mother," she said pointing to the middle-aged woman. She was a big woman in a black body-cloth and she was looking at the camera unsmilingly. "Oh, I remember when this picture was taken," Neikuo continued. "Mother did not want to have her photograph taken at all. She insisted that if you had your photograph taken, it shortened your life because the camera captured your soul by taking your likeness. Of course we had become Christians by then so we didn't believe it at all. But many of the village folk swore that was true. The white officer who took our picture also took the picture of me in your house. When he brought the photographs to our house, Mother kept them in her box as long as she was alive. She really believed it was ill luck to have a photograph taken. We are lucky she didn't destroy it. There were very few people in her village who had had their pictures taken. Look, you can see how unhappy she was about the whole thing. She refused to smile. But Father insisted that we have our picture taken."

I peered at the black and white photograph which had become very brown down the years. I couldn't believe that the smiling young girl in the picture was Grandmother. She was almost pretty in that picture, smiling broadly at the camera and dressed in her best clothes. To think that Grandmother had been a young girl once, to think that she had been the daughter of her mother once. I could never conceive of old people as having once been young. Especially not

Grandmother! I often imagined her as having been there from the beginning of the world, old and sullen with everything and everyone around her. I could never think that she had once been a baby. Somehow, for me, Grandmother just did not have a beginning like everybody else. How stern her mother looked. I wanted to ask Neikuo more about her but I didn't want to sound rude.

Neikuo had another photograph in her hand. I could see she was very eager to show it to me so I went closer to her. It was a young man wearing horn-rimmed glasses. There was a signature across the right hand corner of the photograph but I could not make out the writing.

"Do you know who that is?" she asked. I didn't think the young man was anyone I knew, certainly no one in our family looked like that. The photograph was quite old as well.

"I don't find anything familiar about him," I said.

"Well, do you think he is handsome then?" she asked.

I looked at the picture again. He looked like he studied a lot. I wondered how I should reply to her question. "He looks like a nice person," I said carefully.

She smiled at my answer. "I was to marry that young man," she said.

I waited for more but she was quiet so I asked, "What happened then?"

"He died," she said in a very low voice. All the laughter had gone from her face now and I felt very sorry for her.

"I wish you could have married him and had children. He really looks like a nice person," I said.

I wanted her to know how sorry I was but I didn't know what words to use with an elderly person.

"I know, it was very hard for many years. I didn't want to marry anyone after that though I got two more offers. Then, after that I didn't get any more offers."

"Oh Grandmother Neikuo, I think it's wonderful that you stayed unmarried because we can see so much more of you this way."

"That is true. At the same time, it is good to marry because marriage gives you children and when you are old it is your children who will look after you. That is the way it is with our people. We die in our homes, not in the hospital. Of course some people die in hospital but we try to avoid that happening. If someone is very ill and lying in the hospital, his relatives bring him home before he dies so he can look on his house and beloved things for the last time before his death. He would also have things to say to his close ones. That is why we feel it is right to bring an ill person home to die if he hasn't got long to live. The last hours of a person's life are always difficult so one should have children. That way we won't be a burden on others. I am sorry I never married. I will burden some of you when it is my time to die."

"Oh, I would happily take care of you if you needed help," I hastened to say. I meant it because Neikuo was so good natured she was very easy to be around.

"Thank you, Lieno, I believe that you mean it as well," she smiled at me.

"Would you like to see this picture of your grandparents when they were married?" she handed me a photograph that was bigger than the others. Grandmother and Grandfather were standing outside the church and they were both wearing new body-cloths. Grandmother wore a white body-cloth with geometric patterns on it which looked nice in pictures. Grandfather wore his black body cloth and a pair of dark trousers. There were a lot of children in the picture staring at them. "That was in the village church. The children always gathered at a wedding and they would stare and stare at the newlyweds. So the wedding photographs of this period always have lots of children in them. We cooked three cows. It was a big wedding. But then, your grandfather's family was quite rich. They had many fields and so they could afford to host a big wedding. Of course they could have killed four cows but they didn't because we don't believe it is right to be too extravagant. At weddings, one has to think of those who cannot afford to kill even one cow. So they stopped at three."

The photograph was blurred because it had been enlarged but I could still make out that the couple in the picture were smiling happily. Some of the children wore no shoes. Some of them looked a little shy to have been caught staring. But the rest simply stared at the camera or at the married pair. Grandfather was tall but very thin. I had never seen him so thin. My memory of him was of a large man with rough hands. He used to work a lot and he liked to call us children into the house and give us sweets. If he reached his hand into his pocket he would always take out something to eat, even if it was just a cough drop.

"Who's that?" I pointed to two European looking women in the picture.

"Oh that's the American Missionary's wife and her sister. They came to the wedding because it was a Christian marriage but the ceremony was conducted by the Pastor in Angami. Theirs was the fourth marriage to be solemnised in the new church."

The two ladies stood out in the photograph. They were smiling benevolently. Many houses had framed photographs of the American missionaries. The women's faces looked familiar. That must be because I had seen so many photographs of them and of other missionary wives in many houses.

"Did they serve cake at the wedding?" I asked.

"No, it wasn't that sort of wedding. People liked to eat meat, not cake, at weddings, so it was a wedding with a lot of meat."

The light began to go as Neikuo showed me photograph after photograph. She had a story to tell about each photograph. There was one of Father and his brothers and sister when they were small. I could see that Leto looked a lot like Father and Neno, my Aunt Bino's daughter, looked very much like her mother. I supposed I looked like Mother because I certainly did not look like anyone in Father's family.

There was a photograph of Father as a baby being carried on Grandmother's back. Father had a very big head, almost as big as Grandmother's.

The sun had set when we put the photographs away. I did a good job of dusting the little box. Neikuo gave me a cloth to cover it so that it wouldn't get so dusty again. Then we went to the kitchen and cooked our evening meal. Neikuo liked to eat quite late. We wouldn't cook food before it got a little dark outside. She said it was good to eat food late so that it stayed longer in your stomach through the night. If you ate too early, you would wakeup in the night feeling hungry. It was a new idea for me but I didn't mind because she fed me well when I had my afternoon tea so I didn't feel starved before dinner.

We hardly had any visitors at Neikuo's house. But Sizo did come one day after he had gotten news of her sickness. He carried me on his lap and Neikuo did not object so I stayed there a long time. He said I was doing a good job of looking after my Grandmother and he was proud of me. How good it felt to hear kind words like that from Sizo. They both agreed that I had become a good worker and that I was doing well at school, too. They didn't hesitate to say these things in front of me. I felt very warm inside. I tried to work even harder because I liked what they said so much.

13

I went back to Grandmother's after two weeks. Neikuo was quite well by then and Grandmother sent Bano to call me because she had heard that Neikuo was mended. Now, there were days when Grandmother did not come to the kitchen much. She stayed in her room by her window where the sunlight streamed in and she sat there for a long while. On those days she would call Bano to her and Bano would open her hair and massage it with her hands. She never called me. So I did the work in the kitchen and tried to do all the things that I had seen Bano do. Father came to visit us and he persuaded Grandmother to use electricity. Grandmother refused at first. She said that she had always used the kerosene lamps and they were good enough for us too. But Father said that it was safer to use electricity. Finally she said she would give it a try. A man came to put up the wiring in the house. Grandmother would not use more than two bulbs in the house, one in the kitchen and the other in her room. So when the wiring was completed, Father came with two bulbs from the shop. He put up one in the kitchen and one in Grandmother's room and told her he could easily get more for her.

"That is quite enough," she said in a firm voice. "What use do we have of so many lights in the house?"

"Well," said Father, "Lieno could stay up late and study more if you had electricity."

Grandmother said "Humph, in our day, young girls went to bed early so they could get up early and do all the household work."

I was grateful Father did not pursue the matter.

We used electricity very sparingly in the first month. Grandmother insisted that we put the light on in the kitchen only when it was almost impossible to see. We made more flames in the fire and tried to finish cooking before it got really dark. By the time we were allowed to put the bulb on, one of us would have stubbed a toe on the wooden stools in the kitchen. Now we could no longer use the kerosene lamps. "Why waste more money?" said Grandmother. But if the electricity went off we had to grope in the dark for the lamps and try to light them. Many of our neighbours began to use electricity because the Government announced that it was going to install it cheaply as it was the first time for private houses. The town became brighter and our neighbourhood was well lit by the big street light. Leto said it was so bright you could read a book by it.

I didn't have much idea where Grandmother got her money from. She kept a lot of small change in the cloth belt she wore around her waist. When Bano and I were sent to the corner shop she would take out change from her belt. I vaguely knew that she kept money in a big tin trunk under her bed. But she would close the door and the windows if she was taking out any money from it. She always went on about things being so expensive now, and that we should be very careful how we used soap and sugar and salt and all the things that we couldn't grow. I asked Bano about it once and she said that actually Grandmother received Grandfather's pension. It was a lot of money but Grandmother had been brought up to be stingy with money.

"It's just the way she is, Lieno. When she was young she didn't get very much to eat and that is why she is stingy with food and money," Bano explained.

"You mean that they went through periods of starvation like in the Bible?" I asked.

I instantly had the thought that Grandmother might have lived through Old Testament times, especially the part where it said that the Israelites were starving so badly that a woman cooked and ate her child.

"Oh, not like that, but they didn't have sugar, for instance, nor the rich foods that we get so much of these days. They always had rice and vegetables and dried meat but they didn't often have jaggery or tea or biscuits like we do now," said Bano with some irritation.

I decided not to ask any more questions. I could tell when Bano was getting irritated with my questions especially if I was too persistent.

"Well, our teacher told us that people in India do grow sugar. He said it was a different sort of sugarcane plant that was red and thinner than the sugarcane that we have," I said knowledgeably.

"Ha, I suppose he also told you that the Indians grow soap on little trees?" laughed Bano.

"Is that fire burning?" shouted Grandmother in her shrill voice. Grandmother always shouted when she heard us laughing together.

"Yes, Mother, I'm almost done with the cooking," Bano shouted back.

"Goodness, you don't have to shout back," she said.

We looked at each other and stifled our laughter. Grandmother had rules for others which she would never apply to herself. We were not to laugh too frequently or too loudly. She warned us that girls who laughed frequently ended up becoming wine brewers who had nothing to do all day but brew wine and laugh a lot when the men came. Those women never got husbands and no respectable person ever befriended them. I knew some of them by sight. One was the pink-cheeked young woman who had come to Vimenuo's father's funeral and laid a body cloth over him. When she left, Vimenuo's mother swiftly removed it and stowed it away in a back room. Then there was an older woman with a hard face. She had a harsh voice and the men would either be laughing with her in a vulgar way or avoiding her. The younger men avoided her. Once, when we went to the corner shop she had also come to buy salt. She had a big bruise under her left eye and her mouth was swollen. The shopkeeper asked, "Rough customer?" and she replied, "Neisolie and I got into an argument and I hit him with a bottle but he caught it before it could land and I got the worst of it." She looked terrible but the two of them were chatting as though it was the most normal of things in her life. In a way, I suppose it was.

The women on the street had several men in their drinking houses. It both fascinated and terrified us to walk past their houses, with the open doorways, to go to the corner shop. Some of them knew us by name. Most of them knew Bano.

"Getting some tobacco, Bano?" an old woman had shouted out when Bano and I were going to buy salt.

"No, Aunt, we are going to buy some salt," said Bano.

"Well, you should get some tobacco for that sour mother of yours." She laughed loudly as she said this and people looked at us.

Some of them knew my name now and when I ran down on my own, they would call out, "Shopping, Dielieno?"

I did as Bano did and spoke respectfully to them. "I am going to buy soap, Aunt."

Easterine Iralu

Much of the time they would be friendly. But one day there were some men and women and one of the women called out, "Yes, wash it all off." All of them laughed so much at this. I pretended I had not heard and walked away from them. It was difficult to avoid them because the corner shop lay beside their houses in the same lane. So to get to the shop we had to cross all the drinking houses.

"Don't mind them," said Bano, "just remember to be polite to them and to ignore them if they try to joke with you because they can never tell a decent joke. They love to say something dirty. Pretend you don't understand it." There was a large woman in particular who would sit out in the sun, sprawled out by herself on the roadside on a low wooden chair. She never spared anyone and she would say the most vulgar things.

"Getting to be a big girl, aren't you?" she asked one day when I was forced to go past her chair.

"Thank you, Aunt, I'm nearly nine," I said.

"Hmm, nearly nine? Any boyfriends yet?" she asked.

I blushed against my will and said, "No, Aunt."

"Soon enough, dear, soon enough," she said in a soothing tone that made it seem I was eager to get a boyfriend.

I blushed again as I understood the insinuation in her words. I extricated myself from her grasp saying Bano was waiting for me to bring back oil for cooking.

"All right, you can go, just remember, men are only interested in one thing."

She laughed so loudly that passers-by looked at us curiously. I cursed inwardly because I thought they would surely think something terrible of me.

For a few days, I refused to go to the shop alone. Bano said, "You can't avoid going altogether. You have to learn to ignore what they say. When they find out that they can't touch you they usually stop pestering you and they try it out on someone else. Just don't show them that it bothers you." The next time, we went together. The fat woman was there again. "Hey Bano, have you had some lately?" she shouted as other people were passing by. "Oh, you mean the new potatoes? Of course, Aunt," Bano shouted back. The fat woman couldn't help laughing in spite of herself. I thought that was so clever of Bano to keep her presence of mind and not let the woman embarrass her. "See?" she whispered to me. "You have to concentrate on your reply. Don't stop talking to them. If you do, they'll say you are proud and that will embarrass you even more. Just think of something funny to say back. After some time, she forgets to be vulgar."

I thought hard about what Bano had said to me. I did not expect to live anywhere else other than in Grandmother's house or Father's house in this locality. So I felt it was important to learn to be less sensitive towards the women in the drinking houses. The men were usually not as offensive as the women even though they could be pretty raucous when they were drunk. However, a young girl had had her arm pulled by one of the men who was drunk. He pulled her into one of the doorways and was trying to pull up her skirt when she screamed so much that people rushed into the house from the road and pulled the two of them apart. They threatened to beat him up but the girl begged them not to, saying that nothing had happened. After that they usually stuck to the women in the houses. If the women were being vulgar, one of the men would come out with a mug of brew in his hand and call out to girls on the road, "Hey you want some of mine? I'm pretty good you know." I don't know if Vimenuo's father had ever stood outside and called out to passing girls as the other men did. It was sad to imagine your father doing what the other men did.

Some of the women had children of their own. The children were never well looked after. They wore dirty clothes and played on

Easterine Iralu

the streets all day. Some were sent to school but that had never been a success. The boys got into trouble with the school authorities as soon as they grew bigger. They would break windowpanes and threaten the male teachers. Sooner or later they would be expelled. That was the usual pattern. I felt sorry for the smallest children. One of them had been run over by a bus. After that the Town Municipal Committee put up a big sign which said DRIVE SLOW 20 KMPH. Some cars still drove by in a great hurry but most of the local cars drove more slowly now because the town was not very big and everyone had heard about the child who had been run over and killed. It was one of the out-of-town buses either from Tuensang or Phek.

Many men died in the drinking houses. Vimenuo's father's friend who had wept so much at his funeral became sick. He vomited a lot of blood and had to be taken to the hospital in an ambulance. His wife was screaming and had to be held by two attendants when they took him to the hospital. He was in one of the wards for patients who were too poor to pay. It was an older part of the hospital. The walls had cracks running down them. He lay there for three days. "It's typhoid," his wife said to visitors cheerfully. But they knew. They could see the telltale pallor of the alcoholic on his face, the ugly blue-green of his skin, the way alcoholics looked a few months before they died.

The doctors were not so optimistic. "How much do you drink a day?" they asked.

"A mug or two in the morning," he replied evasively.

"And in the afternoon?" they persisted. "Another mug or two." "And in the evening?" "And in the night?" "And in the middle of the night?" "And in the early morning?"

They were only confirming what their examinations had revealed, a liver damaged beyond repair.

On the fourth day, he could not swallow. "Try some tea," said his sister as she held a cup of warm tea out to him. He sipped a bit of the liquid but began to cough. "Drink slowly," she said. He could not stop coughing, he coughed until blobs of blood came out and his throat hurt. His sister wiped the blood away with a cloth and helped him to sit up but he couldn't stop heaving and vomiting. There was blood all over the floor. Alarmed, his sister called the nurse. His wife, standing in the sun and talking to another patient's wife, came running. When he had stopped vomiting, he wanted to go to the toilet. His wife helped him to get into the toilet that they shared with the man in the next room. He sat on the seat feeling as weak as a baby. He said something warm had flooded his bowels and made its way out. When it was over, his head was swimming. Somehow, they got him back into bed. After a few minutes, he had a nose bleed. The nurse stuffed cotton up his nose and took away his pillow and then she went to get the doctor. When the doctor came, he had stopped bleeding from his nose but his mouth was now filling up with blood.

"I can't breathe through my nose," he said. "Can't you take out the cotton in my nose?"

The moment they took out the cotton, a thin line of blood steadily trickled down, so his wife held a wet cloth to his nose to staunch it.

"I need to go to the toilet again," he said.

But he was too weak to go so the nurse administered a catheter and they could see that the bag was filling up with dark red blood. It was so hopeless. By afternoon, all his relatives had gathered at the hospital and the women tried to assist his wife and sister while the men stood at the doorway helplessly and said, "Try your best, Sonhie, remember you are a man."

They always said that at the hour of death. It was like asking a man to defy death. Some of the men were sitting in the sunny yard. They were already discussing where to bury the dying man. Back in the room, the women took his wife out although she was refusing to leave her husband. One of them fed her some food while another massaged her arms and legs and shoulders. "You must stay strong," said one. After she had eaten, she made her way back to the room where her husband lay.

"Sonhie, Sonhie, don't die on me," she cried. "I need you to help me look after the children, you hear me Sonhie?"

"Hush, hush," said one of the women as she smoothed the sobbing woman's hair from her forehead.

Her eyes were swollen from crying. She had realised that there was nothing the doctors could do for her man. On the floor was a bucket full of her husband's blood. The people standing outside suddenly heard a long piercing cry. Each looked at his neighbour.

"Guess he's gone now."

"Poor bugger, at least it's over."

They waited outside for the frantic crying to be over and then they slowly moved towards the room.

"Let's take him home."

The man said it gently to Sonhie's wife and he signaled to one of the women. She quickly came over and took the woman and helped her away as they prepared the body of her husband to be taken home and buried.

We watched from the road when he was brought in a big truck. His wife was crying loudly as the truck came to a halt and two women held her as she shouted, "Sonhie, we are coming home, do you hear Sonhie, you wanted to come home so much, now we have done what you asked." They lived below the level of the road so the men had a hard time of it, carrying the dead man down the steps to a long and thin house with its floor of cold grey cement. The neighbours had brought chairs to the house and the narrow yard was lined with chairs. Some people were sitting in the chairs but they all stood when the body was brought into the house. The drinking houses were all closed. Some men came knocking to the door, but the women roughly turned them away, "Can't you see our neighbour is dead? There is a time and place for everything." These were men who were not from the neighbourhood and had come to look for a drink. Rebuked by the women, they turned away shamefacedly saying, "Sorry, didn't know."

Sonhie was buried the next morning. All night the family and relatives of the dead man and the women and men from the drinking houses had kept vigil for him. For a few days after that people were solemn and subdued. We could walk to the corner shop without being jeered at. But it didn't last long. In a week, the laughter had returned and the sharp-tongued remarks. I asked Bano about it.

But she only said, "They are desperate people, they have left their villages long back and if they had any faith they abandoned it long ago. So there is nothing left for them to lose. People grow hard, Lieno. They lose interest in staying good. I suppose it is easier to let go and be as they are especially if one had made many mistakes in life."

"What sort of mistakes?"

"Well, some of the girls got pregnant and had no one to marry them. I don't know about the men but I do know that some girls drift to the houses because they have got into trouble. I knew a girl like that. We played together as children. When her mother died, she got pregnant at sixteen and her father wouldn't have her in the house and so she went to live in one of the houses. You know that respectable families do not take in pregnant girls because they are so afraid their daughters will meet with the same fate."

"If that happens, there will simply be more and more girls in the drinking houses and when the old women are dead, there will be the girls to take over the houses. That way we will never get rid of them. Bano, do you think the children who grew up in these houses

Easterine Iralu

where their mothers brewed wine learnt to be vulgar from when they were young?"

Bano nodded her head. Then she poked at the fire in the hearth and made the water in the kettle boil again.

"Yes, maybe they learnt to be like that when they were children."

We didn't want to talk about it again. "Will you get more wood from the pile?" she asked gently.

I walked out to the stack of firewood outside the house. Outside the house, I could look down and see the drinking houses. There were men going in and out of the open doorways. We were able to hear sounds of laughter or raised voices from the road. If I stood outside long enough, I could discern the words they used, curses and more laughter. Somehow, laughter sounded vulgar on their lips, they laughed loud and long and nastily. It was never happy laughter, it was angry, vicious laughter that hurt my ears. I stopped listening and ran back to the house with the wood.

Grandmother was looking at me in an odd way. A long stare as though there was something about me that she didn't like.

"Has she got the curse yet?" she asked Bano rather abruptly.

"Oh no, Mother, I don't think she even knows about it," said Bano quickly.

My ears prickled. I was curious about what "the curse" was but dared not ask Grandmother about it.

"Well, see that you tell her about it. How old is she now?"

"She will be eleven in April, Mother," said Bano.

"Some girls are earlier than others. Tell her soon."

I was surprised to hear Bano say that I would be eleven in April. It was March now. I didn't realise that I had been at Grandmother's for nearly six years now. I was taller and Mother had made me two new dresses, cotton printed frocks from the cheap cloth store in town. I could wear them to church because it was warmer now. I was in the sixth class at school. My teachers were happy with my school work although I was not scoring too well in Drawing. I liked it but never managed to draw good pictures of animals like horses and cows as Vimenuo could. Bano would comfort me and say that I needn't draw anymore once I was in the seventh class and then my marks would pick up again. I was glad to hear that because I liked to score good marks in all the subjects.

Now that I had grown so much bigger, there was more work to do in the house and I struggled to study a little before I slept every night. On some days, if we had been working in the garden and digging soil to plant spring onions or sweet potatoes, Bano and I would be so tired we would fall asleep as soon as we went to bed. But on other nights, I stayed in the kitchen studying under the one electric light until Grandmother shouted, "Go to bed, I don't want a bigger bill next month." Grandmother had agreed to have another bulb in the sitting room so we had a little more light in the house now after dark. But that was only to be used for when we had visitors or for about twenty minutes when we had put off the kitchen light and were preparing to go to bed. One of us would stand in the sitting room and the other in the kitchen and at the count of three, the one in the kitchen would put off the kitchen light and the one in the sitting room would put on the sitting room light. Then Bano and I could make it to our room without having to feel along the walls because the sitting room was next to our room so we could get some light. In the first months, the bills never exceeded one rupee and seventy five paise per month for a long time. It became two rupees in the second year. When Grandmother could see that the electricity did not cost much more than the kerosene lamps, she consented to another bulb in the house.

After dinner, when all the pots had been cleared away and the washing done, I suddenly remembered what Grandmother had told Bano in the afternoon.

"Bano, what was Grandmother saying today? Something about a curse? Am I going to die soon?" I asked fearfully.

We were frightened of curses. If you were cursed by an old woman or an old man, the curse would alight on you and sooner or later it would manifest itself in you. I believed that I might have been similarly cursed as a child.

"Wait till we are in the bedroom," said Bano as she scraped out food residue from the pot.

I did not ask any more. Some days Bano could be moody and if I annoyed her, she would not give me any information until the next day. She said she did it to teach me to respect her. But really, I never felt disrespect for her. "Just because you go to school you don't have to be cocky with me," she burst out one day. Since then, I had been careful towards her and never showed that I thought her inferior because she had not had much education. It became better after that. I stopped talking so much about the way the teacher had praised me if I had done well at school. I would ask her how she was able to do things so well like the embroidery she sometimes worked at or the tablecloths that she made for the sitting room. She was amused that I was so clumsy at holding the embroidery ring and making flowers on the white cloth. I didn't mind. If it pleased her that she was more clever at some things than I, I was more than glad to let her think so, especially since it kept her in a good mood.

"Have you never heard your friends at school talking about the curse?" she asked when we were in bed.

"No, never," I said honestly.

"Well, it is something that women are afflicted with when they are about 13 or 14 and they have it almost all their lives, until one is as old as your Grandmother. You get a flow of blood from your opening for four or five days."

I was shocked by what Bano was saying. At the same time I began to understand many things now. That was probably what the older girls in our class were laughing about one day when one of the young female teachers had a big red stain on her white skirt. She went home early and the girls were smirking and saying to one another, "It was that time of the month. Silly of her not to know." Then they lowered their voices until they were whispering to each other but I didn't make any effort to find out because I thought it was cruel of them to laugh at the young teacher. Sometimes, they would say strange things to each other in class, "I got my guests today, have to be careful." One day I had asked quite innocently, "Did they bring anything nice to eat?" They had laughed so much at this remark of mine. The girl who said she had guests, said between peals of laughter, "It's not that kind of guest. Go home and ask your mother about it, you silly thing." But I never did have much time when I went to Mother's on errands for Grandmother so I did not get to find out. I had forgotten about it until Bano mentioned it.

"How can a girl work if there is blood coming out of her? Don't girls die when they are bleeding for five days? Sonhie bled for two days and Grandfather Sizo was saying that all the blood came out of him, and that was why he died."

Bano smiled a bit at this.

"Lieno, a woman bleeds differently from a man. You won't bleed very heavily every day but on the first and second or on the second and third days, the bleeding is heavy and you must wear something in your underpants or the blood will seep out and your clothes will be stained and people will laugh at you."

"But, Bano, how can I go to school when I am bleeding? What about you? How can you possibly do any work when you are bleeding?"

"Oh, you are quite safe when you use a gauze cloth. If you are at school, you can use a big cloth."

I was very upset to hear all this about what happened to bigger girls. "Couldn't I eat anything that would stop me from bleeding?" I asked.

I was prepared to eat the most bitter of bitter gourds in Grandmother's garden if that would prevent me from bleeding.

Bano looked pitifully at me, "I am not the right person to be telling you these things. You should really have it explained by your mother. But it is entirely normal and you must not be scared if it happens to you, Lieno. You must tell me if you see blood in your underpants. Some unlucky girls get very bad pain in their stomach when they start but you might not get that."

"I don't want to hear any more tonight, Bano, will you tell me some other time?" I slipped under the quilt and lay quiet, thinking. "Do boys bleed as well when they are grown?" I wondered if my brothers and my father had gone through all this before me.

"Of course not, boys don't bleed," said Bano with a little giggle, "that's why your Grandmother and older women call it the curse. If a girl has started to bleed, then she should be very careful because she could get pregnant if she sleeps with a man."

"How could any man want to sleep with a girl who is bleeding?" I asked.

Bano simply sighed and said, "I'll tell you some other time. Just know that all normal girls have monthly bleeding as a sign that they are women and will be mothers one day."

I was repulsed at the thought of blood coming out of me. I had seen Bano slaughter chickens if Grandmother wanted her to cook them for us or for my brothers. When she cut the head of the animal, blood would spurt out in a jet and splatter on her arm and lie in big blobs on the kitchen floor. "Yeu!" I said the first time I saw it. She had simply laughed and shouted, "Stop being such a ninny and get me the basin." We got the floor cleaned up in no time but the

 134 Easterine Iralu

memory of the blood spurting out of the chicken neck was seared in my brain and I imagined that the curse would be something similar. A sudden rush of warm blood that all Bano's gauze cloths could not possibly stem. I would ask Vimenuo about it at school. We talked about everything. If she knew about it and had not told me I would be very surprised. I fell asleep thinking that the bleeding was probably not too heavy because if Bano had ever bled heavily I would have noticed. We spent so much time together, she would never be able to hide it if blood was flowing out of her like chicken blood.

The next day at school, I cornered Vimenuo and asked her if she knew anything about the monthly bleeding.

She looked at me oddly and said, "Of course, my mother told me last year." She said it so matter of factly that I felt betrayed.

"Why didn't you tell me?" I half wailed.

"Is it such a big deal?" Vimenuo could be so irritatingly laid back sometimes.

She didn't understand my fascination with the subject. For me, it was a life and death issue, almost. Imagine bleeding for four or five days and going about your daily routine as though nothing were wrong with you.

"Well, Mother would tell me if she were tired on her days and I would help her more in the house. That is all there is to it. You may not feel as well as you do on other days but it passes," she said conclusively.

She was lucky to have her mother with her so that she treated the whole phenomenon as something entirely normal that happened to girls and women. I was disappointed though. I thought Vimenuo would be able to tell me more about it. I didn't want to ask the older girls in my class because I was not sure if they would tell me the truth or give me some horror stories that were nowhere near the truth. I was determined to ask Mother about it. At school, I found it difficult to concentrate on my lessons. When our female teacher came close to my desk, I imagined I could smell blood on her. At night I dreamed that I was in school, sitting in class when there was a lot of screaming and it was the bigger girls doing the screaming. They were all bleeding and the classroom was filling up with their blood and some of them were drowning in their own blood but they were still screaming. Then all of them began to call me. I woke up with a start but I continued to hear them screaming and calling my name.

Bulie was at the door, banging on it and calling all of us. Bano rushed to open the door.

He stumbled in and said, "Pete is very sick."

He had run to tell us so he stopped to catch his breath.

"What happened?" asked Bano.

"Don't know," he gasped, "he got sick last night but he became worse this morning and now Father and Mother are taking him to the hospital. He can't even speak."

Bulie was getting his words out with difficulty, in great pants.

"Oh, Bulie" said Bano, "rest and then tell us more."

I went to him and touched his arm timidly. Bulie looked much older than his thirteen years. He was not smiling and his eyebrows were knit with worry. I realised that it was very serious. Maybe Pete would even die. I started to cry silently.

"Don't cry, Lieno, we must hope he will be better," said Bulie.

But I felt such dread, like I had never felt before. "Won't you ask Grandmother to let me come home with you?" I begged Bulie.

"Not just now, but I will ask Mother to talk to her."

I wanted to be with my family so much. Of course, Grandmother was family too but I really missed Mother and Father and my brothers and wanted to be with them at a time like this. We heard Grandmother's cane on the floor.

 136   Easterine Iralu

"Who is it?" she asked sharply.

Bulie left us and went to her room shouting, "Grandmother, it's me, Bulie."

"Bulie, come here my darling, what brings you so early?"

We could hear Bulie telling Grandmother what had happened. Bano and I were in the kitchen by then, automatically going about our work. I felt numb and Bano talked softly as though she sensed my anxiety. After some time, Grandmother came from her room and when she was seated, Bano gave her tea in her mug. Bulie followed her into the kitchen carrying her night glass. He was holding some money in his hand. I guessed that Grandmother had given it to him for Pete. I waited for her to say something but she drank her tea without a word. Finally I could wait no longer.

"Grandmother, can I go home?" I asked her with a pounding heart.

I don't know how I dared ask but if Pete was dying I wanted to be by him. He had always been so loving and was the gentlest of my brothers. I loved him dearly. I would never forgive myself if he had died without me at his side to tell him what a lovely brother I thought he was. Bano gave me a warning look. I knew what that meant. Don't overstep yourself. Grandmother turned and gave me a long look. Then she said slowly, "We will decide that when the time comes."

I didn't know what she meant by that. I hoped that she would let me go. But now, all my courage had left me and I did not dare ask her again.

I was sent to school. I seriously thought about playing truant from school and running off to the hospital to be with Pete. But one of the teachers had already seen me on the way to school. He lived nearby and we often walked to school together. I was too scared at the thought of being caught so I went to school. But I was feeling so desperate about Pete I could not absorb the simplest things the teachers were talking about. I could not answer the History teacher's question, "When did the War of the Roses take place?" and he gave me a sharp rap on my knuckle. My eyes filled with tears and I covered my face with my hands and struggled to wipe my tears away with the tassels on my bag because I had forgotten to bring my handkerchief. "You students have not been studying at home, have you?" the teacher asked in an irritated voice. It was more a statement than a question. We were all silent. He noticed I was crying and stopped asking me any more questions. I couldn't possibly explain to him that I was worried about my sick and possibly dying brother. We never had the courage to speak to our teachers about other things except to answer the questions they asked on the subjects they taught.

Mercifully, I got through the morning without any more incidents and without being picked on by the boys or girls. I confided in the fat girl that I was worried about my brother who had been taken to hospital because he was very sick. "Oh you poor little thing," she said as she hugged me. She was the only friend I had in class and I felt grateful to her for the sympathy she offered. Strangely, when she hugged me, I wanted to cry again. It felt so good to be understood by someone. Word had slowly got around after recess because Mother had to send Vini to school with a letter explaining why Pete had missed school. Some of the teachers whispered among themselves when I walked past them. After recess, half the school knew my brother was gravely ill and in hospital. I felt guilty to be at school when Pete was possibly fighting for his life. I decided to insist on going home after school.

The Headmaster called me to his office in the fifth period. I went with a sinking heart thinking he might scold me for not doing my History homework. Nervously, I knocked on the door of his room. I had been there only twice, once with Mother when she was admitting me into school and the other time when we won a prize in the science quiz. The Headmaster was a tall man with glasses. He made me sit down and I stared at my shoes.

"You are Visa's daughter, right?" he asked.

I said "Yes, sir."

"What is your name?" he wanted to know.

"Dielieno" I mumbled.

"Do you know what is wrong with your brother, Dielieno?"

I looked up at him with a bit of a shock because it was so unexpected.

"No, sir" I said.

"Well, he has a congestion in his lungs which means that it is a complication from when he was young and suffered from pneumonia and he may not survive this illness."

Tears rolled down my cheeks at his words. It was like the confirmation of a death sentence. There was no hope then. He reached across the table and patted my head and said, "There, there, don't cry, we must hope and pray for him to get better. God can still work miracles. I want you to go home now and rest. I have spoken to your teacher that you are to be excused today."

I didn't know what to say. So I got up and said, "Thank you, sir" and walked quickly back to my classroom. I collected my bag after telling the teacher that the Headmaster was sending me home and then, I ran all the way home.

It was one in the afternoon when I reached. "Why is that girl back so early?" I heard Grandmother's voice in the next room as I bounded into my room and threw my bag on the bed. "The Headmaster let me go early," I shouted as I pulled off my school clothes.

Plucking up courage, I went into Grandmother's room and asked, "Please, Grandmother, may I go home to my Mother and Father?

The Headmaster let me go because he found out that Pete was very sick."

"How did he find out?" she asked hotly. "Did you tell him? Don't go around telling other people what's going on in our family."

"I did not tell him, Grandmother. He found out because Vini took him an application saying that Pete was sick and could not attend school today. He has even been to hospital with Pete's teacher to see how he was. He said Pete might not recover. I want to see him, too. Please may I go?"

"Oh girl, how you go on, eat your food and go then. But Bano cannot go with you because she is needed here."

I was so grateful to be allowed to go that I did not care if I had to go alone. Now that I was nearly eleven, the way to our house seemed shorter and it wasn't dangerous if I went while it was still light. That way I would not run into any of the drunks who used our road after dark.

I ran to the kitchen before Grandmother could change her mind and I ate a little food and then I dressed to go home.

"Better take a change of clothes," said Bano, "You don't know how long you might stay."

So I took three dresses and my one good pair of shoes and my school clothes and bag and was ready to go.

"You sure you will manage with all that?" Bano asked.

"I'll be all right, I've carried heavier stuff than this," I said reassuringly. "Oh Bano, please pray for him," I said as I remembered the reason why I was going home and felt sad and worried again.

"That I will," she assured.

I took the shortcut home, scratching my hand a bit on the thorny bushes that one of our neighbours used for a fence. I instinctively sucked on the drops of blood on my hand and spat it out. It was still early so I knew I could safely climb over his fence without being detected. If I went the long way round, it would take me thirty minutes to walk home. The shortcut was a rough road through a little wood but I could reach in half the time it took me on the long way round. There was no one at home. "Mother!" I called out urgently but no one answered. I took the house key from its hiding place under the flowerpot and opened the door and let myself in. The house was a mess. Obviously they had left in a hurry. Clothes strewn on the bed, shoes in a huddle in the middle of the room. Father's black umbrella was on the floor instead of its usual place behind the door. I put my bag down and tidied up as best as I could. But I had to think what to do next. If they were all at the hospital, I wanted to go there and be with them. I was undecided about whether I should cook but realised that it would take me a long time to cook and by the time I finished it would be dark and I wouldn't be able to go to the hospital. If they did not return tonight, I would miss seeing Pete for a whole night. I made up my mind quickly and put on my shoes again and locked the door.

I would walk to the hospital. I had been there at least four times, thrice when Pete was sick and once when I had to have my tooth pulled by the dentist. I half ran and half walked the three kilometers to the hospital. It was a big green building. When I reached the gate, I panicked because I had no idea which room he was in and how I was going to find him. Then I saw Father walking toward my uncle Avi's parked car.

"Father," I called and ran to him.

"Lieno!" he exclaimed, "did you come with Bano?"

"No, Father, I came alone, running all the way," I said panting, "I want to see Pete."

Father climbed out of the car again and led me to the last wing of the hospital, the children's ward. Beyond it was the Officers' Ward. It was the same ward where Pete had lain when he got really sick seven years ago. Everything was very still. Pete was lying in a bed with starched white sheets. He was so thin. I could see the veins standing out on the back of his hand. I tiptoed into the room and crept up to him. "Pete," I whispered. Mother, sitting on a chair looked up at me but she didn't seem surprised to see me. She looked immensely tired. "Pete," I called again. This time he stirred a bit. A nurse came in with a little aluminum tray. She took out an injection needle and held up his arm in the light and pierced his thin flesh with her needle. He winced a bit at the injection but he kept his eyes closed all the while.

"Mother, I want to talk to him," I said softly to Mother.

"Lieno, he is beyond speech," she whispered back.

I didn't believe that. After the nurse left, I went to him again and sat on a little stool and held his hand. Periodically, I called his name and every time I called, he would stir. I was sure he could hear me. There was a rasping noise in his throat or in his chest. A doctor came and removed mucus and blood from his throat with a heavy instrument that whirred and made a lot of noise. He was quiet after that. "That helps him," said Mother to the doctor. Father had left with Vini and Bulie. Only Mother and Leto and I were in the room.

I began to tire. I had cried so much the whole day that my head throbbed but I didn't want to leave Pete. I called him again and again. Sometimes he responded to me with a little movement and then he would be quiet. But he was quiet for longer periods. It was frightening how he would seem to stop breathing completely when he went quiet. Just as I was thinking that he must be dead, he would begin to breathe again very gently.

I called to Mother "He's not breathing anymore." Mother was transformed instantly. She began to call his name loudly and she shook him violently saying, "No, my son, no, don't leave us, I won't

 142

let you go." The nurse rushed into the room at the sudden noise and she felt for his pulse. There was a gentle throb. "He is still with us, don't give up hope," she said to Mother but Mother was sobbing wildly, "Ah, Pete, this is not the way, this is not the way it should be." Pete face had turned as white as the sheets. I tried to hold his hand but it felt cold and that scared me. Mother's outburst had unnerved both of us. Leto was standing by the window, looking out, but his shoulders were shaking visibly. I hated what was happening to us.

15

Pete died in the night. He never recovered consciousness. He simply slipped away from us. It was very quiet. I thought he was sleeping but Mother said, "He's gone." Then she started to cry loudly, "No, No! He's gone, my dear, dear son, how can I bear it? Pete, Pete, speak to me just once more." It was the most pitiful sound I had heard. I did not have the strength to console her because I felt such pain inside me as well. Could that really be Pete, my brother, lying on that high bed without any movement? I could only see his ever-smiling face. Whenever he was sick, he would see we were worried and then he would smile weakly and say he was fine. That image remained in my head. Everywhere I looked I saw the smile and I half expected him to open his eyes and smile again. But he simply lay there so still, so unmoving, his face as white as the hospital sheets. Leto was crying openly now but not using the death wail. He was just sobbing out loud. I called Pete by name and touched his cheek. It was still a little warm but when I saw the way Mother was crying, I realised that he was beyond coming back. It felt so strange. I wondered where he had gone. One moment we were all there in the same room and in the next he was no longer there and only his frail body remained. My tears hurt as they pushed their way out. We must have been crying for a long time like that, the three of us. Finally, two nurses came and they were very sympathetic. They asked Mother if she wanted them to bathe him. She stopped crying and said, it would be better to bathe him here. They made us sit outside the room. One of the young nurses brought us three mugs of tea and we tried to sip at it. At first I refused to drink but the nurses were so kind that it felt rude to refuse.

Before they had finished bathing him, Father ran into the hospital. I had never seen him look like that before. He had aged overnight. He came to Mother and then they collapsed into each other's arms. I went to them and tried to get into the circle. But Leto stayed a little away from us. "I knew in my dream," said Father, weeping unashamedly as he said this. Uncle Avi was with him. They said Uncle Bilie was coming with the ambulance to carry Pete home. Then the nurses had finished bathing him and Father could go in and see him. All of us went in then. They had laid him out on the bed and he was looking very fresh and even more white. They had dressed him in a new set of clothes so he looked as though he might be going for a walk. "Ah, my son!" cried Father and ran to hold him. Seeing Father weep, made me cry again. My heart felt as though it would break. Oh, if we could only have had one more year with him, one month, even one day! Uncle Avi's wife, Leno, had come too. She held Mother and escorted her to the waiting car. I was with them and Father and Leto rode in the ambulance.

There was a small group of people in our courtyard. It was amazing how fast news of a death could travel. I saw that my aunt had taken over the kitchen and she was either cooking food or making tea. Some of our relatives came running to the car when it parked. The women wailed with my Mother and they led her inside the house.

Mother insisted on sitting up near my brother though some of the women tried to take her to the bedroom so she could rest. "No, I will have only today with my boy, let me be, I can rest tomorrow," she insisted. So, Neikuo, who was also there, said, "Let her be, let her do what she thinks is best." Then they led her into the sitting room and sat her by a chair. A second cup of tea was forced into her hand but she only drank a bit from it. Four men brought Pete's body to the door in a stretcher. Because the doorway was narrow, two of the men handed over the body and the other two laid him on the bed which had been set up inside. Pete was so much smaller now that he was dead. It was unbelievable. Someone had made up the bed with clean sheets and a pillow and Neikuo covered him with a new body-cloth and she began to wail loudly, "Our child, our child, you have gone ahead of us. Pete, Petekhrietuo, you have lived out your days as your name proclaims, you have always loved everybody equally, we will never know anyone like you again, Hei! Petekhrietuo, there is none to take your place, our child, our best child." She wailed loudly so everyone could hear the words and all the people in the room began to weep.

We must have wept together for about half an hour when the Pastor came into the room. "Dear friends," he began and people controlled themselves, "We are all in deep sorrow over the untimely demise of our dear child today. Let us remember that he has gone to rest from his earthly cares. He has gone to his heavenly home to be with his heavenly father. Our children are not really our children. They are only given to us for a short while. We are none of us our own. We are all children of our heavenly father. Let us pray for this family to be comforted by the Lord and for our own grief to find healing in Him so that we may instead rejoice that Petekhrietuo is no longer in pain but is sitting by his heavenly father's hand. Let us pray that all may go well as I administer the Christian rites of burial

Easterine Iralu

to him. Let us pray earnestly for the family as they deal with their loss." So saying he began to pray and the people in the room began to pray along with him, some saying, Yes Lord, loudly and in the end, there was a very loud Amen when he finished.

The whole day there were periods of weeping interspersed with praying and singing of what were called the funeral hymns, very slow songs that would always make me think of this day in later years. There were women helping everywhere. In the kitchen were many neighbour women helping my aunt to cook. Usually the women made food for the gravediggers and some of the mourners who had come from afar. I found the smell of food nauseating. All of us, Bulie, Leto and Vini, had lost our appetites and we had to be cajoled to eat when food was cooked. My aunt Pfünuo was there too with her six-year-old daughter. She took me aside and said,

"Lieno, if you don't eat, you will be too weak to sit throughout the day. You would not want to miss out on anything would you? You must eat and be strong today. When people talk to you, you must thank them for coming to help you mourn your brother. You may cry as much as you want but you must be able to put flowers on his grave when we have laid him to rest later. If you don't eat, you will be exhausted and you will be angry with yourself afterwards if you are not able to be by him till the end. You know Pete would not like that to happen."

So I ate some food thinking all the while that it was what Pete would want me to do. I did feel so much better after eating. It was so nice to be with Pfünuo again though it was such a sad occasion. I had not seen her for many months, not since the Christmas before this one. After I had eaten, she took me to the boys' room and said,

"Now that you have finished your food you can help me take out Pete's things. You can tell me what things he would like to be buried with."

We opened the little tin trunk where Pete kept his clothes and comic books and toys. There was a slingshot and two or three hardened mud balls. They often shot at sparrows with that. I felt tears burning my eyes again when I saw that. Memories rushed in and I was saddened that I would never see him again, never be with him the way we could be before, never ever see him again. It was so final. I buried my face in the handkerchief Pfünuo had given me earlier and cried into it.

"We won't do this if it distresses you," said Pfünuo.

But I said, "Oh no, I want to do it, I promise I won't cry again."

I insisted and she held me to her for some time,

"It's all right to cry, Lieno, he was such a wonderful little boy, I know." Pfünuo's eyes were swollen and red-rimmed too.

She was also wiping tears away as she went through his favourite comic books. Pete loved to read. He couldn't buy the new comic books but he had his own collection of old comic books from friends and sometimes from our aunt's son after he tired of his new books. I took out his favourite. It was the *Superman Digest*, a big book with some pages coming away and bound together with thick thread. "This one, too," I handed it to Pfunuo. We made up a little box of the things he was to be buried with. Our people always did that. Sometimes it would be clothes like a favourite shirt or sweater of the dead person. Some wives insisted on burying their husband's favourite things. I can't bear to see it again, they would say. Others kept those items with them. But it was the custom to bury the dead with their Bible and a box of their belongings.

There was a strong smell of flowers and pine in the house by afternoon. It was from wreaths and bouquets that people brought. The schoolteachers had brought a big wreath with a card saying, "Deepest sympathies, The teachers of the Mission School, Kohima." Pete's classmates had brought a smaller wreath with little red roses stuck inside the wreath with a card saying, "Rest in Peace." The

Easterine Iralu

smell of pine leaves was something we always associated with death and it was strange to have the house permeated with the smell of pine. I felt a deep sadness at that. A house that has had a death is never the same afterwards. There is always a heavy gloom over the house, one can feel that the very house misses the dead person. Now, our house would become one of those houses.

Grandmother had to be taken out of the room where Pete was laid and she had to be put to bed. She was so overcome with grief, her limbs stiffening every time she went near to mourn him. There was a doctor who examined her with his stethoscope and said, "Aunt, you must rest for two hours at least." So she lay quietly in bed, being fed soup by Bano and after she had taken a white pill from the doctor, she was asleep and snoring. Neikuo, on the other hand, grew much calmer and gained control of herself. Father consulted her on several issues and she advised him on what to say in the funeral speech, who should speak from Father's side and who should speak from Mother's side of the family. She thought that Pete's Sunday School teacher should say a word too. So it was four speeches at the funeral and one by the doctor who would explain the illness of which he had died. Neikuo said that Father should write out who to thank for helping the family when Pete was sick in the hospital and the others who were helping to bury him today.

There were so many people at Pete's funeral. When it was time, one man came in to nail the coffin shut. Mother was hysterical. She was allowed to look on him once more and then she was led away. Everyone in the room surged forward for a last look at Pete. My view was completely blocked and I pushed my way through and stuck my head into the coffin calling his name loudly. I touched his cheek again and said goodbye. Vini refused to look at him but Leto and Bulie called his name aloud and touched him before they pulled us all away and nailed the coffin shut. The girls and boys from his class sang a song. They looked straight ahead of them and looked a little awed by everything around them. We, his family members, sat near the coffin and the rest of the mourners stood throughout the service. The Sunday School teacher said he had been a good boy and she was sure he had accepted the Lord. She said he often asked questions about heaven. When she said this, she paused and wiped away her tears. She said two more sentences about what an obedient boy Pete had always been. Then she sat down heavily. There was a lull after her speech. Then the pastor led us in a hymn and he resumed the service.

It was dark by the time Pete was buried and the soil on his grave pressed down by the gravediggers. Pfünuo, Vimenuo and I laid the rest of the flowers on his grave. Vimenuo offered to sleep with me but I remembered that we didn't have much room in the house so I let her go. Pfünuo stayed on though and fed us and helped us to get on with the routine things that seemed like so much work now. She chopped the wood and made the fire and had water in the big kettle boiling so we could take baths one after the other. "Leave the wood, Pfünuo, I will do it tomorrow," called out Father when he heard her chopping wood. But she said it was only for cooking tonight's dinner and so he let it go. We were all so listless after the funeral we probably wouldn't have had the strength to do any strenuous work. When she had cooked dinner, she made all of us eat a little before we went to bed. But I lay in bed for a long time, unable to sleep. Mother was whimpering in bed, and Father said,

"It will not bring our boy back. You must remember, he will not return to us but we will go to him."

She stopped crying after that, "If only he hadn't had to suffer so much."

Father simply said, "He blest us all with his life. The Lord gave and the Lord has taken away. Try to rest in that. Someday we will see him again. Death is not forever."

 150

They were both quiet after that and then, shortly after, I heard Mother's heavy breathing, an exhausted breathing.

Leto and Vini and Bulie had been sleeping heavily for some hours now. I suddenly felt very lonely. I felt as though I was the only one awake in the house. I wondered if Pete would return like Zekuo had done. But I didn't feel fear. I only felt a thrill at the possibility of seeing him again. I didn't think I would be afraid if I saw him again. But I also thought of what Bano had said one night. She said that good people who believed in Jesus would not return if they died. Pete certainly believed in Jesus. I could only half hope I would see him once more. I don't remember when it was I fell asleep but when I woke it was bright morning. Mother and Pfünuo were working in the kitchen. I could hear them making cooking noises and the boys were still sleeping. But Leto was up and doing something downstairs. I heard his voice as he answered a question Father had asked. Leto had a deep voice now, and he could sound very much like Father sometimes. He was seventeen and a half and turning eighteen in July. He was at second year in college. I heard Leto say that he would fix the cross on Pete's grave.

I got out of bed quickly and changed into my clothes and ran to the grave. Some of the flowers had wilted already. But the ones we had placed in the vase with water inside were still fresh and coming into full bloom. I looked around to see what I could do. There were leaves on the grave, fallen from the wreaths and bouquets. I carefully picked up every stray leaf and took it to the compost pit. The little lantern lit and kept by the cross was still burning. We would probably keep it there for two weeks or so. Some people kept it on the graves of their loved ones for a month. But the time when Vimenuo's family had lit one on his grave, an old woman from the church came by and said to her mother, "*Hou*, Nganuo, he is dead and maybe gone to heaven. Don't keep the light on so long." So they stopped burning the lantern after that. I rather liked that we had a lantern out for Pete. He didn't like the dark and I felt he would have been comforted by the light burning at his grave especially when we were all sleeping and not there to keep him company.

"Lieno, come to the kitchen," it was Mother calling me. I walked back to the kitchen and she handed me a mug of steaming tea. I found a saucer to put it in and cool it. Pfünuo had already cooked food and Leto had a plate filled up very high with rice and meat. "Eat something after your tea" said Pfünuo to me. I was disappointed that everything seemed so normal again. The big crowd of people at our house the day before had gone and we were making food and acting as if nothing had happened. At least it seemed that way to me.

I said aloud, "When can I plant flowers on Pete's grave?"

Mother looked pained when I said that.

Pfünuo looked at me and said, "Oh you can do that in a week or two. We'll do it together. Once the flowers on the grave have all withered, we can throw them out and plant real flowers. But it is disrespectful to the people who gave us flowers to throw out their flowers the next day so we will keep them for at least ten days till they can see they have become brown and of no use anymore."

Vini and Bulie came into the kitchen too and they ate the food offered to them. Soon, Neikuo had joined us and she brought some food for us. So there was a lot of food in the house and Mother and Pfünuo gave away some of the food-gifts people had brought. They sent the boys to the homes of the gravediggers with packets of sugar and powdered milk after checking thoroughly that none of them had brought us those gifts. Then the pastor was given a body-cloth, one of the new ones that Bilie's wife had given. By mid-morning, they had managed to give some little token to all the people who had helped. For the women who had cooked, they made me and Vimenuo carry either packets of sugar or tea because there were a lot

Easterine Iralu

of tea packets that had come as gifts. Some people gave money too but most gave tea and sugar and milk. The old women brought in a loaf or two loaves of bread but we had served most of the bread yesterday while serving tea to the crowd. Later, Mother's cousin who lived nearby, came and she and Pfünuo washed the house and the floors because the floors were muddy from the number of people that had come to the house yesterday. When they finished washing, they waxed the wooden floors so that they shone again. I didn't know there was so much to do after a death.

I was glad Vimenuo was with me. It was so thoughtful of her mother to send her to be with me. I felt a twinge of guilt that I had not been with her when her father died. Grandmother would never have allowed me so I had not asked. I told her all the things I wanted to say but could not because if I said them to my mother they might seem insensitive and hurt her. It was good that Vimenuo had gone through the loss of a family member because she knew what to do and how one feels. I hoped Grandmother would not send for me too soon. I wanted to stay as long as I could and help out. We went to the grave again after we had delivered the rest of the packages and I told her about Father's dream.

"Did your mother have a dream too? Before your father's death, I mean?" I asked.

"No, not her, but Grandmother did dream that some men had come to dig a new grave in our courtyard and she knew then that someone in our family would soon die. We prayed a lot after that but Father died three weeks later. So it was like a preparation."

I told her about Father's dream too. "Father said that he saw Grandfather waiting outside our house and calling one of the boys out of the house. He saw that it was one of the boys, not me. Isn't it strange that dreams always come true especially if it is dreams of death in the family?"

She nodded her head. We were both quiet for some time.

Vimenuo and I rearranged the flowers on Pete's grave. The freshly dug soil had a damp, wet smell about it. We worked together silently, each of us struggling with our own thoughts. When we were done, we walked to the fence that protected our land and marked it out from our neighbour's. The sunlight was getting stronger now. We could see the town before us, very bright, some of the tin roofs reflected the sun and it hurt our eyes. People were on their way to offices and schools. The older folk coming from the village were headed for their fields.

"Do you suppose he can see us now?" I asked her.

"I don't know, Lieno, but I am sure he is in a happy place," she answered in a small voice.

"Do you think he was in a lot of pain?" I wanted to know.

"I don't know about that either. You were with him, Lieno, was he moaning a lot?"

"No, he wasn't, but he was so weak he could not talk to any of us. He did respond when I held his hand. He responded every time, no matter how weakly."

"I am sure he was spared too much pain."

There were so many questions in my mind but I had to accept that very few people could answer them. Some of these questions could only be answered by Pete. Vimenuo and I went back to the house and ate the food Pfünuo had cooked. Later in the evening she would go back to her own house. Vimenuo and I cleaned the yard, and picked up papers strewn on the ground from yesterday. Some visitors came to the house, including the pastor and a small group of men and women with him. They gathered the whole family together and read from the Bible and prayed for peace. We made them tea and they left soon after. Some more people came to visit but they didn't stop for long. Neikuo had been there from morning.

Easterine Iralu

She was a great help because she knew the right words to use when people came to offer their condolences. Sizo came in the afternoon. He said he had not been able to come the day before. He went to the grave and wept aloud calling Pete by name. I suddenly felt my eyes burning when I saw him cry. Vimenuo and I held hands tightly. She had tears in her eyes too.

16

The year that Pete died, many things changed at home. Vini was sixteen at the time. He was in his last year in school but he did very badly in his exams and the teachers reported to Father and Mother that he had become very difficult to handle. He was rude to the male teachers and he would play truant from school frequently. Mother was more worried than Father. She talked to Neikuo about it and they wondered what they could do. One day at school, I was looking out the window when I saw a boy who looked just like Pete. I was so surprised I mouthed his name and at recess, I ran out to see where he had gone. But when I caught up with him, it was Lebu, one of his friends. I remembered with a shock that Pete was dead and I would never see him again. But for many months afterwards, I would see bigger boys on the road who looked very much like him. And when I drew near to them, they would turn out to be someone else.

A week after Pete's funeral, Grandmother sent Bano to fetch me and so I had to go back. I lay in bed at night, thinking of Pete and very often crying over him. One night, Bano caught me crying. "I know how painful it is but some of our people say that it grieves the spirits if we mourn a dead person in excess. Please try to control yourself. You will feel better in a month or so." I didn't believe I could possibly feel better but I did not want to upset her so I made the effort to keep from crying too much. I was sorry I had stayed so long in Grandmother's house and had not been able to spend time with Pete. I never wanted any of my other brothers to die again from now. It was just too sad.

The year passed in a kind of daze because I lost interest in things for a while. I felt that everything was so empty, so temporary. My teacher said my grades were dropping. It was true. I hadn't done well in my second term exams at all. That was a month after Pete's death. Pfünuo came to visit me one day in Grandmother's house. We were all very surprised because I had never had visitors for me. If there were visitors they all came to the house, calling out, "Mother, are you well?" When Pfünuo came she too called out,

"Mother, is it well with you?" and she sat talking to Grandmother while Bano made her tea, but after a while she said, "Actually I came to have a word with Lieno."

"The girl?" asked Grandmother, "Why? Has she got into some trouble at school?"

"No, of course not, Mother, but I want to tell her a few things."

"Well, you can say them here in my presence" insisted Grandmother. So Pfünuo had to stay seated and address me.

"It's about your second term exams, Lieno," she began, "I know you have done as well as you could have been expected to but you are capable of doing better than that. Try and stop grieving for Petekhrietuo, that is not what he would have wanted, you know. Try and concentrate harder on your studies and get help from your teachers if your lessons are too difficult for you. Your Mathematics teacher is a friend of mine. She thinks you can do better."

I hung my head a little. I knew all she was saying was true but to have it said in front of Grandmother was a little more than disconcerting.

"I will try my best," I mumbled.

"Good girl, we are all so proud of you," she said gently.

"I have always said that education is wasted on girls," Grandmother was mumbling, having listened keenly to all that we were saying.

"Oh no, Mother, she is a very fine pupil," Pfünuo put in quickly.

"Humph, only time will tell," said Grandmother in a tone that indicated that she had no faith in what Pfünuo was saying.

After some time, Pfünuo had to leave. I followed her out of the kitchen and held her around her waist. "Oh, Lieno," she said, "don't be lonely, you will soon be back with us." I really hoped that was true. I didn't want to be away from my parents and my brothers any more.

I did pay a lot of attention to what Pfünuo had said and I did much better in my final exams so that by year's end, I was promoted to the seventh standard. Father and Mother were pleased about that. But they were both subdued this year. We were, all of us, very subdued after Pete's death. Even if there was something joyful to share, it was as though we were able to experience only half of it and never the full happiness that it used to give in the past. Father and Mother said that they were pleased over our results, mine and Bulie's. Leto would have his exams next February. Vini was allowed to sit his final exams in March the following year. Vimenuo said that she had heard the teachers saying they didn't want him in the school any more and that was why they were allowing him to sit his final exams. Indeed, Vini had become more and more distanced from all of us. When he came to Grandmother, she would slip him some money and simper at him ingratiatingly. He was often rude to her but she never seemed to mind that.

158 Easterine Iralu

"I want to be rich and generous when I am old, I am not going to be old and stingy like you Grandmother," he said with a nasty laugh.

She laughed right back and said, "Be careful, my boy, you can't just take my money and my love and walk away from me. I want my share of attention. I brought all of you into the world, in a sense, your father and all the rest of you. Remember that, my boy."

Vini laughed sharply and the two of them looked strangely evil, as though they shared a secret the rest of us did not know. I saw that Vini had four ten-rupee notes in his hand when he was leaving. That was a big amount of money. I wondered why Grandmother had given him so much money. He could never have come by so much money on his own. One night he came to the house reeking of alcohol. I don't know if Grandmother suspected that he had been drinking but she said,

"Something smells funny here tonight."

Fortunately, he left soon after she had given him food.

It was around this time that Vini began to stop seeing his old friends. He had new friends now, rough looking boys, two of them who would not come to the house but call to him from the road. I had seen them once or twice when I went to Mother on an errand. Father and Mother did not like them at all but they were helpless, unable to stop Vini from seeing them. Vimenuo had more news about the two. The older boy was Rocky, almost nineteen, a high school dropout and son of a woman from one of the drinking houses. His father was a Manipuri trucker who stopped coming to Rocky's mother three or four months after Rocky was born. So Rocky had practically grown up without a father. His grandmother was the fat woman who owned the largest drinking house. When Rocky was seventeen, he had been arrested for the murder of an Indian trader. The man was stabbed to death and robbed of all his money.

The police had been informed that Rocky was one of a group of four men who had trapped the trader and stabbed him to death after making him hand over all his money. Three of them were arrested and the fourth man was never caught. Rocky, and his two co-conspirators were badly beaten in police custody. But a month later, he was let out on bail because he had not actually stabbed the trader. There had also been some concession because of his extreme youth. After his term in jail, he was completely changed. Many fights broke out on the road, many were started by him. He took to carrying a slim, sharp knife and no one wanted to get into trouble with him.

The other boy was from one of the northern villages. Nobody knew his real name. They simply called him Bai. He always looked shabby and a bit like a big dog. His lower lip tended to hang and sometimes boys would maliciously call him "Brownie", implying that he looked like a dog. That was always the start of a fight. "Hey, hey, Brownie, want to go for a walk?" one of the boys would shout. Another would join in and say, "Let's go catch a big rat, Brownie" and the next moment, Bai would be charging at them, fists flailing and landing blind blows. Sometimes, he would send the boys hollering away with a black eye or bleeding nose. But sometimes they would gang up and twist his hands behind his back and batter his face viciously. Then the older men from the houses would come out and pull them apart. "Enough, enough, do you want to murder him?" one of them would shout and the boys would run off into the darkness. Bai limped home then and nursed his wounds and his swollen face, determined that no one would ever catch him off guard again. These were Vini's new friends, tough street boys who were cruel and terrorised everyone. I was more and more afraid of Vini now. He had changed so much. I thought back on the days when he had let me use his slingshot and I had shot my own finger so badly that it turned blue. I cried for a long time but he put my finger in his mouth and said he would suck the pain away. And, really, my finger had felt better when he sucked on it with his warm tongue.

When I was very young, Vini and Leto would carry me alternately if we went to the forest with Father and I got tired of walking. Back then, I never thought we would ever be parted from one another. Now, Pete was gone from us forever. And Vini seemed to be going a different way too. I didn't want to think about it. Why did life have to be so confusing? Bano was unable to give me any answers. So, I stopped asking her questions. Mother was very distant after Pete's death. She didn't seem to remember the rest of us. She had coped well for a few days and done all the housework when other people were around for the first week. But afterwards, when I went to her, I would sometimes find her absent-mindedly sitting in a chair, holding an old shirt of Pete's and crying, or simply sitting with it in her hand and looking out the window.

It was now seven months since Pete had died but Mother still grieved for him. All of us grieved as well but Mother had been hit the hardest by the tragedy. Her face was pinched and she seldom smiled. She was no longer interested in her garden and her flowers. I tried to sow some seeds on the days that I went home but Mother could never remember to water the seeds. A few straggly plants could be seen after two months which we had to pull out because they looked so bad. I don't know if Father still grieved over Pete. He was getting stones and cement ready so that he would be able to make a proper grave for Pete in January. But Mother did not want him to do that. "It will seem as though he had died a long time ago if you make his grave now," she insisted. So Father was confused about what he should do, whether to go ahead with the grave-making plans or wait until the next year. We were still within the boundary of the village. January was the month for grave-making or repairs on old graves but it was taboo to do this kind of work in any of the other months. Father said that since we lived a little far from the village we could probably do it at another time of the year. But Mother was very much against that. "Who knows what further tragedy we might bring upon ourselves if we violate a taboo?" she said. So, Pete's grave was left unconstructed for a whole year. Old women going to their fields and passing his grave would sometimes say, "*Hei*, this is a very young one." Some others would comment, "Time that they made the grave. It will look bad when the rains come." Father put up a little shelter over the mud grave and Mother would tenderly smooth the red earth with fresh, wet mud every week. I learnt to do it and helped her to plaster the mound of earth. At Christmas, I came home to be with them but there was no rejoicing for us. Mother and I did bake some cakes and we went to church for the White Gift service. Some people from church came carol singing with us and Mother served them tea and cake.

I didn't have a new dress for Christmas but I didn't really want one. By foregoing that luxury, I wanted to show that I was still mourning my brother. It was the first Christmas that Vini spent away from us. He was out with his friends all night. When he stumbled home it was four in the morning and the sickly sweet smell of homemade brew drifted into my room from his. He slept as soon as he got into bed. I think he must have just collapsed into the bed because in the morning, when I went in to wake Bulie, Vini still had his shoes on. Father began to lecture him on drinking when he was having his morning tea in the kitchen.

"Later, later" hissed Mother, "don't talk of these things when the boy is eating. Wait till he has finished."

Easterine Iralu

But Father was in no mood to wait. "Those friends of yours, do you know what they are?" he stormed, "Scum, mere scum, and my son is the greatest fool for having such friends and becoming a hopeless drunk. Which of them has a job? Which of them has any prospects of a good future? Tell me. And you, you want to be the same as them or worse. Don't put me to shame and don't bring shame to our family name. Have you no thought for what people are saying about us? About our family? Do you know they are all laughing at us behind our backs? They are laughing at you. And at me. They think I cannot control my family. That I have no pride that I let my son associate with fatherless boys and prostitutes' sons."

"That's enough, Father, you've said too much already" Vini burst out. His face was red and blotchy from suppressed rage. "You don't have to insult my friends because they were not as lucky as you."

"You call them friends? You call them your friends? You have forgotten your own place in society but that doesn't mean you can pick up people like that and call them your friends. We don't befriend such people."

Vini gave a low growl. He looked terrible, as though he were out of control. I feared he might hit Father because he looked so outraged.

But Father sat down and said helplessly, "Oh son, if you knew the shame you are bringing to our family and the burden your mother has to carry."

Vini didn't say anything then. He finished his tea in silence and took the cup to the washing place. But he laid the cup down roughly so that it made a loud sound. Mother jumped at the sound. But he swung himself out of the kitchen and went to the room slamming doors as he went.

"Visa, I told you not to say anything, but you never listen to me. What if we lose him too?"

"Didn't you see how he was behaving? Don't stop me, Nino, he must listen to me, whether he likes it or not, I am his father and he must listen to what I have to say. It is up to him to act or not act on what I say but I will tell him what I need to tell him so long as he is in my house."

"And if you drive him away? Is that what you want, Visa?" Mother was crying now, "I have lost a son, I don't want to lose any more."

"This is different," said Father coldly.

School suddenly got tougher. In the seventh standard, we were no longer considered children because now we in High School. We went to morning assembly with the senior classes. Vimenuo was still in the sixth standard so we couldn't meet as often as we wanted to. We both turned twelve that year. But we were still thin, Vimenuo thinner than I, her collar bones jutting out over the neck of her white t-shirt. Neither of us had got the curse yet. Bulie was in the ninth standard, he was not doing too well but at least he tried hard and got average grades. Leto was in his third year in college. Vini had cleared his High School examination but not secured good grades.

Grandmother would turn eighty in April or May. She wasn't sure in which month she had been born but her father had said it was the year 1890. So the whole family was planning to have a big celebration for her eightieth birthday. Aunt Bino said she would invite 80 guests. It would be exciting to see how many people would fit into Grandmother's house. Though it was a large house, I didn't believe that more than forty people could be accommodated at one go. Grandmother wanted to stay in her room longer these days. She tired easily and Bano had to massage her feet and legs every four or five hours. Neikuo was slowing down too. Sizo was the only member of their family who was still spry and could work as hard as a much younger man. If Grandmother was almost eighty, that meant Neikuo would be seventy-five and Sizo, fifty-five. I found the age difference between Grandmother and Sizo so ridiculous. Neikuo explained that their father had married at twenty-four and fathered Sizo when he was fifty and their mother, forty-seven. Sizo could almost be Grandmother's son. Yet, he joked with her and would tease her if she was unnecessarily harsh. She didn't like it but she could not put on a haughty air with Sizo and get away with it. He made her look ludicrous if she tried it. I still enjoyed Sizo's visits immensely. He couldn't carry me on his lap any more but he continued to bring me treats and patted me on the head when he saw me. Once he had brought his wife, a large smiling woman who spoke Tenyidie with a funny accent, to see us. Bano and I imitated her accent when we were alone and giggled so much that Grandmother began to tap on the floor with her cane. We went to bed stifling our laughter.

Somehow, old age had not made Grandmother any gentler. However, she was more forgetful now and I could sometimes fool her if I had forgotten a job I was supposed to do. A week ago, she complained I had not swept under her bed. "But, Grandmother, don't you remember, I made you leave the room so I could sweep under the bed and behind the shelves?" "Did you? I suppose you did," she said doubtfully. I now knew how to get away if I overlooked one of my many tasks. I simply had to pretend that I had done it and she had forgotten about it. If I insisted firmly, she would have to believe me. This way, there was less scolding for me. I didn't think of it as a particularly wicked thing to do. It was almost the same as acting in self-defence, I reasoned. There were more things

Easterine Iralu

to do now that I was bigger. I struggled to finish my tasks and find enough time to do my homework and study a bit. Vimenuo and I worked out a way to get to school earlier and come home forty to forty-five minutes after school was over. I told Grandmother the teacher had made us do extra lessons because he wanted us to do well in the exam. She didn't like it but she could not stop me from coming home late because it was a school activity. Every once in a while we did that. Sometimes I actually sat in the school compound and studied my lessons. But on some days I simply followed Vimenuo home and lingered as long as I dared in her house. Fortunately, her mother came home late from work so she was never there to question me.

The big boys in our class had begun to smoke. Not all of them but at least six of the nine who had been promoted along with me from sixth standard. The Math teacher complained that our classroom smelt of stale tobacco. The smokers never looked up if he said that but when he turned his back to write out a sum on the blackboard, they would look at each other conspiratorially and snigger. This year, only two of the older girls were doing well at school. The others were lagging behind. Of the boys, there were four who were bright and the rest were lazy. We were seven girls and nine boys now because two of them had been detained. Some had been in the same class for the last two years, and one of the girls had been in Bulie's class earlier. She knew that if she was detained another year, she would have to leave the school. In Bulie's class there were just four girls and six boys because a number of students dropped out of High School if it got too difficult for them. The older girls frequently got married once they dropped out of school. Of course, fewer boys dropped out but there was one boy from Vini's class who left school and went to work in his father's shop. The drop out rate was much higher for girls. One of the senior girls from Vini's class caused quite a scandal when she dropped out of the ninth standard and got married to her Science Teacher five months later. The school authorities debated for a long time whether they should suspend him, but the Chairman found out that the pair had not really been guilty of misbehaviour when the girl had been a student of the school. So the teacher got to keep his job but the girl refused to be seen outside her house for many months. She gave birth to their first child ten months later. It was only then that tongues stopped wagging. Kohima could be terribly cruel that way and people would discuss such gossip for weeks before something new came along to distract them.

The women at the water spot seemed to know everything about everyone.

"Did you know that Sonhie's sister is pregnant?" I heard the older woman say to the younger one.

"Yes, but it's not her husband's child, it's some guy who was at their house working with her husband for a few days. He's beaten her black and blue and she may lose the child too. Punched her in the stomach several times, he did too. I guess he wanted to get rid of the child as well."

"Has she left then?"

"Nah, stupid woman, she's still there. Should leave if she doesn't want any more beating. I mean, what she's done is stupid enough but since it's done she should just leave instead of staying behind and trying to repair it. He'll never forgive her."

It was always shocking to hear of other people's troubles when we caught these snippets of conversation between the two women. We never doubted that what they said was true. We had no means of finding out. I learnt not to speak of Grandmother's relationship with Bano at school.

One of the older girls had asked, "Lieno, who is that young woman at your Grandmother's house? Is she your sister?"

"No," I replied, "She is my father's sister, my grandmother's youngest daughter." That was the way Bano was referred to at home and so it came to me naturally to say that too.

"Hmmf!" went one of the other girls, "Everyone knows she is not your grandmother's daughter. Is that what they tell you at home? What a silly girl you are to believe that."

I stiffened and stayed quiet but the first girl asked, "Oh, then whose daughter is she?"

The second girl laughed nastily and said, "She is Sizo's daughter but she is not his present wife's daughter. Her mother was a maid in their house and they sent her away after she had given birth. Then they passed the baby off as Lieno's grandmother's daughter but everyone knows that story and it's silly to say she is her daughter when we can all see the age gap between them. Surely her grandmother must have been 55 when she was born!"

The other girls joined in the laughter and I felt my face burn. I was angry and humiliated but I felt even more angry with Grandmother and Sizo for covering up the truth. Why did they have to continue the farce that Bano was not his child? I was angry that I had been forced into this because I had to say what we were taught at home and having Bano's origins publicly exposed in this manner was most unpleasant. I was also put in a very uncomfortable position now. If I participated in the dialogue and agreed with them it could be interpreted as me turning against my family and if I did not, I would be branded a liar or a fool. And whatever it was, Grandmother was still family to me. I stayed silent. The girls laughed about it and they began to say rude things about Grandmother and call her an old sourpuss.

"That's enough!" said the fat girl suddenly, "you wouldn't like it if someone were to say rude things about your grandmothers would you?"

A Terrible Matriarchy   169

The laughter died down then. I felt grateful to the fat girl. But I couldn't forgive the other girls. I told Vimenuo about it after school.

She was angry too and that made me feel better. "You know, they all have some terrible story in their own families. That's why they try to talk about other people so that it will draw attention away from themselves. Zebinuo, for instance, her uncle was caught with the woman who looks after their cows and brings them milk in the morning. They tried to hush it up but everyone knows about it."

Zebinuo was the second girl, the one who had let everyone know who Bano really was.

"I'm going to go say that in class tomorrow then."

"No, no don't" Vimenuo cautioned, "just act as if nothing happened and don't say anything. It will be worse for you if you try to be as nasty as them."

"But they have no business to embarrass me like that."

"Don't worry, they will get their punishment in due course. Don't meddle with them please, you don't know what they are capable of."

I thought about Vimenuo's advice and had to agree that she was right. There was no point getting into a fight with them. Three of them were really foul mouthed. They were the same girls who disliked me and would do anything to put me down. But they were all scared of the fat girl.

"They are jealous of you, can't you see?" Vimenuo went on, "you always score more than them though you are younger than any of them. So they'll do all they can to put you down. Don't let it get to you."

We were almost home by now. We parted and I went back feeling new sympathy for Bano. Father was waiting for me when I reached. I was very surprised.

Easterine Iralu

"Father, is someone sick at home?" I asked because the only reason why he would have come was if someone was sick or some help was needed.

It was not time for any festival like Christmas or Easter so I knew he hadn't come to fetch me for anything festive. He looked old and tired. There were new lines around his eyes and he was thinner than I remembered.

"It's your mother," he said. "She hasn't been keeping well ever since Pete died and now, she is too weak to work in the house. I came to take you home so you could help around the house for a few days."

"Of course, Father, I would be so happy to come, what did Grandmother say?"

"She wants you to help," he said.

I knew Grandmother would resent anyone taking away help from her household but she had no right to refuse my parents. I hurriedly finished eating, got my things together quickly and left with Father.

Everything looked unkempt in our house. I could see that Leto or Father had tried to clean the mess but not done a good job of it. The dirty clothes basket was overflowing with clothes and the floor had been swept but not polished so that a fine layer of dust had settled on it. Mother was sitting in the kitchen by the fire trying to cook lentils and mustard leaves. Father took the vegetables from her and gently asked her to go to bed. She went without protest. I was shocked at how pale she was. I followed her to the bedroom and helped her get into bed. Mother was a tall woman but I had grown a little taller in the past year so I reached up to her ear. I felt young and strong as I tucked her into bed. She hadn't said a word to me. I thought it best not to ask her anything but let her get as much rest as she needed. I stayed by her till I was sure she was asleep. Then I stowed my clothes away and went to the kitchen and finished cutting the rest of the vegetables. I put them into the broth of dried meat, lentils and bamboo shoot and added soya bean and garlic. I could hear Father chopping fire wood so I went to bring it in. After food was cooked, I tried to clean the house but I had to leave some for the next day because it was too much. I heard Leto at the door.

Happily I ran out and called, "Leto, I'm here."

"Hey, Lieno, good to see you and you have grown too," he said as he pulled off his jacket and strode into the house.

Leto was so big now. He was tall as Father and had big arms and hands.

"Do you come home so late from class?" I asked.

"No, I was working."

"Leto! I didn't know you were working."

He looked embarrassed and said, "Ah, it's not a real job. After classes I go to the new store and help till closing time. It's okay. They give me about 200 rupees a month so I am able to pay my own fees."

It sounded wonderful to be a grown-up and be able to have a job, even if it was only what Leto called part-time.

"When did you begin?" I asked eagerly.

"A month and two days now."

"Well, you never told me anything." I felt a little miffed about not being told.

"It's not a real job, it's not as though I am going to be there all my life," he soothed me.

"Still."

I was happy for him but at the same time I felt excluded from the family because I had not been told.

"Wait till I get a real job, one that pays me 800 rupees. That will be something worth talking about, Lieno," he said happily.

Eight hundred rupees was a lot of money to me. I didn't know how much money Father earned. It must be something like that.

 Easterine Iralu

But we would never own a car I could see that, not even on eight hundred a month. We were too many to feed.

Leto was hungry so we ate. When Mother woke, I asked if I should bring food to her in bed but she insisted on getting up. She didn't eat very much, sort of pecked at it and then she pushed her food away. "Try and eat another mouthful, dear" said Father. But she said she felt like throwing up. So he let her be. She wanted to help wash up but the three of us refused to let her help. She sat with us in the kitchen while Father and Leto drank black tea.

"There was some trouble in town this evening" Leto said to Father.

Father looked straight at him and said, "Later."

But Mother had heard and she instantly became alert.

"Where are Vini and Bulie? Why aren't they back yet?"

"You know that Bulie is with Touzo at his aunt Bino's house, don't you? And Vini will soon be home. It is not late yet. We ate early so it seems late. Now, why don't you go back to bed? Lieno can help you."

Father gave me a meaningful look so I got up and helped Mother to the bedroom. She was so weak she had to be helped to walk the steps leading from our small kitchen to their bedroom.

"Are you sure Bulie and Vini are all right?" Mother asked.

"Oh Mother, if Father says they are all right, I'm sure you don't need to worry."

"Will you tell me, Lieno, if anything happens to them?"

"Of course, Mother" I reassured her.

She got into bed wearily. Her Bible was near her pillow. I massaged her forehead and smoothed the creases on her brow. When she was asleep, I tiptoed back into the kitchen. Father and Leto were deep in conversation.

"They shouldn't have tried it," Father was saying.

"Most men would, Father, so it's useless saying that. But it's got more dangerous now that there are so many of our people who cannot be trusted."

I knew when not to ask questions. I worked quietly and listened.

"Did you say there were fifteen who were captured by the army?" Father asked.

"Sixteen actually but one of them escaped. His bonds were loose and he jumped from the army truck a kilometre from the camp. He sprained an ankle but he crawled away. Sometimes he got up on one leg and hopped. He couldn't go home of course so he hid in a clansman's house for the night. I know his cousin well so he told me about him. But it's dangerous to let the story leak out."

I knew what they were talking about. It was the new recruits in the Naga Army who had been captured. The boys in our class would talk about it endlessly, saying they would join up when they were old enough. There were boys as young as seventeen in the Naga army. I had heard horror stories of what the Indian army did to those who were captured. Some men were hung upside down and electrocuted. The boys said that the soldiers especially liked to strip the men down and give them electric shocks in their private parts. We shuddered when the boys said that. And I understood what they meant when some elders would say "better to die in battle than to fall into the hands of the Indian army." When Bulie and I were younger, Father's friend, Vechoi would come and stay with us. He was a man of the Chokri tribe from Phek town. He always stayed three or four days when he came. He said to us, "We are not fighting an unjust war. We were independent before India became a nation. We are fighting for our freedom because it is right." Vechoi's father had been killed by the Indian army when they raided the village and picked out twenty men to be killed as a lesson to the neighbouring villages. Both Vechoi's father and his brother had been shot. The women were systematically raped. Bulie and I made a pact to join the Naga army when we grew up and vowed to avenge Vechoi's father.

"Better warn Vini not to stay out late," Leto was saying, "the police and the army are picking up young men at night. And they have become so brutal. The army especially, they seem to be looking for an excuse to beat up young boys. Kughato's brother was picked up a week ago and they kept beating him and forcing him to say that he was a soldier in the Naga army. Even when he showed them his student identity card, they called him a liar and kept beating him with rifle butts. He would have died if his father had not begged the Member of Parliament to intervene. He's still in a very bad way."

"Don't let your mother hear about this. She has enough to worry about. You know she worries about Vini so much that it's making her sick. She's so scared he'll get into trouble with the army with that temper of his. It's that which makes her ill more than anything else. The doctor says she needs rest but Vini doesn't realize that when he keeps coming home late, she cannot really rest."

So that was what was wrong with Mother. Father had not told me what her sickness was and I didn't know how to go about asking. Just then we heard footsteps.

"Vini!"

Father called out and he came into the kitchen without answering. His eyes were red-rimmed but he didn't smell of drink.

"Got late helping a friend fix his car," he said sullenly.

He saw me but did not smile.

"Don't be out late. The army's sniffing around and picking up young men regardless of who they are. We don't want anything to happen to you," said Father.

"I know the places to avoid," said Vini in a low voice.

"That's not all, Vini. The Government wants to clamp a curfew in the town areas and if that happens and you are caught outside during curfew hours, they could easily bring all sorts of charges against you. You know how trigger-happy the soldiers are. They just need an excuse to shoot."

"I'm careful," said Vini stubbornly.

Father went red in the face and I was frightened that they would argue hotly. Moments passed tensely but Father calmed down and said,

"For your mother's sake, boy, be careful."

"Is she worse?" asked Vini.

"No, but she is not any better," Leto spoke up, "and she heard us talking about the fifteen men who were captured by the army so she was very anxious about you. It wouldn't help if you were to get caught by the army."

Vini didn't look pleased at all. He cared about Mother. We all cared about Mother. But he was so used to his nightly haunts that the idea of giving that up was not something he wanted to consider. Vini's hands were dirty and covered in grease. So he really had been working on his friend's car.

"Will you eat now, Vini?"

I asked.

"Wait, I have to wash my hands. Can you give me some warm water?"

I mixed him warm water in a basin and passed him soap so that he could wash his hands. He smelt of kerosene. But he was not angry anymore. None of them were angry now so I was relieved. I served him food and gave him a spoon to eat with. Father said he would go to bed and then there were just the three of us, Leto, Vini and me.

"Where's Bulie?" asked Vini.

"He's with Touzo, he'll come tomorrow," Leto answered.

"Going to stay here long, Lieno?" Vini turned to me.

"I hope so" I said, "I am here to help because Mother's sick."

I didn't know how much I should say to Vini. He was very close to Grandmother and if I said I didn't like it at her house, he might tell her and then I would get into trouble when I went back.

"Right," he said and finished eating.

Vini ate rapidly. He had always been a fast eater. Pete used to be the slow one, chewing his food slowly and still eating when everyone else had finished.

"I'm sleeping early tonight," Vini explained, "I'm all done in from the work we did on the car."

He shoved his plate into the sink and went to his room. I put away all the pots and washed the last dirty dishes before I put out the fire and went to bed too.

My room was not a real room. I was using the storeroom behind the sitting room having cleared it of much of the stuff inside. There was a curtain across the opening and my small bed was hidden by it. Father had said he would put up a door so that I could have a real room. I didn't fall asleep immediately, I lay awake savouring the feeling of being home again. But I was worried too. Things were so different from what they used to be. When we were younger, we were poorer but we were so close. Now there was an uneasy distance between Vini and Father and Vini and Leto. I could not put a name to it but it was there and I wondered if we would ever recover the deep bond we used to share. Leto had changed too. He had become a man. He could no longer carry me on his back but he was still gentle with me. Vini struggled to be gentle but he seemed to have become so brusque it had grown into him. I don't remember falling asleep but I must have, at some stage, because I dreamt of Pete. He was standing in a garden of flowers, very pretty flowers, all around him and he was wearing a long white robe. "You look like an angel" I said to him before I remembered that he was dead. Then he went away from me to the far end of the garden and after that I did not see him anymore. Next, it was Vini in his place but instead of flowers there were thorns and burnt plants around his feet. In great rage he had pulled up all the pretty flowers so that all that was left was burnt black petals and thorns. I was horrified and woke up sweating. My dream was so vivid I thought and thought about it. I decided that it meant that Pete was in heaven, possibly he had become an angel. But the dream about Vini troubled me, it was so unpleasant.

Easterine Iralu

18

Mother did not get better. This meant that I could stay home
permanently. Grandmother didn't like it at all but there was nothing
she could do about it. I visited her sometimes but she would be
quite piqued at seeing me so I went less and less, using Mother's
sickness as an excuse. I had even more work at home. At
Grandmother's it had helped that two of us shared the workload. At
home, I was alone and Mother could not do very much. The boys'
clothes were difficult to wash and my back ached from the great
amount of washing. But I was so happy to be at home that I never
gave it a thought.

We celebrated Grandmother's eightieth birthday grandly. Sizo
and his family were there. They were our guests because
Grandmother's house had to be readied for the feast the next day.
There were 85 guests in all. Four of Grandmother's friends (three a
year younger than her and one who was the same age) came. They
had to be helped to walk to the doorway. So their escorts made up
the four extra guests, and the fifth was Sizo's mother-in-law who
was 76 and insisted on coming to wish Grandmother. There were so

many gifts, mostly body-cloths, that Grandmother said afterwards. "Give them to the boys, I only need three to bury me in."

"You are not going to die so soon, Vibaü," chided Neikuo.

The Pastor was specially invited to pray and make a speech. When all the guests were seated on wooden benches borrowed from our school, the Pastor got up to speak: "This is an auspicious day. Today we are celebrating the birth anniversary of our mother, Vibanuo, who, by the grace of God, has completed 80 years in her earthly life. Our mother married our father, Letou in the year 1912. But like Hannah in the Bible they did not have children until 1922. After that they were blest with a son, Visa, a daughter, Bino and two more sons, Avi and Bilie. She is our mother, aunt to some and grandmother to many, a mother of sons and daughters who begat sons and daughters in their turn. She is a pillar of the society and of the church. Her upright moral life has been an example to many in our fold. She has also upheld the good customs of our forefathers so that her children and grandchildren know their place in society and none has brought a bad name to our society.

'Rise in the presence of the aged, show respect for the elderly and revere your God, I am the Lord' (Leviticus 19:32). So we revere our mother today and pay tribute to the life she has lived. Her father was one among the first Christians in our village and he suffered great persecution for his faith. Our mother has persevered with the same faith and so we acknowledge that today. 'Honour your father and mother.' He who does that will live long in the land. Our mother honoured her mother and father so she has been blest with long life. May we all live by her example." After that he prayed for Grandmother and all her descendants. My uncles Avi and Bilie were all there with their families and my aunt Bino was supervising the feast. It should have been Mother's role to supervise the kitchen as she was the wife of the eldest son but she was too weak to do it. She sat quietly in a chair throughout the meeting and Avi's wife, aunt Leno threw her a pitying look. I saw her look slyly at aunt Sini, uncle Bilie's wife. I wondered what that look meant. It irritated me somewhat because the two of them could often be found gossiping together about the others at family events like this. They reminded me of the two women at the water spot. Except for that, the celebration went very well. Sizo's children were grown and though they looked a little unfashionable in their best clothes, no one could fault them on their manners which were excellent. Sizo's wife went to help in the kitchen and she did all the washing up.

Afterwards, when most of the guests had gone, and only family members were left, Mother sat on the couch with Neikuo and Grandmother sat in her old faded chair beside them. I was shocked that Mother looked as old as the other two now. A stranger would have thought they were sisters, Mother with that gaunt look on her face. She had more wrinkles and was a little stooped. It was funny I had never noticed before how she had aged. Maybe it was something to do with Pete's death. They were all relaxed and talking about how well the celebration had gone. The Pastor had left but not before grandmother had forced a man's body-cloth on him. Sizo's wife had made a big pot of tea so everyone had a mug of tea in their hands. The men were outside in the courtyard, sitting on the benches and talking about things men usually liked to talk about when they were on their own, hunting and fishing and the new curfew that the government was likely to impose. I took tea out to them and went back to the living room where the women were. Aunt Bino was looking at me as I came in, "You're almost as tall as your mother, Dielieno," she said. I was pleased to hear that. "I guess Neno's old clothes can't fit you any more, she has stopped growing." I secretly thought that was a pity because Neno had very pretty clothes which I had regularly used. She wasn't there at the party because she was studying in Calcutta. I was glad she wasn't there. I didn't like her much because she was still cold to us and I had not forgotten that she'd told her friends that we were distant relatives of her mother's. Aunt Bino always gave us handouts, never anything new though her husband had now become one of the richest men in the town. Father said she was stingy by nature but Mother would shush him when he said that.

We finally left as the sun was setting. I helped Bano to clear the kitchen and the men said they would return the benches the next morning when the school opened. They dismantled the tarpaulin in the yard which had been put up as a shelter for the guests. It had looked very festive, like a small wedding. Vimenuo's youngest sister had been very curious, "Is Bano getting married?" she had asked. Only her grandmother was at the party. The rest of them had not been invited. Mother had had no say in the matter, aunt Bino and the wives of my two uncles had decided who would be invited. But Bano did make me take some meat across to them because so much food was left over. I was a little embarrassed when Vimenuo's mother asked how many guests there were. "About eighty, only very old people" I added so that she would think she had not been invited because she was not old. We also gave meat away to many of the neighbours. Mother and I brought back meat to last us at least four days. The boys would go to help the next day and they would eat at Grandmother's again. So there would be less cooking to do. That was a relief because there was always so much cooking to do at home. Bulie ate with a hearty appetite. He was growing rapidly. He was as tall as Vini but he was very plump. There were never any leftovers no matter how much I cooked.

I wondered if Mother would get better eventually. It was so sad to see her so wasted. She was slowly beginning to talk to me, as though I were an adult. Sometimes she told me about her childhood,

Easterine Iralu

about her father and how he would bring home British officers who gave her chocolate and biscuits. Her father had been a scout in the British army during the war so he had many medals, one for spying on a Japanese camp and leading the British forces to their position. He was wounded in the attack, nearly lost his left arm, said Mother. Hence that medal. Pfünuo had been born many years later, she was about 12 years younger than Mother. They had a brother, three years older than Pfünuo, and all their father's medals were kept by that brother. Mother's own mother had died when they were young. Mother was sixteen when it happened and Pfünuo was just four. So Mother found herself taking on the role of mothering her sister and brother for the next ten years or so.

Her father remarried after the war but did not have more children. Their new mother was a kind matronly lady who cared for them well. I used to call her Grandmother. But she died two years after Mother's father died. So I had only faint memories of the two of them. Two, old, kind people whose faces lit up when we went to visit them. But they were not really that old when they died. Grandfather died at 69 and his wife was 66 when she died. It was as though her job on earth was finished when she had taken care of Grandfather and with him gone, she had really no reason to linger behind. Mother remembered that it was her second mother who taught her how to weave the intricate patterns on men's body-cloths and how to dry herbs in winter. Pfünuo could not remember her biological mother and that disappointed Mother a bit. She often tried to jog Pfünuo's memory by recalling things that they had done together with their mother. But Pfünuo would confuse her two mothers hopelessly.

It was to me that Mother admitted how scared she was of Grandmother when she was first married. How she had struggled to cook and weave and garden so that Grandmother would not think her eldest son had married a woman who was good only for decorating the living room as our people liked to say. Eventually, she won Grandmother's approval because she was such a good worker. But Mother was closest to Neikuo and she told me how Neikuo would help her bathe her babies. She would come over unannounced and quietly weed the garden or do some other job that Mother had not been able to finish because of the babies.

She also had many memories of the war. Of being evacuated from Kohima and travelling to Dimapur in an army convoy with her parents and brother and baby sister. Of returning home in June only to find that their home was too ruined by the shelling to live in. Of huddling in a neighbour's hut while her father and uncle quickly made them a shelter with sheets of tin from the British Government. Of watching while the men buried decomposing bodies of Japanese soldiers and then continued with their work of rebuilding the village and town.

I loved to listen to Mother's stories. They were magical and unreal because I had never been a part of them. She described a Kohima I had never known, with trees and houses bombed out till only black ruins and stumps remained. Before the war, she said they shopped at a bazaar where Manipuri traders came with their special varieties of dried fish as well as jaggery and peanut balls. She and her mother would come home with laden baskets after buying two rupees worth of food. After the war prices shot up, she said. For Mother, life was divided into two periods, before the war and after the war and life was always better before the war. She had been a very young girl then, loved dearly by her parents and getting educated at the Mission School. Mother sang in the choir and learnt to play hymns on the piano. I had seen blurred photographs of Mother in dresses with wide flared skirts. She made life in Kohima before the war seem like a long series of picnics and festivals.

 184

When her mother died in 1943, there were rumours of war all over the town and nearby villages. She heard her father's friends say that Japanese spies had come into the southern villages. But people did not speak of these things publicly. More and more British soldiers came to Kohima and they grew very used to the sight of military trucks and jeeps driving past in a cloud of dust. Most of the bigger boys in her class joined the army or went to work as helpers in the army camps because they had heard that the government would soon close the schools. When school was finally closed, Mother was too busy looking after her siblings to spend time with her girlfriends who went to look at the new troops. The older boys and girls went out on picnics with the young British soldiers and there were football matches in the evening that her friends went to watch. They would return from these outings excitedly discussing which of the soldiers was the cutest. But Mother missed out on all that because she had to care for Pfünuo who was four and had to be bathed and fed and carried around or watched all day. When she fell asleep in the afternoon, Mother did the washing and fetched water. If Pfünuo woke up, Mother would persuade her that they were playing house and give her vegetables to cut up with a blunt knife while Mother herself quickly cooked dinner. Their brother was seven so he didn't need much looking after but he was not of any great help in the house.

One day when they were cooking dinner, a British officer came into the kitchen. He handed a chocolate to Pfünuo. Mother explained that her father was working and would be back late. Suddenly, the officer pulled her into his arms and there was no doubt what his intention was. Mother struggled and desperately called to Pfünuo to get help. Pfünuo began to cry loudly. At this, the neighbour's dog barked and would not stop. The man flung Mother from him and cursed and left abruptly. Mother was very shaken by the incident. When her father came back, she burst into tears and told him about it. Her father was very surprised and asked her to describe the man. A week later, the same officer was arrested and transported to a big jail in central India. He was a German spy masquerading as a British officer. The government seized all the papers that were found in his possession, documents detailing the number of British and Allied troops in the Naga Hills and the location of ammunition depots and British army outposts all over our hills. They also found a radio transmitter with which he kept in touch with his superior officers. A few other women came forward to say that he had tried to molest them but they had been too scared to tell anyone. The cleaning woman confessed that he had once tried offering her money to sleep with him. She had refused and sent him to the local prostitute.

After that incident with the German spy, the government was very careful. New officers posted to the area had their credentials scrutinised thoroughly. The helper boys recruited locally could not bring in their friends to the kitchen as they did earlier. Only certified personnel were allowed into the camp. However, apart from that, life did not become too difficult before the war hit Kohima. The population did not suffer any of the severe starvation and scarcity that other areas suffered. This was because most people cultivated their terrace fields and stocked enough paddy to last them till the next harvest. Mother said even the very poor had grain so no one starved. It was only when the Japanese moved into the town and villages that people learnt what starvation actually was. In great fear, they went to work in their fields only to find that when they returned home at night to salvage grain, they could not because their houses were occupied by Japanese soldiers. Fortunately, the war did not last beyond three months and the civilian population received rations from the government. Mother

Easterine Iralu

and Pfünuo once saw a Nepali soldier being pursued by three Japanese soldiers. When the Japanese saw that they would not be able to catch him, the leader stopped and took aim with his pistol and shot the running man in the back. The man fell with a little sound. Mother fled back to the house with Pfünuo. The next morning they packed all that they could carry with them, locked the house and left for Dimapur. The shelling of Kohima began two days after they had left. They were glad they had left but worried about friends and acquaintances who had stayed back.

In June, when they had been away three months, the government invited people to return and rebuild Kohima. So Mother and her family came back, travelling in a jeep this time with their belongings crammed in alongside. The military jeep was driven by an officer her father worked with. Kohima was unrecognisable. Huge dark holes were visible where the mortar shells had exploded. Shattered tin roofs lay on the roadside and the debris of war was visible everywhere. Out of the corner of her eyes, Mother saw the bodies of dead Japanese. She shut her eyes against the sight and distracted Pfünuo so she wouldn't see it. It was strange how these were the memories that stayed longest in Mother's weakened mind. She also remembered people who had been kind to her before the war, Vimenuo's grandfather for instance, who had built a little cart with wheels so they could pull Pfünuo in it. This was a week after her mother died. Again and again she told me about this. An old woman had brought cooked rice for them to eat for three days after the funeral and she continued to come back every week to see if there was anything else she could do to help. Now that woman was dead and Mother spoke of wanting to do something good for her children. "It is very important to be kind to others," she said, "if you have not been able to do anything with your life, but if you have been kind to others, you'll still have done something good with your life."

How old was Mother now? Forty-six? She looked fifteen years older. I wondered if it was because of all that she had seen and lived through.

Pfünuo came often to see if Mother was better. She stayed a long time when she came, sitting on the high chair and drawing Mother's head to her so that she could massage her gently on her temples and her scalp. Some days, she bathed Mother's long hair and brushed it out. There was more grey in it than black. Pfünuo's own hair was still quite black. She now wore it long and coiled into a bun as all the other housewives did. I had liked the curly short style she sported as a young girl. She was still pretty but not like before. Then she had looked so bright and carefree in her pleated skirts and soft sweaters. I had liked the frocks with flower prints that she wore. There had been no other girl as pretty in her summer dresses the year before she got married. We were always together then. She would tie my hair with a bow on the side and we would go to the shops in town, the little store run by a Nepali lady was her favourite. They sold lots of jewellery, tiny green beads twisted into a necklace and large brooches. They also sold broad belts with very large clasps that were all the rage then. The boys and girls in the tenth standard wore them too. Pfünuo and I sometimes went to the coffee shop which was the only shop where you could buy *rasagollas*, sticky sweet balls made of fermented milk. They came in a saucer of sugar syrup and cost one rupee and fifty paise a plate. That was her special treat to me so we didn't always go to the coffee shop on our trips. If the Manipuri ladies were around we would buy puffed rice rolled in jaggery from them and bring them home to take with tea. It was such fun to go out with Pfünuo. And because she looked so pretty, some boy would come up and buy us Cadbury's chocolates. One time, a woman gave us an extra packet of puffed rice because she said it was a treat to see someone as pretty as Pfünuo. The woman selling guavas called out to us, "Come here my dear, and buy my

Easterine Iralu

fruit. Look, these guavas are as rosy as your cheeks." Pfünuo would simply laugh her delightful laugh and buy a fruit or two or walk off saying we would buy more next time.

I hoped Pfünuo was happy in her marriage. Her husband was a tall man, rather handsome in a rugged way. He worked now at the bank and they had built a small house where they lived with their two children, a boy and a girl. Pfünuo had a maid so she could leave her son at home and come out to see Mother. The girl went to a different school than ours, the Little Flower School. She was pretty but would never be as pretty as her mother. The little boy was very sweet. I liked playing with him when Pfünuo brought him over. But Mother was still too fragile and Pfünuo feared that her boisterous children would tire her out so, most times, she came on her own.

19

On my thirteenth birthday, I finally got the curse. Vimenuo had to wait a month more before she got hers. It was exciting and frightening at the same time. It felt normal to finally be the same as everyone else. That part of it was a relief. But it was a nuisance to have to look out on those days when we couldn't play as hard as the boys and had to be sure we were not staining our skirts. We were both very self-conscious in the first year.

"Check and see if I've stained my skirt?" I asked on the second day.

"No, there isn't anything," she said.

"Are you sure?" I insisted,

"I felt something squirt out, I'm sure its running down my legs, maybe I should ask to go home, do you think I should go home?"

"And what will you tell the Headmaster? Will you tell him you've got the curse?" she asked. That posed a problem. "Look, you have to believe me, there is no stain on your skirt, okay? I'm your friend, aren't I? I would tell you the truth."

She was right so I had to learn to relax and sit still through school hours. We were worried that boys might be able to tell when you were having a period. They had ways of finding out, we were told by the older girls, some could just look at you and tell. So Vimenuo and I avoided the boys as much as we could when either of us was menstruating. "Do you know it's contagious?" Vimenuo asked me one day. I didn't know. Mother had stopped menstruating so I didn't have anyone at home who would be infected when I had my monthly. "Haven't you noticed that we have ours at about the same time every month?" It was true. I was amazed. "Sometimes you are a day early or late but when one of us has it, the other gets it too." There seemed to be so much to learn. I didn't know how women could be so matter-of-fact about it. Vimenuo and I could talk about it for hours. In a strange way, we felt initiated. Pfünuo helped me buy packets of sanitary napkins called *Comfits* which were bulky and uncomfortable. It always worried me that they might fall out some day. I took to wearing two underpants when I had a monthly. Of course, Pfünuo could not be expected to help me buy *Comfits* every month. The first time Vimenuo and I went to town to buy them, we were so nervous. We knew they sold them at the Nepali woman's store and at the pharmacy but the pharmacist was a man so we went to the Nepali store. We could see the packets stacked prominently on the shelves.

"Will you ask for them?" asked Vimenuo.

I said, yes, and we waited for the lady to come to the counter. A smart young man was looking after the store. He looked at us curiously.

"Oh no, what shall we do?" I asked and thought of a solution, "let's come back tomorrow."

"But I'm getting mine tonight" said Vimenuo, "we have to buy some today."

"Let's wait a bit, maybe she will come out."

We pretended to be looking at the jewellery and spent nearly nine minutes at the counter. The young man whistled a little tune and stacked things on shelves. The lady showed no sign of appearing.

We were quite frantic when twelve minutes had passed.

"Should we go to the pharmacy then?" I whispered.

"No" Vimenuo was adamant, "we will get them here."

The young man looked up when we approached him.

"Ladies?" he asked, "found anything you wanted?"

It was now or never. I stepped up to the cashier's counter and tried to be very casual,

"Not today, but could we have two packets of *Comfits*?"

"Certainly" he said and stretched to take out two of the white packages with yellow flowers printed on them. He made it seem very normal, as though I had asked for a packet of sweets or biscuits. I blanked out my mind because I knew if I dwelt on it, I would start blushing and stammering. I paid the money, coolly collected the packages and Vimenuo and I walked to the door casually. Once outside, we fled.

"Next time you do the asking," I said angrily.

But when I looked at her she was convulsed with laughter and struggling to keep it in. We both laughed and laughed because we could see how ridiculous it was.

"You looked like you had been buying them all your life," she laughed.

"Do you think he knew? I'm sure he did," I said.

"Oh he must have sold hundreds, no, thousands of *Comfits* in his life," said Vimenuo with an all-knowing air about her.

"Oh, why do we have to be girls?" I moaned.

"Don't worry," she comforted, "it will get better next time."

"But" I persisted, "don't you see? He will know every time we go to buy them that it's that time of the month for us!"

"So then?" she asked, "What can he do about it?"

"Oh, nothing,"

I had to agree but I was still prickled by an unpleasant thought, "but it's almost as if he were our mother or worse, our husband, to know such an intimate thing about us!"

"Pfah! It's not as though we have to marry him because he knows when we have our monthlies," she said scornfully.

I admired Vimenuo's attitude toward the whole episode. I was so much more self-conscious. I would be horrified if any of my brothers were to find out I was bleeding. Some of the other girls said that if you ate bitter gourd, you wouldn't bleed so much.

Other things began to occupy our minds too. We wondered about childbirth and Vimenuo tried to remember all she had seen of childbirth when her mother had given birth to her sisters. She had not been inside the room but she recollected seeing her mother's belly in the last months. Then she had swelled till she could not see her feet and she had to sit on a low stool to take a bath and Vimenuo's grandmother had to pour water over her. I wanted to ask Mother but she had become so vague these days that she would probably not tell me what I wanted to know. In any case, I didn't suppose I could actually ask Mother the things I wanted to ask. I wondered about how painful childbirth actually was. Vimenuo said her mother had to bite on a piece of cloth to prevent herself from biting her lips from the pain. That sounded terrible! Suddenly I didn't want to hear any more.

Even when we turned fourteen, we had not gotten over our shyness when buying sanitary pads. We learnt to carry money intended for that and buy them on days when the lady was keeping shop. Vimenuo's sisters were growing up too and that meant that they were able to do some work about the house. Being the oldest, Vimenuo had to do the major work like cooking the evening meal and shopping for groceries. Her mother worked as a typist in one of the offices in town. Fortunately for her, she had studied till the tenth standard and taken a six month course in typing with a certificate to show for it. So when her husband died, a relative of theirs had got her the job. It paid poorly but, at least they had money coming in regularly and she would receive a pension when she turned 55 or 57. They said it was more money than they had ever had because their father had squandered so much of his salary on drinks that sometimes Vimenuo and her sisters went for three months without paying the school fees. Then the Headmaster would come to class with a big register to read out the names of those who had not paid. Now, they would never have to face that sort of embarrassment because their mother was good at budgeting and she made it a point to pay off all the dues first. She was a regular church-goer and paid her tithe to the church as well.

Every Thursday evening, Vimenuo would cook while her mother went to the women's service. Lately, she had taken to cooking the evening meal regularly except on Saturdays and Sundays when her mother was home. Then she would come to me and help me with some of my tasks. Mother did not mind her at all, not in the way Grandmother did. So she could stay late and if we finished cooking she would eat with us. But she didn't eat with us all that often. That was because we were all taught that it was a shameful thing to eat frequently at people's houses. They would think we didn't get fine things to eat at home. And no one wanted to be thought greedy where food was concerned. If Vini found Vimenuo at home, he teased her mercilessly. "When are you going to put on some weight?" he asked when she was leaning over and cleaning the rice pot. In deep embarrassment, she dropped the pot and blushed as she picked it up to resume the cleaning. Not only had Vimenuo no brothers, all her cousins were girls and only her uncle had a baby son. So she felt very awkward around boys. With Bulie, she was more comfortable. They would talk about school or food because that was what Bulie liked to talk about. But Vini made her blush and stammer. At school too, she was quite terrible with the boys in her class. They knew they could tease her and make her forget the answers to questions that the Math teacher had set for their test. Leto was almost like a father, perhaps because of the age gap between them. He was very gentle, asking her questions about her family and her mother and grandmother. She answered all his questions without stammering. She would even venture to tell him about the radio they had bought and how her mother was planning to save money to buy a new set of chairs for their living room.

Leto had a job now. He had finished college and been taken on as a teacher in our school. Grandmother asked if he was planning on getting married soon. He didn't reply directly but said he had to work much longer to be able to support a family. She seemed pleased at the news. Aunt Bino sometimes visited and when she came she would say that Leto should get another job and not be satisfied with a teaching job.

"Everyone knows teachers are poorly paid" she said, "if you get work at the D.C.'s office as a clerk you can get promotions and retire as Supervisor and then you will get a fat pension. Girls would think twice about refusing a man working in the D.C.'s office" was her parting shot.

Leto was 21 but he still looked a bit of a boy sometimes. He had reached his full height. He was shorter than Father and just slightly taller than Mother.

"I'm still too young to consider marriage, Aunt," he would say when Aunt Bino spoke like that.

"Of course, dear, you are still young but you should look for a better paid job before you get too settled in that teaching job of yours."

"I'll think about it, Aunt" said Leto in his usual respectful manner.

Leto was so well mannered it was difficult to fault him. He never disagreed with elders. He remained Grandmother's favourite but Vini had a strange bond with her. Later, when Aunt Bino had left I asked him,

"Are you going to give up teaching then?"

"I don't know, Lieno," he said, "there are so many decisions to make when you are a grown-up. I don't want to make a wrong decision. Aunt is right about the job prospects. There is no prospect of a promotion in a teaching job. You know that people respect Government workers and every mother's dream is to have a son in a Government office. If I were to work in the D.C.'s office, I would earn more money and may be able to extend our house. I should love to be able to do that. But I like teaching immensely. I don't know if I shall like working with files and the sort of work that office workers do."

I felt sorry for Leto. It must be difficult to be under so much pressure and have to make decisions for his future life. I didn't want him to marry early. I had been away at Grandmother's for all of six years. I savoured my time with my brothers and my parents. There were many times I regretted having been away and not having spent time with Pete before he died. I wanted as much time as possible with my brothers and it didn't seem such a good idea yet for Leto to bring a young woman into our family circle as his wife. I knew he would have to marry some time but I really did not want that to happen for another two years. I was relieved to hear that he was not contemplating marriage immediately. Two of his friends from school had married. One had a baby daughter now. I could not picture Leto as a father, at least not yet. He didn't even have a girlfriend. In school, there had been a girl in the tenth standard who had fancied him but the other girls teased her and said he wouldn't look at her twice. She had long hair and a sweet face but she was a little short in one leg. I don't believe he ever found out about that girl. I certainly didn't tell him because it didn't seem proper with him being so much older than me. Vimenuo surprised me though.

"Your brother is very handsome," she said one day.

"Oh you mean Vini?" I asked.

Vini managed to look good in a wild kind of way. He never dressed smartly yet he wore fashionable bell-bottomed trousers and loud shirts left open in front.

"No, not Vini," she said.

"Who then? Not Bulie?" I half screamed.

Bulie was not ugly but he was always so busy eating one would never think of him and the idea of being handsome together.

"You've got another brother, or have you forgotten?" she said with a serious look on her face.

"No, Vime, not Leto, you must be joking, he is so old!" I expostulated.

"So what? He is the kindest boy I know. And I think he is very handsome too."

She was almost offended as she said this. I stifled the giggle that was threatening to escape and simply smiled at her. That was a new idea to me and sometimes I caught myself looking at Leto and trying to imagine how Vimenuo saw him. To me, he was just my big brother who was kind, about that she was right, and yet looked ordinary and reliable, that was all, certainly not handsome, I wouldn't say that of Leto.

But it was Vini who occupied Mother's and Father's thoughts all the time. Vini it always was who brought trouble home. The two boys he moved around with when he was sixteen were still around. He never brought them home but we got reports now and then that he had been seen with them. Occasionally, he came back reeking of home brewed liquor. Father got very angry on those occasions. Two nights ago he had stumbled home blind drunk.

"Whose money have you been using to buy yourself drink?" Father shouted.

"Don't worry, it wasn't yours," said Vini in an impudent tone.

"Don't come here drunk again," said Father sternly, "You are slowly killing your mother. If you want to call this place home, learn to respect the rules."

Vini made his way to his room but he didn't apologise for his behaviour. The next morning, Father and Leto were grim-faced.

They drank their tea silently and when Bulie got up, Father said, "Go wake up your brother."

Bulie protested, "He hates to be woken up early when he has had a late night."

"Go, boy" said Father again so Bulie went to wake Vini. Then he came back to get his tea. Vini did not look happy about being woken up.

"What is it? Can't a person get some sleep around here?" he said in a surly manner. I had since learnt to recognise that tone in Vini's voice. He used it when he was looking for a fight.

"Don't speak to Father like that," said Leto. He looked irritated.

"Oh you, you're so good at using your mouth, why don't you use your fists instead?" Vini suddenly challenged him, "It's so easy for you to be the good one but I would like to see if you are as good at using your fists."

"Stop it, Vini, I haven't done anything to anger you. I am your older brother. I shall tell you when I think your behaviour is wrong," said Leto in a raised voice.

 198   Easterine Iralu

Vini moved dangerously toward Leto, with his fist close to his face, "Oh yeah, it's easy for you to talk so piously. Do you think I like being uneducated? Do you think I enjoy people asking why I dropped out of school?"

"Is that anyone's fault then?" Leto asked, "You can join school again, you know."

"What? And sit in the same class with Dielieno?" Vini was red in the face, "Are you trying to insult me?"

"Oh can't you talk without getting angry over every little thing?" Leto sounded exasperated.

The anger had left his voice but Vini was not giving up.

"Listen, I am a grown man now. I am not going to be dictated to by you any longer," he said loudly. Suddenly Mother appeared at the kitchen door.

"What is it? Why are you shouting? Are you boys fighting?" She looked as though she was about to cry.

"It's nothing, Mother," Leto said soothingly, "Don't worry."

But Vini was still very angry.

"It may be nothing to you but it was something to me, it was a great insult to me. You needn't think that I like being insulted because I am uneducated."

Mother looked alarmed. Vini was still shouting,

"We'll get all the ones like you. You are such hypocrites! Go to school. Go to church. Get a job. That's all you want from life. I want more, you hear me? I want more! I'm not like you and I don't want to be like you."

Mother stepped towards him.

"Vini, Vini, my son, my son" she called as she tried to soothe him.

But he roughly shook off her hand on his arm and said, "Don't try to stop me Mother, I've had enough."

He rushed out of the room banging the door behind him.

"Ohh," sobbed Mother as she sat down heavily. I ran to her side and tried to comfort her.

"It will pass, Mother, he won't always stay angry."

Father had not managed to say anything. When he tried to speak, the two were talking so fast and so loudly that he could not get a word in. He was caught between concern for Mother's frail state of mind and his own outrage at Vini's behaviour. He did not want to do or say anything that would push Vini away from us, yet, he felt that it was his duty as a father to scold him. I had seen him get very angry with Vini several times. If Mother had not been there, things would have got more violent, now it was just hot words exchanged every third day or so. It was very unpleasant for all of us. Vini showed his rage by banging doors and throwing things around in his room. After he had gone out, I would go and pick up the things he had thrown, books or a glass of water. I did this quickly, wiping the water away with a cloth so Mother wouldn't see.

Easterine Iralu

20

In the tenth standard, I turned fifteen. From the ninth standard, Mathematics was no longer compulsory for us girls. So we went to another class called Domestic Science where we learnt to cook and knit and sew. We also did some Arithmetic but it was usually simple sums two or three times a week. I quite enjoyed the Domestic Science classes because we could take a break from our studies and sit in the sun and knit or cook. We didn't cook very often. But on Teachers' Day, our teachers decided we were clever enough to cook a meal for them. So, we peeled potatoes and onions and cleaned rice while the peon and the *chowkidar* slaughtered and cut four chickens. The senior girls were quite good at cooking. I watched while they fried onions and garlic and ginger and then added chicken. They also put in spices and red chilly so that it began to smell very good. The rice got a little burnt as we had to cook in an enormously big pot which only the fat girl could stir. But the Headmaster and almost all the teachers complimented us. Leto was there too and he said that it was very good.

The following month was our preliminary test. The school would decide who would be allowed to write the final examination in February the next year. It was a tense month with a lot of revision to be done. But all of us cleared the test. After that it was four months of intense studying to sit for our matriculation examination. Vimenuo would sit her exams the following year. I struggled to look after the house and find the time to study. Sometimes Mother would feel strong enough to do some housework when I was at school. On those days I had enough energy to stay up late and study. But if it was one of Mother's bad days, she would get a terrible headache and not be able to do any work. Then, I would have to fetch water, cook and clean the rooms. I washed clothes every other day. Because if I did not do it for four days it would become too much to wash. So I forced myself to get some washing done even when I felt tired. At the most, Mother would clean the rooms or cook a little food. She was so thin I feared she would break a bone or something when I came upon her scrubbing the pots. Her hair was completely gray. Father did not have so much gray in his hair though he was fifty-one, and three years older than her. Once a friend had asked me rather loudly,

"Is that your grandmother?"

Mother heard her and was ashen-faced. I quickly said,

"Of course not, she's my mother. How silly you are, your mother's just as gray haired."

My friend laughed in embarrassment but I never invited her back.

There were only two or three things I really wished for in life. That Mother would be better, that Vini would become his old self again and that I would pass my matriculation exams well. I wanted Leto to marry a good girl eventually and be happy but that was not one of my priorities. Grandmother sent word through Neikuo that

Easterine Iralu

there was a young woman from a good family that she thought would be suitable for Leto. She did this once every four months or so, even suggesting that she could make offers to certain young women. Leto steadily refused. He used the excuse that he was not earning enough yet. But Grandmother never gave up. If some of the women she mentioned got married in a few months, she would have another lined up. "This one is from a very good family," she would say, "good blood."

Aunt Bino pestered him to give up teaching. One morning she came to visit us. "My dear boy, you must not refuse this offer today because it is not from me, it is from your uncle." She meant it was a job offer from her husband. Leto could go to work as his personal assistant, looking after his correspondence and all the files under his responsibility. After some years, he could get a promotion to Upper Divisional Assistant and after that he would be promoted every four years or so. Father thought it was a good offer. Mother said that Leto should not risk offending his uncle and aunt because it would spoil family relations. Finally, Leto resigned his job at the school and went to work at the D.C.'s office. The school needed three months' notice so he could not join his new job immediately. His pay was almost double of what he received at the school. And though his working hours were longer, he did not have to pore over students' assignments every night. Grandmother hoped that with his new job he would soon marry. She was already thinking of a granddaughter of the friend who had come to her birthday party. The girl had finished her studies and was working at the same office as Leto. She was from the same clan as Pfünuo's husband.

At the beginning of the year, I did fairly well in my Matriculation exams. I thought I had done my English papers remarkably well and hoped to get a second division. With my exams over, I was free in the day and seriously thought of going back to school to work in the nursery classes. The headmaster had offered this opportunity to all of us on the last day of exams. We would be paid too. I was unable to decide whether I should spend more time at home with Mother or take the offer to earn a little money. Mother wavered between good days and bad days, her bad days lasting longer because Vini was drinking so heavily these days. Leto thought I should not miss out on working with children. But I felt a little guilty to go off and leave Mother alone. I didn't know if I would get more free months like this in future. In the end, I chose to work. So in the following week, it was more or less the same routine of rushing through my morning tasks and getting ready for school. Only, this time, I had discarded my school uniform for dresses and skirts that made me look more grown up than my sixteen years. I learnt to sew skirts and simple blouses. Pfünuo gave me some of her old dresses and I liked to think I looked older in them. Passable at least. Some of the other girls were there too so it was all right. The fat girl joined two days after me. She was a great favourite with the children. In the morning, we went through their alphabets and numbers. Then we did some drawing and some singing. All the children enjoyed this but tired easily when we hopped around and sang. So they would have a sleeping break of about forty-five minutes.

I loved working with children. My favourites were a little four-year - old boy who would show me his tiffin every morning and a tiny girl with her hair in a ponytail. She looked like a little doll and had the smallest hands and feet I had seen on a child. Her father was surprisingly large and fat. He would carry her into class on his shoulders every morning and when he left she would look at the door with an expression that wavered between wanting to cry and simply accepting her lot. She brought with her feathers in different colours and shyly showed them to me. Some days it would be a peacock's turquoise blue and green and silver feather. On another day she would have a dove's white and grey feather. She loved her feathers and would stroke them very gently and ask me to do the same.

At the end of the third month our results were announced. Four of us had passed in the second division and the school was very proud of us. But this meant that I had to stop working and prepare to join college. I heard that Grandmother did not think it was a good idea for me to go to college.

"Isn't it quite enough that the girl has finished school?" she asked, "Some men don't like it if their wives are too educated."

To hear her talk one would have thought that I was going to get marriage offers in the next week. Leto was very supportive.

"If you want to study further, I will support you through college. I can do that now I have my own money." I had to find out what Father thought about it though. That evening, I asked at dinner,

"Father, could I go to college, do you think?"

"Your grandmother doesn't think it's a good idea," he said.

Sometimes Father could surprise me by mouthing Grandmother's opinions vehemently.

"But what do you think? I could work harder now that I am bigger. I would love to go," I begged.

"What does Leto have to say?" he turned to Leto.

"I think she should go. Lieno is a good student and she would do well. I can support her on my salary now so it would not be a burden for the two of you."

My heart was suffused with love for my brother at that moment. If only Father would say yes. Bulie was not in college. He was working with cars because he preferred to work with his hands. He found books terribly tedious. If Father agreed, then I would get a college degree and get a good job like Leto and give Mother and Father a better house to live in.

"What do you think, Father? I could apply for a scholarship as well. That way, it won't be such a financial burden on you and Mother to pay for my fees for the next five years."

"All right then, I will go and speak to the college principal tomorrow."

I was happy and excited all at the same time. But there was one thing I had to clear with Father.

"What will you tell Grandmother?"

"Don't worry" Leto spoke up, "I will say that I am sponsoring you and that if you don't do well, I will take you out at any time."

So that was that. I trembled a bit when I went to visit her the first time after Leto's announcement. But she was quite calm about the whole thing. When I was about to leave, she said,

"I hear that you are getting more education, girl."

I said, "Yes, Grandmother."

"That is all very well, but a woman's role is to marry and bear children, remember that. That is her most important role. Men don't like to marry educated wives. Then, if you find no one to marry you, you will be alone in your old age and have no one to bury you. Look at your grandmother Neikuo. Does she have anyone to bury her today? No, no one at all. She has to be good to my grandchildren in the hope that one of you will bury her. See what a terrible thing it is not to have children to bury one? I hope you will think of my words and reconsider your foolishness."

"Yes, Grandmother," was all I could say. I managed to wish them goodnight and left.

"My foolishness," as Grandmother put it, gave me a lot of pleasure. My first year in college was an entirely new experience for me. There were boys lounging around the campus with cigarettes dangling from their mouths. The audacity of it awed me. In school, the boys caught smoking were given warnings three times and, if

 Easterine Iralu

caught a third time, they were expelled. The boys at college smoked openly outside classes and the teachers said nothing about it. Some of the lady lecturers look disapproving. But for the most part, they ignored the goings on of the students. The college was the only one offering Humanities and Social Sciences and it was in an old wooden building in the middle of town. It had been a hospital during the war. We had the largest classroom in the college but even so when all the students were present, some of them had to sit on the window sill. This was a good excuse for many of the boys not to attend class. If their parents asked why they hadn't gone to class they would say that there weren't enough seats in the classroom. On our first day in class, a man came into the room. He swaggered somewhat and said that he was our Political Science teacher. He had a French goatee beard and was very amused because none of us could understand what he said. But when the Poetry teacher came in, a Bengali lady who had the most tragic expression on her face, I was enthralled. Her face was forever etched in my memory, as she half - swooned over the sad fate of Seraphina, who nature had given "hue and note" "but turned to harlotry."

I did well in the poetry paper, better than at History and Economics. At the end of the year we had an exam and we were all very surprised to hear the announcement that we had been promoted to the next class. During the Christmas holidays, Vimenuo and I spent more time together. It had become difficult for us to get time together with me now in college. She was studying for her matriculation examination the following year. Now she twisted her hair demurely into a little bun at the back and would not be boisterous. "Don't be so boring," I said but she simply smiled and said, "We have to grow up now that you are in college." I felt clumsy next to her. She was not so thin now. Her hair had grown and her cheeks had filled out. She wore skirts more often than the frocks we had both worn in high school. I couldn't understand what it was that was different about her that year. We made cookies and baked a few cakes at our house. Leto, sampling our cookies, said he hadn't tasted anything better. Vimenuo blushed at that and was quite flustered. They were neither of them comfortable in each other's presence. There were half-begun sentences between them and long awkward silences. I was foolish not to see what was going on.

In the new year, when she had finished her exams, she said to me,

"Can you keep a secret?"

"Of course" I said off-handedly. We had shared all our secrets all of our lives.

"But this is serious, Lieno."

"Oh, don't you trust me anymore?" I asked with some irritation. It irked me that she had suddenly grown up in the last year.

"Promise not to tell anyone yet, not Bano or your mother?"

"Ooh, have I ever told anyone before?"

Then she caught me close and spoke into my ear.

"I'm getting married!"

"No!" I screamed, "I don't believe it, you are so young, you must be joking."

"Shush! Don't shout, I don't want anyone to know yet."

I looked into her eyes to see if they had that twinkle which meant she was pulling my leg but she was dead serious. It felt like a really bad joke.

"No, Vime, tell me it isn't true!" I begged.

"It is true and you will be happy for me when you hear who it is."

I couldn't believe her.

"Bite your finger and tell me," I said. She bit her finger and whispered,

 208

"It's true. But it is to someone you like very much so you will be happy if I tell you."

I could only think it was some horrible plot by her father's relatives. Very young girls were married off without their consent to men their parents thought were suitable. Girls like Vimenuo with a father dead were even more vulnerable to that sort of thing. She must have seen how upset I was because she came close to me and put her arm around me.

"Don't be sad, dear, be happy for me because I know I will be very, very happy."

"How can you say that?" I accused. "How can you accept that for yourself? If you marry it will be the end of us," I said dramatically.

"How, Lieno, how can it be the end of us? We will be closer than ever before. We will be sisters," she said confidently.

I didn't believe her for a moment. Girls in our school who had got married without finishing school now looked like matrons with a child or two pulling at their clothes all the time, and if they saw us they giggled and spoke of our schooldays as if that had been a childish interlude of their lives. I didn't want that to happen to Vimenuo.

"Don't you want to know who it is?"

"No" I said sulkily and then changed my mind, "Okay tell me then."

She whispered in my ear, "Leto."

I was so surprised I thought I had heard her wrong.

"What? Lezo? But he is so old, Vime."

Lezo was Father's colleague widowed a year ago.

"No, no, not Lezo, it's Leto, your brother."

I am still amazed I didn't faint right away.

"He has proposed to me and I have said yes. I love him so much, Lieno."

"But, but, I thought you found him old."

"It was just you who found him old, Lieno."

I was very surprised by the news. But the more I thought about it the more it pleased me. I could always have Vimenuo with me then, and she would be my sister.

"Does Grandmother know?" I asked.

Immediately her face became anxious.

"No, she doesn't, that's why you mustn't tell anyone about it yet."

I felt a constriction then in my stomach, right in my gut. If Grandmother didn't know yet, she would do all she could to prevent it when she did. I knew that she disliked Vimenuo's family and had said more than twenty times in my presence that they were bad blood. I wondered how Leto would handle this. Father and Mother liked Vimenuo very much and I couldn't imagine that they would be displeased with Leto's choice of a wife. I wished the deep sense of foreboding inside me would go away.

"What! The dead drunk's daughter?" Grandmother roared when she was told of the news. "This is what happens when people get it into their heads to educate young girls! Folk forget their status and try to marry above their station. If my mother were alive, the news alone would kill her. If you knew the kind of family they are descended from, the scandals in that family, you wouldn't have anything to do with them. But it is all these modern ideas to blame. Educating girls indeed! Education can't rid you of bad blood I say!"

I thought she would have a stroke. I had never seen her get as angry as this and I had seen her angry plenty of times. I wasn't supposed to be present at that unfortunate outburst but I was delivering some herbs that Mother had got from Pfünuo and was washing cups at the sink when Father announced it to Grandmother. Though it was distressful, I could see the funny side of it, Grandmother blaming it on education when Vimenuo had not been all that good at school and had no plans to get a college degree. I could see it was me she was angry with. She partly blamed me for my friendship with Vimenuo which had brought her into our lives. I wanted to rise to her defence and explain that Leto would be just as lucky because Vimenuo was a gem of a girl. But I knew that anything I said in her favour would have the reverse effect. Especially coming from me, Grandmother would turn around and ask, "What is she hiding that you have to protect her?" and because I knew how perverse Grandmother could get, I kept quiet and vowed to pray extra hard for the two of them.

As a parting shot, Grandmother rose from her seat and said loudly, "Well you may marry anyone you want, I won't prevent it. I am just a poor old woman after all. No one remembers what I did to bring my children into this world and to raise them up. But I will not be there at the wedding. And I don't want to hear another word about this... this *marriage!*"

She spat out the word as though it were the most vulgar word.

"Mother, Mother" Father was trying to calm her down, "Please Mother, you will have a heart attack!"

"Yes I will," she said as she stumbled out and Father scrambled after her to make sure she didn't fall in the hallway.

After that, we didn't talk of the wedding for a long time. Aunt Bino visited and spoke to Leto for a long time. But they were talking in his room and although I wanted desperately to eavesdrop, I knew that the floor would creak if I went there. Leto didn't tell us what she said. When it was over, she said to Father, "Really you must talk him out of it, it is most unsuitable, no wonder Mother was in such a state over it." She cast a sly look at me but I pretended not to have heard her and busied myself with watering the flowers.

21

Hoping Grandmother would change her mind, Leto and Vimenuo waited the whole of that year to get married. But Grandmother would not relent. She snubbed Vimenuo's mother who had come to visit her with a gift of a cake. After that, Vimenuo's family did not try to win her over. I was proud of the quiet dignity with which they conducted themselves. By now, they knew that it was aunt Bino and Grandmother and my uncles' wives, aunt Leno and aunt Sini, who were strongly opposed to the marriage. But they were never rude to them. If they met in church, they would greet them politely but without any familiarity so that they could not really fault them. My aunts, however, repeated what others had said of Vimenuo's father and his family, how her grandfather, when he was alive, would get drunk and wave his walking stick at people on the streets and threaten to beat them. How his wife had tired of his drunkenness and had an affair with a younger man and had a baby by him. The baby was a boy who became an alcoholic too and died at 26. There were so many stories of Vimenuo's family that were doing the rounds that year. On the days that I met her, she looked pale and defeated.

Finally, they married in early December. It was a small wedding, very subdued and quiet. But Vimenuo said that she would have felt uncomfortable with a big wedding. The new couple went to live in one of the small government houses in Bayavü Hill. It had four rooms, two bedrooms and a tiny kitchen but they were just so happy to be together. Vimenuo insisted that I spend as much time as possible with them in their new house. So I stayed a couple of nights when they first moved in, helping to arrange their new pots and pans and stitching curtains for them. They were still shy with each other. I wondered how many years would pass before they got to be familiar with one another like Mother and Father. Leto was not all that shy but Vimenuo would be startled when he called her name and walked in the door. She would blush, a rich bright red, and sometimes drop whatever she was doing at that moment.

"Heavens, it's only Leto" I said in exasperation one day.

She smiled across at me and said, "You don't understand, Lieno, he may be only Leto to you, but to me he is the most wonderful man I have met. I can't help being nervous around him."

"How will you ever live together then? You'll be forever dropping things and getting into such a state that it will not be possible to settle down. You have to stop jumping every time he comes into the room," I said.

She didn't say anything again but she had a secret smile on her. I didn't like the change in her. It embarrassed me that she would get such a daft smile on her face whenever my brother was around. After a few weeks of that, I preferred to spend more time at home. It was not that I was unwelcome in their home. Vimenuo insisted that nothing had changed between us, that we were closer than before because we were sisters now in the real sense of the word. But I felt that I should not always be around them. They were so happy it seemed unreal.

Grandmother never really accepted them into the family fold though. She was harder than before. When they visited her with a gift, she sat there unsmiling and asked what they were going to do about building a house for themselves or were they going to spend their lives in government quarters, and this, nastily.

"There are other things in life than love," she said. "People need a house to live in, a field to have one's own rice harvest for the year. These are the important things in life. I am afraid you have married a man who has neither a house nor a field and not very likely to inherit one from his father or uncles."

Vimenuo looked shocked. I could see she was searching for the right thing to say. Eventually she spoke up in her soft voice and said,

"We will both work hard, Grandmother and someday we will have those things as well."

"Humph" said Grandmother.

There was an awkward silence for some time. Bano was stirring sugar in the tea and for a few minutes that was the only sound we could hear.

"We should also visit grandmother Neikuo while we are in the area" said Leto finally.

They awkwardly took leave of Grandmother and walked in the direction of Neikuo's house. I was secretly glad they had left early because we never knew what other horrid thing Grandmother might say if they stayed longer. At least they would be warmly welcomed in Neikuo's house. I was sure of that.

"Foolish young puppy, he doesn't want to listen to me, me with my years of experience about human beings. When there is bad blood in a family, it always repeats itself. That is why we always consider the background of a girl's family when we want our sons to marry well. Look what happened to your aunt Pfünuo," Grandmother looked fiercely at me.

I was glad that the two of them had escaped hearing that. I

would certainly not repeat it to Mother or to them because I knew Grandmother well enough by now.

"People think marriage is simply two young people going to live with one another. It is so much more than that, it is a mixing of blood. So one cannot be too careful but does anyone listen to me these days?"

I had to sit out the rest of this litany because I knew Grandmother hated to be interrupted when she was raging about something. I stole a look at Bano but she was busying herself with some needlework. Grandmother didn't want to know how many water pots the newly wedded pair had got as wedding gifts. She was certainly not interested in the embroidered tablecloths that Vimenuo's other friends had made for her. As far as she was concerned it was an unsuitable match and she was waiting for the day someone would come and announce that something terrible had happened to them. She said she had resigned herself to that.

The other thing that happened after Leto's visit was that Vini began to spend more and more time at Grandmother's. There were many nights when he wouldn't come home. Sometimes, if it was early in the evening, Bano would come to say that Grandmother had asked Vini to dinner and he would spend the night as well. But, more often than not, he spent the night without telling anyone. In the morning, when he came home, Father would have left for the office.

"Where were you last night, dear?" Mother asked when he came home.

"I have been at Grandmother's," he said.

"Oh I didn't know, I worried," said Mother.

"Well, you shouldn't worry. I am a big boy now," he said rather brusquely.

Vini was losing his good looks now. He had the ruddy complexion of an alcoholic but I knew he would soon turn green if he didn't stop drinking the way he did. He didn't work regular hours. He had a job at the store selling women's clothing but he would stroll in an hour after opening time and take a long lunch break as well. The woman who owned it was a friend of Aunt Bino and that's how he got the job in the first place.

"Will you have some food, dear?" asked Mother anxiously.

She always tried to placate him when he was annoyed.

"I have no appetite in the morning, I told you before," he said unpleasantly.

I disliked Vini so much when he had a hangover. He could be quite brutal to any of us who tried to speak to him in a loving manner. When Mother showed her concern, he brushed her off and made her feel small and insignificant. Father had given up disciplining him. Most of the time, Vini behaved as though it was our fault he was drunk. On the nights he came home drunk, he'd complain, "Don't you ever cook meat in this house?" and he would angrily push his plate away. It had been even worse before Leto got married. "Ah, the educated government officer" Vini would taunt if Leto protested at his behaviour, "I must apologise that we are not all of us, educated and able to behave in a civilized manner. Some of us will cater to our lower selves, I'm afraid, brother dear."

Vini had the most vicious tongue, he had learnt to talk like the people in the drinking houses, very cleverly insulting Leto so that he would hesitate to say anything further because it would seem as though he was being priggish. Twice they had come to blows. The first time, Vini had insisted that Leto thought poorly of him. Leto had slapped him then and shouted, "Don't ever say that again!" Vini's face turned red with rage but he did not strike back. The second time was when he came home drunk and pushed me. He was angry and when I did not answer him immediately he became even angrier and pushed me violently. Leto saw it and shouted, "Are you going to strike the only sister we have?" His fist landed on Vini's left cheek. Vini swung back and hit Leto in the nose so that he started to bleed. I was screaming and trying to stop them but they were so strong, both of them, and kept going at each other. Father and Mother came running at our cries and separated them.

"What's got into you, Leto? Why provoke him?" Father was asking.

"He pushed Lieno, it isn't right for him to come back home and bully those who are weaker than him."

"Are you all right?" Father asked me.

I said yes because I didn't want any more trouble and we cleaned Leto's bleeding nose and Mother put some balm on Vini's bruised cheek. After that we all went to our rooms but no one could sleep. I heard Mother sighing in bed for a long time.

With Leto out of the house, Vini calmed down for some weeks. But he started to get violent again shortly after. It was as though he couldn't get drunk without getting violent. Lately, he had started to insult Father if he got drunk. "Couldn't you have built a bigger house?" or "Why didn't you get a car like your other friends did?" or "Why didn't you get a better job?" According to Vini, there was always something that Father had done wrong in his life which Vini brought out and used as a reason to get angry. Father had stopped getting into an argument with him long ago. At fifty-two, he looked much older. I sometimes saw in his place, an old man stooped over with the burden of an alcoholic son and an ailing wife slowly dying because of their son's alcoholism.

But Bulie was growing up fast too. He was strong and well built. In a fight he could have thrown Vini easily. Usually, Vini did not pick on him but in later months he had begun to make Bulie the butt of his cruel jokes.

"Buffoon" he said one night to Bulie, "Isn't that right? You are my buffoon of a brother who couldn't study further and had to satisfy himself with working as a mechanic in a garage, hands full of grease, clothes permanently smelling of grease, ha ha, we are a family of buffoons, right, Bulie?"

Bulie laughed good-naturedly along with him the first time. But the next time he didn't find it so funny because Bulie was not so unintelligent he could not catch on that Vini was actually insulting him. He didn't laugh when Vini came back and started to call out "buffoon" in a high-pitched voice. Vini was jumping up and down in little jumps and crying out "buffoon, buffoon" but Bulie stared at him angrily and said loudly,

"I am not a buffoon. My boss says I am very clever at my work. I don't want to be called a buffoon."

Bulie was taller than Vini and much broader. He had muscular shoulders and at twenty, he was very fit because he ate well and worked with his body all day. Vini simply laughed when Bulie rose to his full height and then he said,

"Well, if you are not a buffoon then, what are you, a big gorilla? That's right, you must be, oh my God, you are King Kong, why didn't I see it before?"

How I wished that Vini would stop it. But he seemed to get a big thrill out of testing how far he could go with Bulie. Now he took up the refrain of "King Kong, King Kong, who's the gorilla now, its B-U-L-I-E, hear that everyone, B-U-L-I-E!" I'm sure Vini could see that Bulie was steadily growing angrier but he would not stop. On and on he sang the stupid refrain. Maybe Vini was counting on the fact that Bulie would never touch him because he was his younger brother and even if you were younger by a year, you could never strike an elder brother. Bulie was not unaware of that fact either. He was three years younger than Vini. I watched the pair of them, fascinated. It was like a movie gone terribly out of control, Vini doing his ridiculous little hopping dance and Bulie going red in the face and struggling to control his anger.

By then, the neighbours had congregated by the fence. Some of them were kneeling in the undergrowth and watching this macabre dance. The others pretended they had come out for a bit of fresh air. No one could actually interfere if they weren't scuffling. Most of them enjoyed the spectacle of a good fight. But the women felt sorry for Mother and expressed their sympathy and begged the men to pull the brothers apart before they could start fighting. One of them, a woman about Mother's age was very brave. She came up to the two of them and said,

"My sons, please do not break up your brotherhood in this manner. You have fine parents, the finest in our neghbourhood, why do you want to break your mother's heart? Come, Bulie, let us go home. Come, my son."

Bulie was past hearing anybody.

"Then will you come with me Vini?" she pleaded, "I have cooked a fine dinner and you may eat it and you may also sleep in my house, my son."

"Not tonight, Aunt," said Vini to her.

She had a son who was Bulie's age and the two of them had been playmates. Bulie was no longer embarrassed by the people who were watching. It was as though he had lost complete control. As Vini danced up to him, he suddenly swerved and brought his fist up against Vini's face. He followed it up with another blow. Vini slumped to the ground, bleeding from his nose. "Oh my God!" said a voice behind me and I turned to see Mother's ash-white face. I didn't know she had come out of the house. She was trying to go down to help Vini but fainted from the effort and the shock of seeing him bleeding. The next moment was a mad flurry of activity. I caught Mother as she fell. The woman who had been trying to break up the fight moaned and came to my aid. I didn't know where Father was but Leto and Vimenuo came out of the darkness and I gratefully let them take Mother from my arms and carry her inside the house. "Mother!" Bulie screamed and came running inside. We had all forgotten about Vini. Fortunately, two of the men's wives helped him to his room and they bathed his bleeding nose and made sure he was all right, He had been knocked out by the blow from Bulie's hard fist but no bones were broken. Mother took a longer time to be revived. When she came round, she mouthed Vini's name.

"He's all right, Mother, we have seen to him," said Vimenuo.

Leto gave her a small, white pill and she slept heavily through the night.

"This can't go on," said Leto as he paced up and down the living room, "Vini has to stop drinking or go to live on his own somewhere else. At this rate he will be the death of Mother."

He then turned round and looked at Bulie, "And you, Bulie, how could you let him taunt you into fighting with him?"

Bulie was looking shamefaced.

"I am sorry, Leto, but he infuriated me so."

"Try and stay out his way next time, you know he spoils for a fight when he is drunk," warned Leto.

Mother had an enormous headache when she woke up. I pressed her head and tried to ease the pain by gently massaging her throbbing temples but she was in so much pain we sent for the doctor. He gave her some aspirin but he said that her blood pressure was dangerously high and that we were not to let her get excited or worried.

"She must have absolute peace and quiet," he insisted as he was gathering up his bag. "I will return in the evening to check on her," he added as he was leaving. In the next room, he took me aside and said, "Give her some warm soup, Lieno, but most important of all, give her a rest from your brothers. Get your uncles to help. This is serious."

Vini slept the whole morning. His pillow was stained with congealed blood but I didn't want to clean it for fear he would wake up and start shouting again. We had had enough of that for now.

 220

"But if we moved him out of the house, he would probably go to live with the women in the drinking houses. Then we would lose him completely. You know how Vini is, he is so proud and if he suspects that someone is treating him badly, he really takes that to heart. If only we could get him to stop drinking," I said.

It didn't seem to be such a great idea to get him to go away, even for a short while. Vini was our blood brother, whatever he had done, and I desperately tried to make them see that we would not be doing the right thing by sending him away. We were all so fed up but we were still family.

"Lieno" called Mother very weakly from her bedroom.

She could not finish the soup I had given her. I took it away from her. How thin she was! Mother was not getting better. It hit me then. She would not get better as long as Vini was the way he was. It was not just grief over Pete that had reduced her to this, she could see that Vini would soon die if he went on drinking. The skin on her hand was stretched tight over bone. Every vein was clearly visible and the pulse at her throat beat violently.

"Oh Mother!" I said involuntarily.

"Is Vini okay?" she whispered.

"Don't worry, he is quite all right, he is sleeping.

"And Bulie?" she asked.

"Bulie is just fine, Mother, don't worry about them."

"Lieno, I don't want to stay in bed. I am not sick, I must get up and help you," she said as she tried to get off the bed.

"No, Mother," I held her back, "the doctor said you were to stay in bed till you got better. You are not better yet. In any case, I don't need any help. Vimenuo is here too and she has taken over your kitchen."

"Bless her," whispered Mother.

Just then Vimenuo walked in and crept to the edge of the bed. She began to massage Mother's feet very gently.

"Thank you, my child" said Mother.

The two of them looked at each other and smiled.

"It will be all right. Mother" said Vimenuo, "it will pass. He will not always be like this. God will listen to our prayers."

Mother smiled down at her again. I was so grateful for Vime's calmness in the face of all this turmoil in our family. I went to look for Bulie. He was nursing a sore hand and trying to put some balm on it.

"Does it hurt?" I asked.

"I think I broke a bone here, a little one, can you feel it?"

I felt along his hand until he startled me with a squeal.

"Ahh! That's it, there, I must have broken it, it hurts so much if I flex it. It's a little bone."

His fist was swollen and bruised. I took it in my hand and asked if I should bathe it in lukewarm water. He said all right. I didn't know what else to do. I had never treated a hand swollen from a fight before. But I thought it might feel soothed in warm water and so I put water in a basin and laid his hand in it.

"It does feel a bit better," he said.

I found a cloth to bind it with. Trying to be very gentle I bandaged Bulie's hand, winding the cloth firmly but not too tightly round his hand.

"Lieno, you don't really believe that I am a buffoon do you?" asked Bulie so softly, it was almost a whisper.

"Of course not, how can you be a buffoon? You can do so many things the rest of us cannot do. If you were a buffoon, you would not be able to do that."

He looked relieved at my answer.

22

Things got so bad that Father had to confer with his brothers. Both Avi and Bilie came to our house.

"How old is Vini now? Twenty-three?" asked Uncle Avi.

"He's twenty-four, he will be twenty-five next January," said Mother.

"Have you thought of getting a wife for him?" Avi asked.

"Who would marry an alcoholic?" asked Father angrily. "The only time he is not drunk is when he is sleeping. If I were not his father, I would never allow any daughter of mine to marry someone like Vini. He should not be allowed to make some innocent girl miserable."

"Well, marriage might tame him, I have seen that happen to others, Visa," stated Avi.

Father gave him a strange look. But Uncle Bilie also thought it was a good idea and they began to consider it quite seriously.

"Who then?" asked Father.

"Visa, don't forget that we are a respectable family that many mothers would like their daughters to marry into our family," said Avi.

"Leno and I have been talking about it for some time now. There is that nice daughter of Lhouvi, the one who always comes to church on Sunday mornings. She's not too pretty but we have heard that she is a good worker. The family is not very rich, but they come of good stock. Leno and I could pay them a visit one evening if you are both agreeable."

I only heard snatches of their conversation as I could not sit in with them, being a child. At least that was how they regarded me. I did listen keenly as I served them tea. But afterwards I made Mother repeat to me every word of the conversation.

"Do you think Vini would agree?" I asked Mother.

"He will, he will, she is a sweet girl and perhaps she will help him to stop drinking and become a responsible husband and father."

This was the first time I had seen Mother look so hopeful in years. Her face was bright and cheerful. She asked for the curtains in her room to be pulled so she could get more sunshine. She began to eat well after that, finishing her food to the last grain of rice. We were all happy about the plan. Only Leto seemed doubtful it would work. "Let him get a real job first," he advised, "then he can learn to work like other people do and learn something of real life before he gets married." But it was not easy for Vini to get the jobs he wanted because for those he had to compete with college graduates. Not wanting to make him frustrated again, the search for the job was kept in abeyance. Grandmother was happy about Vini's marriage. I learnt from Bano that it was actually Grandmother who had suggested that he marry the young girl. She would herself make an offer of marriage to the family. That way, they would be sure the family would not be able to refuse. Vini surprised everyone by agreeing to the idea when he was told.

"Marry? Sure. Why not? That's one thing left that I am yet to do in life," he said cheerily.

It was a big relief that he was not opposed to the plan at all.

"We will have a big wedding," said Grandmother decidedly.

"Are you sure, Mother?" asked Father, "we don't have to spend so much money on Vini, you know, the important thing is to get him settled."

"I'll pay for it, for the wedding" said Grandmother, "because he is marrying into a family I approve of. I have no hesitation in paying for the wedding."

So Vini had a grand wedding, grand by our standards because they killed five cows and a *gwi*, so there was much meat in the house for the next two months. The girl's family were overwhelmed by our generosity and they had no reservation left about marrying their daughter to a young man whose alcoholism had done the gossip rounds. My aunt Bino, accompanied Grandmother on her one visit to the girl's family.

"He is a fine boy, I was there when his mother brought him into the world, oh you never saw a finer baby, masses of black hair and tough little fists and legs. He was already kicking and screaming when he came out. We, older folk, take it as a sign of good health when a child comes out like that. The quiet ones are the ones to watch out for, for they may ail in later life. Vini has always been my favourite. His name is Vinilhoulie, you probably don't know that. It's this modern habit of shortening names which I don't approve of. Children should be called by their full names because they have such good meanings. Vinilhoulie's name means live a wealthy and good life. We give our children names that we want them to inherit because we want them to live good lives. Vinilhoulie has always showed himself to be a boy full of life and energy. No doubt, you have heard that he is fond of drinking. That will go. In this day and age, one cannot expect a young man to keep from tasting a little drink now and then. People make too much of it, you know how tongues wag when a boy is seen weaving his way home once. They multiply it until it the rumour spreads that he comes home drunk every night. Don't think too much of it. He is a young man with the natural appetites of all young men and in fact, it should be taken as a reverse kind of blessing that he is doing his drinking before marriage and not after. I have known young men who never touched a drop before marriage but after they got married, they would spend all their time in the drinking houses till they died of drink. Our daughter should learn to be firm with him and then there's no reason why they should not have a happy life together. I am settling the Vürie field on him which is the biggest in the area. We have always got a harvest of seventy tins from that field. His elder brother, Leto, is not getting any of my fields, as you might have heard. He is a hard one, that one, he married a girl I did not approve of. The family background is so important, don't you think?"

Vini's wife's name was Nisano. Her mother's family had come from the village of Rüsoma. Her great-grandmother still lived there. Her son had married a woman of Kohima village and in turn, their daughter married a man of Kohima village and so they became bona fide residents of the bigger village. Nisano was a quiet girl, who was nervous in crowds. Vini teased her endlessly by calling her "wife" on the second day. She was nineteen, three months younger than me and she had been to the same school but she had been in Vimenuo's class. Grandmother wanted them to live with her as she insisted she had a big enough house. But Father and Mother thought they should learn to live on their own and so they rented a small house about twenty yards from us. There, Nisano put up her new curtains and cushions with light green and lemon flowers on them. I went to help her a bit. Her younger sisters were also there and they giggled a lot and placed the wedding presents of teasets and plates and water tumblers on the shelves in neat rows. The youngest sister was fourteen. She liked to talk a lot and she jokingly said,

"Maybe you should keep the glasses out of the way so Vini won't break them when he comes home drunk."

There was a long silence. Then, she clapped her hand to her mouth and exclaimed, "Oh, I'm so sorry, Lieno, I was only joking, we were told by aunt Benuo that he often breaks his glass in the drinking house when he gets drunk."

The woman she mentioned was the older of the two women at the water spot. So I knew that the two of them had gone to gossip with Nisano's family when the proceedings for the wedding were going on.

"It's all right" I smiled at her, trying to break the awkwardness of the moment. "Everyone knows that Vini gets a little aggressive when he's drunk. He becomes an entirely different person but we are hoping that he will not drink anymore now that he has got such a sweet bride. He has gone a month without drinking. He must have tired of breaking glasses."

The tension eased somewhat after that. We even laughed over the things Vini had done when drunk, like stand in the middle of town on the traffic policeman's stand and try to direct traffic. Luckily, it had been late at night, past midnight so no one had reported him but a friend of Leto, driving home from another town, had seen him and that was how we got to know. Nisano blushed a bit to hear the antics of her husband but she seemed happy enough so I tried not to worry too much.

Vini got another job as an assistant in the engineering department of the Radio Station. It sounded impressive but it was largely menial tasks of lifting equipment and setting up microphones or recording equipment. But it certainly sounded well to say that he was working at the Radio Station. His boss said that if he got a degree from the evening college he could get promoted in another four or five years. He would also get a pension if he stayed steadily at the job. Mother was very pleased now and Grandmother was almost patting herself on the back because she said that she had done the right thing by fixing up Vini's marriage. I hoped that it would last. I didn't want to be pessimistic but it seemed too good to be true. Vini, working at a regular job and coming home sober to a loving wife, I couldn't have dreamt that up even if I'd tried. Since they lived closer to us than Leto and Vimenuo, it was easier to visit them and help Nisano with work in the house if she needed help. She was easy to be with though I had never been close to her in school. We talked of people we'd known at school and laughed over the drawing teacher who everyone knew had a big crush on our nursery teacher. It appeared that almost the whole school had known about it. Nisano's sisters were still at school. Her mother often visited her and sent over cooked food frequently.

One morning Nisano woke up vomiting and nauseous. Vini asked me to come over and help so I ran over as soon as I could. Mother was well enough to finish the rest of the cooking so I went to them and found Nisano in bed. She was pale and tired from the retching.

"Was it something you ate last night?" I asked.

"I don't think so," she said, "we had some beef broth but I am fine with that, I have never reacted badly to beef broth before. I don't think it was the food."

"What then?" I asked.

She blushed a bit and stammered when she answered,

"Um, I think, I do believe I am pregnant."

"What!"

I was surprised but realised that it shouldn't be so surprising. They had been married five months now and folk got pregnant even in the first month of marriage. I couldn't imagine Vini as a father. But it was a nice thought. A baby might help him to settle down completely.

"That's wonderful, Nisa," I said, remembering to come up with the right response, "You must just take things slowly then and rest more. I know it's important to be rested in the first three months. Maybe you could get one of your sisters to come and live with you for a while. Does Vini know?"

She stopped smiling.

"That's the trouble, he's not very pleased about it. I suppose he will come round but he felt it was too early."

"Don't worry, " I soothed, "He will come round, men usually do and babies are so adorable and irresistible."

She smiled then and looked a little less nervous. I made her a clear soup which she sipped slowly.

"Oh, that's much better" she exclaimed, "I can keep it down."

When I told Mother the reason for Nisano's nausea, she was ecstatic. "I'm going to be a grandmother then," she said with a beatific smile on her face, "I wonder if it will be a girl or a boy? It doesn't matter though, I shall love it all the same." Poor Mother, it must have come as a nasty shock to her that being the mother of many sons was not always a pleasant thing to be. That was one of the blessings that her age-mates had pronounced on her when she was getting married. Half-jokingly and half seriously, they had proclaimed, "May you be the mother of many sons, may your offspring be as numerous as that of crabs and spiders." It was one of the traditions we still had at weddings but the words of blessing were now treated with humour and the married couple could be blest with progeny as numberless as the stars. The man's best friend would, then, stand up and offer the age-group a rooster as bride price. At this gesture the mock rebukes came immediately: "Is our age-mate only worth a rooster? Is she not worth more? Give us back our age-mate." The others joined in this refrain, "Give us back our age-mate, give her back." This was the cue to produce the second rooster. "That is more like it, we value our age-mate and her place in the age group cannot be replaced so you have to make good compensation for her loss." Some men gifted the age-group with piglets. Then the leader of the age-group would take the gift and lift it high for all too see. "Is this enough do you think?" he asked "should we ask for more?" After two roosters the age-mates would say in unison, "It is enough, we should not ask for our age-mate back." They always left amid much laughter and good will because it was a part of the wedding festivities.

"Oh, Lieno, I hope your brother will be a good father. Do you think he will do well?"

"Don't worry, Mother, everything will go well, Nisano is a good wife."

It was funny how all of us had slipped into the role of mothering Mother. Especially me. But we longed so much for her to be happy and at peace. She had had such a hard life. Now, with Vini married and on the way to being a father, she was calmer than she'd been for a long time.

"Do take her some of the chicken broth I have made this morning. She must eat well. She must eat for two. I hope they have enough food in the house."

"Mother" I said firmly, "will you stop worrying? They have a lot of food. Her mother sends her cooked food once every week. And when I was there they had dried meat hanging over the fire to last them a month."

"I'd like to visit them later this evening."

So, in the evening I took Mother over to Vini's house. Nisano was alone in the house.

"Where's Vini? Isn't he home yet?" asked Mother.

"No, not yet, I suppose he had to work overtime," said Nisano cheerfully.

Mother admired the new curtains and the tablecloth.

"Have you embroidered that yourself, child?"

           Easterine Iralu

"Yes," said Nisano shyly "it's an old thing I made in school."

"Oh it's so nice," said Mother, examining the intricate pattern of flowers, "how clever you are." Nisano blushed further at this. "You know, I did learn to embroider as a young girl but after I married, I never had time to do it and now, I finally have the time but my eyes are too weak for this sort of activity. We learnt to weave our own cloths as young girls. But I cannot weave with my bad back. I could teach your children how to weave waist bands though. But I suppose you both know how to do that. Lieno, you did do some weaving at your grandmother's house, didn't you?"

"Yes, Mother I know how to weave the waist cloths that Bano weaves. Mine are not as smooth as hers but if I had time, I could learn to weave as finely, I'm sure."

Nisano joined in the conversation and then she brought waist cloths that she and her mother had made. The geometric patterns on the white waist cloths were very intricate. Woven in very fine cotton, the patterns were picked up along the borders, very delicately worked at by women who pored over the cloth as they sat at their loin looms in the afternoon. I imagined Nisano's mother doing something similar, her small head bobbing up and down as she used the sticks to pick out the patterns. The black cloth which both men and women used were also beautiful but I thought the white ones were more lovely. Used by young girls and women, men could use them only at festivals along with a black cloth. There was an old man in the village who would use the white women's cloth of the western villages. But no one laughed at him because he used it ever so often that people had got used to him. I had never seen any other man using a woman's cloth. Nisano's mother had also woven wool body-cloths which were all the rage in winter. They didn't look as good as the cotton ones and the patterns looked clumsy because they were picked on much thicker yarn. But they were popular because they were so warm and so one got used to them.

"Look at this one," Nisano spread out a new cloth in the usual black background but it had bright blue and orange borders. It was unfamiliar. Neither Mother nor I had seen a pattern like that before.

"I think it might belong to one of the tribes of Burma. Did you get it as a wedding present?"

"Yes, but we can't figure out which tribe it is. It is very warm but Vini doesn't want to wear it because he thinks it is outlandish."

We laughed at this because it certainly was outlandish. We were not used to such bright colours on our own cloths. Amongst the tribes, our Angami cloths were rather subdued and looked somber, especially the black with red and green stripes. But I thought it looked dignified on men. It was already dark when we put the cloths away. There was a sound of boots on the wooden verandah outside their house. "That must be Vini" said Nisano and she looked excited as she turned hopefully to the door. He came into the house and was surprised to find Mother there too.

"Why Mother, what brings you here?" he asked.

"Well, son, I have come to congratulate you on your good news."

"What good news?" he looked a little puzzled and looked at Nisano.

"Well, I think it is marvellous that you are going to make me a grandmother," said Mother with a big smile on her face.

"Oh, you mean that?" he said and he looked at Nisano again.

Then he glanced over at me, "Is she better now?" I nodded yes.

"Good, you had all of us worried this morning."

He looked over at Nisano and she blushed again. I was seated at the end of the bed, right below where they hung their jackets. Vini walked over to where I was seated and hung up his jacket. It was when he bent over to untie his shoes that I got the distinct smell of home-brewed liquor on his breath, the sickly sweet smell that wafted out of the entrance of the drinking houses when we walked past them. There was another smell too, cardamom and *paan* leaf. I knew then that Vini had started drinking again. He had not been working overtime but he had been at the drinking houses, and the cardamom was an attempt to disguise the smell from his wife. My heart constricted within me. Why, Vini, why? I longed to ask him, when everything was going so well?

23

Vini was dead drunk the night his wife delivered a healthy eight-pound baby boy. Vimenuo and I stayed up helping his wife through her long labour. Nisano had an extraordinarily long labour lasting at least twelve hours. She refused to drink the soup we kept making every hour. But in the third hour, her mother insisted that she needed to keep her strength up by drinking as much as she could. So, she drank a little each time. But she was in such pain throughout the labour that I pitied her and tried to stop her mother feeding her soup.

"You don't know how much she needs it, childbirth is a life or death event. Never underestimate the strength a woman can get from feeding well," she said.

As for Nisano, she alternately broke out into a sweat or lay limp and exhausted from the contractions. The midwife attending her said, "This one is a big one, it will take all night, his head is not engaged yet."

I felt so sorry for her. She didn't cry out when her pains came. I had heard that some women would scream when their labour pains were upon them Nisano would close her eyes tight and bite down on her lip. Then we knew she was having her pains and we took turns at holding her hand and tried to do anything to alleviate her pains, massage her lower back which she said was hurting terribly or simply let her hold our hands very tight. The bedsheets were damp from her sweating. But the midwife did not want them changed because she said that we would have to change them anyway, after it was all over. So Vimenuo and I pulled a flannel cloth over the damp sheet. At least the flannel would absorb the moisture better than the cotton sheet she was using. The midwife bent over Nisano's bloated stomach and felt the baby every twenty minutes or so.

All night Nisano struggled to give birth. A little before dawn, the midwife's voice became urgent,

"Push, push, my dear, that's it, it's very close."

Nisano lay back exhausted from the pushing, "Am I doing it right? I can't remember anything when the pains come."

"Don't worry, my dear," soothed the midwife, "just do it a couple more times and your worries will be over."

The second pain came so fast that her face was contorted from the pain.

"No, no," she cried, "I can't push anymore."

"Give her some soup, fast," called out the midwife and I came running with the bowl of soup, happy to be of some use. I had just about managed to ladle two spoons of soup into her mouth when she started to close her eyes tight again.

"No more," she said to me so I took the bowl away.

But she was reaching for my hand so I quickly held her outstretched hand.

"Push, my dear, push, this is it, push some more, it's coming out, almost there."

Nisano was no longer biting her lip. She was in such terrible pain she was screaming, a long, low, drawn-out scream.

"No, no, push, just concentrate on pushing, just this once more," begged the midwife.

"I can't," whispered Nisano in a ragged voice, "I can't anymore."

"Oh, you can, you can, just this last time, then it will be over, please my dear, try," urged the midwife.

Mother had been praying quietly in the next room.

"Pray harder, Mother please," I screamed out.

I saw the pallor of death on Nisano's face. If she couldn't push the baby out this time, she would probably die. All of us were praying aloud now. "Oh my Lord, help us." And then, miraculously, she lifted her listless head and began to concentrate on pushing even as her pains overwhelmed her. She pushed and pushed like she had never before pushed, pausing a while to draw breath and then pushing again.

"It's almost there, come on, you're doing beautifully, good girl, give us one more push," the midwife encouraged.

The wet black head of a child emerged from between her legs. Nisano lay back exhausted. The baby was trapped between her legs.

"Good girl, give us one more push and it's all over, see it is already halfway out."

But her pains did not return for what seemed like a long time. We were all alarmed and worried for the baby. Would it die having struggled so much to be born? Would it be strangled between its mother's legs? The midwife was looking very worried now. She frantically begged Nisano to push again.

"I can't" whispered Nisano.

Then, as suddenly as it had gone, the pain returned in a rush and she was arching her back and pushing mightily. Vimenuo held her back down gently and we were soon rewarded with an infant's weak cry.

The midwife held up the very red baby, cleaned its mouth and nose and wrapped him in a cotton cloth and made me hold him. He was a big baby, a boy.

 236 Easterine Iralu

"Nisa, it's a boy!" I cried to her excitedly.

She smiled up at me weakly and fainted. She had slipped so quietly into a faint, we first thought she was simply sleeping. Fortunately, the midwife was very experienced in these things.

"Look after the baby," she said, thrusting the little bundle into my hands as she rushed to Nisano's side.

"Warm milk or tea quickly," she shouted to Vimenuo and then she began to rub Nisano's hands and call her loudly, "Here, here my girl, you can't do this to us, you have the most beautiful baby and he needs you."

Vimenuo was back with lukewarm milk in a flash. They got some inside Nisano. I watched in horror as the milk trickled down the corner of her mouth. But she was roused after that. How close we had come to losing her, I realised from the way the midwife had tried to revive her. One of us constantly sat by her side now and tried to keep her awake. When she slept, we kept watch over her breathing. I had never worried more over the drawing of another person's breath. It was late morning when Nisano woke, still looking tired and pale. But she was happy and smiled weakly. She rose to have a bath and try to feed the baby. The midwife had said that she should finish the five-day lying-in period. So I helped her to the bathroom and brought her warm water to bathe in. When she was finished she called out to me and I helped her get to the bedroom. Vimenuo and Nisano's mother had finished cleaning the room a while ago. There were clean new sheets on her bed. The open windows let fresh air into the room. Nisano's mother had finished bathing the baby and Mother carried him proudly. Everyone ignored the fact that Vini had been too drunk to be of any help during the birth. It was painfully embarrassing for my family. But Nisano's mother had been gracious about it, "He's probably nervous, many men are." I hoped that Leto would take him to task about it.

The baby kept us busy in the next days. Nisano was slowly recovering from the ordeal that childbirth had been for her. She was out of bed in a week, washing the baby's clothes and making food for her family. Vini seemed happy with his son.

"We'll name him Ruokuolhoulie, because he has been lucky to be born safely. Likewise, the rest of his life should be full of fortunate events," said Vini.

But Mother wanted to name him Kesalhoulie,

"It means live a new life. Vini should learn to live a new life now that he is blessed with a wonderful healthy son and a kind wife."

Finally, they arrived at a compromise. The baby would use the name from his father officially but he would be called Salhou for short.

"Don't worry, Mother," soothed Leto, "we'll use the name you give to our baby."

Everyone laughed at that. Vimenuo was six months pregnant already and we were all very excited about it. Soon, our family would be overrun by babies, so it seemed.

Nisano was a neat and orderly mother. She had her baby's nappies stacked in a row by the baby's crib. It was a pleasure to help her care for the baby. Mother and I took turns to go to her and carry the baby so she might finish some housework. After the first month she was able to manage fairly well. It helped that her mother or sisters would come to spend the night often. I hoped that Vini would be encouraged to stop drinking completely. By about the third month, baby Salhou began to be very fretful. He didn't sleep well anymore and he woke up his parents constantly in the middle of the night or toward early morning with a steady whining sound which, if left unattended, developed into a full-throated scream that would be quite impossible to quell. The doctor called it colic and gave him a syrup to drink at night. It was quite a job to get it down the little fellow. He would close his mouth or cry loudly every time we fed him a spoon of the syrup. I was convinced it must be awful and tasted some. To my surprise it was a honey sweet mixture that tasted quite wonderful and I couldn't understand why the child hated it so. The doctor's medicine did not help very much. If we got a bit of it down his protesting throat, he would throw it up immediately. One night, Nisano's sister came to call me at home. I was surprised because I was preparing to get some rest at home having been with them the night before. She said that Nisano had specifically requested that I come over. I put on my shoes because there was a light drizzle outside and it could develop into a heavy shower. The rains had come early this year.

"Did she say anything? Is she unwell?" I asked anxiously because it was most unusual for Nisano to send for me.

"No, she is quite well. She didn't say why she wanted you," answered her sister.

She was a young thing, turned fifteen now but still very naïve and irritatingly silly. I worried that it was something to do with Vini. At their house, I called out "Salhou, Salhou" and Nisano shouted from inside,

"Come in, the door is open."

I pushed the door open and walked into the small house that Nisano had worked so hard to turn into a home. Her bright curtains were drawn because it was early evening and she had already put on the lights in the living room. The bedroom was small and dark, darker than the other rooms but they could not turn any of the other rooms into a bedroom because there wouldn't be enough privacy with the doors opening from one room into the other. That was the trouble with all the government quarters. They had a standard design and the occupants could not do much with them. Some people extended the houses so that they had an extra bedroom thrusting out of the main house at an odd angle.

"Did you want me to spend the night then?" I asked Nisano.

"If you don't mind. I was hoping we could talk."

"Of course."

But the talk had to wait until later at night when her sister had parked herself in front of the television set to watch a Hindi serial.

"What is it, Nisa? Any trouble with Vini?" I began.

"He never comes home on time. I know he is drinking regularly. Oh, Lieno, I am so afraid to say anything because he gets very angry then. Last night he accused me of trapping him with the baby. He said he didn't really want to marry me but he had been forced into it."

She was crying now as she said this. I knew then that Nisano had been struggling with this for a long time. My heart went out to her.

"No, you mustn't believe all that he says. Men say the most foolish things when they are drunk. Vini cares for both of you. He just forgets everything when he is drinking."

Even as I said them, I felt the falseness and futility of my words. And I felt very angry with my brother. How dare he do this to her? She was so young and trusting, deeply in love with her husband and he, he would leave her every night and go out drinking. Or not come home early because he had stopped by the drinking houses to laugh with former cronies and a drink for old times sake would lengthen into five or six drinks before he was ready to go home. I didn't know what to say to Nisano. If a wife and child could not do the trick of taming him, I didn't know what could possibly make Vini a better man.

"That's not all, Lieno, he is with his friends, you remember Rocky, the boy on the road that we used to be so scared of when we were in school?"

With a sinking heart, I recognized the name.

"He was at school with us, wasn't he?" I asked, desperately hoping it might be someone else with the same name.

Easterine Iralu

"He was a few years senior, but he never finished school. He was handsome in a rough way and always in a fight with some boy or the other. He was expelled for beating up a teacher."

It was the same Rocky. He was the sort of boy whose name made your stomach churn if you heard it used along with any male relative of yours. He had been in jail a couple of times for breaking into a shop and making off with the cash box. The second time he had thrown a brick at an elderly man because the man had not given him money when he asked for it. No one ever said anything good about him.

"What about him, Nisa?" I asked reluctantly.

"Vini has been with him a lot lately. He even came to the house once."

"What!"

I was amazed that he had had the audacity to step into a self-respecting home.

"Why? What would he want here?"

Nisano had a pained look on her face, "Vini invited him home. The other boy also came with him."

"Which other boy?" I asked.

"The one they call Bai, the ugly one with scars on his chin and cheek."

Nisano said that they had not been disrespectful when they were there. In fact, Bai had been very embarrassed to be there. He was apologetic to Nisano. But Rocky was cocky and familiar. He made some joke about Vini becoming a father too early.

"I know that when he doesn't come home early, he is always with those two. Rocky recently beat a man so badly he had twenty stitches on his face. I am so worried, Lieno, I don't want Vini associating with boys like that but he won't listen to me. He gets very angry when I try to tell him anything. I fear that I will make things worse if I nag him. Last night he got so angry, he shouted, "Why don't you leave if you are so tired of my drinking? You are free to leave, you know, leave the baby behind and go!" I was so scared of him and at the same time, I didn't want the neighbours to know. I have heard from my sister that aunt Benuo goes around telling people we are already having problems in our marriage because of Vini's drinking. She was saying, 'You can't change a drinking man.' Oh, Lieno, I am so tired of thinking of what to do."

She wiped away her tears on one of the nappies and leaned back on a pillow. How thin she was! The veins in her neck stood out sharply. I spoke up,

"I don't think he will listen to me but I will tell Leto to speak to him."

"Oh Lieno, will you do that? I haven't told my mother or my sisters about it because I don't want them to worry. And you mustn't tell your mother anything. It would kill her. As it is, she is so happy with the baby."

I promised her that I would do as she said.

"Oh, I am relieved I could talk to you tonight" she sighed.

24

The talk between Leto and Vini did not go well. I didn't expect it
to go well but it was worse than I expected. It ended in a slanging
match with Father accusing Leto of being too harsh on Vini.

"You have to be patient with him. This way, we will lose him
altogether" said Father. We were at Leto's house and the talk had
taken place at Vini's house.

"Oh Father, can't you see that he has held us to ransom all these
years? We haven't had any real peace in the family since Pete died.
And it is now eight years since Pete died. We are all so weary of it.
Vini should not be allowed to blackmail the family any longer. Not
now that he has the responsibility of looking after a wife and child.
Someone has to tell him the truth and if you and Mother won't do
it, I must."

Leto looked stern as he said this. But I knew he was right. We
had coddled Vini too much because we had been afraid of his terrible
outbursts of temper. Before his marriage, he had come back many
nights from brawling on the streets and on the nights he had been
beaten up by others, he would take it out on Bulie. Thankfully, it was

not too often that he was at the receiving end of the blows from others. On such nights, we tiptoed around and Father would either pretend he was asleep or call out to him gently to go and sleep. Mother got up from bed and served him food which he ate desultorily or pushed away roughly as the desire took him. I was not sure if he was as badly behaved with Nisano. But from the things she had told me, I did suspect that he was quite brutal with her now. She had a blue bruise on her neck one day. When I asked her about it, she said she had slipped and fallen against the bed in the night. I didn't believe her but she had pulled up her shawl to cover it so I did not mention it again. Grandmother was the only member of the family who continued to welcome Vini into her house. We knew now that she gave him money regularly. When Leto protested, Grandmother had simply said,

"Didn't I tell you, Leto, that I would reward you if you married a girl of my choice? Yet you would marry against my wishes. You have no right to tell me what I may or may not do with my money. If I want to give it to Vini, that is up to me. If he is drinking with it, that is his business. In any case, a man has to sow some wild oats before he settles down."

"But, Grandmother, he has a wife and son now so it is time he settled down,"

Leto protested but Grandmother accused him of being jealous of his brother so Leto let the matter go.

"You can't make me change my mind, I am settling the field on Vini, not you."

It was useless to talk with Grandmother when she became stubborn and impervious like that.

She couldn't see that she was contributing to Vini's problem by giving him money that he would only use to drink. It was hard for Leto to talk to her because she would always accuse him of being jealous of Vini's inheritance. The only thing to do was to talk to

Easterine Iralu

Vini again and again and hope that Nisano would not suffer too much. Mother spent even more time in prayer for Vini. When we were angry with him, she would say, God will change him some day. We stopped hiding it from her because she knew. She had always known. Not all of it perhaps, not the terrible brawling in the streets nor all the violence because Vini went to a lot of trouble to hide his bruises from Mother. I suspect that he was the one doing much of the beating because he had more bruises on his knuckles with which he must have been landing blows on some poor unfortunate. There were times I wished he were the sort who drank quietly without feeling the need to do something violent afterwards. But Vini got a thrill out of brawling. He had told Bulie that it made him feel more of a man when he felt the blood rushing to his head as he pumped into another human being and delivered blows to the most vulnerable parts of his body. We didn't tell Mother about that. It was bad enough that she had to live with the guilt of a son who was drinking himself to death. Almost.

Things came to a head when Rocky was killed in one of their drunken brawls. Someone had picked up a huge rock and crushed his head with it as he bent over another boy whom he had pinned to the ground in order to smash his face. Rocky's head was completely crushed. He was unrecognizable. The police said that the killer had used the stone with incredible force. They had to keep the lid of the coffin closed at the funeral. Vini went to his funeral but none of us accompanied him because we had never really known Rocky or his parents. The women at the water spot were very blasé about it.

"He had it coming," said the older one,

"Did I tell you he threatened to flatten my face if I did not give him brew?"

We were horrified.

"When was that?" I asked.

"Two weeks ago at least. That boy was born to trouble. I have never seen a more violent man. He loved hurting people. That was the greatest pleasure in his life. The only other person I have seen come close to him is that brother of yours, Lieno. He loves to brawl almost as much as Rocky did. And you had better believe me. I have seen what the two of them did to a couple of fellow drinkers."

I should not have been shocked to hear that but it was painful to have an outsider tell you things about a family member that you were not aware of. I had not realised that this was what others thought of Vini.

The day after the funeral, Leto visited him at his house.

"You have to choose now, Vini. If you go on the way you do, you will come to the same end as Rocky. We don't want that to happen to you, Vini. You must stop drinking, see how it has destroyed your family and yourself. I wish you could see how much you are hurting the people who love you. Mother has lost a son already. She must not lose another. And consider your wife, she chose to come and live with you, giving up her family and loved ones and now, you have reduced her to a wreck."

That stung Vini.

"Who says that? She is happy with me still. She loves me and she will not leave me. Do you know why I drink, Leto? Have you ever once thought about that instead of condemning me every time? Do you know why Rocky was killed and no one did anything to the killer? You have a good job and you don't drink and you think you are so safe. But it will come to all of you as well."

"What do you mean by that? You are not making much sense, Vini," said Leto.

"Do you want to know why I drink? Why all of us drink and brawl? It's because life here in Kohima is so meaningless. Do you know the reason why Rocky was hitting the other guy? Well, they were arguing about politics and the other chap said that it was no use fighting for independence because, in any case, the Naga cause was a dead cause. That made Rocky mad and they kept arguing and the man said that Rocky was a fool because he couldn't see that the people who were getting anything out of the conflict were the Parties and those who sided with them. Rocky said that he would rather die than give over his country to another nation. The man called him a fool, he said he was the greatest fool and he hit out at Rocky first. Do you know how frustrating it is to be a Naga and live with the fear of being shot all the time? Do you know what it does to your insides when you hear about the people tortured and killed by the army and you can't do anything about it? And then, along comes this smart alec who thinks it is all right to stop fighting for freedom, to stop being men and be sitting at an office desk, having sold your identity away for a bundle of money. You didn't know that Rocky's father was killed by the Indian army, did you? You don't know anything but yet you are so quick to accuse. You won't be so safe anymore, it will come to you, it will come to all of us soon."

Leto looked quite shaken at Vini's words. He calmed down and addressed him in a quiet voice, "Is that why you drink, my brother?"

Vini looked surprised at Leto's sudden change of tone. He didn't reply immediately. After a few moments, he said,

"I didn't start out drinking because of that reason but now that I have been drinking for some years, I feel the futility of stopping because things are going from bad to worse. Leto, haven't you heard that they killed Lato's mother? Put a gun into her mouth and shot her dead after they had raped her. Do you know that when Lato went to avenge his mother they beat him until he was half-dead and then they released him. And no one could do anything to help him, certainly not the government. Tell me, Leto, what is the use of trying to live life well?"

Leto was grey-faced.

"I know about some of those things, Vini. But we have to hope that God will help us and bring peace to our land soon. How can you live as though there were no hope left? You have a son, Vini, don't forget, you have a beautiful son. I wanted a son but I got a daughter. Nevertheless, I am happy with her, very happy. You should be happy you have a healthy son, you should try to live as a good father so that your boy grows up to be an obedient boy. Stop drinking, Vini, we will all help you, just please stop drinking."

Vini simply sat there quietly without saying a word.

Later that night, Nisano ran over to us, clutching her son to her. She had not had time to bind him to her with the binding cloth.

"Lieno, oh Lieno, Vini is drunk and in such a temper, I am afraid to stay at home alone with him. He threw a chair at me but it missed. I feared he would hurt our son so I came away. I cannot go back tonight. Please let me sleep here. I don't want my family to know about this."

I was shocked yet could not help wondering why I should be so shocked at what had become standard behaviour from Vini. I made up a bed for them and bade them rest but I could not sleep. Stealthily, I pulled a shawl around me and made my way to Vini's house. All the lights were lit in the small house. I could hear the sound of plates crashing to the ground. I quickly stepped into the kitchen. Vini stood in the middle of the room throwing china plates to the floor which broke instantly. He had broken at least five plates.

"Please, Vini, don't do this anymore," I said gently.

"Please Vini, don't do. this, don't do that," he mimicked me sarcastically.

"Where is my wife? I won't stop until you bring here back."

"Please let her sleep in our house tonight. She is frightened now but she will be all right tomorrow, she will come back in the morning."

He lifted a plate high above his head.

Easterine Iralu

"Bring her back now or I will break all the plates in the house."
I lost my temper then and with it my fear of him.

"How dare you behave like this? You are the most selfish person I know and you have made life difficult for everyone. I wonder how Nisano can love you and stay with you. I'm ashamed to call you my brother. We should all leave you to yourself and get on with our own lives."

I was so angry I didn't even regret what I had said. He looked very surprised to hear me say that.

"What Lieno, you dare to raise your voice at me? Do you know I used to carry you on my back when you were small? I saw you as a baby and I have seen you grow up and now, you think you have the right to scold me? Grandmother was right. Girls should never be educated. They always forget their station in life."

I felt a little abashed then because he was right that I had spoken out of turn. But I was so fed up of his drinking and violence that I had not chosen my words well.

"I'm sorry, Vini, I have always been respectful to you. But you have hurt us all with your drinking. Now, we worry afresh for your wife and child. It is embarrassing because her family knows it too. But they are too polite to say anything."

"What!" he exclaimed, "How did their family get to know? Has Nisano been telling tales?"

"I don't think she does that" I said, "but the other women talk and they tell her mother you are a heavy drinker. You should know that actually Nisano does not want her people to know about it at all."

I was grateful the awkward moment had passed and he was actually listening to me. He surreptitiously left the plate on the table.

"Who then? Who has been telling tales about me?" he wanted to know.

But I knew that if I mentioned names he would go and threaten the persons involved and it would become very unpleasant.

"You know I don't have the time to go around listening to other people's gossip. But it must be that they have seen you drunk or brawling at some time. Does it matter who said it?"

He sat slumped into a chair now. I could see that his skin had turned green, the chronic alcoholic's colour.

"Ah!" he suddenly cried clutching at his side.

"What is it, Vini?," I asked.

He seemed to be in pain.

"A sharp pain there in my side. Caught me by surprise," he began to heave, "Lieno, I must throw up" he said as he stumbled toward the bathroom.

I followed him and held him as he put his head over the sink and heaved again. Bright spots of blood lay on the white surface of the sink.

"Vini! You're bleeding!" I screamed as I held him up.

He was still heaving and vomiting blood in a steady stream. I was horrified. I struggled to stay calm and think of how best I could help him. It was so late in the night we would not be able to get a doctor but if we got him to the hospital, the emergency doctor could treat him. He stopped vomiting after what seemed like ages to me.

"Lie down" I urged when we had got him into the bedroom, "I am going to take you to the hospital now."

"No, I'll be all right" he protested.

"Vini, you will die if you vomit any more blood. Just lie there and wait. I'll be back soon."

I put a blanket over him and ran back to the house, got Bulie and ran back to Vini. We did not wake the others. Bulie would borrow a friend's car that he was fixing up. Vini was so pale and bloodless I feared he would not be able to survive the night. Mercifully, the doctor was on duty and he immediately administered an intravenous injection to him after examining him thoroughly.

"How long since he's been drinking?" asked the doctor in a very impersonal manner.

I was thinking back because Vini's drinking had gone on for so long,.

"Ten years?" prompted the doctor.

"That would be about it," I answered.

"Rice brew or hard drinks?" he asked.

By 'hard' drinks he was referring to whisky and rum which were readily available in the drinking houses.

"I think he drinks rice brew," I answered again but Bulie said, "Lately, he has been drinking a lot of rum."

"I thought so," said the doctor, "that's a quick killer. Well, he has to stop drinking if he wants to stay alive. There are no two ways about it. I can see his liver was probably very inflamed two weeks ago. But now it is shrinking rapidly. He has got cirrhosis of the liver and if he goes out to drink again, he will simply bleed to death. That blood vomiting is an indication that his liver has collapsed completely. I am not even sure if he will recover the use of his liver again. It is so damaged already. You understand he has to stay in hospital for some days. It's very tough on the family. You are his wife then?" he turned to me.

"No, I am his sister, but he has got a wife and a child."

"How old is the child?"

"Six months now," I replied.

"Bring them both in the morning. If that doesn't help him to stop drinking, I don't know what will."

I stayed by Vini's side at the hospital all night. Bulie left to bring Mother and Father and Nisano and the baby the next morning. We agreed that we would not wake them as Vini's condition had become somewhat stable. The night nurse brought me tea and asked me to sleep saying that she would watch over him. But I was scared something would happen during the night if I slept. Sometimes he slept a deep sleep, twitching a little. Then I dozed too. But I would wake with a great sense of premonition. When it was nearly dawn, he woke and said,

"Lieno, I am sorry for all this. I feel terrible to put you through this."

"Please just get well. All we want is for you to be well. Stop drinking and be a father to your son."

"I will try my best."

But we both knew that death was close now. We would need a miracle for him to survive.

"The doctor says you must never drink again."

"I won't."

"Oh, Vini, that is all that we want."

I stroked his temple gently and he fell asleep again. But I could not sleep any more. I silently mouthed a prayer for him and padded to the window. Outside, morning was breaking slowly. It was June so it was rare for the skies to be completely clear of rain clouds. Yesterday it had been sunny in the morning and the sun made the moisture on the grass rise up in a thin mist from the ground.

Nisano and my parents came before it was quite morning. Nisano had strapped the baby on her back. I raised my finger to my lips to indicate they were to be quiet. I had never seen my father look so grim before.

"He needs to rest a lot, says the doctor," I tried to speak naturally.

But they were not fooled. Nisano went fearfully to the bed where her husband lay. Timidly she reached out a finger and laid it on his cheek. Vini slept on.

"We brought tea and biscuits for you," said Mother as she unpacked a flask of tea.

 Easterine Iralu

I was very grateful for the tea. It had been a long weary night. I remembered being mortally afraid that he might die during the night and I would be the only one with him when it happened. Leto and Vimenuo came too and we sat around the room and on the extra bed because there were not enough chairs. We spoke in whispers but soon Vini woke and when he saw that we were all there, he looked very startled. "All of you here? I am sorry to bring everyone out like this," he said. There was no attempt on his part to be sarcastic as he would have been before. Leto and Vimenuo drew close to him along with all the others and spoke to him kindly. Vini was very surprised. He probably expected to get a scolding. Instead, everyone was voicing concern for him and wanting him to get better. He turned away then but not before I saw there were tears in his eyes.

25

The end came swiftly for Vini. The next night, Bulie and Leto
and Nisano were with him when he started to cough and vomit
blood. The doctor gave him an injection to stop the vomiting but it
did not help. He was too weak and he died before we could reach
the hospital. After that, it was a long wait for them to bring the
body home to be buried. I felt sad but suddenly freed as if a burden
had been lifted. I also felt very guilty. It wasn't that I didn't love
Vini. He was my brother. I loved him dearly though I had hated
what he had done to himself and the way he had hurt those who
loved him. But I had a sense of deep gratitude because in the end he
had come to see how much we all loved him. When the pastor visited
him in the afternoon, he had asked if God would forgive him.

"Oh my son, God's forgiveness is for everybody," said the pastor.

"Tell Him I am sorry for having hurt so many," said Vini.

"Why don't you tell Him yourself?" urged the pastor.

"No, you tell Him first. And after that if He is willing to speak
to me, I will speak to Him too but I am too ashamed to make the
first move."

"All right, my son" said the pastor as he took Vini's hand in his and led him through the prayer of repentance.

Vini fell asleep peacefully after that. He woke towards evening and began to vomit.

Mother was incredibly calm. It was such a difference from how grieved she had been when Pete had died. "He has gone to be with Jesus and with Petekhrietuo. Why should I grieve as though he had died in sin? I know God forgave him in the end. Now Pete will not be alone. And soon we shall see them both." She spoke to all who came to the funeral in the same calm tone. The pastor preached a short sermon and said that he was sure Vini had received God's salvation before he died. Mother joined in the hymn singing at the end of the service. It was a very quiet service. When Leto spoke on behalf of the family, he added, "My brother was a disobedient son much of his life. If he has hurt any of you in word or in deed, we beseech you to find the grace to forgive him before we lay his body in the dust." It was the customary thing to say especially at the funerals of violent men. When the grave was covered over, it began to rain again. Then there was such a terrible downpour, the fresh soil on the grave was muddy and the flowers were washed out. Nisano was heartbroken but she tended to her son and said, "At least I have our son." I felt so sorry for her. I had always wondered how she could have loved Vini. She must have seen some good in him to have loved him so devotedly throughout their short married life. I hoped so. I hoped he had not always been cruel to her.

Grandmother was grieved beyond consolation. Bano said that she woke in the night calling for Vini. "Vinilhoulie-o" she would call several times before Bano could manage to quieten her down. She would get very angry when interrupted by Bano. It took several days for her to accept that Vini was dead and would never come back. After Vini's death, we had to concentrate on taking care of

Grandmother. She was so distraught with grief, there were days when we feared she would lose her mind. The doctor had to be called to attend to her. He gave her tranquilizers for a week because Bano said she rarely slept. Neikuo now spent the night at Grandmother's house but Grandmother would push her away. Bano was the only person she could bear to have near her. She refused to leave her room except to answer the call of nature. Bano brought her food in her room and patiently waited till she was done and then she cleared the plates away. Though she had refused to eat anything in the beginning, she was now beginning to relent and eat small portions. Very cleverly, Bano made her favourite dishes, pork broth cooked into soft pieces and flavoured mildly with country ginger in which she added squash leaves and red chilly. Twice, she made her rice with chicken so that the rice was soaked in the flavour of the chicken broth. Grandmother could not hold out for long and soon, she was eating normally again and asking for jaggery in the afternoon. Sizo visited and stayed for a week. It comforted her that Sizo was around, doing the men's jobs around the house. She let him arrange her will. Now that Vini was dead, she would settle her good field on Vini's son. Bulie would get the other one. Nothing for Leto. Not that Leto was interested in inheriting from Grandmother. He had taken all that into account when he was getting married and firmly decided that he did not want a field if he had to give up Vimenuo.

Grandmother spoke as though she was ready to go too. She was eighty-eight now but she was as healthy as her mother when she was that age. If she got over her grief at Vini's sudden death, she would live a long time. She wanted Nisano and her son to live with her. So, when it was time to vacate the government quarters, Nisano and Salhou went to live with Grandmother. It was a strange arrangement. Tongues wagged as we knew they would: "The girl is Vinilhoulie's widow, she should live with his parents for a year before she goes back home to her father's house. She should tend his grave for a year. That is the way of our people. Why should she go to live with his grandmother? Has anything like that ever been done before? Doesn't the old lady know that there is no such custom? Or is that family trying to create new customs? Humph!" Oh, how people talked! As though what Nisano was doing was something totally taboo. Indeed, people only talked like this when there was a real violation of a taboo. When I met Aunt Benuo, the older of the two women at the water spot, she said,

"Well, Lieno, it seems your grandmother is starting a new custom. She has given shelter to your sister-in-law and taken that privilege away from your parents. Unfortunately, none of us is as rich or as headstrong as your grandmother so I don't think we can do that when it is our turn to lose a grandson."

I simply said, "We have considered that aspect too, Aunt. But Grandmother is very old now and she may have forgotten how things are done in our culture. And she is grieving so much over Vini that this is one way of making her feel better…"

She smiled in a nasty way. I quickly filled up my pitcher and walked home. The last thing I needed was to get into a conversation with the neighbourhood gossip and have my words distorted and repeated to all and sundry.

Not surprisingly, Grandmother recovered rapidly when the two went to live with her. Nisano saw it as a temporary stay and she had shifted her belongings to her mother's house and ours. But Grandmother insisted that they should consider her home their home. She said she wanted them to live there even when she was dead. Though they were not too far from us, Nisano found it difficult to visit us. She told me that Grandmother did not like them to go out frequently. And she was impossibly possessive about the baby. So we went to visit them instead. I carried Salhou when I was there and played with him. Nisano was always happy for the respite from carrying her very heavy son. But twice it happened that Grandmother would snarl from her bedroom when she heard me playing with Salhou.

"Don't spoil the child, girl. He has to get used to his mother."

"But, Grandmother, I am only trying to help. Besides he is here with you all the time and we don't get to play with him unless we come here. Don't you think I should help care for him when I am here?" I reasoned.

"Still as impertinent as ever, aren't you, girl?" she said impatiently.

Nisano gave me a look so I held my tongue and quickly said, "Sorry Grandmother, I didn't mean to interfere in his upbringing."

"Humph!"

She made sure the sound was loud enough for me to hear.

"Nisano, bring Vini here for a while" she called.

"What?" I hissed, "Is Grandmother out of her mind? She called him Vini!"

I was shocked. But Nisano did not look surprised.

"That's her name for Salhou and none of us is allowed to call him Salhou anymore."

Nisano picked up her son and took him to Grandmother's room. I followed them.

"Here, my darling," she cooed, "come to me, Vini, my darling boy." The baby crawled happily to her.

He was a big and happy baby. He ate very well and went to anyone who held out a bit of food to him. Grandmother had a biscuit in her hand which she was holding out to him. When he reached her she held it up out of his reach and then he climbed into her lap. She gave him the biscuit and held him to her happily.

"Ah, you are surprised I call him by his father's name," she said to me, "but I see no reason why I should not call him Vini. I gave

Easterine Iralu

his father his name and Vinilhoulie means live a good and prosperous life. It is a good name. I am happy he has a son to inherit his name and his house. This house will go to the boy when I am no longer here."

"That's very nice of you, Grandmother," I said, knowing when not to argue with her.

I stole a look at Nisano and made a face at her.

She looked away from me and busied herself with the baby's socks which were falling off. But I felt very uncomfortable about the whole thing. This was no life for Nisano. She was still very young, not yet twenty-one. It was so unfortunate that she was widowed but there was no reason why she should be made to live under Grandmother's roof like a prisoner. In time, if she should meet a nice man who knows what might happen? I didn't think Grandmother would allow her to take the baby with her if she remarried. She still mourned for Vini. I could see that in her hollow cheeks. Once every week, she would come to his grave and change the flowers and clean the grave.

I felt uneasy about Grandmother's plans for the two of them. For the moment, Nisano was too docile to protest when Grandmother made unreasonable demands such as ordering her to stop long visits to us and to her mother. But, surely, she would tire of being cooped up in a dusty old house with a cantankerous old woman who was no blood relation to her and would have been a stranger to her if not for her marriage to the old woman's grandson. Then what would happen? Grandmother gave her generous amounts of money every month to spend on the baby. She spent only half the amount and gave the remaining amount back to Grandmother. But the old woman would be displeased and so, Nisano was forced to use all the money on the baby. Grandmother dictated what she was to spend it on, clothes and every kind of new toy.

"What's that on Vini's arm?" asked Grandmother pointing to a little blue bruise he had.

"He hit himself against a chair when he was crawling in the kitchen," said Nisano.

"See that he is watched all the time," said Grandmother sternly. "Tell Bano she is not to spend so much time sleeping in the afternoon. That girl naps when she thinks I am resting, but I can hear her snoring from my room. Let her help you to look after the child."

I wondered how Nisano would put that instruction to Bano.

"Please don't worry, Grandmother, I can look after him myself. I wouldn't want to trouble Bano. She always has so much to do," said Nisano.

"Well, you must see that no harm comes to the child," continued Grandmother, "a male-child is to be brought up very carefully. He will shelter all of us in turn when he is grown."

Of late, Bano had become very difficult to be with. She was now thirty-two but there was no suitor in sight. The man who had made an offer to Sizo thirteen years ago was the only one to have done so. Over the years, she had grown obese and slowly lost her looks. A newcomer could mistake her for a fifty-year-old woman because she had grown so slovenly. She no longer bothered to pretty herself up in case a suitable man might come along and make her an offer. When she went to the shops she waddled like a giant duck.

I felt sorry for Bano but she had grown so sour it was difficult to be around her for long. I wondered how Nisano put up with her. Perhaps she was not as unkind to Nisano because she had lost her husband too and therefore could be considered to be in the same boat as her. Her face was coarse to look at now, her skin lustreless and scarred by old acne. It was only for a short period in her youth that Bano had been close to pretty. To console her lack of suitors, she snacked on food frequently. The other thing

Easterine Iralu

she liked to do was nap. So, if Grandmother was in her room, she would take a quick nap in the daytime. It became such a habit with her that she would doze in the middle of the afternoon even when there were guests. Grandmother put up with it because if she were to send Bano away, there would be no one to take care of her and cook for her. I was no longer a potential source of domestic help as Mother had never recovered her full health. So they were stuck with one another in a way. And Bano had never known any other home so I suppose she wasn't missing out on anything.

Yet Bano could do surprisingly kind deeds like bathing Salhou in the evening if she had finished her work. She would tell the child many stories as she dressed him. Salhou grew to be very fond of her. So, these were the two women apart from his mother who nurtured him. We were not able to spend as much time with him as they did. Father did try to tell Grandmother to allow the two of them to come and spend a few nights with us. After much persuasion, Grandmother agreed. We were ecstatic when they came with their little bundle of clothing. I had made up a fine bed for them and Mother had been waiting for them all afternoon. Salhou cried a bit because he had not been with us much. But we brought out some old toys and he soon settled down and played happily with them, crawling around the floor and putting every toy he found in his mouth. He was scared of Father and Leto because the only man he had seen in Grandmother's house was Sizo and that too, very infrequently. He would begin to whimper if they came near him. Father thought up a trick. He carried the little puppy we had, on his lap, and spoke to it and dandled it on its lap so that it yapped happily. Salhou was fascinated by the sight. He slowly crawled over onto his grandfather's lap and let him dandle him. The rest of the evening he was quite happy to play with Bulie and Father. We were all tired out when it was time to sleep. But it had gone well and so we were tired in a happy way.

At our house, everyone called the baby Salhou. He looked confusedly from one to the other the first few times. But soon he grew used to it and responded by turning his head in the direction of whoever called him. Mother picked him up frequently but the little fellow wanted to play on the floor and preferred to crawl around so she let him after she had checked that the door to the outside entrance was shut fast and he could not crawl out onto the road. Nisano looked happy and I believe she felt more relaxed at our house than at Grandmother's because Mother did not expect her to be in constant attendance on the child. In fact, she insisted that Nisano should go out with me to town and go shopping.

"He'll be all right with me" said Mother.

So after she had fed the baby, we went to town and lingered at shops looking at dress materials or shoes. Once or twice she expressed some anxiety at having left her child behind but I managed to calm her by reminding her that Mother had both Bulie and Father to help her if Salhou became too energetic for her. She was eyeing a dark blue flower print longingly.

"Can you make a dress out of it?" I asked her "Or a skirt?"

"Perhaps a skirt" she replied thoughtfully, "if I had two metres, a long skirt that is not too girlish."

"Oh, do get it, Nisa, you are a girl still, you know, you don't have to go around dressed like a matron."

"Oh, but I am a matron," she smiled as she said it.

Nevertheless, we bought two metres of it and went home feeling very pleased.

"Mother, did he cry?" asked Nisano anxiously.

But Mother said he had not even missed his mother. He had played contentedly with his toys and then, fallen asleep on the floor so she had got Father to put him to bed and he was still sleeping when we returned.

"I'm so relieved," said Nisano, "I have never been able to go anywhere without him."

"You should let him get used to us, then we could babysit him whenever you need to go somewhere," suggested Mother.

"Thank you, Mother, that is very kind of you, but Grandmother does not want me to leave him in anybody's care. I suppose it will be better when he grows up. He is already growing so big."

I felt so sorry for Nisano.

"Well, she did allow you two to come to us so maybe we can do that again," said Mother slowly. "I know it does her good to have Vini's son and wife in her care. Of all my children, Vini was her favourite so she has taken his death very hard. Thank you for being patient with an old woman, Nisano."

"We are lucky that she is willing to feed both my child and I," said Nisano in a quiet voice.

Even then, it was very hard to live under the constant surveillance of Grandmother. Here, Nisano had learnt to relax a bit, laughing at Father's jokes and not always so tensely looking after her young son. But, ever so often she would stop laughing, as though remembering herself, and try to be more sombre.

On the morning of the third day, Bano came. We all knew why she had come.

"Mother thinks the two of them should not exhaust your hospitality any longer," she said.

"Oh, Bano, forget that, we are their family, for heaven's sake, does Mother really think that?" asked Father.

That made Bano ease up and she said, "Well, she's been saying that the house is too quiet with the little one away. Last night she kept asking me to come here and bring them back but I begged her to let me go in the morning as I can't see so well in the dark. Actually, it is not a problem but I thought it would do them good to be here for at least another day."

"Go and tell Mother we will bring them tomorrow. She did promise us that they might come for a week and it is not fair that she start sending for them after two days. He is our grandson too and she is our daughter-in-law," said Father with some irritation.

"Please don't let me go back without them, Visa. You know how Mother is, she gets very agitated and then it is not good for her heart when she is so worked up" pleaded Bano.

"All right then," agreed Father, "but next time, they must come for the whole week without anyone coming to fetch them back."

"I'll see to that," said Bano.

It took a long time for the two of them to get ready to go back to Grandmother's because they had to pack all the clothes and toys they had brought. Nisano looked forlorn but Salhou was quite happy to see Bano whom he recognised immediately. I went back with them, carrying their bag for them. We were a sad little procession. The baby made cooing sounds and that was the only sound for a long while. Nisano was sad to go and I was too upset with Grandmother to make polite conversation.

26

Salhou was a year and six months old when his father's first death annivesary came around. He and his mother came to lay flowers on his father's grave. We would make a proper grave for Vini in January, with a gravestone and cement. For now, it was only a mud grave that Mother and I smoothed in turns every week. The wooden cross above it bore his name and date of birth and the day he died. Vini's son was a year and seven months when he was allowed to come to us with his mother for a week. What a change from the sweet eight-month-old we all remembered. Now, he was demanding and dictatorial. If his mother could not give him a toy he wanted, he would lie on the floor and cry and scream his little lungs out.

"Nisa, when did he become so difficult? I did not see him acting like this when I was last at Grandmother's. And that was two months ago" I said.

"Oh, I can't tell you how demanding he has become and I am unable to do anything about it. He has learnt to cry if he is denied anything at all. And he knows that Grandmother will indulge his every wish so he goes to her when he wants anything. She can't bear to hear him cry. She calls out to me, "Nisano, why is Vini crying?" If I say he is asking to eat more candy but he is not supposed to because it is close to his mealtime, she insists that I give it to him. She always says, 'You will not deny him anything, not while I am alive' so I have to give in every time" she finished wearily.

Nisano looked very different. She was worn out and tired. There were tiny wrinkles around her eyes and she had grown bone thin.

"Haven't you been eating, Nisa?" I hissed at her.

"Oh, it's not that, I cannot sleep so well because Vini wants to feed at night and I can't sleep when he is feeding."

"What? How old is he?" I asked incredulously.

"One year and six months now."

I knew very well that our womenfolk usually stopped breast feeding babies by the time they were nine months or a year old.

"That's ridiculous, Nisa, you can't possibly have any nutrition left in you. Stop feeding him now, he's a big boy. He needs to eat more solids."

"I know that, but he cries and cries until I feed him and if he cries, Grandmother wants to know why he is crying and then she insists that I feed him."

At first we indulged the boy too, giving in to him every time he cried. But Bulie soon put a stop to it. "Do you know this is not going to do him any good at all? If we keep giving in to him, we will succeed in creating a monster who grows up thinking the whole world should revolve around him. We have to learn to start saying no when he asks for something he should not have." Bulie was right but it was a tough struggle to get the little boy to obey. He had become so used to being pampered by the adults he had grown up with that he resented it deeply. When Bulie held him as he threw a tantrum he bit down on Bulie's arm. But when Bulie threatened to bite him back, he calmed down a little. Of course Bulie would never do that. Bulie was the gentlest person I knew. When we were children, he allowed me to bully him, not because he was afraid of me, but because he knew he was so much stronger than me and could hurt me if he tried. With Vini's son, he took matters in hand and managed to make the boy understand that he could not always have things his own way at our house.

Miraculously, Salhou was happily following Bulie about the next day and responding correctly whenever Bulie said no. He had tried to pick up a wrench to play with when Bulie saw him and said no. Nisano thought he would cry but he surprised us all by putting it back in its place and smiling up at Bulie as though he had done something very clever. We all cheered him and by the third day he had understood that his good behaviour would be rewarded and his bad behaviour would come in for a ticking off. It was quite amazing to see how he had taken to Bulie. There was a quiet authority in Bulie's voice when he spoke to Salhou. I think Salhou understood it and respected it. The two became inseparable in the next few days. When Bulie left for work, Salhou would cry and want to follow him. He learnt the sound of Bulie's voice and ran to the door if he heard him coming home. Bulie remembered to call out "Salhou" instead of "Mother" when he came home after work. He fashioned a small car for the boy out of some machine parts he had found in the garage where he worked. It was a clever little thing and he must have spent many hours beating the metal into the shape of a neat low-slung racing car. Salhou loved it and played with it all evening. When he went to bed, he kept it by his pillow. He drove it up and down on his side of the bed until he tired of playing. Then he would fall asleep with the car in his little fist.

We were very happy with Salhou's new behaviour. He was basically a good child and seemed happy to be disciplined. I wished they didn't have to go back to Grandmother's. Perhaps the day was coming soon when they could leave and set up a house of their own or go to live with Nisano's mother. Now that it was a year and a month since Vini's death, some tongues had started to wag about how odd it was that Nisano was still with Grandmother. "The young have no respect for our customs" we had heard some elderly women say, "Vini's wife should be preparing to go back to her father's house because it is already a year since her husband died. Certainly it is our custom for the widow to stay on in her in-law's house and tend the husband's grave for the length of a year. But beyond that period, her mother should know that it is shameful to let her stay on and impinge on the hospitality of her in-laws. They are two extra mouths to feed, she and her child. Imagine what would happen if our sons' widows did not return to their parents but stayed on with us. How would we feed them?" But we knew this sort of talk was what malicious people like Aunt Benuo and her sister indulged in. Fortunately, there were others who thought it was wonderful that Nisano and her son were with Grandmother. They were kinder. Father's cousin who often came from the village said,

"*Hou*, how people will talk and be so concerned about other people's affairs when they have not lifted a finger to help them. Don't let it bother you, Nino, our daughter can stay with Mother as long as she wants. It must be her choice, not ours, and certainly not that of the village gossips. What harm is she doing by making an old woman happy in the last years of her life? I have visited Mother and she could only talk of the boy. Of course she can confuse people because she insists on calling him Vinilhoulie. But it is not a bad thing, it is not a bad thing at all. How long will Mother be with us? Another year, or perhaps two? Let her be happy in that short period. Is the girl unhappy there? That is the one question we have forgotten to ask. Is she happy where she is?"

"She does not complain," said Mother.

Easterine Iralu

"There, you have it."

Father's cousin was a large woman who we called Aunt Pfenuo. She was most uncomplicated and could think up the most simple solutions for any problem. I wished more people were as generous as her. Aunt Pfenuo, along with all of Father's and Mother's relatives, called Grandmother, Mother. She visited her at least once in two months bringing with her a laden basket of freshly picked herbs or squash from her field which Grandmother would share with us. She was one person who could not see ill in any situation.

But Nisano was having a hard time. When they were back at Grandmother's, she had gone to fetch water. Aunt Benuo, the nastier of the two gossips, sneered and said, "Nisano, it is a year now since Vini has died. Not waiting for Bulie, are you?"

Nisano was shocked by her insinuation and stammered as she spoke, "Aunt, I am here because Grandmother feels comforted by Vini's son. There is no other thing on my mind."

She was close to tears as she said it. So the older woman's tone changed and she began to speak in a confidential tone,

"Oh don't mind me, girl, but I am your relative on your father's side, even if a little distant, so I will tell you one thing. If a widow stays too long with her in-laws after the normal period of waiting, she makes tongues wag. When there is a younger brother around, people talk even more. If I were you, I would talk to my mother about returning home soon."

"It is not up to me, Aunt. If we went away, Grandmother will be very sad. I suppose you know that Vini was her favourite grandson and so she has taken his death so hard. We are all trying to help her to heal from this loss. That is why I stay on here. There is really no other reason," said Nisano.

She had never spoken so many words to the older woman before. If they met, Aunt Benuo usually teased her and she would smile it off in a respectful way. No one dared get on Aunt Benuo's bad side. She could make anyone who crossed her regret that they had ever tried it.

In a week's time, a rumour was being spread that Nisano was very unhappy staying at Grandmother's. I felt uneasy about it and though I did not want to make her sad, I felt I had to know how she truly felt. So I went to Grandmother's house in the evening with some of the toys that Salhou had left behind.

When we had a moment to ourselves, I quickly whispered, "Listen, are you really content to be here?"

She looked straight at me and asked, "Why? Have you heard anything?"

I hesitated to tell her about the rumour but we had also grown close over the past two years so I repeated what I had heard. I added that I was concerned about her happiness. She thought for a while and then said,

"Lieno, I do long for my mother and sisters. But now that I am a widow I know that things will not be the same when I go back. At the same time, I am grateful that even if Vini is no longer here, your family has continued to care for me and for my child. As for Grandmother, I have learnt to love her in spite of her harsh ways. I can see how much she loved Vini. She is trying to love him beyond the grave by loving his son. I cannot deny her that. In any case, I don't feel like a stranger here in your family. Isn't that strange? I feel that you are my family and that I have a right to be here so long as I am welcome. I do think of looking for a job when my son is old enough to go to school. But for the time being, I am content to be looking after him. He is my reason for living."

It came as a big relief to me to hear what Nisano was saying. She had suffered a lot during her marriage to Vini. It wouldn't be fair if

Easterine Iralu

she was being made to suffer by being forced to stay at Grandmother's. I was also amazed at how mature her attitude had become.

"I have heard all the gossip about me but I have chosen to ignore it and live here for as long as Grandmother wants us."

It still didn't feel right to me that a young woman should be cooped up with a woman as dominating as Grandmother. But I had to admire Nisano's loyalty to Grandmother. I had myself never learnt to feel anything of the sort and always wondered how Father and his siblings could be so devoted to her. They tried to fulfil her every wish. They quoted her constantly and it irked me that they would expect their spouses to be awed by her wisdom and her philosophy of life and try to abide by it. Old age had not taken the hard edges off her. She had instead become more domineering than ever, taking even greater advantage of her advanced age. Of course, this was my opinion and I kept it to myself because I could never get Father or Mother to agree with me. They would always maintain that I would feel differently when I grew older. But I was twenty-one now and not in any danger of having a drastic change of opinion. Aunt Bino once said that I was unfeminine and it was the result of having grown up with so many brothers.

"Only daughters can become very manly in behaviour and outlook. It is a pity that staying with Mother has not had much impact upon Lieno. She can still be as hot-headed as ever."

I resented that. I didn't think I was hot-headed but I did have strong opinions and had expressed them in the past. Now, I was learning to keep my opinions to myself.

One afternoon, Mother said, "You mustn't be so harsh on your Grandmother. I know you were unhappy in her house but she was trying to teach you to become a good woman. Men don't like women who are aggressive and outspoken. They like their wives to be good workers. You are a good worker, Lieno, but you must try to be more docile."

"That is not fair, Mother, you don't know how I was treated at Grandmother's house. I never told you that I was not allowed to bathe with warm water in winter. That Bano bathed me in icy cold water following Grandmother's instructions. And I was only five and a half."

Mother's face fell. She looked shocked but had nothing to say.

"Oh my child," she said finally.

"That is not all, Mother, I would have to stand in the dark counting her chickens and if I counted them wrong she would make me go out in the dark again. I was so terrified. There are so many other things that I will not tell you. You say that Grandmother loved me but I know that she held it against me that I was a girl and not a boy. I used to feel I was being punished for being born a girl. For many years, I hated it so much, I wished that I was not a girl."

Everything was coming out in a rush. In between sobs I poured out all the terrible things I had felt. I had my head on Mother's lap.

"Hush, my child, hush, it will be all right. You must forgive and forget. I am sorry I never knew it was so hard for you. But now, calm down and listen to me. I will tell you things that may help you to understand Grandmother better."

Her soft hands smoothed down my hair and I felt better so I stopped crying and prepared to listen.

"Your grandmother was the eldest of three children. She grew up in the village and moved to the town only when she married. When she was young she lived through a very hard time. In the village, widows without sons lost all their husband's property to other male relatives. So she understood that it was very important for a married woman to produce as many male offspring as she could. Her mother did not have brothers and they lost all their lands and fields when her

   Easterine Iralu

father died. I think she said that her grandfather had given them a small field to cultivate as long as he was alive. But people were unkind and mocked those who could not produce male children. The understanding was that a woman without a male heir would be sheltered by her in-laws but her daughters could not inherit the father's property. Their best bet would be to marry a man rich enough to have property of his own. Then they would devote the rest of their lives to trying to produce a male heir. Grandmother saw her own mother suffer hardship and poverty and exclusion from many aspects of social life because she had no brothers. It hardened her and made her determined not to suffer as her mother had. I think your grandmother looks at her sons and grandsons as a kind of insurance and she is inclined to take a very conservative attitude toward your brothers by pampering them as she saw other boys being pampered in her childhood. You know that our people say we should love our sons because they are the ones who look after us in our old age. That may be true but for your father and I, it is you, our daughter, who has brought us the greatest comfort. We love all of you equally. You must always know that.

"Try and understand why Grandmother feels that she has to be more generous to your brothers, why she was so loving to Vini. But sometimes one can love wrongly by loving too much. Try to see her as a weak, old woman who has lost her husband and therefore, she has to make sure one or more of her grandsons and sons will look after her. She tries to secure their loyalty by giving them food and money and the field as happened to Vini. But she did not have the foresight to see that she was doing more harm than good to Vini by plying him with money. That was a tragic mistake. We cannot buy love. We can only hope that when we have loved our children well, they will, in turn, grow up to love us. Please do not hate her, you are wise enough to understand that she is the way she is because she did not want to suffer as her mother's mother did. It is not possible to change her. But you are young and you can change your feelings towards her. You could start by learning to forgive her."

Mother's words made me cry. I didn't know she understood so well all the bitterness I had felt for Grandmother all these years. She made me want to forgive and that was something I had never felt before. How do you forgive someone who has borne a grudge against you for being born a girl? Yet if I didn't forgive, I would probably end up as embittered as her. I certainly did not want that.

"Was she angry with you for giving birth to a girl?" I had to ask.

"No, of course not, that would be sinful. But she was not as interested in you as she was in your brothers when they were newly born. I guess she had grown up to believe that girls were weak and not as good as boys. We were all told that as children. But I know differently now. I am amazed at your strength sometimes, Lieno. The way you took over the household when Pete died. You were just eleven and a half and yet you took over my role in our family so naturally. I can see that women are not weak. They just have a strength different from men. Unfortunately, Grandmother will never see that. She will always think women have to be dependent on men. That was the way it was when she was young. It is difficult to unlearn things learnt in childhood. In her mother's day, men were still going to war, leaving women to do all the field work. No one expected a man to help with field work. He would help in times of peace but otherwise he had the much more important role of defending the village."

"But we have specific works that are men's work" I protested.

"In the old days, women were expected to do those works as well," said Mother, "in fact, they pushed their men to go to war.

That was what they saw their mothers doing that and they grew up to do the same."

"But why, Mother?"

"Because they would be safe if their men were good warriors. Others would think twice about attacking their village if their men could earn the reputation of being good warriors. Strange though it may sound, they did this to protect their children. If their men were good in war, their village became feared and their children, would be safe from being invaded and taken captive. I know women do the strangest of things but you are a woman too and will understand these things by and by."

27

After talking to Mother, I understood the deep sense of insecurity that led Grandmother to hold the worldview she did. I think I mellowed somewhat towards her. My fear of her changed to pity. Indeed, Grandmother was to be pitied. Imagine living all of one's life trying to buy love. That was what she had been doing with Vini all along and Vini had been too foolish not to see it. I was looking at Grandmother in a different light and it also helped me see myself in a better light. I felt a new sense of worth. I was not unfortunate to have been born a girl. Mother and Father were grateful for the things I was able to do at home. My brothers would not have been able to do what I did, the cooking and washing and cleaning. Bulie often said, "I'd rather work overtime at the garage than have to cook and scrub as you do, Lieno." But I actually enjoyed it and it was my contribution to the family so I was proud of my domestic skills. I resolved to be kind to Grandmother from now on. I am sure she knew that I did not always mean the polite words I used with her. She was shrewd enough to know when one was insincere. Now, I would say nice things and mean them too. But we were all in for a rude shock when Bano came suddenly to our house the next morning.

"It's Mother, she slumped over after her morning tea and we have not been able to rouse her," she said between panting and sobbing.

Father quickly rose to his feet, "Is anyone there with her?"

"Nisano and the boy."

"Any others?"

"No, I came running immediately, I thinks she's almost gone. We have laid her on the bed, Nisano and I, and she was faintly breathing then, but she did not respond to my calls."

Father, Bulie and I ran all the way to Grandmother's. We requested one of the neighbours to tell Leto and Vimenuo that Grandmother was very sick. Mother and Bano were to come slowly.

The only sound coming from the house was Salhou's whimpering. We ran inside the open door and found Nisano by Grandmother's bed, wiping the saliva running down the side of her mouth with a little cloth.

"How is she?" I whispered.

"Barely alive but she is responding a little more now."

"Grandmother," I whispered.

"Mother, Mother," Father called in a louder voice.

She did not open her eyes but she moved her hand very slightly. I took the cloth from Nisano and bade her tend to her child.

"Grandmother," I said in a louder voice.

She did not open her eyes but she moved the hand that I held. I looked up at Father enquiringly.

"Is Bano back?" He asked impatiently.

Then he remembered that Bulie was there.

"Go phone your uncles," he said to Bulie.

Bulie ran out and went to borrow the neighbour's phone. In a few more minutes, Mother and Bano were there too. I stayed where I was, dabbing the saliva running out of her mouth time and again. She never once opened her eyes. I sat on a low wooden stool and tried to massage her hands. They were icy cold. The rest of her was just as cold.

"Can you make a hot water bottle," I asked Mother and she went out of the room.

In moments she was back with the water bottle. But Grandmother refused to get warm. It was as though she was dying on us. I rubbed and rubbed her hands and feet. It felt rather hopeless because when she got warmer in her hands and I started to rub her feet, her hands would get cold again in seconds. We got a second water bottle and kept it on top of her feet.

The first hot water bottle was kept on her stomach so that she could lay her hands on top of it.

"Will you drink something?" I asked. "Squeeze my hand if you want some warm milk."

But she stayed very still. So we did not give her anything to eat or drink.

"What did she have this morning?" I asked Bano.

"She's had two cups of tea, one as soon as she woke at four, and the other one just before she fainted. She ate a biscuit with it."

Very soon, my uncles were there too and they conferred on whether she should be taken to hospital or a doctor should be brought home. In the end they agreed that it was less trouble to bring a doctor home than try to carry Grandmother to the hospital. She had grown so large that she would be too heavy for the standard stretchers that the hospital used. Bano and Nisano had dragged her to bed that morning. Soon, the doctor was there, a dapper young man with a moustache and nervous hands. He sweated a lot and kept wiping his hands on a kerchief he carried.

"It's a stroke," he said, "it's not unusual at her age. She is quite paralysed on her left side. I can see that she is having difficulty speaking and opening her eyes. She should recover a little in a few days. But if you are thinking of home care, you will need a professional nurse who can administer a drip at regular hours. Because of her advanced age, I should warn you to be prepared for a change in her condition for the worse. Here's my telephone number in case you need to contact me urgently. But I shall be coming to check on her again in the late afternoon. I would still recommend that you bring her in to the hospital but it is entirely your decision."

Before he left, he had hooked up Grandmother to an intravenous injection and her left hand was strapped down to the bed so that the liquid could flow uninterrupted into her. The nurse who had assisted the doctor would stay until we decided whether we were going to take Grandmother to the hospital or get a fulltime nurse. Father and my uncles thought that it was best not to move her until her condition was more stable. I stayed by her side constantly. Vimenuo insisted that she take turns with me when I had sat for at least three hours. Her daughter was with her mother and sisters. Grandmother looked like a felled tree. She was really a very large woman. Her stomach swelled beneath the blanket and she looked as though she were sleeping. But her breathing was very faint. It was in complete contrast with her size. Grandmother was a snorer. She had not snored once since morning. So I realised she was probably not asleep although she had her eyes closed. Vimenuo's hand on her pulse showed a steady rhythm. "Grandmother" I called close to her ear. She did not stir at all.

Nisano led me away to the kitchen where Bano served me chicken broth which I ate rapidly. I didn't know I was that hungry. Salhou sat quietly in a corner eating his food and playing with a toy car simultaneously.

"Nisano's mother is coming to take him for a few days" said Bano when she noticed the direction I was looking at.

"That's very kind of her," I said.

Everything had happened so suddenly I still felt a little dazed.

"Has she been ill before?" I asked Bano.

"No, just the usual complaints. This morning, she said she couldn't taste her food. Just before she fell over, she said that her biscuit and tea tasted like nothing at all."

"Did she?" I asked wonderingly.

It meant that she had lost the sense of taste and the stroke must have come upon her gradually. It felt odd to see Grandmother's chair empty. The whole house was very quiet. People spoke in whispers to one another. Even in the long corridor. I guess it hit me then, that Grandmother would not recover from the stroke. It would be cruel to take her to hospital only to have her die in some cold hospital bed where she would feel alien and unable to tell us she longed to die at home.

Grandmother didn't die immediately. She lingered for two days, breathing in great gasping breaths and making all of us gather round her bed, thinking she would surely go now. But her breathing would ease and she would sleep on. We were exhausted by the waiting. No one was pretending anymore that she would recover. We saw death on her face every minute. The coldness in her body was incredible. We directed all our efforts to keeping her warm. In the end, we were using five hot water bottles to warm different parts of her body. Every hour, someone would rush to the kitchen to change the water. Bano kept the fire steadily burning under the big water kettle. I wished I could be with Grandmother alone so I could tell her that I had forgiven her. But there were always people around. Nisano and Vimenuo in turns, Aunt Bino or Sini and Leno. Once, when Mother and I were alone with her, I began to say,

"Grandmother, it's me, Lieno, I want to say that it is okay, I forgive you for being harsh with me."

As soon as I had uttered the words, her immobile face seemed to be cracking up.

Easterine Iralu

"Stop," hissed Mother, "don't you see she is crying?"

And indeed she was crying silently. A tear rolled down her useless cheek. I wiped it away. Mother forbade me to speak again so I sat silently holding her hand and trying to squeeze it but there was no responding squeeze. I was not surprised. Grandmother could be amazingly emotionless at times. The only time I had seen her agitated was when she had to be tranquilized at Vini's funeral. Before that she had never displayed grief openly.

Outside her bedroom, the sun was setting. The intravenous injection dripped steadily. The nurse sat in a corner of the room. She would sometimes doze on the same chair in the evening. If we tried to get her to rest on a spare bed, she would refuse saying that Grandmother might suddenly need her. There was a lot of cooking to be done for all the extra people who were there to care for Grandmother. Furthermore, news had gotten out that Grandmother was near death so her relatives and clansmen had gathered and were keeping vigil in the night. Sizo and his wife arrived on the second day. As before, his wife immediately made herself useful in the kitchen. She had kettles of tea ready for the visitors and for the family members. Then she helped Bano to cook big pots of rice and meat for every meal. When we had all prepared ourselves for at least another week of caring for Grandmother, she suddenly stopped breathing. Just as suddenly as she had had her stroke. Mother and I were sitting by her. I did not notice anything. But Mother looked at her face closely and let out a little cry,

"Oh Mother, so soon?"

Then she was no longer whispering but crying out loud and calling Grandmother in the way we mourned the dead.

"Mother, Mother, it is too soon, Mother, we are not tired of taking care of you, did you think we were tired? We have not done enough yet, Mother."

I saw that Grandmother had indeed stopped breathing and her head lay in an awkward position, a little inclined to the right and hanging with difficulty over the edge. The nurse and I quickly put it right and we took off her bedclothes so that she might be bathed for the last time. Aunt Bino had gone home earlier so it was up to the nurse and I to do the job. She went to the door and said to the men outside,

"She is gone. Allow me to bathe her. It won't take time. Can you fetch me some warm water?"

Bano burst into the room with a basin of water, a washcloth and soap.

"Mother, Mother" she sobbed loudly, "how can you leave me alone? What shall I do now?"

I saw that she would be of no help so I took the basin and wash things from her and sent her out of the room with Mother. The nurse was very efficient. She rubbed Grandmother with the wash cloth very carefully in all the cracks and wrinkles of her skin until it was shining a bit from the rubbing. Then she dried her gently as one would a baby. And then, she took the fresh change of clothes I was ready with and clothed her without any effort. The new clothes let out a strong whiff of naphthalene balls. They must have been taken out from her tin trunk recently and readied for this day. While we were washing her, the others had been busy laying out a bed in the sitting room. "Tell the others she is ready now," said the nurse, so I went out and told Father the bathing was over. "Bulie, go with Leto and carry your Grandmother out." I was surprised that Father did not do it himself but when I looked up at him, he had tears in his eyes. Bulie, Leto and Vimenuo and the nurse together carried Grandmother to the sitting room.

As they carried her in, her relatives and clansmen began to cry loudly so that the house resounded with the mourning sounds of a funeral house.

"Mother, Mother, are you ready now? Oh, Mother, you have readied yourself to go? But we don't want you to leave now. Mother what shall we do without you? Who shall we call Mother?" they wept aloud.

Some of them simply cried, "Mother, Mother" loudly and beat on the floor with their body-cloths and some of the women stamped the floor a bit. The sound of weeping was deafening. I felt tears, hot and threatening to overwhelm me. I felt so sorry for all the people who were crying and strangely sorry too that she had finally gone. Bano crying like a madwoman, tearing her hair and needing to be restrained, Nisano quietly crying and Mother stroking Grandmother's cheek and calling her again and again. I didn't feel terrible grief over Grandmother's death but I felt very sad that the others were so sorrowful. I couldn't cry if I thought of her. But the sight of other people weeping prompted me to cry too.

Then the Pastor made his way into the room. He spoke in an authoritative voice and all the mourners quietened down.

"Dear ones, today our mother has gone to the place of eternal life. We are all grieved but let us remember we do not grieve in vain. She is in a better place. Her suffering here is over. Let us quell our grief and best prepare ourselves in a dignified manner to take leave of her. There are many details that we all need to take care of. Our mother is not our mother alone. She is known to many other people so we expect that many will come to pay their last respects to her."

At this Bano began to wail aloud again so Nisano led her outside the room. The Pastor continued when the sound of her crying had retreated somewhat.

"Let us remember we are her representatives today. We must not forget to thank those who have helped her in her sickness, those who have spent nights here keeping the family company and those who have prayed for the family, brought food and taken care of all the myriad details that a funeral involves. We all want our mother to have a good funeral and so we will pray for God's guidance to enable things to proceed smoothly. I need your prayers so that I may be able to share about the great blessing her life had been to all who knew her. Our heavenly Father, we beseech your help in this hour of our grief. Our Father, you know how sad we are all feeling over the loss of our mother. Let your spirit comfort all of us. Dear Father, we thank you for the life of our mother and all the years in which she has been a blessing to all of us. We thank you that in your great wisdom and mercy you have put an end to her earthly suffering and allowed her to go home to you and be with our father who preceded her. Help us to look after all the details well, to thank all who should be thanked and to share her blessings with all who come to us today as well as in the coming days. Amen."

When the prayer was over, things settled down a bit. The weeping began again but it was now subdued and though Bano ran into the room again to join, she grew tired after some time and sat by Grandmother's bed on a woven seat made of cane. Now and then she called out "Mother" and laid her head on Grandmother's pillow. Then women came in with new body cloths to place over the body so she had to pull her seat out of the way. The pungent smell of chrysanthemums filled the room. It was October and someone had brought a bouquet of white chrysanthemums. It was a sickeningly sweet smell and I was glad to leave the room to prepare Grandmother's other belongings which would be buried with her. Nisano and I sorted out body cloths that she had expressly stated should be placed in her coffin. One was really old because it had been her mother's. There were grey lines between the white portions because the cloth was so old.

"Look," I said to Nisano as I tore at a corner of the cloth and it came away easily.

"Don't!" she hissed, "someone might see you."

 284   Easterine Iralu

We got the other cloths together and piled them up ready to be taken out when it was time for the burial.

"Bano will have to check the collection," said Nisano. I agreed because we knew she would be very upset if any one article had been forgotten.

"Later," I suggested to Nisano, because Bano was in no frame of mind to see to these things at the moment. I was surprised she was so distraught. But I realised that Bano had always regarded Grandmother as her real mother, never having known her own biological mother. She had stayed on not only because of her circumstances but because this was home to her no matter how brusque Grandmother could be some times. We could hear a group of women singing hymns in the room. After every hymn, Bano would weep aloud but subside when the women resumed their singing again. Finally the women left and Bano gave free rein to her grief. She howled aloud. I discerned other voices weeping along with her. After at least a half hour of that, another group came in and began to sing. This time, they sang for about two hours and a half. The hymn singing by different groups was done so that the family would not exhaust itself from weeping. If the hymn singers were not there, the family members would weep constantly and many would fall sick before the dead could be buried. So, many churches were paying more attention to the importance of funeral singers. This seemed to be the right time to get hold of Bano.

"Can you check to see that we have all the right items?" I asked her in a matter-of-fact voice.

She came quietly, happy to be of service in the funeral. She checked the items meticulously.

"Where is the red waist belt?"

I didn't know what she was talking about so she dived into the trunk and rummaged through the clothes there. The sight of

Grandmother's belongings upset her again and she was crying again.

"Ah, Mother, these are the work of your hands," she wept.

I felt it would be inappropriate to remind her of the task at hand so I let her be.

"See, see" she said holding up an old faded orange body-cloth, "She wove that one for Father. I was four when she was weaving it and it was a beautiful bright orange then, Oh Mother, how your cloths have faded too."

Then she recollected herself and searched for the red belt, finding it in a corner of the trunk, hidden by a cloth we had lifted over it. Now the collection was complete so we set it aside. I persuaded Bano to remain in Grandmother's bedroom while I fetched her some food. She did not refuse so I came back to the room with a plate of warm food. Poor Bano! She was looking totally lost and not at all like her capable self. She allowed Sizo's wife to take over the kitchen completely. I massaged her legs a bit and spoke gently to her,

"It will be all right, Bano, she knows how much you loved her. That is the important thing."

"But, but" she cried again, "I didn't get to speak to her at all. Not one word before she died."

That renewed her weeping. I asked if she had tried to hold her hand.

"Yes, many times," she replied.

"Didn't she squeeze back?" I asked.

"Yes, every time," she answered again.

"That was her way of speaking, don't you see, Bano, she could not speak but she certainly could hear us."

She drew a lot of comfort from that fact and quietened down.

"Poor Mother," she said eventually.

"No, Bano, she had a full life, don't you think? She is at peace

Easterine Iralu

now. We should stop feeling sorry for her. We are crying because we feel sorry for ourselves."

All day, Bano alternated between paroxysms of grief and periods of calm. We worried for her. She repeatedly said that she was alone in the world now. "You are not alone, Bano, we are all here still. Besides, Nisano and the baby are with you too. We will make sure that you are never alone," I soothed her. Mother came and stayed by her constantly. My aunts helped with the other preparations such as the lining of the cofffin with black satin cloth. One of us continued to see that Bano was well nourished. We plied her with mugs of soup and tea because she refused to eat any more food. The doctor had been in to see to her and he said she was too stressed and so, her blood pressure had shot up and we would need to keep her calm until the funeral otherwise she would have to be hospitalised. That gave her a bit of a shock because Bano thought that people who went to hospital never returned alive. She quietened down and tried to be less dramatic.

Neikuo surprised everyone by taking her sister's death very well.

"Ah, Vibaü, you are the eldest, it is right that you should go first. I will soon come to you. I will try to be a good grandmother to your grandchildren but no one can fill your place. Be happy in your new home. Ah, ah, there, I am crying again. But we have only this day to see your face, that is why we forget ourselves and shed tears."

Neikuo mourned her sister in the peculiar chanting that the elders used to mourn the dead by chanting their praises and telling of their own loss. Then she went to sit by the door and greet people who came to attend the funeral.

"Thank you for coming to be with us" she said to every one who stepped up to greet her.

When we served her food, she ate it without any fuss and then she went back to her place by the entrance. She would alternately greet people and stand by Grandmother's bed. There were many elderly guests. This was one of the reasons why the funeral was held early in the afternoon instead of in the evening as was usual when an elderly member of the community died.

"It will be a long service" said Father, "so those who come late can still mourn her."

The service was not conducted by the new young Pastor. Instead, we got the former Pastor to come. He had retired some years ago. He was seventy-four but he too addressed Grandmother as "Mother." He spoke of her long Christian life, how she was baptised at the age of fifteen and how she had been a member of the church throughout her life since then.

There were two more speakers, old men who had known her and her husband and they spoke of Grandfather's long and faithful years of service to the government. The speeches were long-winded and by the time the service was over, it was four in the evening. It was a good thing we had started early. The Pastor said, "Now, we will put our mother to rest because it is not fitting that her grave should be covered up in the darkness of advancing night. So let us join in a hymn while we lower the coffin into its final resting place."

It was an abrupt end to the long funeral service but it was necessary because many of the elderly grew maudlin and wanted to say something too. After the burial was completed, the mourners began to leave. But some of Grandmother's clansmen remained with us. They cleared the chairs and took down the tarpaulin covering in the courtyard. When they had finished we bade them eat the evening meal with us. They were reluctant but we insisted that they eat too. At the meal, one of them said that Grandmother had given him a body cloth when he was baptised. "I still have it. It's quite faded now but it was what she had herself woven for me so I did not want to throw it out." They all spoke lovingly of her and declared that the clan had lost a great mother.

 288   Easterine Iralu

"At that age, a person has seen three generations and has accumulated so many stories. It is a great loss to all of us."

The man who was speaking was a thin, tall man. He was related to Grandfather, a nephew of his first cousin, and infrequently visited us to find out how Mother was. I remembered him coming to enquire after Grandmother when I was living at her house. He had had thick black hair then. Now he was completely grey and looked older than Sizo though they were about the same age. The men left after the meal. We thanked them for their help and declined their offer to sleep on benches to keep us company that night. Bulie and I would stay with Bano and Nisano for some days till things were sorted out. There was the major job of going through her things and deciding what to give away to whom. Aunt Bino would supervise but Bano and I would have to help her distribute them.

28

Three days later, Grandmother came back to us. It sounds funny when I put it that way. What I mean is that she showed herself to us three days later. I was the first person she showed herself to. I was surprised because I thought it would be Bano. I was walking into the kitchen in the afternoon after having cleared a trunk in her room. When I was at the entrance I saw her sitting in her chair as before. I did not think anything was odd about that because my mind was distracted by the work I had been doing. It took a few seconds for me to register that she should not be there at all. In those few seconds, I saw that her face was turned from me so that I saw her only in profile. I think I stood there for many minutes trying to grasp that I had actually seen her. By then, she had completely disappeared from my view. I went over to the chair and touched it thinking I might find a hollow where she had sat or feel some warmth. The chair was cold to my touch and I thought again that my eyes might have deceived me. But I knew that I had really seen her. It was incredible that I did not feel any fear. All around the dark kitchen, I felt her presence. I sat for a long time in the semi darkness taking it all in, before I told the others about it.

"Grandmother was in the kitchen when I went inside" I said to Nisano and Bano.

"No!" they both said in unison.

"Yes," I said quietly trying not to alarm them, "it was only for a very short while."

They wanted to know all the details so I told them what I had seen. It is not unusual among our people to sight the dead a few days after they died. We say it is their way of bidding a last farewell to their loved ones. After Grandfather died, Grandmother had seen him working in the garden a few days after his funeral. When she called out to him, he looked up and smiled and then turned and walked away. She swore that the hoe he had been using was still warm to her touch. I wished I had not been the first one to see Grandmother. I thought that Bano would be hurt by it. But she surprised me by being quite happy about it.

She said, "I am glad you were the first. I know that I will soon see her but if I were the first, I would be so frightened, I would probably have a heart attack!"

"You know, it is usually quite peaceful. Others who have seen their loved ones always say that it gives them peace," I said.

I didn't want her to be upset if she saw anything. The sighting put all of us in a mood of heightened excitement and we couldn't talk about anything else the whole day. That afternoon, Bulie had returned home. In the night, it was only the four of us, Nisano and Salhou, Bano and I. Sizo was supposed to return in the evening but he sent word that he was sick and would come after two days. We ate our evening meal together. But we were all awed by what I had seen earlier. So we instinctively drew closer to each other as darkness drew nearer.

Nisano asked, "Will you come to the bedroom with me as I have to get another pair of pajamas for Salhou? He has wet this one."

I got up and followed her but Bano ran after us saying, "Don't you leave me alone."

We all laughed at that.

"Are you scared?" asked Nisano,

"Of course I am, silly," Bano burst out, "it will be my turn now, don't you see?"

We joined our beds in Grandmother's room and slept together. But no one could fall asleep for a long time. I heard Nisano sigh deeply when I thought she was asleep. Bano kept tossing and turning.

"You two want some tea?" I spoke out loud.

"Who's going to the kitchen now?" snapped Bano, "not me."

"Oh, I'll go if you want tea" I said, "It's better than lying here sleepless, isn't it?"

The clock on the wall showed a quarter to twelve. I got up and went to the kitchen. I felt the hair on my neck rise but I controlled myself and switched on the light and got the fire going. The water in the kettle was still warm so it boiled in no time and I had the tea ready. Soon, they were both sitting up in bed with their tea mugs whispering to each other. Something fell from the shelf to the floor in the kitchen. "Shh!" one of us said and we all froze. Then we all heard it; the heavy footsteps on the floor shuffling toward the corridor and coming closer and closer to us. There was a small step as the corridor began and Grandmother would always make a sound like, "heish" when she lifted herself over the step to get to her room from the kitchen. I knew it so well because I had used it so often to calculate the time it took her from the kitchen to reach our bedroom. I would jump from my bed to the floor and be out of the room in a flash when I heard the "heish" and I would pretend to be working so that she would not scold me. It used to take about twenty steps for her to get to the front door from the step on a good day. Tonight I found myself counting automatically when we heard the footsteps.

Easterine Iralu

I didn't know what we would do but if we heard the "heish" we would be sure it was Grandmother and not Sizo suddenly come home on a late bus. On the eighteenth footstep we all heard it, a loud exhalation of air and Grandmother's "heish" before we heard her footsteps turn, not toward the bedroom but toward the front entrance of the house. We were frozen where we were. None of us could move even if we tried to. And we could hear every sound as though it were magnified. She lifted the bolt from the door so that it made its usual clanking sound and then she opened the door and walked out. There was silence after that.

It took a good ten minutes for us to regain our senses.

"Who's going to close the door now?" asked one of us.

"We'll worry about that later," I said as I tried to take control of the situation.

Bano was grey-faced. If Grandmother had shown herself to her, she would have died of fright.

"It's only Grandmother, why are we so scared? We know that the dead return like this. Didn't Grandmother tell us that she saw Grandfather in the garden after he died?" I said, trying to be very casual about the whole event.

But neither of them smiled. After some time, Nisano looked over to her son to check that he was still sleeping.

"Come on," I tried again, "it was no ghost, it was Grandmother coming to tell us she is all right where she is now. I'm going out to close the door."

I swung off the bed abruptly as I said this. I was secretly hoping they would both follow me out. But neither of them moved as I went to the door. I didn't dare go out into the dark corridor alone.

"Well, come on now, aren't you coming with me?" I finally asked and they both came, laughing a bit because they had seen through my bluff. It helped to laugh at ourselves. It eased the terrible tension of the whole evening. Strangely, the door was locked and the bolt in its own place when we went to check. We ran back to the bedroom.

"Goodness, if the neighbours could hear us, what would they think?" exclaimed Bano.

I was glad to hear that. I took it as a sign she was beginning to start living again. When we woke in the morning, we had to laugh at ourselves all over. We had been clinging to each other tightly in the night and we were a tangle of limbs and Salhou pointed at us and laughed delightedly.

After that, Grandmother did not return to the house. I was the only one who saw her. It continued to confound me but Mother had her own explanation for it:

"She was showing you that in her own way she loved you and though she had been harsh with you, she wanted you to know that it was for your own good. We say that spirits show themselves to stronger people, never to the weak-hearted, so you should be proud and happy that Grandmother chose to show herself to you."

"But it doesn't mean that her spirit is not at rest, does it, Mother? What about the spirits of all the white soldiers from the war that we keep seeing around here? Don't people say they are unquiet spirits? What about them, Mother?" I asked.

"These are things we only speculate about. We cannot ever say for sure that they are this or that. I know that our people say that the spirits of the white soldiers return because many of them were very young and did not want to die. Many of them had not married. We say that they felt such remorse at dying so early that they keep returning to the place they were last alive on earth. But we also say that our loved ones return not as unquiet spirits but to say farewell in a manner that we would instantly recognize. It is in familiar noises that we associate with them. It is unusual to sight them as your grandmother did with your grandfather but it has been known to happen sometimes. If the living ones are very grieved over their going, the dead show themselves to them to comfort them and assure them that they are happy where they are. In our ignorance, we assume that they might still be suffering some earthly pain in the afterworld, especially if they died of some painful disease. So we are granted the grace to see these things. I don't think we should be alarmed by it. Rather, we should accept it as privileges that are granted to certain special people"

Mother's face was serious yet gentle as she explained these things. I always felt comforted to talk to Mother about things that confused me.

"But, Mother," I had to ask, "you never saw Petekhrietuo though you were so grieved over him."

She smiled slightly at that and said softly, "Actually I did."

"No! Mother, you never told me!"

"Yes," she said absently, "but you were too young then and I didn't want to frighten you or your brothers. You know that non-Christians spit on the graves of those who return and they even take out the fences around the graves to prevent the spirits returning. So, I had to be very careful that no one who could misinterpret it would hear of it."

"Won't you tell me how it was?" I begged.

"Hmm, let me think again. It was so long ago. I was out at the grave very early in the morning before any of you were up. The doctor wanted me to stay in bed but I struggled to walk slowly to his grave and I was standing there talking to my boy. I imagined him being crushed by the earth on top of his coffin and that hurt me. I tried to pray and I was asking God to please let him be all right wherever he was. As I stood there, weeping, I felt a slight breeze and a voice calling "Mother" very softly, so softly I could just barely hear it. I thought it was the wind but it called again. I wiped my tears and turned in the direction of the wind when I saw him,

Petekhrietuo, standing in front of me, smiling at me and holding out his hands to me. But I could not move. I was paralysed by the sight, I suppose. I could see and hear perfectly well but I could not move at all. He was at a little distance from me and at his feet were many flowers. I shall always be amazed at that, my boy surrounded by so many flowers, just a mere few feet from me. 'Mother, He is looking after me, I am not there in the grave there, I am in another place where He is.' I saw that he was holding the hand of a man who stood by him, a tall man with a very kind face who kept looking at me with a smile.

"I am not sure how long I stood there but when I felt the blood returning to my veins, they both slowly faded away. I came back to the house and I told your father about it many days later. But he thought I had imagined it because I was so sick then. I did tell Neikuo about it and she believed me but she thought I should keep it to myself because people were so superstitious then, even more so than now, and she feared that unpleasant rumours would spread about Pete's spirit being seen. And now, you are the third person I am telling it to. I wouldn't have told you if you hadn't seen your grandmother yourself. You know that you really saw her and that the three of you heard her in the house. That is wonderful, at least I think so. But don't tell others about it. There is such fear of spirits among our people and we don't want anyone to spread a rumour that your grandmother has returned and is haunting her relatives. You know well enough that there are vicious people who would quickly spread a story like that and make every one fearful to pass her grave or her house. We want people to remember her as the good person she was, not as a fearsome ghost."

What Mother was saying made a lot of sense to me. I remembered the time after Vimenuo's father's death when our neighbours had been too scared to venture out after dark. People who saw a dead leaf stirring in the wind would jump and think it was Zekuo's spirit. I think it took at least six months for the rumours to settle down and allow life to come back to normal. Still, it was the kind of cruel thing that made people talk about details of his life, his alcoholism and his father's drinking habits as a young man. They remembered that his mother used to see spirits as a young girl. When she died her spirit haunted her grave for a long time so that people who passed it had their body cloths pulled from them and people coming home late from the fields felt something lifting their baskets as they came close to her grave. The older folk simply said, "Hou, Neilhounuo, you are as kind as ever, my poor back was bent over by my heavy load." The spirit would carry the basket till the turning on the road and at that point, the basket carrier would suddenly feel the load again. They would say, "Ah, she is just playing with us, she liked a good joke in her lifetime, that one." But the younger people would be very scared, especially young girls and they would spit on her grave and throw bitter wormwood on it, shouting, "You are dead, don't return." That angered her a lot and she would give chase to them and pull their hair and their clothes, so that they raced home like maniacs, out of breath and crying and frightened out of their wits.

This was very damaging for Vimenuo's family. When her younger sisters came of a marriageable age, their suitors were intimidated by these stories of the family. Someone would slyly repeat one of the stories and add, "You don't really want to marry someone who has ancestors like that, do you?" Many suitors were put off by it and though the girls were pretty and good workers, they did not get many suitors. But now they were being courted by young men from the neighbouring village who did not mind the stories because they could see the advantage of marrying women from a village bigger than theirs. Such families were called by a special name, "terhuo ze" which meant those who befriend spirits. It was a pity Vimenuo's family were called that behind their backs and that was one of the reasons Grandmother had been so opposed to the match. People who didn't know them well believed that they had nightly visitations by spirits of their dead relatives. However, Leto's friends had found out that Vimenuo was a wonderful wife and they changed their opinions when they had met her and seen how good she was to Leto and to all of us. But the stigma remained to this day.

Mother had been right not to tell anyone about Pete's showing himself to her. Not everyone would think it was a sacred vision. They would expect to be haunted every time they crossed by Pete's grave which lay rather close to the road. Vini's lay close to it. Grandmother was buried outside her house next to Grandfather's grave. It was a readymade grave. She had insisted on constructing her grave when she turned eighty-five. Everyday she supervised the work, pointing with her cane where the men should lay the gravestones and how wide they were to construct it. It was rectangular and built in two layers. Salhou was allowed to climb on it and play on its surface. But the rest of us remembered to treat it with the respect it demanded. We never dried clothes on it and certainly not paddy though we knew many people thought nothing of drying paddy on a smooth grave surface.

The public path lay to the right of Grandmother's grave and we still had a little lamp burning at the grave. People were even more fearful of old women and the most feared of spirits were those of old women. So the sighting I had of Grandmother had to be laid to rest: I just hoped that Nisano and Bano had not told anyone about it. But when I returned to them two days later, the whole neighbourhood was abuzz with it. At the water spot, Aunt Benuo said to me,

"So you saw the old lady, hey? Hope she didn't try to get you with her cane, Lieno?"

 298   Easterine Iralu

She laughed raucously at this.

"I don't know what I saw. It could have been that my eyes had deceived me. It was quite dark too."

I said this carefully because I didn't want her to spread any stories about Grandmother, especially through her.

"Oh, you needn't try to protect her, we all know she had it in for you, so it figures that she would try to scare you," she said with a toss of her head.

I was too outraged to remember to speak cautiously, "That's not true, you know that the dead always return to show their loved ones that they are fine, not to frighten them!"

"Oh, you three were all certainly frightened by her in the kitchen weren't you? Don't try to deny it. Why do you want to protect her after all she has done to you?"

I saw that either Bano or Nisano had told her of the night's events. They had probably been too scared to think about the damage it could do.

"Well, aunt, if you came back after you had died and I were to meet you here some morning, I am sure I would be very frightened. So you must excuse us for doubting that we ever saw or heard anything the other night."

I smiled as I said this and she retorted,

"Oh you cheeky girl, you are a sly one aren't you? But I know all the details even if you are not willing to part with then."

Saying this she turned away to fill her waterpot.

I questioned Bano and Nisano and they both admitted they had spoken of it to others when I was away. There was nothing to be done about it but to let the rumours die a natural death and hope that Grandmother would not show herself to anyone else after that. We could do without that. We tried to concentrate on other things. There were the pumpkins to be gathered from the garden and stored for the winter. There were a lot of mustard leaves too. Bano could keep herself busy drying them and making sure that she and Nisano had enough food in winter. We left the dry leaves and plants in the garden to rot so they would give good manure for next year. Slowly, the thought of any of us seeing Grandmother grew more remote and after a month we were able to go into her room alone in the dark.

Easterine Iralu

29

"But Bano has never known any other home" Bulie was protesting, "we are being very unfair to ask her to move to Sizo's home at this point."

He was making his opinion heard after the unexpected turn that had taken place in the family discussions about what to do with Grandmother's house. Two months after Grandmother's death, Uncle Avi and Aunt Leno surprised everyone by suggesting very strongly that Bano should now move to Sizo's house so that the rest of the family could use Grandmother's house for some profitable purpose, perhaps rent it out and get some income from it.

"What about Bano?" Father had asked.

"Oh, she will have to move to her father's house. After all, everyone knows that she was there basically to look after Mother and now that is done, she should be happy to be with her father." Aunt Leno was very cold as she said this.

Uncle Avi, Uncle Bilie and Aunt Sini did not seem shocked at this suggestion at all. They all agreed that it was an ideal plan. Leto was astonished at the idea and the way Father's two brothers and their wives seemed to be agreed upon it. But he was wondering if he should express his opinion on the matter considering that our people taught that it was rude for a young man to air his views strongly when his elders were around. The young men would sit in on family conversations but they were deferential, most of the time. But Bulie was both simple hearted and impetuous. He didn't think it out of place to speak up for Bano. That was Bulie all over, he didn't much care if his rights were trodden over, but if another was being treated unfairly, he rushed in to help.

"Whose house is it anyway?" he demanded.

Then in a gentler tone as though he was remembering his manners, he said, "Excuse my roughness, I just don't want Bano to suffer any further."

Father spoke up then, "Your grandfather left the house to all three of us and our male heirs. Technically speaking, it belongs to all of us men in the family. Whatever decision we make, it will have to be done in full agreement of all the male members. We should also listen to the womenfolk and what they have to say on this."

Mother was also sitting in the room with the others. I felt it was not my place to sit in on a family meeting where the discussion was about family property. I was automatically excluded and if I had sat with them, my aunts would throw looks at each other and I knew Mother would find some excuse to make me leave the room. So I busied myself with making tea for them. But I could catch snatches of their conversation when I served them tea. In the kitchen, I kept the door open so I could hear them better. Uncle Avi and Aunt Leno argued that Bano had, in any case, had her share of staying in Grandmother's house. At this, Father sternly reminded them that none of them had been able to look after their mother as they had all been preoccupied with their own families. I wondered if I should remind them that Grandmother had actualy left the house to Salhou, Vini's son. How much weight did

Easterine Iralu

Grandmother's opinion have in this matter? Could Grandfather's will be overridden by Grandmother's edict? Father was in a difficult position because if he argued that Grandmother had left the house to his grandson, he would appear greedy to have the house remain in his family. Wasn't there somebody they could go to who could give an impartial decision that would serve everybody's interests? There was a strained note in Uncle Avi's voice as he pressed his former argument again.

"None of us has much property from Father and it seems a shame that the only property we have should lie fallow. The income will be shared by all of us."

"That is all very fine, Avi, but we must think of the people who are involved in any decision we should make regarding the house" said Father in a placating tone.

After they had all left, I joined in the talk with Mother and Father and my brothers.

"Father, why didn't you say that Grandmother had left the house to Salhou?" I asked Father.

"Lieno, we are not the ones to make that claim. If we did, my brothers would immediately suspect that I was trying to cheat them out of the house. Yet, I cannot let them throw Bano out so long as she wants to live there."

Bulie thought that we should have been more open in our conversations and they might have understood that we really were interested in Bano's welfare.

"Ah, it is easy for us to see that but they would misinterpret it. Men are not men when they have wives," said Father mysteriously. I asked him to explain that but he refused.

"You will soon know when you are a wife too," was all he would say.

I thought that over and it made me suspect that Aunt Sini and Leno were behind the idea to move Bano out of the house and rent it out. It was more complicated than they had made it sound.

Two days later, I was surprised to see Sizo at our door, but Father did not seem surprised at all.

"I came as soon as I could," Sizo said.

So Father had summoned him. They sat in the kitchen where I made them tea and served rice and meat broth to Sizo after some time.

"Visa, I can see that you mean well for Bano. I have also thought much about this after getting your message. But the only solution I can think of is to let her go to stay with Neikuo. That way we can explain to her that she is to keep Neikuo company and I think she would not be so reluctant because it means she can stay on in Kohima. Neikuo has enough rooms. I will support both of them. I have already seen to it that Bano will receive some of my pension after I am dead. None of us can hope that she will miraculously receive an offer of marriage at this stage of her life. Most men want young wives. This is the best solution I can think of. If I tried to take her to the village, she would resist it and she can be unbelievably stubborn, that one. So our best bet is to keep her in Kohima. I am sorry for Salhou and Nisano because it means that they will have to move too. But don't worry, greed has its own punishment."

Sizo could speak very lucidly at times and then confound me by slipping in a mystifying sentence. That was the way the older people spoke and they expected us to understand them. Father obviously could follow the drift of his conversation and it was a relief to see that Father thought of Sizo's words as a solution to the problem of what to do with Bano.

"I will speak to her myself," Sizo promised.

Afterwards, it was decided that Bano would shift to Neikuo's house in a month's time. Nisano and Salhou would come to live with us and Grandmother's house would be put up for rent. Neikuo did not oppose the plan and Bano moved in with her. She used my

Easterine Iralu

former room as her bedroom and filled it with all the knick-knacks she had collected over the years. Among her things were Grandmother's cloths, greying cotton body-cloths that Grandmother had woven forty years ago. She insisted on keeping them with her. She also took the white mug that had been Grandmother's tea mug for as long as I remembered. It was broken off at the edges and stained brown inside. Along with her went the tea kettle blackened by years of tea-making. We had to make as many as fifteen trips to carry all the things Bano wanted to take with her to Neikuo's house. In our carrying baskets we took all sorts of things, much of them fit for the garbage dump but we didn't have the heart to tell Bano. Last of all, came Grandmother's chair, the same one in which I had last seen her.

Neikuo's empty house was filled up with Bano's things. But Neikuo was her usual generous self. "Let her bring all she wants, I shall enjoy looking at each item and remembering my own memories of them." It was evening when we finished shifting Bano's things to Neikuo's. She was still fretting that she had not brought Grandmother's needlework box. So we promised to bring it to her in the morning. I had to sleep with Nisano and Salhou that night in Grandmother's house. We could not let them come away before Bano did. Salhou wanted me to tell him a story but I was exhausted from shifting things back and forth and went to bed early. I felt guilty about not telling him at least one story, so I called him into my bed and began to tell him a story of a boy and a bird but I fell asleep in the middle of it. The next morning, Nisano teased me about my story. "I have never heard anyone snore so much while telling a story," she said with a big laugh. As I was drinking the tea she had made for me, she said, "You don't have to work as hard today. We have already packed what we need to carry. There are just a few items left for this morning." I was relieved to hear that because yesterday had been so hectic with Bano wanting to take everything she could possibly take. She had this great fear that if she left anything behind, the people who came after would burn it all and then Grandmother would never forgive her.

Nisano and Salhou moved in with us the next day. Her mother wanted them to come to her but we explained that we really wanted them to stay with us. They had few things to carry, two suitcases of Salhou's clothes and toys, a box of Nisano's body-cloths and three of their blankets bound into a slim bundle. Salhou was happy to carry a little rucksack filled with his toys. He was most unsentimental about moving out of their last home and rather looked forward to living with his uncle Bulie in the same house. In the end, it was Nisano and I who still lingered in the house.

"Maybe we should have a cup of tea?" I suggested.

"That's a fine idea," she agreed.

At the hearth, I stirred the embers into life again. The very dry wood that I placed over them caught fire easily and we warmed water in Grandmother's old water pot. Ten minutes later, we were sipping our tea. I had found enough sugar and tea leaves but no milk.

"It feels so strange, doesn't it?" she said, voicing my thoughts. "I know, I always thought that Grandmother's house would be a place where some of us would live on forever. It feels strange to be leaving it so permanently."

I felt a sense of loss which I had not wanted to talk about. I understood why Bano had wanted to take as many things as she could from the house. It was as though she were trying to carry off the whole house itself by insisting on taking what to others were apparently useless articles of no worth at all.

"Come on, Mother, let's go."

 306   Easterine Iralu

That was Salhou calling to us for the third time. Bulie had taken the heaviest of the suitcases and we were left with a light bundle of clothing and a little bag.

"Why don't you go ahead with Salhou?" I said to Nisano, "I will lock up and come soon. We shouldn't keep the little one waiting."

She reluctantly agreed because Salhou had begun to whine. He had been so good up till now, not getting in our way and playing with his toy car when we were tidying the house. I watched the two of them climb the road that led up to our house. At the turning in the road, their small figures became indiscernible and a few seconds later, they disappeared from view. I knew if I stayed long enough they would reappear a little higher up above the bamboo grove. But I didn't wait any longer.

I walked back inside the house and looked into every room. Bano's bedroom where I had spent so many years of my young life was already looking as though it hadn't been lived in for many years. Her bed was stripped of bedclothes and I could see how old the bed was. There was dust in the corners of the steel frame. There was a musty smell about the room already and I guiltily remembered that we had not opened the windows after she left yesterday. Now there was no point in opening them because I would have to lock the whole house and go in a few minutes. So I closed the door and walked to Grandmother's room. The bedclothes gathered into a round heap in the bed startled me. It looked as though someone was lying in bed. But I instantly remembered that Nisano and I had rolled the bedding instead of making the bed as no one would lie in it for a long time. "Grandmother" I said softly and waited with bated breath as though she would answer me from somewhere. It was the oddest of feelings, as though the darkening emptiness still housed another, not a human being, but a presence. So many memories returned to me. I didn't know how I really felt after some time.

I stepped back into the kitchen. Almost everything was still in its place. The big pots and pans Sizo's wife had cooked in at Grandmother's funeral still lay on the shelves. Only a very keen observer would notice the missing tea-kettle and the empty spot where Grandmother's tea mug should be standing. We had moved another chair into the space where Grandmother's chair used to stand. Mother had not wanted us to take away anything from the house. It was all right for Bano to take all that she wanted. But it would have looked odd if we were to strip the house of all the things inside it. In any case, many things were so old they would not survive the move.

A sudden wind blew up outside the house. The kitchen windows rattled and the whole house heaved in the wind. I felt the same fear that I used to feel, as a child, of the wind in the night, when it shook Grandmother's house the way it had just done. After that, I didn't want to stay there anymore. I really didn't need to recheck that all the rooms were in order because we had done that twice before. The wind started up again outside. That was odd because it was not windtime at all. Wind in early December was unusual. I didn't want to think about it anymore. I quickly hoisted the last of the bags onto my back and stepped out of the house. The heavy lock still hung on the door. My fingers trembled and I fumbled to fit the key into the keyhole. Finally I managed to steady myself enough to turn the key in the lock. At the threshhold, I looked behind me. There was a shadowy figure moving around inside the empty house. I couldn't believe what I saw. "Bulie, Bulie, is that you?" I called out. No one responded. I ran back to peer into the windows but there was no one there.

Easterine Iralu

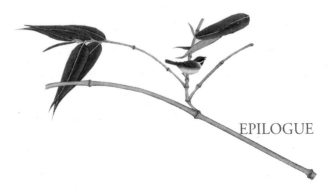

Grandmother's house was put up for rent for exactly twelve months. In that space of time, four different families lived in the house. The first was a young couple with two children aged three and four. The children kept crying because they saw an old woman sitting in the large chair in the kitchen. The same old woman would stand at the door to their bedroom and glare angrily at them. At first, adult members of the family brushed it off as a child's excuse to get more parental attention. But one night the woman of the house woke up suddenly in the night. The whole room was terribly cold. She thought they might have forgotten to close the windows and got out of bed. The first window was shut when she went to close it. She was puzzled but went to the second window. On the windowsill sat an old woman malevolently looking in at her sleeping family. The young woman fainted in fright and was revived with difficulty. She recalled that the old woman looked just like the descriptions her children had given her. In less than a week, they were out of the house, not bothering to be repaid the security amount deducted earlier. Uncle Avi sought them out and returned their money to them.

The next tenant was a young man. He preferred to live alone in the old, by now, almost crumbling house. He used Grandmother's room as a study and slept in one of the other rooms, not Bano's but the one next to it, which used to be the sitting room. He came home late many evenings and often in an inebriated state. But he paid his rent on time and though Aunt Benuo often complained that he made a lot of noise when he was drunk, no one thought he should he asked to leave. Things went well for three months. There were no reports of strange sightings from the young man. He said that he was puzzled that the front door sometimes opened of its own accord and so he requested Bulie to fasten it well. This Bulie did. But the next morning the young man came to say that the door had opened out again and he had found it wide open and clanging in the wind. Around this time, the young man's mother fell sick so he went to be with her and was away for a month because she died. When he returned, Bulie went to keep him company for a few nights. One night, they were sitting and talking when he saw an old photograph of Grandmother. He asked who she was and Bulie explained that she was the former owner of the house. He asked if she lived elsewhere. Bulie explained that Grandmother had been dead for a year and eight months. The young man exclaimed that she had come to his room two afternoons in a row and asked him to leave. He thought she was one of the neighbours and did not take any notice of her. When he learnt the truth about Grandmother, it was just a matter of days before he packed his bags and left.

The house was empty for the next three months. Uncle Avi was in touch with the young man and hoped he could be persuaded to return by lowering the house rent. The tenant was non-commital. After a month had passed he sent a message through a fellow villager known to us that he would not be returning. Fortunately, a family that had moved from Mokokchung was interested in renting the

 Easterine Iralu

house. Uncle Avi and Uncle Bilie consulted Father and they lowered the rent. The new tenants were a family of three, a widower and his sister and seven-year-old daughter. They were very pleased to get a house in Kohima at such low rates. They moved in almost immediately. In the first three weeks, there were at least eleven people in the house because the widower's mother and brother had also come with the brother's four grown up children to help them settle in. There were two men with them, his elderly uncle and his uncle's friend, who was in Kohima for some business. For the first time in many days, there was a festive air about Grandmother's house as the man's mother and sister cooked big pots of rice and meat for all. After a week, the uncle and his friend left. In the generous fashion of their tribe, the two men had contributed a lot of dried fish and meat to their hosts. With the two men gone, it was still a large group of nine people in the house. Nothing happened for two days. After another two weeks, the man's mother and brother left taking with them the four siblings. The three occupants felt that perhaps the house was too large for just three people. But it had been a good beginning and the housewarming had made them feel at home in their new surroundings. Bulie visited them often to make sure they were not wanting for anything. The man's sister and daughter had learnt to fetch water at the water spot and go early enough so as to be able to get good water.

In the fourth week, the man's sister felt a presence in the house. She did not want to tell her neice about it. But she took care to shut all the doors and windows before it grew really dark. Her brother had to travel to Mokokchung for two days because his office wanted him to deliver some files personally. She thought it would be silly to go with him when they had just settled in. Besides, she didn't want to worry him unneccesarily. So that night the two of them were quite alone in the house. Around midnight strange sounds came from the kitchen. The woman got up to see what the sounds were and saw an old woman menacingly approach her with a kitchen stool. She ducked as the old woman threw it at her. The stool fell heavily against her shin and she heard a loud crack before she fell. The doctor said her bone was broken in two places. He looked strangely at her when she said an old woman had thrown a kitchen stool at her. But the rest of us knew it was Grandmother. We persuaded them to move out of the house. We even found another in the vicinity for them which was not as big but had a reasonable rent.

The house was empty for the next month. The gentleman from Mokokchung came to Bulie twice to request him to ask Father to let him rent it again. Finally Father had to tell him that the family was considering pulling it down. Word had gotten out by this time and Grandmother's house gained an infamous reputation as a haunted house. People added more to the stories already in circulation so that in the end, folk feared to go near it. Then one day, two young men came to Uncle Avi saying they had heard all about the house but they were not afraid of spirits and were willing to rent the house. They quoted a ridiculously low sum. Uncle Avi was offended at first and thought of refusing them. But Aunt Leno said that it could be a last attempt to rent out the house. So the two young men came to stay. We don't know half of the things that happened during their stay because they would not tell. Aunt Benuo said that Grandmother troubled them so much they couldn't sleep for weeks on end. But they were immensely stubborn and did not want to admit their defeat. They were men of Grandfather's clan so they were determined to stay on. Sometimes there were slanging matches between them and Grandmother. "No room here for the dead," they would shout, "Don't trouble us, old woman, we have done you no harm or do you want us to spit on your grave?" The threats went back and forth. No one heard Grandmother reply to their insults but she would bang on the walls of tin outside and make a terrible sound. And she would get up on to the roof and stomp on it until the men would come out of the house, shouting, "Stop that" and shoot in the air with their guns. Then the stomping would mysteriously stop. But Father and my uncles felt it was not right that their mother's memory be sullied in this way. They asked the men to leave. Then they brought in a pastor to pray over the abandoned house, praying especially for the unquiet spirit. The pastor dreamt of Grandmother that night: "My house is not for strangers. It is for my family members. How can I be at rest when they have thrown out of my house those who cared for me?"

After that, Uncle Avi and Aunt Leno themselves asked Bano to return to Grandmother's house. They also asked Nisano and Salhou to return. But they were unwilling to move as they had shifted house so many times before. The day Bano returned to Grandmother's house, none of the strange sounds and happenings were heard of again. Bano said her evening prayers every night and she also added a little prayer to Grandmother, "Mother, remember I have never been ill to you all your life, do not show yourself to me but keep yourself busy with praying for all of us." I sometimes kept her company in the old house. Sometimes Nisano would take Salhou and spend the night there. We never felt the presence again after Bano returned to the house. Slowly the stories subsided.

Bulie proposed to Nisano a whole year afterwards. He had needed that much of time to make up his mind that it was all right to love her as more than a sister. Before the proposal, Nisano and Salhou went to live with her mother who had been ailing for some months. It was a very quiet wedding. I was already 23 when an offer of marriage came for me from one of Bulie's friends. Mother and I found out that this was not the first offer I had had. There had been three others but the boys' families had gone to speak to my Aunt Bino as was our custom. Each time, she had rebuffed them saying that I was probably too out spoken to be considered as good wife material. Unknown to us, the other families had been deterred from pursuing the offers with my parents because they did not dare marry a girl whose paternal aunt did not hesitate to speak ill of her. Bulie's friend was persistent. He was the fourth boy who had gone to my aunt, but fortunately for me, neither he nor his parents believed my aunt's report. They decided to come directly to my parents and so we were married in about six months after the offer was accepted.

Now, Bano, Nisano and Bulie and Salhou live on in Grandmother's house. Bulie has done a great deal of work on the house so that creaking floorboards are a thing of the past. After a few months, Uncle Avi and Uncle Bilie themselves told my father that they were sorry they had tried to take the house away. They both agreed that the house should go to Salhou. In February, Leto and Vimenuo had another child, a son this time. Leto received two promotions in his job and they were able to buy property and build on it before he turned forty.

Before the end of the year, Aunt Benuo died of a stroke. She was returning from the water spot when she fell ill. They found her dead a few yards from her house. Her sister still frequents the water spot and tries to draw the women who come there into gossip. But the women who know of what happened to Aunt Benuo usually shun her. Ocassionally a new woman joins her in her favourite activity and the pair sit and jeer at the others who come to fetch water but want to mind their own business. But sooner or later, the new woman is warned by others and Aunt Benuo's sister finds herself companionless again.